Hold Me If You Can

If You Can Series: Book 2

Cheryl Terra

Bang It Out Writing

Author's Note

This is the second book of the If You Can series, however if you want to jump into Hold Me If You Can without reading the earlier books or just need a refresher on what happened, a summary of the series **containing spoilers** begins on the next page.

There is also a character summary **at the back of the book** featuring names and basic descriptions of important characters.

Please note that this books is written in Canadian English, which has rules and spellings from both UK and US English. It also contains phrases and words specifically from Québécois French. Translations of those can be found **at the end of the book**.

Content Warnings: Full content warnings can be found on my website (**cherylterra.com/trigger-warnings**), but please note that the If You Can series contains characters who engage in casual relationships with characters not involved in the main relationship dynamic. This will not include adultery of any kind between the MCs.

This series contains an age gap teacher/student relationship, toxic parenting and family situations, slut shaming, references to non-consensual activity, and multiple explicit scenes. This book contains a scene that includes on-page emotional abuse, discussions of neurodiversity including harmful misconceptions (which are corrected on page), and discussions of the death of a friend (does not occur on page or within the timeline of the series).

The Road So Far

The If You Can series is intended to be read in order, however if you want to jump into Hold Me If You Can without reading the earlier books or just need a refresher on what happened, here is a summary of Nellie's story so far.

THE FOLLOWING TWO PAGES CONTAINS MASSIVE SPOILERS FOR THE PREVIOUS BOOKS IN THE IF YOU CAN SERIES. Turn past them if you do not want to see these spoilers

If you would rather read the full books, get your copies here: geni.us/iycseries

If You Can Series Recap

The Boy Next Door: Set the summer before Nellie starts university.

After realizing she can't afford to pay for university on her own, she asks her insanely wealthy but probably sociopathic father for help behind her mother's back, not understanding why her mom has told Nellie to cut ties with her dad. With the help of her best friend, Anne-Marie, Nellie decides she doesn't want to start university as a virgin, but also doesn't want to get into a relationship after her high school boyfriend spread horrible rumours about her that ruined her reputation.

After an unsuccessful summer of misadventures and bad dates, Nellie unexpectedly connects with JP, Anne-Marie's older brother, when she gets locked out of Anne-Marie's room in nothing but a towel. Telling him about her ex-boyfriend telling everyone she was a slut. JP tells Nellie it's okay to want sex but not a relationship and Nellie decides she wants to lose her virginity to him, though she doesn't tell him she's a virgin until after they've started hooking up. When they're done, Nellie asks him not to tell anyone and rushes away because she's afraid her religious, conservative father will find out.

Want the full story? Get your copy of The Boy Next Door here:
geni.us/bndct

Kiss Me If You Can: Three years after The Boy Next Door, Nellie is a self-described "joyfully promiscuous" college student who doesn't do serious relationships, but does do anyone who seems like a good time...

except JP, who she's successfully avoided seeing since that day in his bedroom, despite his attempts to get in touch with her.

After unexpectedly running into JP, who is now a successful junior associate at his dad's law firm, at a social event, Nellie's dad tries to get him to convince Nellie to go to law school. Much to Nellie's dismay, JP offers to tutor her for the LSAT if she doesn't get the internship she's applied for. Well aware of her dad's toxic nature and tired of him trying to control her life, Nellie tells him she's so certain she'll get the internship that if she doesn't, she'll take him up on the offer so she can take the LSAT and consider going to law school.

Unfortunately, after offending a former flame who has connections to the internship, Nellie isn't accepted. She decides to hide this from her dad and gets a job at a restaurant to pay her bills, but her dad discovers her lie and tells her that until she takes the LSAT and attends the events he wants her at with a date who Nellie despises, he will withdraw all financial support. Upset, Nellie impulsively spends the weekend hooking up with Ben, her former psychology professor who she's been regularly flirting with all summer.

Not able to avoid JP any longer, Nellie finally tells him she's been avoiding him because he kept trying to get in touch with her and she didn't want a boyfriend. JP tells her he wanted to make sure she was okay after they hooked up, not be her boyfriend. He tells her he only offered to tutor her for the LSAT because he didn't think she'd need it and encourages her to stand up to her dad. They eventually agree to a friends-with-benefits situation since Nellie will be spending a lot of time in Montreal over the summer and hook up again. With casual hook ups arranged in both Ottawa and Montreal, Nellie is surprisingly looking forward to her summer even if she has to spend more time than she wants with her dad.

Want the full story? Get your copy of Kiss Me If You Can here:
geni.us/kmiyc

Prologue

Jerk Pants

NO MATTER HOW I twisted it, I couldn't figure out why everyone was laughing.

It had to be something really funny. My mom had both hands over her mouth and a tear snaking down her cheek as she stifled her laughter.

"Jesus-Mary-and-Joseph," my dad said as the bride let out a loud cackle while the groom grinned at her and the wedding guests descended into chaos. My mom leaned forward in her chair, her head nearly on her lap and her shoulders shaking.

"What does it mean, though?" I whispered.

"Lower your voice," my dad snapped, since I wasn't actually whispering. But half of the people around us were laughing the same way my mom was and I had to speak over them.

"But Dad, I don't understand—"

"As you shouldn't." His voice was clipped and he turned to my mom. "For God's sake, Victoria. Enough."

"H-He said—" She coughed, shaking her head. "He-He-He s-said—!"

"Yes, we all heard what he said," my dad said.

"But what does it *mean*?!" I repeated, then reached across my dad's lap and shoved my mom's thigh. "Mom, why is everyone laughing? I don't get it. What's so funny about—"

"Nellie!" my dad hissed. "It is not at *all* appropriate for you to know what that means. Just know that it is something you should never say."

"But—"

"Max, let me—It's n-not—" My mom coughed, shaking her head before heaving a deep breath and leaning across my dad's body so she could whisper to me. "Honey, it's a… a term for a grown-up thing. It's n-not something you s-say in your wedding v-*vows*."

"Or in a church," my dad muttered.

It wasn't enough of an explanation to satisfy my nine-year-old self, but if even my mom wouldn't tell me more, I knew it was hopeless. And since my dad had already scolded me three times for talking too much during the ceremony and kicking the back of the pew and somehow getting gum in my hair even though I wasn't even *chewing* gum, I didn't want to make things worse. Sitting back in my chair, I pinched my forefinger and thumb together and swung my legs impatiently, waiting for the ceremony that was taking for*ever* to finish so I could ask Anne-Marie, who was sitting next to her mom farther down the row, what it meant.

I mean, she had to know. Her mouth had opened into a wide "O" and her eyes went almost as large as everyone was laughing.

But she couldn't tell me what it meant, either.

"*Je sais pas*," she whispered as we lagged behind our parents, who were gossiping wildly while waiting in the line outside the church so we could tell the bride and groom we were happy for them.

"Why did you look so shocked then?" I whispered. "If you don't know what it means?"

"Because people do not laugh like that if it's not something extremely scandalous," she replied. "And because did you see the lady in the gold dress? That is the bride's mom. She almost *fainted*."

"She did not almost faint," said a voice from behind Anne-Marie. "Don't make things up."

And *ugh*.

"Why are you eavesdropping?" I asked, folding my arms across my chest as I turned to glare at Anne-Marie's older brother, JP. "Don't you have anything better to do?"

"No, actually," JP said.

Which was fair, unfortunately. I'd never been to a wedding before and had originally been excited, but now that we were here, I had no idea why I'd wanted to go. The ceremony was boring except for the joke that everyone was laughing at that I didn't understand. All we'd done so far was sit around, listen to people talk, and watch the bride and groom kiss for way too long.

At least my mom had bought me a pretty new dress to wear. It was purple and didn't have any itchy lace on it. And that morning, we'd gone to the Marchands' house to get our hair done by a lady Anne-Marie's mom had hired. My mom had gotten her makeup done, too, but she said I wasn't old enough to wear makeup.

Even though Anne-Marie's mom let her wear lipstick and eyeshadow.

"Well, no one said you could listen in our conversation, Jean-Paul," Anne-Marie said. "So unless you're going to tell us what the joke was, perhaps you should find someone else to bother."

He shook his head, pulling his shoulders back to make himself look more mature. "Someone'll explain it when you're older."

I rolled my eyes. "You don't even know, do you?"

"I do," he said.

"Yeah, right." I looked at my nails, which the makeup lady had painted for me and which already had a chip in them because I'd put a sticker on the backseat window of my dad's car and then had to hurriedly pick it off before he noticed when we got to the church. "You're just trying to make us think you do too look cool."

"I already look cool," he said.

Which was also, very unfortunately, kind of true.

Like, not totally true. Boys were gross, obviously, even though Anne-Marie said they weren't so bad. And JP was still a smelly, rude, primeval boy with a nose that turned up just enough to make him look like a pug and a crooked tooth on the left side of his mouth. And he was mean and annoying and stupid and smelly, which was worth mentioning twice because he was a teenager now and that meant he needed, like, deodorant and stuff.

But like, objectively, he did look kinda cool in the royal blue suit and matching tie he'd worn for the wedding. But his mom probably made him wear it or bought for him, so it wasn't even like he picked the outfit himself.

"Well, you would look a lot cooler if you proved you actually know what it means," I told JP. "'Cause otherwise I think you're lying."

"I'm not lying," he said. "But I'm also not telling you."

I huffed, picking at the skin around my thumbnail. "But I want to know."

"Yeah," Anne-Marie agreed. "What good is it to have an older brother if he won't even explain a joke to you, Jean-Paul?"

He smirked. "Alright. I'll tell you—"

"Finally," I sighed.

"—if you tell me what I'm gonna get out of it."

I frowned. "What do you mean?"

"If I tell you what it means, you gotta do something for me."

A mix of anger and annoyance began building up in my stomach. "You could just do it as a favour."

"That's not how negotiating works," he said. "I do you a favour, you're gonna owe me a favour."

"You're a jerk," I said. "Jerk Pants Marchand."

"Fine," JP said. "Ask someone else, then."

So I did.

We were at the end of the line now. My dad was saying something to his friend, the bride's dad, as they shook hands.

"He makes Kendra happy," I heard my dad's friend say. "Somehow. I asked him to see Madame Villeneuve for some basic etiquette lessons, but apparently that was too 'one-percent' of me, whatever *that* means."

My mom was talking to the groom's mom animatedly, even though as far as I knew, they'd never met before. Mr. Marchand and Ms. Kinsley were talking to the bride's mom, who had a strange look on her face that I think was supposed to be a smile. Anne-Marie was standing in front of me, her shoulders square and chin tilted up as she introduced herself to the groom, who looked semi-uncertain what to say to a nine-year-old he didn't know.

Which left me standing in front of the bride.

Kendra.

"You are Nellie, right?" she asked, smiling at me. "Mr. Belanger's daughter?"

I nodded. "Yeah. Happy wedding. It was nice."

She laughed. "Thank you."

"Also," I said. "What does —"

"Nellie, no!" JP gasped from behind me.

I didn't ignore him, mostly because I didn't bother acknowledging him at all. "—'blow your dad' mean?"

Because that was what the groom had said during his vows when he told everyone how he'd met Kendra.

"Y'all know how Kendra is," he'd said. "I never seen a girl so sweet and proper with such a mouth. First time we met, she's standin' there wearin' a Gucci"—and he said it funny, like *goo-shee*—"dress and some Lewd Baton heels or whatever they're called, a Bud Light in one hand and a cigarette in the other, just swearin' like a Newfie trucker. And ya know, I say to her, I say, 'Damn, girl, you gonna kiss your mother with that mouth?' And not missin' a beat, the love of my life here turns to me and goes, 'Nah, but I'll blow your dad with it.'"

I'd known it was kinda bad because my dad said so. But I didn't think it was *so* bad that the second I asked Kendra what it meant, the world would shift into slow motion as a bunch of things happened all at once.

First, Kendra's mouth dropped open and her eyes went wide. Next, the groom's neck snapped towards me. His cheeks had barely started turning red when just ahead of me, my mom whirled around, but the giggles she'd had earlier had disappeared into a look of horror. In the background, my dad's friend closed his eyes and his wife pressed a hand to her forehead. A hand clamped down on my shoulder and I thought it was my dad's, but he was in front of me, turning around with grey eyes burning and his lips forming words that seemed to take far longer than usual to say.

"Ele-an-or Bel-an-ger—"

And that was when time started working normally again.

"—come here," my dad finished, his voice clear as glass and hard as the enormous diamond on the bride's finger.

"But—"

"*Now.*"

"It's my fault," said a voice behind me, and I realized it was attached to the hand that had grabbed my shoulder. I twisted my neck to watch as JP stepped forward, still holding onto me. "I'm sorry, Mr. Belanger."

My dad looked at JP, his lips pressed into a thin line. "I fail to see how—"

"I was teasing Nellie and told her to ask," he said. "I didn't think she would because I meant it as a joke, but I should have made it clearer that I wasn't serious."

A bubble of silence enveloped all of us standing there as my dad studied JP. My heart was vibrating so fast that it felt like it wasn't moving at all, but a billion heartbeats passed by before the groom let out a peal of side-splitting laughter and nearly keeled over.

"Oh, Lord thunderin' Jesus," he gasped. "This is the best fuckin' wedding I've ever been to."

Kendra looked at him, a laugh playing on her lips as she feigned offense. "It damn well better be, asshole. It's *our* wedding."

The bubble popped as the groom's parents joined in on the laughter. Not the bride's, though, and my dad set his eyes back on me, jaw clenched as he motioned for me to obey his order to *come-here-now*. I started forward without even glancing at JP, who let go of my shoulder as soon as I started walking. When I reached my parents, my dad put his hand on my upper back and started walking, nearly making me stumble. He kept his hand there, pushing me faster and faster as we left the receiving line until my mom caught up and smacked his arm away from me.

"Victoria—" he started.

"I'm not disagreeing with you," she hissed. "But stop shoving her like that. She is still your *daughter*."

I didn't know what she meant by that, which seemed to be the theme of the day. But my dad's hand fell away from my back and my mom reached down to take my hand in hers. I chewed on my lip as we walked to my dad's car in silence.

It wasn't until we got into the car and both doors were shut that my dad took a breath and turned around in his seat to look at me.

"Eleanor, you need to grow up and control your impulses," he said.

"Max—"

He lifted a hand, silencing my mom.

"We brought you today because we thought you were mature enough to handle it. You should be able to understand that a wedding is an important day and you must respect the people being married enough to pay attention. It is not the place to be loud and obnoxious. It does not matter that the groom couldn't seem to behave himself. *My* daughter will stop embarrassing herself by asking inappropriate questions, regardless of what her friends or the boy next door or *anyone* dares her to do. Do you understand me?"

He probably wouldn't have been upset if I spoke to agree with him, but there didn't seem to be any words in my body, so I nodded and didn't say anything else. Not even after he drove us to a restaurant and my mom asked what I wanted as a snack since it would be a while until we had dinner at the reception. Instead, I pointed at chicken strips on the menu before flipping it over so I could go back to colouring the pirate ship on the back. When we got to the reception, I glued myself to my mom's side and only said hi to people when my dad introduced me and told me to say hello.

When Anne-Marie came to our table and plunked herself next to me so she could whisper what JP had told her the groom's joke had meant, I just nodded.

"He also said to tell you he was sorry you got in trouble and that you can ask him for a favour to make up for it, if you want," she whispered.

I nodded again, but I knew there was no way I would ever in a million-billion-trillion years *ever* ask JP Marchand for a favour again.

Chapter One
My Vibrator Would Never Do This To Me

"Nellie, I mean this in the nicest possible way: Fuck you."

"I thought you were straight."

Sydney sighed, shaking her head. "I'm offended at the audacity you have to look so good in that. And a little pissed I can't pull it off myself."

I blew her a kiss and winked as I checked my ass out in the mirror. "You can pull it off anytime you want, baby cakes, but maybe not in public."

"I look like a goddamn granny here," she grumbled, shaking her head as she stood in the mirror beside me.

"How many grannies do you know that wear strappy one-pieces with ribcage cutouts?" I asked. "And more importantly, where do I meet them? Because it sounds like we'd be friends."

She rolled her eyes. "In comparison to *that*? Yes, I look like a grandma."

"Well, I guess I've learned I think grandmas are sexy," I said.

"Grandma or not, there isn't enough sunscreen in the world to keep me from burning in this."

"You have SPF 50."

"Yeah, and I get a sunburn by looking at vacation photos too long." She pursed her lips as she studied me. "Though I guess we'll have to get some for you. I wasn't expecting your ass cheeks to look like they haven't seen daylight in years."

"Well, fine," I said, sighing. "But you need to rub it on for me."

She cackled. "Why are you so horny today?"

"Hell if I don't ask myself the same damn question pretty much every day," I said, adjusting the bikini top again. "So are you getting the swimsuit?"

She shook her head. "When I said I wanted my ass turned red, I didn't mean with a sunburn."

"It might be your only option. I don't think Olivier will ever spank your ass that hard."

She rolled her eyes. "His ass, on the other hand..."

"The other hand is probably a good idea. If you keep using your right one, his ass will end up the colour of this bikini."

She snorted. "I doubt it. He'd probably come hands-free if I managed to spank him this hard."

"Really? He's that into it?"

"He'd be blasting in every direction. Just"—she flapped her wrist in sporadic, jerking motions that were clearly meant to represent a cock flailing with wild twitches as it came—"fucking everywhere."

"So... you ladies *are* finding everything okay?" the saleslady asked.

"Oh, yes," I said. "We're fine. Thanks."

She nodded quickly, then turned on her heel and scurried away. I glanced at Sydney from the corner of my eye and she looked back at me, her lips pressed together to hold back the giggle sparkling in her eye. As soon as the saleslady rounded the corner, we each choked on a laugh.

The first thing I'd thought when I saw the bikini was that it was the most beautiful swimsuit I'd ever seen. Candy apple red with a triangle halter top highlighted the fullness of my breasts. And the bottoms weren't so high-waisted as to hide my belly button ring, but were high enough that the leg holes curved high above my hips before dipping into a thong back, showing off an expanse of untanned skin on my ass cheeks since I'd never dared to wear a bikini like this at my dad's before.

The second thought I had was that my dad would hate it for those exact reasons. So obviously, when I arrived in Montreal a few days later to attend yet another stupid social event so he'd look marginally human to the other stuck up high society types, the first thing I did was put on the bikini and make my way down to the pool in the backyard.

I mean, sure, I probably wouldn't have done that if my dad had been home to *see* me in the skimpy thong bikini, but that was beside the point.

After grabbing a floatie out of the pool house and putting on my sun hat, I grabbed my phone and nearly spilled the tumbler of juice I'd poured for myself in the kitchen. After murmuring my usual silent prayer that I wouldn't drop the aforementioned phone in the water while I was floating, I climbed into my floatie and tucked the juice into the cup holder.

And then I nearly dropped my phone as it vibrated with a message.

Bastard

Welcome back, babe

I glared towards the Marchands' house. It accomplished nothing since my eyes were hidden by my sunglasses and also the only part of the house I could see from the pool was the deck, which was empty.

Me

I thought you didn't sit at the window watching for me. When did you turn into such a pathetic loser?

Bastard

Allegedly on a snowy day in February approximately twenty-six years ago. Unless you believe life begins at conception, in which case, you'll have to ask my parents for exact dates

But even if I hadn't just got home and noticed your car parked in the driveway, I didn't have much of a choice. AM would be better at keeping water in a mesh bag than she would a secret

I sighed heavily as Anne-Marie unintentionally proved, yet again, why she couldn't know about *this*.

Because even though she was my childhood best friend, even though she not only approved of but was attempting to manifest a relationship between me and her brother, even though I told her *almost* everything about me, she couldn't know.

You know. Because of the whole aforementioned "trying to manifest a relationship between me and JP" thing.

Me

You sure know how to flatter a girl

Bastard

Oh, sorry. Let me try again

Yes, I was staring out my window with the yearning of a sailor's wife on her widow's walk, watching for the illustrious curves of your noble Honda Civic to grace the cobbles of your father's manicured driveway

Me

Yikes. Sounds like you've got a serious thing for my car

Bastard

I'm not saying I grabbed my cock the second I saw it, but I'm not NOT saying that

Me

Yeah but when DON'T you have your cock in your hand?

Bastard

When it's in your mouth, for starters

I twisted said mouth to the side, trying not to laugh.

Because yeah, I'd had JP Marchand's cock in my mouth a few times. Five, to be exact, not that anyone was counting. But if they were, that would include the initial cock-in-mouth situation three years earlier, plus the four times I'd blown him over the last month-and-a-half.

Not that we'd only hooked up four times. No, that was sitting at a somewhat alarming seven times since he finally cornered me after years of avoiding him.

More alarming was how impressive it was considering how much of a pain in the ass it was for us to fuck. My dad was making an annoying point of being around as much as possible. And when he wasn't around, he made an even more annoying point of trying to get me and Kimberlee to spend time together.

And since JP was twenty-six and living with his parents—because "his condo wasn't ready yet," not because he was a spoiled rich kid who had no reason to move out—hooking up in his room was just asking for trouble. Sure, the Marchands' house was easy to sneak in and out of—Anne-Marie and I had discovered that when we were about thirteen—but the house was almost never empty.

Plus, JP's bedroom was beside Anne-Marie's. And that was *far* too risky.

But even though I hated to admit we had anything in common, JP and I shared a mutual level of unreasonable horniness and dedication to getting laid.

The easiest option was his car, of course. Especially since there was a semi-private parking lot near a nature trail a couple of blocks away from our houses. And since my dad didn't have any interest in learning anything about me that wouldn't benefit him, he didn't care enough to question why I'd suddenly started going for jogs while I was visiting. Which was great, since it gave me a good reason to get out of the house and explained why I was red-faced and sweaty when I returned.

And there was the pool house in my dad's backyard. After he and Kimberlee had gone to bed one night, I slipped out to meet JP there. When I let myself in, he was just disconnecting the air compressor from one of the air mattresses.

"I don't think that's gonna work," I'd said.

"Why not?" he asked, letting the air mattress settle on the ground.

"Because if you think an air mattress can hold both our weights without popping, you're clearly not fucking me hard enough," I said. "And then why am I wasting my time here?"

"Because your travel vibrator isn't as good as my dick," JP said as he stepped around the mattress. He slipped a hand behind my back, cupping my ass and pulling my body forward so I was pressed against him when he dipped his head down to kiss me. "And besides, that's not what it's for. I figured you might appreciate the extra padding when you're on your knees for me."

"How very thoughtful," I replied, trying not to smile as he kissed me again.

"Your comfort is my top concern."

"And yet you want to cram your cock down my throat."

"I said it was a concern. Not a requirement."

I scoffed in disbelief. "You're such a bastard!"

"You like it."

"My vibrator would never do this to me."

He kissed me again, fingertips digging into my ass cheek. "Let me show you a couple other things your vibrator can't do for you."

I never did find out how well the air mattress thing worked. JP was the one who ended up kneeling on it, my pyjama pants pooled around one ankle and my leg hooked over his shoulder as he ate me out. And after I came on his face, biting the base of my thumb to keep my moans at least semi-muffled, he'd stood up and kicked the air mattress out of the way.

"Turn around," he said, his voice rough.

"Thought you wanted a blowjob," I said, still trying to catch my breath.

"After all that work I did getting your pussy even wetter than it usually is?" He grabbed my arms, spinning me around and bending me over the back of a wicker armchair. "You're insane if you think I'm going to deprive my cock of feeling that."

He fucked me hard enough that I didn't notice the stiff reeds of the chair digging into the softness of my belly. And I didn't notice the scratch-like marks on my forearms as I braced myself against the chair while he brought me to another orgasm that would've definitely popped an air mattress, leaving me a shaky, melted mess of a person.

My phone went off in my hand and I nearly lost my grip on it again as I jolted out of the memories of my and JP's various hookups.

Bastard

Speaking of my cock in your mouth, wyd?

Me

Sitting in the pool in a thong bikini

Bastard

Liar.

Me

You could literally go onto your deck to see

Bastard

Would love to, babe, but between seeing your incomparably sexy car and all this talk about me having my dick in your mouth, I'm up, but not for walking through the kitchen where my mother is having her weekly book club to prove you're lying.

If you get what I mean.

Oh, God.

I pressed my thighs together. The thought of JP being hard right now should *not* be doing it for me the way it was. I lifted my thumb to my mouth, sandwiching the nail between my teeth, then glanced over the edge of my phone towards the Marchands' house. Then, as carefully as I could, I reached down into the pool with one hand and slowly paddled until I was facing the other direction.

A few minutes later, I sent JP another message.

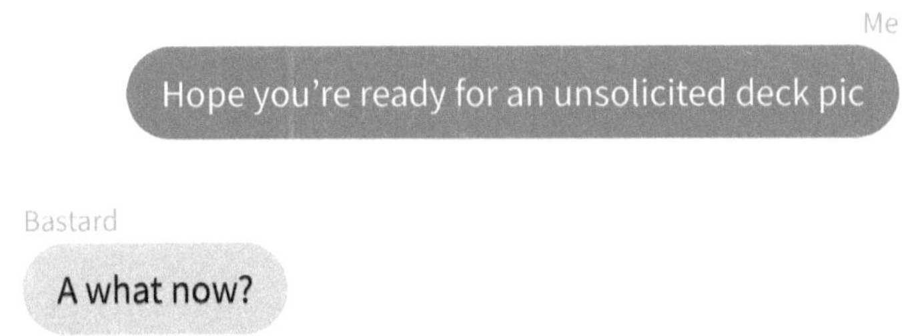

He'd responded before the picture finished sending, so I didn't reply. The photo sent and the checkmarks confirming he'd seen it appeared instantly. A second ticked by, and then another, and then multiple more seconds because that's how time worked, and just when I was about to double-text because Jesus Christ, JP, this was not the time to leave a girl on fucking *read*, his response came through.

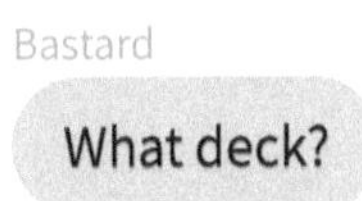

I bit back a smirk.

There was definitely a deck in the picture. It was in focus, even, right near the top of the frame.

It was just that the rest of the photo showed me sitting in my floatie, a few errant drops of water on my chest catching the light, and the slightest hint of my nipples poking through the stretched red fabric across my breasts.

Me

You don't see the deck in the picture? The one attached to the back of your house?

Bastard

Babe, fuck me if I'm wrong, but there was no deck in that picture

Me

You're wrong.

Bastard

Thank God. When are we meeting up?

Chapter Two
The Exorcist

"You know, this would have been so much easier if you'd just pretended I was tutoring you for the LSAT," JP said.

"I know it must be hard to imagine what it would be like to sell your soul since lawyers don't have one," I said as he turned out of the parking lot we usually fucked in. "But trust me. Your dick isn't worth it."

"I'd say that remains to be seen, considering you sound like you're casting out a demon when you come."

"Selling my soul has nothing to do with being possessed."

"Yeah, but you beg me to fuck the hell out of you so often that you might as well call my dick the exorcist."

I tightened my mouth, refusing to let so much as a smile flicker on my lips. "How was I supposed to know other people fuck in that parking lot? You're the one who lives here. I've never even seen another car there, let alone three."

"Well, we normally don't meet there during prime hooking up time." He let the car roll up to a stop sign, thinking for a moment before flicking the turn signal on. "It's either earlier or later."

"Normally I don't drive to Montreal early when my dad forces me to go to one of his stupid galas or events," I said. "But it's Sydney's birthday tomorrow and she wanted to spend it getting dicked down by her hot cop fuck buddy, so I said I'd suffer through an extra night here."

"That was the only reason?" He merged onto the main road. "Not because you *also* wanted to spend her birthday getting dicked down?"

"I could've done that in Ottawa."

"True. How is Professor Sexy doing? You're still hooking up, right? Or did he leave already?"

"Of course we're still hooking up," I said. "He's not moving to California until next month."

"Nice. Are you getting him a goodbye present?"

I gave him a weird look. "Like what?"

"I dunno. Something special to remember you by."

"I'll ask him if he wants a pair of panties as a keepsake or something, but I don't know how special that would be. It's not like it's the first time I've given my panties away."

He scoffed. "How come he gets keepsake panties?"

"Are you saying you want keepsake panties?"

"Maybe. You've never even offered me a pair."

"What would you even do with keepsake panties?"

"Add them to my scrapbook or something."

"You're disgusting."

"And yet here you are, demanding I find another parking lot for us to fuck in."

"You know, the only thing my vibrator ever says is *bzzzzzz*." I looked out the passenger wistfully. "I miss him."

"Him? Does he have a name?"

"Yeah. Buzz Right-Here."

JP chuckled. "So when are you back in town after this? I'm assuming we can't meet up tomorrow since you're going out to celebrate Sydney's birthday after the gala."

I looked over at him. "How do you even—"

"Anne-Marie."

"Does she seriously tell you everything?"

"Imagine how out of the loop I'll be in September when I get into my condo and don't have daily access to the Anne-Marie News Network. Hopefully she's got someone to replace me so she doesn't implode under the weight of everyone's secrets."

"Maybe she should start a blog," I said. "Gossip Girl style."

"Except everyone would know it was her," he said.

"True." I tapped my fingers against my thigh. "Well, yeah. We're doing a girls' night tomorrow. Between Bruno liquoring me up at the gala and the amount of shots I'm assuming Syd'll want to do, I won't be in much shape to meet up."

"Fair. And Bruno's still taking you, then?"

I frowned. "To the gala? Of course. Why?"

He shrugged. "I'd just heard that Clinton—"

"God*damn*it, Anne-Marie," I grumbled.

JP laughed. "She was saying he seems *really* into you."

"You'd think after trying to break his arm at that luncheon and telling him to his face that I find him disgusting, he'd take a hint."

"He's one of those guys who wants something until he has it," JP said.

"Well, there's no way he's getting it," I said. "If something happened to Bruno, I'd find someone else."

"Anne-Marie would help you, I'm sure."

I snorted. "Like I'd ask her. She'd tell me to go with you. I'm half-surprised she hasn't told Bruno to pretend he's busy one weekend so I'm forced to ask. She hinted as much last weekend when he was running late to pick me up."

A solemn pause filled the space I expected a laugh.

"Is that what you want, babe?" he asked.

The gravity in his voice was so strong that it pulled my gaze towards him. Heat rushed up my face, not from the stereotypical enthralled breathlessness of wondering if someone had feelings for them, but from the absolute fucking *terror* of wondering if someone had feelings for me.

"JP, I—"

"Because I need to tell you, from the bottom of my heart and with all the soul I apparently don't have, I would rather drink a pint glass of day-old *steamé* water from the bottom of the pan at La Belle Provence than take you to a gala."

I tried not to sigh in relief as he turned into a parkade near an office building. "If all I had to do to get out of these galas was drink steamed hot dog water, this would've been a very different summer."

He steered around the parkade to one of the higher levels, which was nearly empty. "Yeah, but then you would've missed out on getting to fuck me all these times."

"I'd still pick the hot dog water."

He grinned. "In fairness, so would I."

"See? So you have nothing to worry about. You'd have to be the last man alive for me to ask you to be my date for something," I said as he pulled his car into an empty spot near a concrete wall.

He turned off the car, the sudden absence of the engine and air conditioning and radio settling around us. "Really? You'd go with Clinton before me?"

I undid my seatbelt and opened the car door. "In this scenario, Clinton had an accidental falling-into-the-St.-Lawrence-and-tragically-not-resurfacing incident."

JP mirrored my actions. "I see. Were one or both of his arms broken before this alleged accidental fall?"

I got out of the car. "How premeditated would that make this accident seem?"

"Does it matter? I'm assuming if I'm the last man alive, there are no other lawyers to take his case."

A firm bang echoed, first through the parkade as he closed the driver's side door and then again by me bumping the passenger door closed with my hip. "Don't tell me you've forgotten female lawyers exist."

He chuckled as we opened the back doors in unison. "Babe, I said lawyers who would *take his case*. You think any woman in her right mind would defend that prick?"

"Well... you're not wrong." I climbed into the car and closed the door.

"You could just say I'm right, you know," he said, closing his door and reaching for me.

"Yeah, but then your head might get even bigger." He helped me onto his lap and I straddled his thighs. "And there'd be no room left in the car for me."

"And that"—he slid his hands up my legs, gripping my thighs through the thin fabric of my leggings—"would be a goddamn tragedy."

I didn't have an immediate response to that, but that was okay. One of his hands slipped around to my lower back as the other moved up to my neck, drawing me forward so he could press his lips against mine. An unintentional sigh slipped from my mouth as I settled, shifting from side to side and trying not to shiver from the friction.

"I was going to remind you we have to be quick, but you're more than ready, eh?" I murmured, my core prickling awake as I ground myself against his already straining cock.

He let out a low chuckle. "Oh, I'll be taking exactly as long as I need to, babe."

"So not very long at all?"

"You knew what you were doing when you sent me that photo earlier. Just like you know I can make you come with a couple of minutes and a well-placed finger."

His teeth sank into my bottom lip, tugging at it as he moved both his hands back down my sides. Smooth palms pushed along my hips until he reached my ass, cupping it and digging his fingers into the soft curves.

"Ready, babe?" he whispered.

"Don't call me—"

Before I could finish, he squeezed my ass harder and pulled me down as he thrust his hips up, grinding himself against my pussy. A surprised whimper slipped from my lips.

"What was that, babe?" he asked.

"Stop calling me—"

He did it again, this time pulling my body forward and creating more of that delicious friction. I cut myself off with another cry, clenching my teeth after in frustration at the betrayal of my voice.

"It sounds like you're trying to say something, babe," he said, smirking.

"You know what I—"

He did it again and I let out a frustrated shout. JP chuckled and I decided I'd had it.

The chuckle turned into a startled laugh as I reached down, wrapping a hand around each of his wrists and yanking them away from my ass. It should have been easy for him to take back control considering he went to the gym a few times a week and most of the time, the closest I got to working out was pretending I jogged when I was in Montreal. But apparently, pinning his arms against the back seat redirected enough of his blood that the only thing resisting was his dick against the fabric prison of his pants.

"What's it going to take to make you stop calling me that?" I asked.

"Why don't you start trying things and see if any of it works?" he said, a hint of uncontrolled breathlessness in his voice.

"Like duct taping your smart-ass mouth so you stop annoying me?"

"I was thinking more like sitting on my face, but I can take you to a hardware store if you want. The closest one to here is probably a RONA."

"You do have a perfect face for sitting on," I said. "But seeing as we're limited by the constraints of a car, I'm gonna have to go with the duct tape."

There was laughter on his lips as he kissed me, his wrists flexing beneath my grip until I gave in and released them. He slipped his hands beneath the hem of my shirt, pulling it up and tugging the cups of my bra down so he could lift my breasts out. He took one of my nipples in his mouth, pulling in a breath through his nose and letting out a controlled sigh like I couldn't tell how much he was craving me. Smirking, I rolled my hips, letting out a sigh at the friction between us.

"Fuck," JP whispered, though it came out more like "muhk" since he said it at the same time that he bit down on my nipple, not too hard but firm enough that a startled squeak escaped my throat. Arousal surged through me, heat and promised bliss travelling through my veins and into my bones, up my spine and down to the tips of my fingers and toes.

"Fuck, I love that," I hissed, the words coming out mindlessly.

He did it again. "I know you do, babe."

"Shut up."

"What's so bad about me saying I know what you like?"

"The fact that you'll use it against me."

"You think I'd do that?" he asked innocently.

"Yes."

"Well, no one said you weren't smart." He nipped at my nipple again, then soothed it with slow, flat licks that made my head spin. Determined not to let him control everything, I rolled my hips again, grinding against him until he made a mindless noise of his own and shuddered beneath me.

"I can't take it," he said, his voice hoarse. "I want your pussy so bad, babe."

"Bad enough not to call me babe?"

He made a noise like a dry laugh, then captured my lips with his.

"Please fuck me, Nell," he murmured.

And how was I going to say no to that?

I stripped my leggings off quickly, but all JP had to do was pull his pants and boxers down to mid-thigh and take his cock out. He wrapped his hand around his shaft, stroking lazily until I set my panties on the seat beside us.

"Are you finally ready?" he asked, his tone unhurried even though his cock was so red and swollen it looked like it ached and there was already pre-cum collecting on his tip.

Instead of responding, I threw my leg over his, grabbed his cock, and lowered myself on it in one smooth motion. Without so much as a pause, I started riding him as hard as I could.

And suddenly, JP seemed a *lot* less self-assured.

"Fuck," he hissed, tilting his head back and closing his eyes. His hands moved to my thighs and he inhaled sharply, then pressed his lips together as he fought to keep from panting.

"You're not going to come already, are you?" I asked innocently.

He scoffed, despite his fingertips digging into my thigh. "Of course not."

"I can slow down if you need me to."

"Don't you dare." He looked up at me, his eyes heavy lidded. "Fuck me hard, babe. Use every fucking inch of this dick."

And oh, God.

How could I *not*?

So I did. I bounced on his cock as hard as I wanted, holding his shoulders for balance, before rolling my hips back and forth, grinding my clit against his pelvis. JP's chest rose and fell far more rapidly than usual, and I was half-certain I was moments away from the admittedly guilty pleasure of feeling him unload inside of me.

But after a few deep breaths while he moved about as much as a suction cup dildo on the side of a shower stall, he finally loosened his grip on my legs. Reaching up, he pulled me in for a kiss and made my movements stagger. He made up for it by thrusting up into me, hips raising and meeting the backs of my thighs to create a new, deeper, more intense rhythm that I couldn't stop myself from matching.

It wasn't long before I felt the telltale heat in my core, that place deep inside me sparking each time I took JP's cock fully inside me. My legs were trembling when JP let out a groan, followed by a gasping breath as he grabbed my hips.

"Shit," he said. "Babe, I—*fuck*. I'm too close. If you don't slow down—"

I fucked him faster.

His fingertips dug into my hips, his eyes slamming shut and head tilting back. He moaned again, a gorgeous, addictive sound that sent a rush of pleasure through my body, and a moment later his cock throbbed inside of me.

"Fuck," he gasped. "Fucking... *fuck*." He moaned again, blissful gasps of breath escaping his parted lips as he came. I kept riding him hard, not stopping until his hands relaxed and his eyes reopened.

"Okay," I said, moving off his lap and twisting so I could spread my legs. "Give me your fingers so I can—"

"No."

My mouth dropped open. "*Excuse* me?"

Unbelievably, he grinned, shoving his dick back into his pants and zipping them up before opening the door beside him. A thousand things burst in my mind as I gaped at him.

"Are you fucking for real?" I asked. "Where do you think you're..."

But I trailed off as instead of getting out of the car, like I thought he was, he stuck his legs out before looking over his shoulder.

"Move so I can lie down," he said.

I stared at him.

"Babe," he said patiently. "Don't you want to come?"

"But there isn't room. And you just—" I gestured towards my lap as if that would finish the sentence. "And you don't think someone'll hear us with the door open?"

"I'll make it work," he said. "And as for that"—he gestured the same way I had—"seriously? You think it's going to bother me?"

"Well..."

"Trust me. If you can take my cum in your mouth, I can handle it."

I glared at him and he grinned.

"And I should be able to keep quiet with that phenomenal ass of yours smothering me. But if you think you'll need a gag, we can put your panties in your mouth."

In hindsight, I probably should've tried putting my panties in my mouth, even though they wouldn't have been very effective. Because yeah, one of my legs was crammed between JP's shoulder and the seat and the other was bent at a semi-strange angle in the wheel well. And the mix between of the two plus the noticeable lack of pillows or anything to help with angles meant I hovering more than I was sitting, which was fine except that I was a "If you want me to sit on your face, how you breathe is a you problem, not a me problem" kind of person.

But also, *fuck*.

I bit down on the base of my thumb when I came, trying with everything to keep the pleasure I wanted to let out in shrieks from echoing in the parkade. JP's hands were on my thighs, holding me as close to his face as he could. Waves of pleasure rocked over me, his tongue keeping steady until my legs unclenched and the hand that was sort of covering my mouth moved to the seat so I could steady myself.

There were also very few times I knew JP would be completely silent, but he always was in those moments after we finished fucking. For a minute or two or twelve—okay, probably not twelve, but who actually knew how long we sat there in the buzz of bliss—after he wriggled out from beneath me and flopped against the seat, the only sound was his breath and mine, my heartbeat thundering and then drumming and then pulsing in my ears.

And it was nice. Unreasonably nice, to just sit there and exist and recover with him.

But of course, JP always ruined it.

"You know, I was wrong," he said.

"Usually," I said.

"You don't sound like you're going through an exorcism when you come. It's more like a bleating goat."

I slapped his bicep, but I wasn't quite recovered enough to say anything else. He waited, then grinned.

"So, I was right about there being enough room for you to sit on my face?" he asked.

"Baa," I said.

He let out the loudest, most unattractive and unrestrained snort I'd ever heard. It was something I'd never heard him do before and seemed to surprise him as much as it did me. So of course, that made me laugh, and for a minute, neither of us could speak.

After cleaning ourselves up and redressing, JP drove back to our street. He dropped me off at the end like he usually did, promising to drive around the block a few times before going back to his place so we didn't suspiciously return home at almost the same time. And as usual, I got out and started jogging just fast enough that by the time I got to my dad's driveway, there was a light sheen of sweat on my forehead.

Then, like always, I walked up the driveway, breathing a little harder than I usually did.

However, unlike always, the door flew open the moment I stepped onto the stairs, surprising me so much I nearly tripped and smacked my head on the concrete pillar beside the door.

Which honestly, might have been preferable to seeing JP's sister standing in the doorway, hands on her hips and a maniacal grin on her face.

"Nellie Belanger, how *dare* you keep this a secret from me?" Anne-Marie said, her voice glimmering with excitement.

Oh no. I stared at her, my eyes wide.

"Look at you, all red-faced and out of breath with your messy hair. Did you really not think I would find out about your little escapades, *chérie*? You know I find out *everything*."

And just... shit.

Shit.

Chapter Three
Spit Take

"You know, I prefer the other kind of cardio we do," I said.

Well, sort of said. It came out more like a gasp and Ben chuckled, pulling the water bottle from his running belt and twisting the top off as I leaned against a fence post to catch my breath.

"You're doing well considering you said you're not a runner," he said, taking a casual sip of water before passing the bottle to me. "Which I still find hard to believe since you're keeping up with me." He checked his watch, which was one of those fancy runner ones that measured how oxygenated his footsteps were or whatever. "And I'm not slowing my pace all that much."

"Yeah, which you can credit to all that other cardio I do." I took a glug of water from the bottle before handing it back to him. "I hate running."

"I wish I would've known that before I suggested all this gear," he said, frowning a bit as he gestured at me.

"Seriously, stop feeling bad about it. My dad won't even notice the charge on his card."

"Yes, but for a charity race... and with only a couple of weeks, I can't even do all that much to help you train..."

"Ben, it's okay. You told me that up front." I took another deep breath and reached for the water bottle I'd given back to Ben. "It's still helpful. I needed to make it look like I've been jogging all summer. And this way I'll at least be able to know how hard I can run during the race so no one realizes I was making the whole thing up."

And also how far I could run in case Anne-Marie ever found out the *actual* secret I was keeping from her, but I didn't add that part.

Ben laughed again, waiting as I drank nearly half his bottle of water before giving it back to him.

"Sorry," I said. "I guess I should have brought my own."

"It's okay." He sipped his water again. "We're not too far from a bathroom that has a water fountain if we need to refill it."

I nodded, wiping sweat off my forehead as I looked at the sunlight glinting off the water in the Rideau River and silently regretted every moment of my life that led to me thinking *jogging* was a good excuse for sneaking out to fuck JP.

But for now, I had to consider myself lucky that Kimberlee had told Anne-Marie I was running when she'd stopped by my dad's place to see if I was around for an impromptu wine night on my last trip to Montreal.

Even if it didn't feel lucky once I'd found out why she was so excited.

"You sneaky, sneaky girl," she'd said as I tried to catch my breath after realizing she wasn't talking about me fucking her brother. "If I had known you were a runner, I would have hounded you about Illumi-Nite years ago!"

"About what now?" I'd gasped.

She pressed her lips together, her eyes bright with excitement and her voice taking on a distinctly sales-like tone. "The Illumi-Nite Race. Each summer, dazzling runners such as yourself come together to brighten up the night with a race like no other, raising money and awareness for Montreal's vivid neurodiverse communities, including a number of programs targeted to assist children, students, and adults with diagnoses of autism, ADHD, and dyslexia supported by the HueManity Foundation."

I blinked three or four times, trying to follow everything she'd said. "Uh... a race?"

"But not just a race!" She gestured as if there was a Powerpoint presentation behind her, so convincingly that I looked before remembering we were standing in my dad's foyer and there were no projectors there. "The HueManity Foundation was created and is still spearheaded by neurodiverse leaders who want to celebrate neurodiversity while creating supports and accommodations in a world designed for neurotypical people. The Illumi-Nite Race challenges the standards of a typical race. By racing in the evening and creating an atmosphere of celebration with lights, colour, and music, we show how there is space in the world for minds that exist outside the box. And at the end of the race, a live dance party and beer garden extend the party into the night."

She finished her presentation by knitting her fingers together, an expectant look on her face. I was especially thankful for that since I'd gotten about halfway through her canned—though admittedly well-prepared and cheerful in a soulless corporation sort of way—speech before zoning out.

I couldn't help it. Jargon like that felt like verbal melatonin to me.

"Right," I said slowly. "And you want me to... sponsor you?"

She laughed. "Oh, *chérie*. You are too funny. I will be there, of course, but I work with the HueManity Foundation as the community outreach coordinator for Illumi-Nite."

"Really? I thought you were still doing the personal stylist thing."

"I am, but I am both picky and relatively new, so I do not have that many clients," she said, waving her hand. "So I spend my extra time helping the organizations I enjoy supporting. Illumi-Nite is close to my heart based on the personal connections. Remy is Autistic and has worked with the HueManity Foundation in the past, but Jean-Paul also had a friend who helped create this event and it has become very meaningful to me."

From the way she said it, I was pretty sure it was a volunteer thing, kind of like what I assumed Kimberlee did for all the organizations she supported. Which made sense. None of the Marchand children really *needed* to work. Jean-Luc Marchand was a successful lawyer who made very good money, but the Marchands also had family money that ran a lot further than one or two generations.

I guess that was technically true for me, too. But between realizing what taking my dad's money actually cost me and my certainty that I'd eventually annoy him enough that he'd fully cut me off, I'd never even considered not trying to support myself.

"Oh, a family thing. How nice," I said. "Well, I know I would hate to impose on a tradition like that, so—"

"*Bien tenté, chérie,*" she said. "You must run this year. It would mean the world to me and I *know* now that you are a runner!"

"Well, yeah," I said unconvincingly. "But I'm not sure I'm good enough to do a full race."

She waved her hand. "It is all for fun, Nellie. Many people walk it. But I expect to see you sprinting across the finish line. I told Kimberlee I would wait for you to return even though she said you always take a very long run. I nearly gave up waiting, *chérie*. You ran for a *very* long time!"

And what was I going to do? Tell her that no, actually, I wasn't running for a very long time, I was sitting on your brother's face in the backseat of his car in a parkade because we've been secretly fucking all summer?

Of course not.

So instead, I'd gone back to Ottawa and complained about it to Ben after we'd Netflix-and-chilled our way through the next episode of some alien conspiracy docuseries we'd been "watching" together whenever he came over.

Or at least, I think it was about alien conspiracies.

I don't know. I was naked most of the time.

"And I don't even have an excuse not to do it," I'd whined as we curled up on the couch, a throw blanket over us and my head on Ben's bare chest. "I have to be there that weekend for a gala anyway. *And* when I told Syd about it, the traitor said it sounded like *fun* and decided to come along!"

"How dare she," Ben had said.

"I know, right?"

He'd trailed his fingertips down my bicep. "You know I'm a runner myself, right?"

"You've mentioned it."

"I'd be happy to help you get ready for your race."

"You would?" I'd fidgeted again, picking at my thumbnail. "You wouldn't worry about someone seeing us running together?"

He'd slipped his hand between mine, his fingers warm as they tapped against my palm. "I don't think it would be likely for anyone to see us, but even if they did, I don't think it would be an issue to see a former student running with me. We would just need to ensure it's not obvious that there's any more to it than that."

I'd traced the side of his index finger. "And what about the fact that you're at a way higher level than I am?"

"There's nothing wrong with that," he'd said.

"I'm going to hold you back. Like, I can hold my own, don't get me wrong, but I'm not as active as you are."

"I very much doubt you could hold me back, Ms. Belanger," he'd said, his voice a low rumble. "I've seen just how *active* you can be."

"That's different from running," I'd said, shivering as he brought my hand up to his mouth and kissed my knuckles.

"A little, sure." He'd traced my fingertips along his lips, kissing them gently before guiding my hand to his jaw and letting me cup it. "The biggest difference between running and riding is distance, after all."

Which was fair, since even though we ended up in my bedroom not too long after that and I rode him until my legs were shaking, I didn't move a single inch until we woke up the next morning. Then we'd gone to one of Ben's favourite running stores so I could get some actual running shoes and shorts and stuff before taking me to a trail that ran along the Rideau River.

He'd said it was an easy trail. I'd started believing it would be the site of my death.

"Maybe that's why I'm struggling so much," I said to Ben as he lifted the water bottle to his lips. "I'm overdoing it after riding your dick for whatever the equivalent of five kilometers is last night."

Ben choked and his cheeks went bright red as he glanced around. The only person anywhere near close enough to have heard what I said was standing right in front of him covered in the water that had sputtered from his mouth when he choked, and considering she was the same person who said it, I wasn't particularly worried.

In fact, I was almost crying with laughter as I wiped water from my face.

"Oh, God," he said. "I'm sorry."

"It's okay," I said, shaking drops of water from my hands.

He coughed, holding a fist to his mouth so I couldn't tell he was laughing at the same time until he moved it. "*Where* did that come from?"

"Your mouth, mostly," I said. "Although maybe a bit sloshed out of the bottle, I'm not sure, but—"

"Not that," he said, chuckling as he unzipped his running belt. "What you said. About, uh… your riding distance. I'm not entirely sure how you got there from me saying there's a water fountain nearby."

I opened my mouth, then closed it thoughtfully. "Huh. I guess that was kind of a weird connection."

Ben shook his head, still smiling. He glanced around again and then, seemingly satisfied that no one was around, stepped forward and lifted the small towel he'd pulled from his running belt to my face. I kept my eyes on him as he gently dried my cheek, but his gaze didn't meet mine until he'd finished.

"Thank you," I said softly.

"Gladly." His throat flexed as he swallowed. "And you may be, ah... correct. About being tired because of, ah, last night. Or it could be that we're three-quarters of the way done this loop, which is impressive considering you say you're not much of a runner." He cleared his throat. "In fact, I'm concerned that perhaps I've pushed you a bit too far and risked causing you an injury."

"That doesn't sound good," I said, even though an injury that prevented me from running a race in the next couple of weeks wouldn't be a bad thing.

"No," he agreed. "It doesn't. So I think we should head back to my building. So I can, ah, help you with a post-run treatment to... ah..." He cleared his throat again. "To avoid that."

"What kind of post-run treatment?" I asked, blinking up at him.

And honestly, if every run ended with a treatment that involved a shower, being washed from head to toe, and a leg massage that just so happened to end with his face pressed against my pussy, I would have been a lot more likely to take up running permanently.

Chapter Four
No Kink Shaming

"This is the best day of my life."

I glanced at Sydney from the corner of my eye before looking back at the road. "Did Olivier finally agree to put you in a ball gag and call you a bad, bad girl?"

"Better." She grinned, tilting her phone from side to side. "Reid and Alison are breaking up. Bye-bye, squeaky toy sex."

I refrained from pointing out that her roommate-she-totally-wasn't-in-love-with breaking up with his girlfriend probably shouldn't be "better" than her sort-of-boyfriend finally doing something in bed that was for her instead of him and held my hand up for a high-five. "About fucking time. What happened?"

She propped her elbow up on the little ledge beneath the closed car window, resting her cheek on her hand as she looked at her phone. "It has to be something good because he just asked me to tell him if he's being a dick."

"Ooh, gladly," I said. "Tell Reid I say he's a dick."

"I haven't even read you the message."

"My statement stands."

"Okay, well, we need to tell him if he's being a dick about *this*," she said, then read from her phone again. "'She said I'm kink-shaming her.'"

I grimaced. "Ugh."

"Yeah, but he says it's not kink-shaming to not be into the same thing as someone else."

I hmm'ed in reluctant agreement. "Tell him establishing his dick status can't be completed until he tells us specifically how the conversation went down."

Syd tapped on the screen, pausing and thinking for a moment before typing more. Probably because she was asking Reid what he said in a much clearer way than I'd suggested. She tapped her foot cheerfully in the wheel well, humming along to the radio until his response came through a few minutes later.

And once it did, her face darkened.

"Ohhh," she said, drawing the word out in a low tone. "Yeah, no, Reid was definitely not kink-shaming her."

"No?" I asked, glancing in the rear-view mirror and shoulder checking before switching lanes to pass a small grey car doing ten below the speed limit.

She shook her head. "Nope. He even sent me screenshots."

"Wait, did he break up with her over *text*?!"

"No, they argued and I guess she stormed out partway through and then texted him." She half-laughed, the sound almost incredulous, before she started reading. "'You're a goddamn hypocrite. No one should have to be ashamed of what their'—she used the wrong *they're*, ugh—'into and I hope you know how much of a dick that makes you.'"

"That was Alison?"

"Of course." She kept reading, moving on to Reid's response. "He goes, 'I *never* said you should be ashamed of that or that it was a problem, Ali. I said I don't want to watch my girlfriend cheat on me or—'"

"Wait, *what*?!" I interrupted.

"Yeah. Because apparently she's into cuckolding."

"You're joking."

She shook her head. "Which wouldn't be so bad, except she wants the whole 'I'm doing this because you don't satisfy me' aspect of it. And pulled that out mid-sex without telling him first."

My mouth dropped open. "She didn't."

"Mm-hmm. So of course, he got upset and said he was still into her, but he would never be cool with her telling him he'd never be able to satisfy her or to hurry up and finish so she could go find a real man to do what he couldn't."

"That seems more than fair."

"Yeah, but Alison took him setting a boundary personally and told him she couldn't be with someone who wouldn't respect what she liked sexually and he told her he—"

She cut herself off, paused for a heartbeat longer than it should have taken to read whatever it was she'd read, then made me jump as she started *cackling*.

"Oh, he's such a dick!" she said through her giggles.

"What did he say?"

She pushed her hair back off her face, taking a breath to control her laughter. "'I can't be with someone who talks about me like that, even if it's a fantasy. Syd's the one with the humiliation kink, not me.'"

I raised my eyebrows high enough that I felt it in my cheekbones. "Your *what* kink?!"

"Hey. No kink-shaming," she said, wagging a finger at me.

"I'm not. I just... how did I not know that about you?" I asked.

She shrugged and from the corner of my eye, I could see her face staining pink beneath her freckles. "I dunno. I mean, it's kind of embarrassing to admit."

"Isn't that kind of the point?"

"The... oh, shut *up!*" she said, though she grinned and joined in when I started laughing. "It is, but it isn't. Like, I don't love being embarrassed. I just kinda like being told, like..."

"You're a bad, bad girl?" I finished when she trailed off.

"Sorta," she admitted. "Or, like, being called a, um... slut."

I nodded in understanding, even though she didn't say anything more. Sydney and I had exactly one conversation over the course of our friendship about being slutty and calling ourselves sluts and the concept of sluttiness in general.

Not that we'd only talked about it once. It had been countless times, often over strong drinks and skimpy dresses after someone felt the need to share their judgements on the way we lived our lives. The memories of all those talks had folded together, blending and mixing until they made up the one conversation we'd had time and time again.

That there was nothing wrong with enjoying sex as often and with as many people as we liked, so long as we respected the people we were with and ourselves.

That we weren't ashamed of being so-called sluts, even though I felt like that word had ruined my life in high school.

That the word only had as much power as we gave it, and that we both felt like we were ready to stop giving it power.

And that if either of us ever heard someone refer to the other as a slut, we'd physically or emotionally slap that person. Because while the *word* only had so much power, the intent behind it was often negative, and I wasn't going to stand for someone trying to insult my best friend like that.

"You know I'm not judging you for that, right?" I asked.

"Of course," she said, though there was relief in her voice. "If anyone would get it, it'd be you."

"I mean, shit. If it's that hot, maybe I need to try it some time," I said. "But I *am* a little surprised Reid knew about that when I didn't. How'd that happen?"

"Oh, God," she groaned, though she started laughing. "Let's just say Truth-or-Dare gone wrong. He's never going to let me live it down."

"That's kinda kink-shame-y on his part, though," I said.

She shook her head. "It's fine. Honestly, Nell. You know how Reid and I joke with each other."

And oh, did I.

On the day the two of them got their heads out of their respective asses and admitted they wanted to bone each other exclusively for the rest of their lives, I was going to buy a pack of cupcakes. The fancy kind made in the correct way, with icing piled higher than the cake part because we all knew the cake was just a vehicle to get the icing to your mouth.

Then I was going to bring those beautiful cupcakes downstairs to Reid and Syd's—because I could not handle the prospect of this not happening in the near future—and sit down at the kitchen table with them to celebrate. There would be an assortment, so I'd ask them which cupcake they wanted. Syd would pick one with purple icing, regardless of flavour; Reid would pick chocolate, regardless of any more interesting flavours.

Once they'd chosen their cupcakes, I was going to carefully remove them from the box. Then I was going to take one in each hand, lean across the table, and mash it into their faces as payback for the *years* I had to put up with them dancing around and pretending they weren't going to fuck one day.

Because they were. And God help the city of Ottawa when that happened because I imagined getting all those years of pent-up pining out would shake the ground hard enough to bring down buildings and cause the Rideau to overflow. I'd already planned out the sermon I was going to give Reid when they announced they were dating, which culminated with me reminding him that there was no guarantee he'd be standing at the front of the room during Sydney's future wedding, but that as her best friend, I most certainly would be.

But there was no way Reid and Sydney were getting together anytime soon. They were inconveniently almost never single at the same time and both of them were too stubborn to do anything but hide their internal angst at how much they wanted the other. And I sure as hell wasn't going to press Sydney's buttons and pressure her into dating someone just because I thought they were meant for each other.

I wasn't Anne-Marie, after all.

When we finally arrived at the park where the Illumi-Nite starting line would be, Sydney was still breaking down all the details from Reid and Alison's breakup. I wasn't intentionally ignoring her, but there was a *ton* of stuff going on around us that stole my attention.

Despite Anne-Marie's description of what Illumi-Nite was, it wasn't until that moment that I realized what we were actually in for. I didn't know a ton about neurodiversity, but Reid had ADHD and Remy, Anne-Marie's boyfriend, was Autistic. And from talking to them, I knew enough to wonder how "Overstimulating Nightmare" became the theme for an event that supported neurodiverse people.

I mean, it was a lot, even for me. Thumping music and excited shouts filled the air the moment I closed my car door. The sun was still up, but not for long; the race was scheduled to start three minutes after sunset to really lean into the whole *night* part of it and I could already see the towering structures with black lights and disco balls marking the race route.

And then there were the people. I thought Sydney and I had gone a bit overboard with our outfits, but the people milling about made us look like we'd done the bare minimum. Anne-Marie said we'd registered too late to get the racing T-shirt they were giving to people and *definitely* too late to get a team name or custom message added to it, so to wear white or bright colours. Syd had gone with a neon yellow shirt that clashed horribly with her reddish-blonde hair and added a rainbow tutu over her running shorts. I'd cut up an old white shirt, using strips of fabric to tie parts of it together and morph it into a racerback tank with plenty of fringe so the tanned skin on my stomach and back peeked through as the fringe swished around me. I'd added a neon pink sports bra beneath and while my spandex shorts were black, they had a metallic rainbow leopard print pattern on them that I figured was colourful enough to count as part of the theme.

But around us, people were clad in everything from full one-piece neon jumpsuits to pure white bikinis with mini-shorts. There were multiple people walking around in morph suits of all colours, a shirtless man who had painted his chest and back with body paint, and a group of guys wearing unicorn onesies with rainbow manes.

There were normal-looking people too, of course. Old people with walkers and T-shirts tucked into Bermuda shorts. Old people with thin, leathery legs poking out of baggy running shorts, white tube socks pulled halfway up their calves and running belts like the one Ben had with full water bottles around their waists. And also teenagers and kids and parents and college students and whatever you call adults who aren't parents or students, like a group of women in their thirties wearing those sports bras you could fill with a bottle of wine to sneak it into hockey games and some hippie-esque women who you just knew leaned into their identities as the cool childless aunties, and JP.

"What the fuck," I said, stumbling as I realized he was about twenty feet away from me. Then, as I realized the *rest* of the goddamn Marchand family was standing with him: "What the actual fuck?!"

"Ah, *mes chers!*" Anne-Marie squealed, noticing me and Sydney and waving us over, her long blonde hair pulled up into a high, flouncy ponytail that seemed to bounce with her excitement. She was wearing an electric blue shirt paired with a bright pink vest declaring she was

Event Staff and there was a temporary rainbow infinity symbol tattoo decorating one high cheekbone. Beside her, Della Kinsley was wearing the white racing T-shirt and a pair of pink running shorts, while Jean-Luc Marchand was wearing a tight pair of running shorts and a light grey sleeveless shirt with the race bib pinned directly to it. Marc-Andre milled nearby in a pair of navy blue dress shorts that were completely inappropriate for running, his head tucked down as he tapped on his phone.

And then there was JP, wearing the white racing T-shirt, though he'd obviously registered early enough to get a custom message on it because bold rainbow letters spelling "SIX FOR SAM" were sprawled across the back. He was wearing a baggy pair of basketball shorts that were such a light shade of grey, they were almost white, hitting just above his knee so you could see a hint of his toned thigh muscles when he moved the right way. He also had a set of sweatbands on his wrists and forehead that were faintly stained with coloured powder, a word I couldn't quite read embroidered on the headband, and that telltale amused smirk playing on his lips as my eyes met his.

The bastard.

I looked away, knowing damn well that his smirk grew even as I did, and waved at Anne-Marie.

"There you are." She shuffled forward on her tiptoes, giving both me and Sydney a hug hello. "I was wondering if you had backed out, *chérie*!"

I frowned, looking down at my phone. "You said the race didn't start until sunset."

"Yes, but people usually come early to enjoy the festivities," she said.

"And to get ready to run," Mr. Marchand added, grumbling a bit. "You can't accurately track your time if you're not at the starting line when the race starts."

"We said you could go get lined up, Dad," JP said.

"And it is okay, *chérie*," Della said. "There is still plenty of time."

"I didn't know your whole family would be here," Sydney said, trying to divert the conversation. "It's so cool that you all do this together."

"Well, our children are very involved in this cause, so we wanted to show our support, too," Della said.

Mr. Marchand chuckled. "And it's the only place JP doesn't get to follow in my footsteps, since he'd better be ahead of them." He clapped JP on the back. "Right, son?"

And I didn't know if it was because I was more in tune with JP's face now or if something had changed, but instead of the laugh and cheerful agreement that he was just like his dad, JP's jaw tensed and his usual easy smile was forced.

"Of course," he said, then straightened his shoulders. "Well, I just spotted Ibrahim and Nic so I think we're getting set up. I'll see you all at the finish line."

"We'll head to the start, too," Mr. Marchand said, and Della and Marc-Andre went with him.

"What was that all about?" Sydney asked.

"What?" Anne-Marie replied, confused, then glanced after her brother. "Oh, you mean Jean-Paul? He and his friends run this together. It is... Well, something of a tradition for them."

It wasn't quite what Sydney meant, but it did answer two of *my* questions, which were where JP was going and also if anyone else noticed the weird tension. But before Sydney could clarify, the only person in a five kilometer radius dressed in all black came up and threw a relieved arm around my shoulders.

"Oh, thank *God*," Bruno Lemaire, also known as the guy who agreed to be my date to all the bullshit events my dad had insisted I attend this summer, gasped. "I was going to hide in the outhouses if I didn't see someone else I knew."

"Ah, Bruno!" Anne-Marie said excitedly. "You came! I have your racing bib here."

He glared at her. "Of course I came. You roped me into it."

Anne-Marie tutted. "I did not *rope you in*."

"You used my weak spot against me." He looked at me like I was going to agree with him. "I bet she used it against you, too."

"I don't think your weak spot would work against me," I said. "It's *your* weak spot."

He rolled his eyes. "Okay, but she used *your* weak spot against you."

"I did not," Anne-Marie said. "Nellie just never told me she was a runner until I caught her jogging one night."

"Wait, seriously?" Bruno groaned. "You're a runner, too? How did you ever trick me into thinking you're cool?"

"Jerk," I said. "I was going to be nice and not even ask what your weak spot is, but now I want to know. It could be useful information."

"Trust me, it would be the opposite of useful for you," he said, sniffing.

"That just makes me want to know more."

"Well, too bad, *ma nouère*," he said.

"You know Anne-Marie will tell me if I ask her," I said.

Anne-Marie nodded. "It is true, I'm afraid."

Bruno scoffed, though a hint of pink appeared on his otherwise pale white skin. "Well, she's a liar."

"Hey!" I said, pushing his arm off my shoulders. "Anne-Marie may be a gossip, and she might be sort of materialistic and really pushy and way too involved in everyone's drama and far louder than she needs to be, but you can't sit here and call one of my best friends a *liar*."

"Thank you, *chérie*," Anne-Marie said, folding her arms. "I do not *lie*, Mr. Lemaire."

Bruno ignored her, instead turning to me with an amused look on his face. "That's how you talk about your best friend? Yeesh. What do you say about people you don't like?"

"Oh, she would probably call them lovely and kind and generous," Anne-Marie said. "That is how you know Nellie likes you. If she says too many nice things, watch out."

"Hmm," Sydney said, leaning in and lowering her voice as Anne-Marie pulled Bruno over to safety pin the bib to his shirt. "Is that why you keep calling JP a bastard?"

"Syd, you're the sweetest and prettiest person I've ever met in my entire life," I grumbled, and even though I stormed away, Sydney burst out laughing.

Chapter Five
Start With A Shot

GIVEN HOW MANY PEOPLE were there—well over a thousand, according to Anne-Marie—and the fact that he'd walked in the opposite direction of the eventual direction me, Sydney, and Bruno walked, the chances of us lining up anywhere near JP and his friends were slim.

Of course, that didn't take into account the fact that the universe seemed to conspire against me at any given opportunity.

"Where did your secret crush get Jello shots?" Bruno asked loudly.

"Secret crush?" I repeated, insulted. "I don't—"

"Sure you don't, *chérie*," Bruno and Sydney said in haunting unison, their voices eerily similar to Anne-Marie's.

"You're both dicks," I muttered.

"You must have been dropped on your head as a baby if you're just figuring that out," Bruno said.

About twenty feet away, JP was reaching into a gallon-size Ziploc bag and pulling out Jello shots, handing them out to a bunch of other people wearing the same "SIX FOR SAM" T-shirt he was wearing. I watched as he handed a shot to a woman with glossy black hair, medium reddish-brown skin, and a similar embroidered sweatband to the one he was wearing. She said something to JP, who smiled and responded before she threw her arms around him. He chuckled and hugged her back, and I definitely wasn't jealous in any way, especially after they parted and the woman wiped a hand beneath her eyes before laughing again.

"Or maybe her secret crush has railed her head into the headboard a few too many times," Sydney added.

Bruno let out a howl of a laugh, loud enough that it caught JP's attention. Sparkling blue eyes met mine and I couldn't help but raise an eyebrow in mock judgement, my eyes flicking to the woman he'd just given a shot to.

Because of the shot. Not because of the hug.

Which JP clearly understood because that telltale smirk of his crossed his face. He glanced around, seemingly confirming something, then side-stepped a few of his friends and half-jogged over to us, digging into the Ziploc bag.

"What's this for?" I asked as he handed me a plastic cup full of cherry red Jello.

"We start the race with a toast," he said, putting the shot in my outstretched hand before turning to Sydney and passing her a lime green one. "You have to wait until they set off the starting pistol, but take the shot the *second* you hear it, okay?"

"So specific," Bruno said as JP gave him a lemon yellow shot.

"Trust me. Take the shot when you hear the shot." He looked up at me, the corners of his eyes crinkled. "No matter how much you hate it when people tell you what to do."

"Bastard," I said under my breath, and he grinned.

"Have a good race," he said, then turned and headed back to his group of friends.

"Wait," Bruno said after JP had walked away. "Is there actually something going on with you and him?"

I scoffed, taking the lid off my Jello shot and running my finger along the edges. "What makes you think that?"

"Uh…" He held up his lemon Jello shot.

"So because my friend's brother gave us some of their extra Jello shots, something must be going on?"

"Well no, but—"

Sydney started snickering and Bruno looked at her, then at me, an eager look blossoming on his face.

"Oh my God. He *has* actually railed your head into the headboard a few too many times, hasn't he?"

"It's more like the roof of his car," Sydney said.

"Shut up," I said, glaring at them. "Seriously. Anne-Marie absolutely cannot find out about this."

"That sounds like exactly the kind of thing Anne-Marie should find out about, *chérie*," said a voice from behind me.

My face went cold and my head went light. Every ounce of blood in my face seemed to drain into the pit of my stomach, making it drop so low I wanted to shit my pants. Whirling around, I ended up staring straight at Anne-Marie, who was…

Well, she wasn't grinning maniacally. Instead, there was a curious look on her face, her long blonde ponytail dangling over her left shoulder as she tilted her head.

Which meant she hadn't heard what I said. Or if she had, she didn't know I was talking about her brother. I was half-certain that Anne-Marie carried around pockets of glitter confetti for the sole purpose of being able to throw it in the air if JP and I ever did get together. Unfortunately for her, that would never happen, so I guess she was just going to be stuck with pockets full of glitter for the rest of her life.

But even if she wasn't wearing something with pockets for some reason, there was no way Anne-Marie would ever hear me say I was hooking up with her brother and not immediately shriek with joy.

"Busted," Sydney said, sighing dramatically. "I knew she'd catch us the second we broke the shots out."

"The shots?" Remy, who I hadn't noticed walking up with Anne-Marie, stepped forward with a frown creasing his forehead. "What sho—"

"Ah, *ostie de câlisse de crisse*!" Anne-Marie swore, noticing the plastic cups in each of our hands, a scandalized look shadowing her eyes. "Where did you—ah, *tabarnak*, let me guess." She whirled around, glowering in the general direction of JP and his friends. "My goddamn brother gave those to you and told you not to let me find out."

"Uh… obviously," I said.

"Ah, *il est un trou d'cul*," she grumbled. "I told him and he promised—*he promised*! Complete *trou d'cul*. He knows—he *knows*!—I still haven't heard the end of last year and—*aghhh*!"

Without another word, she stormed through the people milling between us and JP's group of friends, Remy tailing not far behind her. Sydney and I exchanged glances, a guilty look flashing on her face.

"Shit," she said. "If I'd known I was actually throwing him under the bus…"

"Don't worry," Bruno said. "I'm sure he won't mind if Nellie makes it up to him on your behalf."

He wasn't wrong, but he also wasn't right. I mean, yes, I could've absolutely made it up to JP if I needed to. And somehow, I'd gotten to know JP well enough to know he wouldn't throw *me* under the bus and tell Anne-Marie about us hooking up or anything. So I wasn't worried that he'd say something he wasn't supposed to when she stormed up and yanked on his arm, forcing him to turn and face her.

But instead of looking ashamed or chastised as Anne-Marie reprimanded him in rapid French, JP grinned. He waited patiently for Anne-Marie to finish speaking, then waved over the woman he'd hugged earlier. She glanced at Anne-Marie and burst out laughing, then swung a drawstring bag I hadn't noticed off her back and scurried forward in excitement. Anne-Marie frowned as she took the bag, working the strings open and peering in before slapping JP on the arm. He snickered, then waved another person over, and another, all of them passing matching drawstring backpacks to Anne-Marie until she was juggling five of them. There was an exasperated huff of an expression on her face, but beneath it, I could see her fighting back a smile. Remy took three of the bags from her so she could hug the first woman and slap JP on the arm again, then they started back towards us.

"What a twit," she said, rolling her eyes. "Last year the station volunteers got word that Jean-Paul and his friends had brought Jello shots, but they ran out before the first checkpoint. Even I did not get one! And so I told him they could not bring shots again unless they made enough for everyone. So what does he do?" She brandished one of the backpacks she was holding. "He makes sure they made enough for every one of the volunteers and set them all aside for me!"

"How dare he," Bruno said, his voice flat.

"Exactly. As if I did not have enough to do, now I have to hand these out." She scoffed again, but before she could say anything else, a creaky voice thundered out of the sound system, even louder than the thumping, blaring music.

"*Bienvenue, coureurs, à la septième* Illumi-Nite *annuelle!*" There was a pause as a loud cheer rose from the crowd before repeating the announcement in English. "Welcome, racers, to the seventh annual Illumi-Nite!"

Again, a rousing shout vibrated the air around us, even though I was pretty sure almost everyone understood both languages. Still, the energy was contagious, and even Bruno started clapping as the announcer reminded us of the race etiquette—have fun, don't spit when other runners are down wind, there's no official timing or winners so don't elbow people to get ahead of them, which I imagined was directed at people like Mr. Marchand—and the exciting activities waiting for us at the finish line.

"*Nous souhaitons rendre hommage à l'un des premiers membres de la Fondation—*"

"Ah, *crisse de tabernak,*" Anne-Marie said, wrenching the bag open and grabbing one of the Jello shots, flicking the lid off in a smooth motion and shoving it at Remy before grabbing a second one from the bag. "Already?!"

"What do you mean, already?" Bruno said. "They've been talking for ages."

She waved a hand at him. "Shut up. Get ready."

"We *are* ready," I said, trying not to laugh.

"—tribute to one of the early members of the HueManity Foundation, Samay Mehra, who organized the first Illumi-Nite race seven years ago," the announcer said. "And who would be personally offended if we took a moment of silence in his honour instead of starting with recognition of one of his favourite holidays: the festival of Holi."

"Six years for Sam!" someone hollered from somewhere to my left, and an echoing shout responded. When I looked over, I couldn't see JP, but all the people with the SIX FOR SAM message on their shirts had lifted small, colorful plastic cups in the air.

"*Maintenant, sans plus attendre: prêts,*" said the voice on the loudspeaker. "*Partez...*"

I don't know if they finished the statement or repeated it in English. Everyone around me shouted "*Feu!*", an echoing blast went off and I immediately understood why JP told us to take the Jello shots as soon as we heard the gunshot sound effect.

I slammed the plastic cup to my lips, watching as huge clouds of coloured powder puffed into the air from the cannons surrounding the starting area. People around me shrieked and laughed in excitement and the crowd started pulsing forward before I even registered the burn of what I was guessing was vodka mixed in the cherry Jello.

"Bleugh!" Anne-Marie said, wincing and shaking her head as she lowered her plastic cup a few moments after everyone else. "That was gritty."

"Mine was fine," Sydney said. "You should try to do it faster next time."

Anne-Marie stuck her tongue out at Sydney, then let out another *bleugh* sound and made a face as more of the powder floating in the air settled on her tongue. Bruno laughed, then choked as he inhaled a lungful of the coloured powder, which made Remy shake his head.

"Come on, Anne-Marie," he said. "We should get ahead of the racers and bring those to the rest of the volunteers."

"Get ahead of them?" Bruno said through his coughs. "How fast d—" He hacked for a moment, then cleared his throat. "How fast do you think you can run?"

"Oh, I am not running," Anne-Marie said, fishing a tissue out of her pocket so she could wipe the powder off her face. "Remy will drive me on one of the golf carts. We will meet you all at the finish line!"

And with that, she shuffled away through the throng of people surrounding us, now doused in colourful powder and with Remy close behind her. The crowd kept moving forward and I'd barely blinked before I lost sight of both of them.

They weren't the only ones I'd already lost track of, either. The stream of bodies to the left of us seemed to move faster for some reason and JP's group was already long gone. But Sydney, Bruno, and I all stuck together as the people in front of us finally picked up speed and the cluster spread enough that we could start jogging.

The loud music and black lights were nearly constant along the race route, but each of the distance markers had an extra little gimmick or bonus at it. At the first kilometer were a bunch of actors dressed up in the kitschiest spectator gear they could find and holding signs that said "You're almost there!" and "She's not so good at numbers" and "PAIN" with a picture of bread. The one-point-five kilometer marker had more confetti, though there were also people giving out candy, but the two kilometer mark had an inflatable mini-obstacle course filled with foam.

"*Why* would I want to get all soapy?" Bruno complained as Sydney and I dragged him over to the inflatables.

"Why *wouldn't* you?" Sydney asked. "It's like a bouncy castle for adults!"

"Do I look like the kind of person who enjoys a bouncy castle?" he grumbled.

The answer to that ended up being yes, he was the kind of person who liked bouncy castles, because even Bruno was grinning like an idiot when we got to the end. A pile of white suds had collected on top of his dark hair after we slid down a tall inflatable into a pool of foam at the bottom.

And then there was the two-point-five kilometer mark.

We rounded a bend and saw volunteers spraying down racers with Super Soakers and bottles full of coloured water. It was a welcome sight. While it might be night, it had been a particularly humid day and the heat had lingered after the sun went down. I turned to say as much to Sydney when a brown-haired man with a thick mustache jogged past us wearing a white muscle shirt that showed off his swollen biceps and brown chest hair, his skin a rich shade of tanned beige.

"Hey, Bruno!" He clapped Bruno on the shoulder, making him stumble. "You made it!"

"N-N—" Bruno cleared his throat. "Niko. Hey. Didn't expect to see you here."

The man grinned, his eyes flicking down and back up. "You thought I'd ditch out after mentioning it at trivia? I'm running for my little brother, remember? He's dyslexic?"

Bruno sputtered again, his sweaty, flushed face turning a deeper shade of red. "I, uh... I... must've forgotten. My... my friend, he's Autistic. Not that I'm... I mean, his girlfriend, she—" He cleared his throat again. "My friend's girlfriend is a volunteer and she asked me to come. To run in honour of Remy."

I raised my eyebrows. Remy wasn't exactly shy about sharing that he was Autistic since it was just part of who he was, not some negative thing about him. But there was a pretty big difference between raising money and awareness for something in general and saying you were running in "honour" of a singular person. I wasn't sure Remy would appreciate Bruno acting like it was some big personal act.

"Fair enough," the man—Niko, I guess—said, still grinning at Bruno. "Well, maybe I'll catch ya at the finish line. Have a good run!"

"You have a good… running… time," Bruno stammered, though Niko had already taken off and likely didn't hear any of it.

"So who was that?" Sydney asked teasingly.

Bruno blinked. "No one."

"Huh," I said. "I thought he said 'Niko,' not 'Nemo,' but if you're saying it's no one…"

"Shut up," he grumbled. "I mean he's… Niko. He's a guy I know. Who's friendly. That's it."

"Mmm," Sydney said. "So he's the weak spot?"

"Of course not!" Bruno said.

"Oh, so you really are here 'in honour of Remy,' then?" I asked. "I thought that might just be you stumbling for an excuse because you were flustered and maybe didn't know that Remy would find it insulting."

Bruno's face flushed pink. "I was just… like… Whatever. You're making a big deal out of nothing."

"She literally said one thing about it," Sydney said, frowning.

The embarrassment on Bruno's face grew, but before he could say anything, a loud shout of familiar laughter caught his attention from the station of volunteers ahead of us. All of us glanced over just in time to see Niko take a small plastic bucket from a volunteer and lift it over his head, tilting his face up as he tipped the bucket over to let it splash all over him.

"Oh my God," Sydney murmured as blue-tinted water dribbled down Niko's thick neck and soaked the white muscle shirt until it was clinging to his round pecs and showing off a defined set of abs.

"He just might be," Bruno breathed, his eyes glued to Niko.

"You do have good taste," I admitted.

Bruno didn't take his eyes off Niko. Not as one of the volunteers sprayed him with pink water from a Super Soaker. Not as we jogged past Niko. Not as he slowly started to veer towards the edge of the path, his head swivelling to keep watching the display behind him until—

"Wait, watch out!" Sydney said.

Bruno did not watch out. Instead, Bruno crashed into a garbage can. Luckily, he bounced off it, but before he could right himself, he stumbled into a blue bin meant for collecting cans and bottles.

And I mean *into*.

As in, he tripped and went down ass-first, the cans and bottles clanging and crunching as he half-fell, half-sat on top of them.

"*Oh*," I gasped, clapping a hand to my mouth as if it could hold in the laugh bubbling up from my chest.

"Oh, no," Sydney added, her voice shaking with giggles trying to escape. "We have to go help him."

I bit my lip. Bruno had said something kind of dick-ish, but that didn't mean I wanted to leave him in a garbage can. Still...

"Would it be horrible if I took a picture first?" I asked.

"Nellie! Of course it would be."

"So... do it?"

"If you don't, I will."

I took the photo, but before Syd and I could go over to help, Niko burst past us. His eyes were wide with worry as he bounded over to the recycle bin Bruno was stuck in.

"Oh my God!" he shouted. "Are you okay, Brun-Brun!"

I pressed my lips together, curling them in as I glanced at Sydney. She looked back at me, mirroring my expression.

"Are you hurt?" Niko asked, reaching out to take Bruno's hand. "Let me help you... and excuse me! Someone come move this. What a horrible place to keep a recycle bin. Who put this here? You could've hurt my... my friend!"

"Keep going without him?" Sydney whispered.

I barely hesitated before nodding and the two of us started jogging again, not saying a word until we were far enough away that we knew Bruno wouldn't be able to hear us laugh.

Chapter Six
Finish With A Bang

I lost Sydney at the four-kilometer marker.

Not, like, literally. Or emotionally. Or physically.

Well, I guess physically. Like, she was no longer physically with me, but I knew where she was and had said it was fine for her to ditch me even though running the last kilometer by myself would suck because the only thing worse than running was running alone.

"Oooh," I said as we got near the marker, eyeing the flashing lights on the firetruck parked next to the route. "Is this a sexy firefighter station?"

"Maybe," she said. "Or maybe they're going to hose us down again."

We were both wrong. As we got closer to the marker, it became clear it wasn't just firefighters, but also police officers and paramedics. The firefighters were shirtless and posing for photos with runners, including the group of women in the wine sports bras I'd seen earlier. The paramedics seemed to be milling around, so I wasn't sure if they were just on call in case anyone got hurt while running.

And then there were...

"Oh my God," Sydney said, suppressing a giggle. "The cops are giving away donuts?"

"Apparently," I said.

"Think Olivier will be mad if I take a photo and text it to him?" she asked as we veered to the side to claim our powdered donuts.

"Why would he be mad?"

"I mean, the whole cop-donut thing?" she said. "Obviously some people think it's funny, but I don't know if he does."

"You don't?" I raised my eyebrows, glancing at her. "Really?"

She frowned. "It's not like I've asked him about it."

I glanced at the donut station, then at Sydney. "And do you think you *need* to ask him about it?"

She looked even more bewildered. "I guess not, but how else would I—"

"*Bonjour, ma minoune.*"

Sydney blinked, then whirled away from me and saw what I'd seen way before she had, which was an officer with messy brown curls, beige skin that was far tanner than the last time I'd seen him, and a wide grin on his face.

"Olivier!" Sydney gasped.

His grin widened as he stepped away from the table. "Surprise."

It was the fastest Syd had run the entire time. She bounded the last few feet towards the station, though when Olivier's shoulders tensed and he glanced around, she skidded to a stop as if remembering he was surrounded by his coworkers. He grimaced regretfully, though after another quick look, stepped out from behind the table and reached for Sydney. Her shoulders hunched almost imperceptibly so he didn't have to tilt his head up when he pressed a quick kiss to her lips.

"I thought you were working late tonight!" she said when they parted.

He gestured around us. "When you said you were here for the run, I did not want to tell you I had volunteered. So I could surprise you. I have been watching for you all night."

She bit her lip, but it wasn't enough to stop her eyes from sparkling. "How long are you volunteering for?"

"Until the last racer is done." He sounded apologetic. "Or until we run out of donuts. But if you want to, you can help me pass them out. I think it might go faster that way."

Sydney glanced at me.

And here's the thing.

If I'd thought she wanted an excuse to say no because she didn't actually want to stay and help him pass out donuts, I would've happily thrown a fit about her ditching me. I would've *absolutely* made myself the bad guy so she wouldn't feel bad about turning her down her fuck-buddy-but-also-kind-of-more-than-that.

Because that's what best friends do.

But I knew Syd, and the look she was giving me wasn't a "help me out of this" look. It was a "how mad are you going to be if I ditch you here so I can get laid sooner rather than later" look.

And sure, that might annoy some people. But part of the reason I loved our friendship so much was that Syd and I knew each other too damn well to be annoyed if one of us wanted to run off to get laid.

"Well," I said, reaching over to grab a donut off the table. "Let me do my part to make things go even faster."

Olivier's tongue poked out, wetting his lips as a pleased smile spread on his lips. "*C'est gentil. Merci.*"

"It's definitely a sacrifice," I said, powder puffing off the donut as I took a bite.

As expected, it sucked to run alone, so I didn't. The wine sports bra women were finishing up their shirtless firefighter photo shoot as I passed by and adopted me for a few minutes when I stopped to ask for a photo.

Not from the tall, bald, beautifully sculpted shirtless firefighter. Or the tall, red-haired, beautifully sculpted shirtless firefighter. Or the other tall, bald, beautifully sculpted shirtless firefighter. No, I wanted a photo with the slightly shorter, brunette, beautifully sculpted firefighter who was wearing a shirt because even though it wasn't illegal in Montreal, baring your tits in public wasn't exactly common.

Not that it mattered. I mean, she was so hot that I finally understood the whole "fighting fire with fire" analogy. Frankly, the tousled undercut, long eyelashes, and strip of midriff showing beneath the hem of the tight-fitting navy blue T-shirt worn beneath her beige firefighter jacket was doing *way* more for me than the muscle guys.

After I got my photo with the hot firefighter, I jogged past a group of college guys who apparently ate edibles before starting the race and were astounded by how light could make colours, like, *glow*, man. Not too long after, I passed a couple standing to the side in morph suits, the woman using her vape through the fabric while the man unzipped a hood that had multiple wet marks on it, peeling it away to reveal a face dripping in so much sweat that his hair was plastered against his forehead. I joked with them for a moment before continuing past a bachelorette and her bridesmaids, another set of morph suits, and JP.

He was laughing and chatting with a short, chubby man with dark brown hair and pale beige skin, but I didn't make eye contact or wave at him or anything. Not because of anything weird, but I didn't want to impose on whatever this tradition was. It didn't take a genius to put two and two and two together; the SIX FOR SAM T-shirts, the toast at the start of the race, and the literal announcement about a guy whose name sounded like Sam made it pretty clear they were running in memory of someone. A teacher, maybe, or a coach, or some other mentor.

But just after I claimed a four-and-a-half ounce plastic cup of beer from the four-point-five kilometer marker, he jogged up and fell in pace beside me.

"Tired yet?" JP asked, holding his hand out for my empty cup.

I scoffed and passed it to him. "Of course not. I could run another one of these. In fact, I might circle back and start the race all over again."

"I dunno about that," he said, stacking my cup into his and veering to the right so he could throw them both in the nearest garbage can. "You look pretty tired to me."

"Looks like you need your eyes checked."

It wasn't my best retort, so I was a little surprised when JP let out a bark of laughter. "Maybe. I don't have my contacts in. I made that mistake one year and between the Holi powder and the foam pit, my eyes were red for three days afterwards."

I looked at him, bewildered. "Since when have you worn contacts?"

"My dad said I couldn't get them until I turned thirteen, so the day I turned thirteen."

That just raised more questions. "I have zero memory of you wearing glasses."

"Because between the ages of ten and thirteen, I pretended that I hated reading and that writing in straight lines was for losers." He smirked. "Trust me, I've made every effort to make sure no one knows I wear glasses."

"Why?" I asked. "Afraid they might make you look smart or something?"

"It's more convenient if my fans and admirers don't know about the glasses so I can take advantage of the whole Clark Kent effect."

I rolled my eyes. "Okay, Superman."

From the corner of my eye, I saw him grin as he glanced at me. "You think I'm Superman, babe?"

I chose not to respond to the pet name, even though I knew he was trying to get a rise out of me. "I think *you* think you're Superman. But I'm not going to take your word for it without proof."

"There you go, proving why you would've made a great lawyer again," he said. "How am I supposed to prove I'm Superman?"

I shrugged as we ran past an elderly couple who were strolling peacefully under a string of black lights, white golf visors glowing on their heads. "You could tell me your kryptonite."

"Nice try, Lex Luthor. If I tell you, you'll use it against me."

I shrugged nonchalantly. "Fine then. I guess I just don't believe you."

He chuckled, but didn't say anything else. For a while, we ran next to each other in silence.

Which was weird.

JP and I didn't, like... *do* stuff together. We fucked. We were polite to each other in social situations. But while he was my best friend's brother, JP was almost five years older than me and Anne-Marie. It was enough of an age gap that he'd never complained about his parents making him let his little sister tag along with his friends because no one in their right mind would send a twelve-or-thirteen year old girl to hang out with a bunch of seventeen-year-old boys.

Those four-almost-five years didn't matter quite so much now. Yeah, there was definitely a difference between me being twenty-one and him being twenty-six, but it wasn't as intense as it seemed when he was starting CEGEP while Anne-Marie and I were technically still in elementary. But still. We weren't *friends*. We didn't hang out.

So it was weird to just... run together.

And it was *really* fucking weird that it didn't actually feel weird.

"What happened to your entourage?" he asked after a while.

"Bruno fell in a garbage can," I said. "And Sydney's hanging around the donut table so she can fuck a cop."

"One of those things raises more questions than the other," he said.

"I've told her a million times that him being a cop is a huge red flag, but Syd insists he's nice."

JP chuckled. "That's what I meant, obviously. Since it's a well-known fact that Bruno's a distant relative of Oscar the Grouch."

"Well, technically it was a recycle bin. He was staring at a hot guy and tripped."

"And you left him there?"

"I considered it, but the hot guy got him out and I'm assuming Bruno's off 'showing his gratitude' or something."

He let out another soft chuckle. "So you're on your own, then?"

"Until Anne-Marie inevitably tracks me down." I glanced at him from the corner of my eye. "Why?"

"Well, I was thinking you might like to earn it."

"Earn what?"

"The right to know my kryptonite."

"You seem to think I'm a lot more desperate to know what it is than I am."

He shrugged. "Fine. If you really don't want to know what my weak spot is, I won't tell you."

The bastard.

I glared at the race route ahead of me for a moment, telling myself not to give him the satisfaction of knowing he called my bluff, then promptly gave up. "What would it take to 'earn' that information?"

"Race me."

I twisted to look at him, raising my eyebrows. "Excuse me?"

JP's grin widened. "We're almost at the finish line. Race me to the end. If you beat me, I'll tell you my kryptonite."

"And if you beat me?

His eyes flicked down as his lower lip curled between his teeth. My heart rate was already higher than usual, but it skipped an extra beat and made my breath hitch as his eyes traced my body.

"There's a stage with live music set up at the finish line," he said, his voice low. "Behind that and to the left are a bunch of outhouses. Behind *those*, there's a gravel trail that leads to the other end of the park, where there are a ton of trees. If I win, you slip away from the party, follow that trail, and meet me in those trees."

Fuck.

In the best possible way, *fuck*.

"Are you serious?" I asked.

"There are only two things I take seriously, babe," he said. "One is winning."

"And the other?"

"Fucking."

I tried not to laugh. "You think that's a good idea?"

"Why wouldn't it be?"

"Hmm, I don't know." I tapped a finger on my chin. "Let's start with your entire *family* being at this event."

"My dad texted me five minutes ago to compare finish times and admonish me for not being done yet. They're already in the car. Marc-Andre never even started the race. He left to go to a friend's place. And Anne-Marie—"

"The worst of them all."

"She's busy being in the thick of the action."

He wasn't wrong, but I didn't want to admit that. "I don't know why you think a quickie in the trees is that good of a prize."

"Maybe it's because I'm jealous of your heart."

I frowned. "What?"

"You know." He elbowed me. "It's pumping inside you right now and I'm not."

I gagged loud enough that a few heads turned towards us and JP almost tripped as he laughed.

"So?" he said.

"I just about died because that joke was so bad and you still think I want to race you?"

"Don't you?"

I tried to tell him he was delusional. That there was no way I'd race him to "earn" the right to know something he was joking about. That his dick wasn't good enough for me to risk us getting caught with our pants literally down by the last person on Earth either of us wanted to be caught by, also known as his sister.

The problem was that his dick was definitely good enough for me to risk that.

"You're on," I said.

Chapter Seven
Magical Dick Reasons

JP WAS NOT THE only one who took winning seriously.

Unfortunately, JP's prize for winning the race was better than mine. I didn't really care what his kryptonite was. I doubted *he* even knew what he'd answer with. JP and I may not have been friends, but I knew him well enough to tell when he was talking out of his ass.

Which was most of the time.

But even though he was full of shit and I'd rather fuck him in the bushes than listen to him lie about kryptonite, I wasn't going to let him win. I was too competitive to throw a race, especially when I was pretty sure I could talk him into meeting me at those trees anyway.

You know, since I would be the winner and all.

And then we started running and I realized I had a lot going against me.

Like how he was the one who did the whole "Get ready, get set, go" thing so he had a split-second head start on me.

And how he had to be at least six feet tall and I was five-four on a good day.

And how he went to the gym and my so-called "training" for this race had mainly consisted of riding my former professor's dick.

"Took you long enough," JP said when I met him in the trees at the far end of the park a while later.

"Not long enough for you to clean up, apparently," I said, lifting an eyebrow.

He ran a hand across his cheeks, doing nothing to brush off the coloured powder his friends had showered him with after they caught up at the finish line. His hair was still speckled with pink and orange and purple, and blue and yellow streaks ran down his arms. Splotches of orange and green stained the back of his T-shirt and there was a smear of teal that started at the edge of one nostril and followed his smile line down to his jaw.

"The price I pay for finishing first," he said.

"You get to look like you got bukkaked by a bunch of ancient, dehydrated clowns?"

"It's tradition. For us, at least." He grinned, the teal line curving along with his smile. "Ever since the first year. First person to cross the finish line gets pelted. Although most years, it's more of a shoving match to get someone across the finish line. I think I might be the second person who did it on purpose."

"Hmm. Seems like a heavy price to pay just to get me in some bushes."

"Trust me, babe." He jerked his head to get me to follow him. "I'm gonna make sure it was *well* worth it."

I pretended that didn't make a warm sensation coil in my stomach. "You could've waited an hour for me to get home so we could meet up in your car instead of a forest.

He stepped off the path and moved a branch to the side so it wouldn't smack me as we ventured deeper into the trees. "No, I couldn't."

"My ass is good, but it's not that good."

"No, I mean I've been doing this race for years and not once have I gone home with the contents of my stomach still in place. If I go home at all."

"You take the after party seriously, eh?"

"Of course." A branch snapped beneath his foot. "It's the whole point. And tomorrow night's not an option because you've got that benefit and I've got a dinner meeting with a client in Sherbrooke. Besides, a change of scenery might be nice."

He pushed a few branches out of the way, then took my hand and pulled me into a clearing sheltered by a tangle of brush on one side and a few closely spaced trees on the other. We were far enough off the path that I could barely see the lights lining it illuminating the deserted section of the park. In the distance, the music at the after party thumped loud enough to drown out the buzz of the people dancing and celebrating.

"There," JP said. "It's not as good as a bed or anything, but it'll do."

"What makes a bed so good?"

He raised his eyebrows high enough that they almost touched the colour-stained sweatband on his forehead. "You don't like fucking in a bed?"

I shrugged. "I mean, they're nice, but not necessary. You proved that when you showed me I had plenty of room to sit on your face in the back of your car."

"Yeah, but I can't tie you to the backseat of a car," he said.

"You think I'd let you tie me to a bed?"

He tilted his head in concession. "You would probably try to scratch my eyes out."

"Damn straight."

"Okay, well, not having a bed means I can't hold you afterwards."

I rolled my eyes again. "The romantic shit doesn't work on me, JP. It does the opposite, actually."

"I don't mean romantically, smartass," he shot back.

"Oh, of course. You want to platonically hold me after we fuck. That makes total sense."

"It does."

I scoffed. "Seriously? Why would you want that?"

JP returned my incredulous scoff with an expression of disbelief. "Are you legitimately asking, after I've admitted multiple times how goddamn hot you are, after you've seen how hard you get me again and again, after I subjected myself to a so-called ancient clown bukkake to get you alone so I could fuck you for what is far past the world record for how many times I've fucked the same person, why I would want to have your naked body pressed against me?"

I opened my mouth to respond, but JP wasn't done.

"You seriously don't think that after I've buried my cock as deep inside your pussy or your throat as you'll let me, after I've felt you clench around me when I've made you come so hard you can't even think anymore, that I might want to sit there and enjoy watching you come back to your senses and realize you just screamed my name for me?"

His voice was like silk, light and smooth at first, like it was blowing in the breeze and rustling like the leaves in the trees above us. But each word brought more weight to it until it was draping over itself and pooling around us, dulling and dimming the world until all that was left was us in that clearing, his question hanging unanswered on the humid air like seconds hanging on a clock.

"I've never screamed your name," I finally said.

He took a slow step towards me. "Are you gonna stop me from doing my best to change that?"

I tried to control the shake in my voice so he didn't realize how his words had fucking *gotten* to me. "Can you at least take the sweatband off? You look like a fucking dork."

I half-expected him to argue, but he reached up, tugged the sweatband off, and shoved it in his pocket. "Better?"

"Well, you still look like a dork," I said, reaching up to rub the teal line off his face, though there wasn't much I could do for the band of beige-white skin now cutting through the coloured powder. "But it's tolerable."

"I can work with tolerable," he said.

"You'll have to be quick. I have *maybe* fifteen minutes before Anne-Marie realizes she's been squealing about Bruno to an empty chair and wonders where I went."

"Squealing about Bruno?" He took another step.

"Oh, apparently Niko—" My voice betrayed me on the *k*, crackling just enough that JP's smirk widened. "Niko carried Bruno across the finish line piggy-back style, took him straight to the beer gardens, and knocked half a table of drinks over while putting Bruno down so they could start making out." I bit my lip as JP moved another step closer. "I only managed to sneak away when security told them they had to tone it down and Anne-Marie went over to... help. I think."

"Well, good for them. Anne-Marie's been saying they've been dancing around each other for weeks now and the only thing more unbearable than Bruno's obsession with Niko is how obsessed Niko is with Bruno." He took one more step towards me. "Are you done with the story?"

"I... yes."

"Good. I wanna fuck you now."

And after everything he'd said, *that* was what sent goosebumps skating across my skin. *That* was what made the core of my body scream at me to shut up and get on with things. That simple statement, those simple words—"I wanna fuck you now"—was what it took to move me forward into his arms.

His lips tasted like salt in the most addictive way and his tongue like sweetness and peppermint, like he'd crunched one quickly before I got there. I let out an unintentional sigh and JP pulled me closer so I could feel what I'd already seen, which was the hard bulge tenting the fabric of his shorts. It pressed against my lower belly, thick and enticing, and I reached down to cup my hand around it.

"Fuck." He nudged his fingers through the cut-up fringe at the bottom of my shirt and slipped them beneath the stretchy fabric of my sports bra. A moment later, I stifled a cry as his fingers pinched the hard little nub, and he choked on another soft moan as I tightened my grip and stroked his cock through the fabric of his shorts. "I've been thinking about this since you walked up to my family like you had no idea how goddamn good your tits look in a sports bra."

"Oh, I know." I sighed as he cupped my breast and squeezed. "The only downside is they don't bounce as nicely when I run."

He slipped his hand out of my bra and trailed it down my body. Both hands moved behind me and he palmed my ass, squeezing and groaning as he pulled my body into his. "This isn't fucking fair. I won our race fair and square."

I frowned. "And here I am."

His lips moved to my jaw, then my neck. "Yeah, but you're getting both prizes."

"Are you saying your kryptonite is my ass?"

He squeezed my ass again, then he whimpered.

He fucking *whimpered*.

And yeah, I knew it was fake. I knew he was joking, that he was pretending my kryptonite ass was draining his energy. I knew JP, of all people, would never let me get him into a position where he'd legitimately make a noise like that.

But my pussy did not know those things. And it apparently *really* liked it when men fucking whimpered for me. So much so that I was almost worried I'd soak through my running shorts before JP pulled them down.

"It's weakening me already, babe," he said, still faking a feeble voice like he wasn't at all aware of the arousal that had just scorched its way through my body.

"Oh no," I said, swallowing hard. "Isn't long term exposure super dangerous? I should go back to my friends so you stay nice and safe."

"No, it's okay," he said. "We can reverse the effects if you, uh... let me fuck it."

His face was still buried in my neck, so he couldn't see the way I raised my eyebrows, but I assumed he felt the way I stiffened. "Did you just ask me for—"

"No," he said quickly, kissing my neck. "I'm not asking you to take it in the ass."

Damn. That was too bad. Not that I was going to tell JP, but I would've said yes. Like, not right that second, but maybe the next time I was in town for an event.

Like the Diamond Gala, which was the weekend after next, and which marked the end of my commitment to my dad for attending events as a Perfect Daughter Barbie. And it might also mark my last time in Montreal overall.

Because my dad would be paying my tuition and rent not too long after that. And yeah, he was still my dad and yeah, I felt like a garbage person for thinking I would put up with him until he was done paying for my education and then never have to see him again.

But I was starting to think the hurt of not having him in my life would be less than the hurt of having him there.

That was a thought for another time, though. Preferably a time when JP wasn't pressing kisses to my collarbone and grinding his dick on me, since the whole point of that thought train was that my potential last visit to Montreal would be a great time to lose my anal virginity.

"The kryptonite effects are just, uh, getting to me," JP continued, moving his hands to my hips. "I meant that you gotta let me fuck you"—he turned me in place until he could push his throbbing cock against my ass—"like this."

"Like this?" I shifted my hips from side to side and JP made a noise that wasn't quite as earth-shattering as the whimper, but was definitely full of genuine desperation.

"Yeah, babe," he said in my ear.

"And how is it that fucking your kryptonite is going to help?"

"Because of... you know." He thrust himself forward. "Magical dick reasons."

I snorted. "Magical dick reasons?"

"Mm-hmm. Trust me. I'm not making any of this up."

"Sure you're not."

He pressed a kiss to the top of my head and let go of my hips, hands wandering to the waistband of my shorts and pulling them down. "You wet for me, babe?"

"Find out for yourself," I replied.

He didn't say anything, but I could almost hear him smirking behind me. A moment later, he hooked the waistband of my thong and tugged it down to join my shorts under the curve of my ass. His fingertip dragged down my crack, tracing a path down lower and lower until his fingers dipped between my legs from behind.

"You're not wet," he said, his voice rumbling and low and pleased. "You're fucking *soaked* for me, aren't you, Nellie?"

I wanted to deny it, mostly because I wanted to deny that I ever did anything *for* JP Marchand.

But I couldn't. I absolutely couldn't deny my panties were soaked for JP when we both knew damn well I was aching for him.

That didn't mean I had to say it, though.

Instead, I pushed back against him, making his fingers slide along my slit. "Are you gonna do something about it?"

That was how I ended up with my hands pressed to the trunk of a reasonably sturdy tree, my feet shoulder-width apart and my shorts tight around my thighs, bent forward as JP slipped his cock inside me from behind. Both of us sighed as he entered me, a contented sound that wrapped our little clearing in relief and pleasure underscored by the thumping bass of music pounding at least a million miles away.

"How the fuck do you always feel so goddamn good, Nellie?" he groaned as he started moving inside me.

"I've got a grade A pussy," I replied.

He laughed. And like every time I made him laugh while he was inside me, his cock jostled the slightest bit and I had to bite back a moan because something about that felt *so* good.

So goddamn good.

"You've got grade A everything," he said, sliding his hand around me. "Grade A pussy"—he brought his hand up, grabbing my breast over top of my shirt and squeezing—"Grade A tits." He kneaded my breast for a moment before letting go, tracing the lines of my body until his hand was on my ass. "And this. This grade A fucking *ass* that just—"

And then he pressed his thumb against my hole.

I slammed a hand to my mouth to muffle the noise I made. It was like a mix between a yelp and a moan, the yelp not from pain but from surprise and the moan from... well, he was...

He was playing with my ass.

Which made me wonder how sincere he was when he said he wasn't asking to fuck it. I mean, it wasn't the first time he'd played with my ass. Though, I was pretty sure it was the first time he'd done it while we were fucking like that.

Luckily, I didn't have to wonder long.

"I'd love to have this around my dick," he murmured, pressing his thumb inside me. "You're clamping down so tight right now and it's only the tip of my thumb. If this was my cock—"

He started moving faster and my elbow buckled, leaving me no choice but to rest my forearm against the tree.

"You're so fucking hot," he gasped. "So hot, babe, and so—"

"Oh, God," I hissed as he pushed his thumb in further.

"Close," he said. "But it's actually pronounced 'JP.'"

"If you have enough brain power to make that joke, you're not fucking me hard enough," I gasped.

"That's fair," he said, then proceeded to fuck me *hard*.

God, I hoped no one was around. They would have definitely heard the way JP's hips were slapping against my ass and the high-pitched noises escaping my throat each time he drove his cock inside me. There was no fucking *way* they didn't hear his gasps as he brought us both closer and closer to the edge, though I doubted anyone would have been able to hear the things he was whispering to me.

"You gonna come on it for me, babe?" he asked.

He pushed his thumb in deeper and I squeezed my eyes closed, heat building up in my core as I cried out.

"Answer me, babe," he insisted.

"Please," I whispered. "Fuck, *please*—"

"Say it. *Say* you're fucking coming for me."

"I am," I gasped. "I—*fuck*, I'm... gonna c-come..."

"For who?" he demanded.

"For you," I whimpered. "I'm c-coming for you."

And then his hand was over my mouth, muffing the sound of me losing myself around his cock and in his arms. He buried his face against my neck, his moans rumbling against my skin. I was still mid-orgasm when I felt him come inside me, a pinprick of guilt cutting through the bliss because I knew he shouldn't be fucking me bare. I shouldn't be letting him *do* that.

But God, was it addictive.

My ears were ringing as we came down. JP took his thumb from my ass and pulled his cock out carefully, pulling my panties up quickly so they'd catch anything that leaked out before it hit my shorts.

"Thanks babe," he said as he tucked his cock back into his shorts. "Glad I won that race. I've never been so happy to fuck a loser before."

He laughed obnoxiously after I smacked his arm and I rolled my eyes. "Whatever, bastard. I'm going back to the party now. You wait here for a bit."

"What?" he asked. "Why do I have to wait?"

"So we don't suspiciously get back to the party at the same time."

"Yeah, but why do I have to be the one to wait?"

I made an aggravated noise. "Because I'm the one who has to deal with Anne-Marie and because I said so."

He looked like he was about to argue with me again, but his eyes flicked down my body and back up. Once they met mine again, he grinned and shrugged.

"Alright. Go for it."

And him giving in so easily should've been my clue that something was wrong. But it took until I found Anne-Marie at the party and she put an arm out to hold me in front of her, a suspicious look on her face, for me to realize JP had left a powdery blue and orange hand print directly over my right breast and that I was now stuck trying to convince her I'd been elbowed in the tit and instinctively grabbed it as a reflex at the beginning of the race.

Chapter Eight
This Ain't A Sin, It's A God Damn Tragedy

I WAS FAR TOO overdressed for a place that had a dish called Dee's Nuts on the menu.

So were my dad and Kimberlee, and it was obviously bothering them a lot more than it bothered me seeing as I was the one who picked the restaurant. But neither of them had said a single word about it since they were both stubborn as all hell. Kimberlee was absolutely not going to admit she was wrong for letting me pick where we went to brunch, and my dad was absolutely not going to step in to fix what he'd deemed as her mistake.

"You made the reservation at Beaujolais Park?" my dad had asked after we'd climbed into his Bentley to go to brunch that morning.

"No," Kimberlee had responded, her voice light.

From my spot in the back passenger seat, I saw a sliver of my dad's face frowning in the rear-view mirror. "No?"

"No," Kimberlee repeated, fastening her seatbelt. "We are always going to the same places."

"Have you made the reservation at a different restaurant, then?"

"No," she said again.

"Kimberlee," my dad said, his voice so tight the annoyance couldn't seep out of it, even though we all knew it was there. "Could you please let me know, my dear, where I am to drive us to?"

"No."

He almost snapped.

It was almost funny.

I almost rolled the window down and shouted for Pierre to throw a bag of popcorn in the microwave because of all the times my dad had broken up with someone, they'd never aggravated him to the point that I'd actually *witnessed* it. If I was around, he'd tell them to go to his office or to another room and the next time I saw him, it would be like whoever she was had never existed.

But while all those things *almost* happened, none of them actually did. I didn't roll the window down and it wasn't really funny and my dad, most shockingly, didn't snap.

Instead, he took a deep, steadying breath.

"Why have we not got a reservation for brunch today, Kimberlee?" he asked.

Kimberlee turned even more in place so she could peer at me in the back seat, a gentle smile spread on her lips.

"Because I thought it might be nice if Nellie got to pick where we went for once," she said.

And oh, no.

Oh, *no*.

"That's okay," I said before my dad could say anything. "I don't like picking. You guys wouldn't like the places I like anyway."

"How would we know if we have never tried?" Kimberlee said. "We are always going to the same places. I think it is time to broaden that and see what kinds of places you like to go."

"I can have Pierre call and get us a table at Blanchette Café," my dad said. "They usually have availability."

"That sounds great," I said. "I love Blanchette Cafe."

But Kimberlee shook her head. "I think it is important to try the kinds of places Nellie would like to go sometimes, Max."

"Nellie does not want to choose a restaurant," he replied. "She has already said that."

Kimberlee was silent for a moment. I thought she was pouting as she accepted defeat, but her hand went out and touched my dad's thigh.

"Max," she appealed softly. "Please."

And then, like the asshole he was, instead of telling her enough was enough and to drop it and if she didn't like it, she could leave, my dad sighed.

"Nellie, where would you like to go for brunch?" he asked.

My mouth fell open. "I don't—"

"Pick a restaurant," he said. "It is not a big deal."

To anyone else, it wouldn't be. To anyone else, it probably seemed like nothing, but to me, my dad had just destroyed one of the precious few things I'd counted as his good qualities.

I'd told my dad ten years earlier that I'd never pick a restaurant again. Well, I screamed it, actually, about a millisecond before I screamed that I fucking hated both my parents and about three seconds before my mom told me I was grounded for swearing and sent me to my room, even as I'd sobbed that I'd been invited next door to hang out with Anne-Marie while her stupid brother had a stupid birthday party.

But after they'd stopped fighting—or at least, after my mom had stormed away and they couldn't continue fighting—my dad had come upstairs and told me I wasn't grounded. I said I'd rather be grounded than pick a restaurant again, and he said I didn't have to and for ten *years*, I'd believed him.

Even before they officially told me they were getting divorced, I'd believed he got why it mattered. It might have been a small throwaway promise made to a child, but it meant something to me, and I'd believed—no.

Not just believed.

I'd *trusted* he understood.

He didn't, though. He didn't see what the big deal was. And since where we went wasn't a big deal and I was petty, I pulled out my phone and Googled the place my mom had wanted to go that day, which was called Tee Dee Daisy's. Unfortunately, Tee Dee Daisy's had closed down five years earlier, but my search brought up a place that had an appetizer called Dee's Nuts, which seemed promising.

And that was how I'd ended up at a place called John Jean's Pub and Eatery wearing an Alexander Wang mini-dress and heels while my dad made a pimply-faced server question his existence.

"...and the beef is fresh?" my dad asked, staring at the laminated menu.

"Of course, *monsieur*," the server said in a flat voice like he didn't get paid enough for this shit because he probably didn't. "We take it fresh out of the freezer every morning."

My dad fixed his cold, grey eyes on the server. For a moment, I thought the guy was impervious to my dad's iciness, but the wall of sass crumbled under the weight of my dad's gaze.

"I am only joking," the server said. "The ground beef is not frozen and the patties are made by hand daily. But the smoked brisket sandwich is made with, ah, better quality beef."

"Fine. I will take that," my dad said, setting the menu down.

"Fries or salad?" the server asked.

"Salad," my dad said.

"House?"

"Caesar."

"There's an extra charge for that."

If my dad clenched his jaw any more that day, he was going to end up at the dentist with a cracked tooth. "Fine."

The server jotted that down, then turned to Kimberlee. "Madame?"

"The summer berry salad, please," she said, closing her menu. "With grilled chicken and extra dressing."

"There's an extra charge for—"

"The extra charges are fine," my dad said, his tone clipped.

The server nodded and turned to me.

"The chicken strips," I said innocently. "And is there an extra charge to upgrade my fries to poutine?"

The server fought back a smile. "There is. Will that be okay?"

I turned to my dad, who had pressed his lips into a thin line. "Dad, is that okay?"

"No," he said.

"Great." I closed my menu. "I'll take the poutine. Oh, and I think we should start with an appetizer." I re-opened the menu. "Is one of Dee's Nuts enough for the whole table?"

"For three people, I think you will need two," the server said, his voice completely deadpan. "And that way, you don't need to decide between the sweet and spicy or the dill and cheddar varieties."

"Is that okay, Dad?" I asked. "Or is that too many of Dee's Nuts?"

"It is fine, Eleanor," he said.

"Great." I picked up the menus from the table and handed them to the server. "We'll take both of Dee's Nuts."

"Wonderful." He took the menus from me. "I'll bring you Dee's Nuts in a minute."

"Can't wait to get my mouth on them," I said. "They sound good, don't they, Dad?"

"They sound delightful," he said.

The server's shoulders shook as he walked away. Kimberlee let out a short, silent sigh and took a sip of water. My dad eyed the silverware in the middle of the table warily, as if he didn't know what the paper thing wrapped around them was—a napkin, for the record—before taking one and setting the cutlery next to him.

"You have a dress for the Harmonies for Hope benefit tonight, *ma fille ange*?" he asked, his tone crisp and business-like, as if he was resuming a conversation we'd been in the middle of when the server interrupted us to take our order.

Of course, since we hadn't been in the middle of a conversation, I was confused by the question. "Uh, yeah. Why wouldn't I?"

He reached for his water glass. "We are nearby that boutique Kimberlee likes, so I am ensuring you have an outfit prepared for this evening."

For a split second, I took him at the line between his words. Not quite at his word, because he hadn't outright said it, but I took him at the hope the line between them represented. That it was an implied apology for making me pick the restaurant and crossing one of the few boundaries he allowed me to have.

I shouldn't have. If there was one thing I knew about my dad, it was to never let my guard down. Because it only took a moment of hope to make it hurt when I was inevitably wrong.

"After all," he continued. "I don't want a repeat of the choral event a couple of weeks ago."

I swallowed back my disappointment as my dad took a sip of water. "There was nothing wrong with that dress, Dad."

"We were in a church, Nellie."

"How was I supposed to know God would be offended by a sliver of my shoulders?"

"I am sure God was fine with your shoulders." He set his water glass down. "However, He may have found the V-neck dipping to your sternum beyond inappropriate."

"It was an accident," I said. "It sometimes happens with wrap dresses. The tie came loose and I didn't notice."

Which was true. I'd loosened it myself to take a picture of my cleavage to send to JP, but I thought I'd retied it tight enough.

"Be that as it may, there is an especially important prospective client attending this event. It is the largest client I have ever attempted to manage and I do not want to lose this investor. So it is imperative they leave with a good impression of me and my family."

"Oh, I see," I said. "So you want me to wear the wrap dress again?"

Kimberlee pressed her lips together. If I didn't know better, I would've said she was trying not to laugh, but given that she was dating my dad and my dad was looking at me like he sincerely thought there was something wrong with me, I figured she wasn't.

"I was joking," I said before my dad said anything else. "I'll wear the *appropriate* dress. Don't worry."

He nodded briskly. "And your date? Mr. Lemaire?"

"I'll ask Bruno to wear an appropriate dress, too."

His lips tightened. "The investor I am working with is quite elderly. Following traditional etiquette, such as a young lady being escorted by an appropriate date, will be noticed. So Mr. Lemaire is still escorting you tonight?"

"Of course."

"And he will stay for the entirety of the event this time?"

I sighed. "It was *one* event that he left early, and it was only because there was an emergency."

That was also half-true. Bruno had only left one event early, but the emergency was that a guy he was crushing on was a musician who had a set that night. But my dad didn't need to know that.

"And in his absence, you decided it was acceptable to camp out at the table next to the chocolate fountain, staining your shirt, before insulting a *député* I have supported for a number of years."

I gritted my teeth. "I didn't do it on purpose. How was I supposed to know he doesn't believe in human rights?"

He held up a hand. "We are not getting into this again."

"But—"

"Eleanor, everyone is entitled to their opinions."

"Human rights aren't a matter of *opinion*."

"Enough." He set his hand on the table. "Bruno may not be the most ideal date, but he has been successful at ensuring you make a good impression when needed. If for some reason he is not available this evening, I happen to know Clinton Thibault is available and would be very interested in attending with you."

Ugh.

Of course he was.

It was news to exactly no one except my dad that there was something *wrong* with Clinton. After the luncheon at the Marchands' place, Clinton had been doing his best to worm his way into my life since my disdain for him was apparently more of a challenge than it was a deterrent. Not only had he requested to follow me on two different social media accounts since that weekend, but Anne-Marie had told me he'd asked around for my contact information. Luckily, Anne-Marie had made it clear, in her subtle and powerful way, that if anyone gave my number to Clinton, she'd make their lives hell.

"I'm not going with Clinton," I said. "I'd rather go alone."

"It is not acceptable for you to be at any event alone, but especially not this one, as I have *just* said," he said testily. "I have made this expectation very clear all summer. There are only two events left that I am requesting you attend, and you are required to have a date for both of them." He picked up his water glass again, but didn't sip it right away. "This client is exceptionally particular about appearances and the people they associate with. It is imperative that I display the same values in my family as they have in theirs."

"Well then, if Bruno can't make it, I'll find someone else," I said.

My dad nodded, lifting his water glass again and taking another sip. Awkward tension circled the table as no one spoke, but when I felt a pair of eyes on me, I looked up. My dad was staring at something on the other side of the restaurant, but Kimberlee was looking at me with a strange expression on her face.

Before I could think too much about it, though, the server returned.

"Here we are," he said, setting a dish down in front of me. "Let me get Dee's Nuts on the table for you."

My dad reached into the bowl and popped a couple of the nuts in his mouth, chewed, then nodded his approval.

"Excellent," he said to the server. "Please let Dee know I am impressed by his nuts."

And not that I said it out loud, but I also hoped the server would let everyone know that I'd choked on Dee's Nuts as I started laughing.

The rest of brunch passed by uneventfully. My chicken strips were slightly above mediocre, but my dad didn't have any complaints about his sandwich and Kimberlee said her salad was delicious.

Then, shortly after the server set the bill down, I nearly had a heart attack.

Bruno

What are you doing right now?

Me

Brunch. Why?

Bruno

Need to talk to you asap

Oh God. What fresh hell was this? Was he sick or something? I tried to panic as subtly as I could, bowing my head and hoping my hair would block my dad and Kimberlee from seeing the heat rushing up my neck.

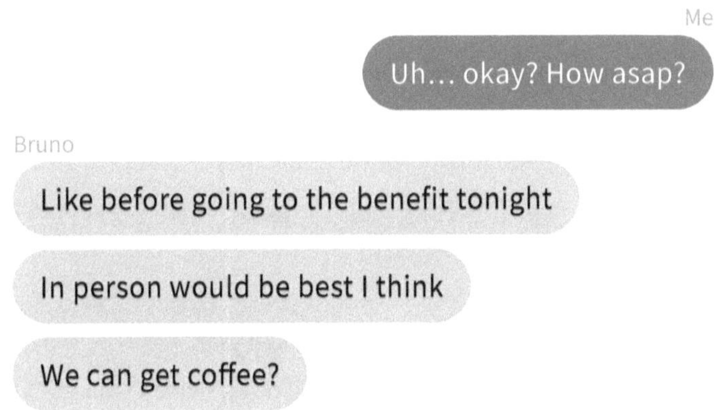

I breathed a sigh of relief. If he wanted to meet, he couldn't be sick. And he said before the benefit, so he was clearly planning on going.

I told my dad I'd made plans to have coffee with a friend, so after he paid the bill, I walked a few blocks to the café I'd said I'd meet Bruno at. I'd just gotten my latte and sat down when Bruno entered, spotted me, and beelined across the restaurant.

"I have good news and bad news," he said, slamming his body into the chair without even saying hello.

He didn't look good.

Like, he looked *fine*. He didn't look sick or anything. But there was tension pinching his eyebrows together and his shoulders were hunched forward and he was sitting with a weird sort of stiffness that was very unlike the chill person I was used to.

"Do I get the bad news first?" I asked.

"Uh…" he said.

"Good news first," said another voice. The chair next to Bruno moved and I looked up to see Niko, the muscley mustached man from the night before, lowering himself into it. Unlike the night before, he wasn't smiling, and there was a wary look on his face.

"Right," Bruno said. "The good news is that you get to meet Niko."

Niko nodded and I thought he was going to say something, but when he didn't, I stuck my hand out across the table.

"Hey," I said. "I'm Nellie. Nice to meet you."

He looked at my hand, then shook it tentatively. "I've heard a lot about you."

"All bad things, obviously," I said.

"Mostly," Niko said.

I laughed, but I wasn't entirely sure it was a joke.

"The worst things," Bruno said, forcing out a weird chuckle. "Like how you could only name four Fall Out Boy songs despite claiming you had a Pete Wentz poster on your bedroom wall as a teenager."

"Oh my God," I groaned. "This again? There are *books* with less words than some of their song titles. Of course I don't remember them exactly."

"You thought one of them was called *The Big Lebowski* because you mixed up Mia Wallace from Pulp Fiction with Bunny Lebowski."

"It was an honest mistake! There was the whole thing with the toe being cut off and I thought that was from a Tarantino movie." I rolled my eyes. "Anyone could make that mistake. And clearly you knew I was thinking of *Mia Wallace* when I explained it."

Bruno frowned. "What?"

"The song. *Mia Wallace*. I just called it by the movie name."

He stared at me, then sighed heavily. "*Uma Thurman*."

"What?"

"The song is called *Uma Thurman*. Not Mia Wallace. That's the character she plays in Pulp Fiction."

"Same difference."

"It's not at *all* the same difference."

I shrugged. "Could be worse. Wait until you find out the poster was actually of Brendon Urie because I mixed up Fall Out Boy and Panic! at the Disco."

Bruno's mouth hung open for a long moment before he closed it again. "This might actually be easier than I thought it would be."

"What is?"

"Giving you the bad news."

"Oh, it can't be that bad," I said. "It's not like you're breaking up with me."

Bruno's dark brown eyes were hidden beneath his eyelashes, but I saw them dart towards Niko all the same. Niko stared at me, unblinking and unimpressed. I looked from him back to Bruno, who finally tore his eyes off Niko, but didn't meet my gaze as he grimaced apologetically.

"Well, actually…"

Chapter Nine
What's More Valuable Than Altruism?

"I KNOW IT'S SUPER last minute," I said. "I will definitely owe you one. Like, massively."

"Nell, I'd—appy to help—could." Brandon's booming voice was cut by the crackling static of bad phone reception. "But—up near Petawawa. Even if I lef—"

I waited, then pulled my phone away from my ear and looked at the screen. The call was still connected, so I lifted it to my ear again.

"Hello? Are you still there?" I said.

"—no chance of getting—oh," he said. "Hello? Can you hear me?"

"I can hear you," I said. "You just cut out for a sec. But I got the gist of it."

"Sorry," Brandon said. "We're near the d—"

He cut out again. I waited for a moment, staring blankly at the window looking out over my dad's driveway.

"—luck finding someone. Maybe Cal—"

That time, the line beeped its notification that the call had dropped. Sighing, I took the phone away from my ear again.

"Fuck," I said.

Sydney looked up from where she was sitting on the floor in Anne-Marie's bedroom. "Brandon's a no-go?"

I nodded, then took a breath. "I'm running out of time. But it sounded like maybe Calvin could help."

But she held up her phone and shook her head. "He's in Toronto for his mom's birthday."

"Matthieu is already attending with Jeanette," Anne-Marie said, sighing as she put her phone down. "Remy tried asking his cousin if she would like to stay home and you could go with her husband since she complained the other day that she does not enjoy going to these events now that she's nine months pregnant."

Sydney grimaced. "That went as well as we all think it did, I take it?"

"He has been apologizing for half an hour now. He did not realize it was one of those situations where she did not say what she actually meant."

As they talked, I scrolled through my contacts for what felt like the hundredth time. It was more useless than the first time I'd done it; most of my friends were in Ottawa, so even if I found someone who could come, they'd have to leave Ottawa in the next thirty-six minutes to make it to Montreal with enough time to get ready for the event.

Still, we kept trying. We went through all of my close guy friends, from Brandon and Calvin to Jake, a guy I'd had a threesome with at the start of the year.

Then all of my guy acquaintances, who ranged from guys I'd made out with a couple of times to guys I'd had more than one class with in the past three years.

Then all the guys who I had a semi-cordial relationship with even if I thought they were massive idiots, like Kevin Huang, a guy in my year who was Cs-get-degrees-ing his way through the forensic science program and who had bewilderedly asked me how I'd gotten his number.

"We did a group project together last year," I said. "In Forensic Photography. I know this is out of nowhere, but if you'd be willing to come to Montreal for this and maybe one other thing in a couple of weeks, I'll help tutor you in some of our classes next semester."

"I'm still confused about how you got my number."

I took a slow, deep breath in through my nose. "You gave it to me. When we worked on our Forensic Photography project. With Mindy. Remember?"

"Right, but it's just weird that you called me out of the blue."

"I *know*, Kevin," I said. "But I'm really in need of some help right now."

"For what?"

"For this event I have to go to tonight in Montreal. I need someone to accompany me"—God forbid I say I needed a date in case he thought I was asking him to be my boyfriend or something—"and I was hoping you could help me out tonight and in exchange, I'll help you out with some tutoring next semester."

"Oh," he said. "I mean, maybe. When's it happening?"

"We'd have to be there around seven."

"Yeah, but like... what day?"

I hung up without answering, mostly because the things I wanted to scream could probably be used against me in court if Kevin ever met some kind of untimely end, or at the very least, gotten me charged for uttering threats.

"That did not sound good," Anne-Marie said.

"I have no one to blame but myself," I replied.

"Except you can fully blame someone else," Sydney said as she tapped on her screen. "Like remember that whole thing where Bruno—"

"Do not even say his name right now." Anne-Marie's voice was absolutely vicious. "We do not talk about him. I am so disgusted with that *chien sale. Il est un esti de mange de marde.* I will never, *never* forgive him for this. How could he even—I mean, honestly. *How* can he even live with himself knowing—"

"I told him it was fine," I said, staring at my phone screen because I didn't want to look anyone in the eye.

"What?" Anne-Marie asked, bewildered. "Why would you say that?"

I half-shrugged.

"Seriously, Nellie," she pressed. "Why—"

"Because I didn't want to upset either of them," I snapped. "And how would it actually go if I did insist he still go as my date? He'd be miserable, which would piss off my dad, and I'd still be in the same position as I am now. At least this way I know what I'm dealing with. And I get a bad feeling about that guy, so I didn't want to, like, isolate Bruno."

"You get a bad feeling about Niko?" Sydney asked.

I nodded, but Anne-Marie scoffed.

"Bruno is as stubborn and sassy as you are, *chérie*. He will not do anything he does not want to do, and seeing as he has been obsessed with Niko for ages—"

"That doesn't mean Niko didn't pressure him into doing this," I said. "Look, it's easier for me to believe that Niko's an insecure asshole who told Bruno they couldn't get together if Bruno was publicly 'dating' someone else. I'd rather ask you to keep an eye on Bruno over the next little while to make sure he's okay than sit here and accept that yet another man has let me down."

Anne-Marie's face had softened. "*Chérie*—"

I put my phone down on the bed and stood up. "I need a break. I'm going to get a drink."

Before either of them could tell me I didn't have time for a break, that I needed to get back on my phone and start looking up escort services in Montreal so I could *Pretty Woman* a guy into spending the night pretending to be the long-lost prince of some faraway country that sounded real enough for people to think they'd just never heard of it, I left Anne-Marie's room and padded down to the Marchands' kitchen.

When I got there, the TV was on in the nearby living room. I froze for a moment, worried it might be JP, but the dark brown hair beneath the curve of a black headset meant it was Marc-Andre. A first-person shooter was on the screen, frantic clicks coming from the controller in his hands.

Marc-Andre was quiet and reserved to begin with, so not wanting to interrupt his game, I didn't say anything before opening the fridge and staring in. It was meticulously organized the same way my dad's was, probably because the Marchands used the same housekeeping company my dad did. The dedicated beverage drawer had cans of beer and seltzers along with Coke Zero, mango Bubly, and diet ginger ale. I reached for one of the Bublys, but stopped when I saw the two-liter of chocolate milk in the door.

My dad never had chocolate milk. And I never bought chocolate milk because I never thought of it.

Grabbing the milk, I closed the door. Twisting my mouth to the side, I glanced around the kitchen, trying to remember which cupboard had the glasses.

"The far one on the left," came a voice from behind me.

My eyes darted to the side, hoping against hope the voice only sounded familiar because I hadn't heard Marc-Andre speak for so long that I didn't know he sounded exactly like his brother. But the youngest Marchand was still facing away from me on the couch, eyes focused on the TV. A moment later, the edges of the screen flashed red and he sighed heavily.

Damnit.

"Thanks," I muttered.

"Anytime, babe."

I whirled around. Behind me, JP was putting a mug into the dishwasher. I glared at him, refusing to be distracted by the sight of him in a pair of fitted khaki-coloured pants with a leather belt, a collarless denim-blue button-up shirt tucked into them, the top few buttons undone and showing off a peek of warm tan skin. And I definitely wasn't distracted by the slightly messy blonde hair on his head or the way the kitchen light caught the natural highlights in it or the height of his cheekbones or the way the sleeves of his shirt were rolled halfway up his forearms and the biceps were fitted because of course the bastard worked out and—

"What?" he asked.

Right. I was in the middle of glaring at him.

"Don't call me that," I hissed. "Especially when—" I gestured towards the living room.

"He's wearing headphones."

"Headphones. Not magical-can't-hear-anything-else-ever-phones."

"Trust me, he can't hear shit." He closed the dishwasher, then crossed the kitchen to the farthest cabinet on the left. "I gave them to him. Those headphones are the reason I kept my sanity when Remy and Anne-Marie were first figuring out how the whole insert-rod-A-into-slot-B thing worked and he could go four or five times a night."

"What are you even doing here? I thought you had a dinner meeting in Sherbrooke."

"I do." He opened the cabinet door. "I'm about to leave."

I rolled my eyes. "Whatever. Give me that."

He held up a tall glass. "This?"

"Yes."

"Why?"

"Because I need it, JP," I said, clenching my teeth.

"Hmm." He examined the glass. "What do I get out of this?"

"What?"

He glanced towards the living room, then stepped towards me. "I said, what do I get if I hand this over to you?"

My heart felt like a trampoline with a bunch of rubber balls bouncing on it. "The satisfaction of helping someone out in their time of need?"

He wrinkled his nose. "I was hoping for something valuable."

"What's more valuable than altruism?"

He took another step closer, eyes flicking down. "I'd say a kiss from the hottest girl in the room."

"I'm the only girl in the room," I said, then belatedly realized what he'd said. "And oh my God. Are you fucking insane?"

"Did you change your name to Insane recently?"

"*JP!*" I hissed, glancing past him.

He chuckled. "C'mon, babe. It helps both of us. I get something to think about while I'm driving to Sherbrooke. You get a glass of milk and something to cheer your grumpy ass up."

"I'm not grumpy," I whispered grumpily. "Why would you even think that?"

"Your general vibe," he said. "Is something wrong?"

"Oh my God," I huffed. "I don't have time for this. Can I just have the glass, please?"

He twisted the glass in his hand. "You know how to get it, babe. One kiss for one glass. Seems like a fair trade."

It was not at all a fair trade. But instead of pointing that out, I looked at the back of Marc-Andre's head.

Then I stepped forward, grabbed the front of JP's shirt, and tugged him forward until his mouth met mine.

I meant it to be quick. So fast that I wouldn't even be able to feel JP's smirk or the victorious puff of laughter exhaled through his nose.

But then his lips were on mine and I just...

I...

Fuck.

I hated how addictive his kisses were. I hated how familiar he tasted. And I refused to even consider that his kisses were addictive *because* of that familiar taste. Instead, I let myself be distracted by the shiver of desire spreading over my body, the result of the chemistry between us, ignoring the fact that we were doing something stupid in the stupidest fucking place.

Or maybe not.

Maybe I was aware of how stupid this was, and that's why I was melting against his body.

"Damn, babe," JP breathed when I finally pulled back. "I would've settled for a peck on the lips, but *that*—"

"Shut up," I whispered, glancing back at the living room, where Marc-Andre hadn't moved. "Give me the glass."

He handed it over with one of those shit-eating grins I wanted to wipe right off his face. "Feel better now?"

I glared at him, grabbing the glass and storming out of the kitchen without another word.

Because yeah, I did feel better. My steps felt lighter and my body felt warm and there was a pleasant fuzzy memory of JP's lips on mine.

And I absolutely did not want him to know that.

When I got back to Anne-Marie's room, I took a steadying breath before letting myself in. Almost in unison, Anne-Marie and Sydney looked up at me, Sydney with her phone pressed to her ear and a grimace on face.

"I told you," she said to whoever was on the other end. "I'm his roommate. Sydney. I—" Her round eyes widened as she listened. "Are you serious? It's a *two bedroom*." She paused. "Why would I pretend to be his roommate?" She listened again, then let out a disbelieving chuckle. "Okay. Well, since you're refusing to get him, you can be the one to tell him—oh, hey Reid."

She waited, annoyance rolling off her. "Sure. Next time I don't know you're staying at a one-night-stand's place, I won't call so the crazy person you slept with doesn't answer your phone while you're in the shower." Another pause, then a scoff. "'Kay. Whatever. Bye, asshole."

There was a heavy pause as she hung up.

"So I'm gonna say Reid's a no," she said.

"Want me to tell him he's a dick?" I asked.

"Nah. I'll do it when I get home. It'll be taken more seriously when he's not in the middle of dealing with what must be the most insecure rebound girl in the history of rebound girls." She took a deep breath and let it whoosh out. "Okay. What about Ben?"

My stomach dropped, as did my lips. I turned to Sydney, not even trying to hide the disbelief on my face that she'd bring up the former psychology professor I was hooking up with in front of—

"Ohhh," Anne-Marie said, her voice wavering up and down with intrigue. "Who is this 'Ben,' *chérie*?"

"A friend," I said, sharpening the pointed look I was giving Sydney, who shrugged unapologetically.

"Desperate times," she said.

"A friend?" Anne-Marie repeated. "A friend you are sensitive about?"

"I'm not *sensitive* about him," I said. "It's just complicated. And I can guarantee my dad would lose his shit if I brought him."

"Hmm," Anne-Marie said. "Is he scruffy?"

"Huh?"

"You know." Her lips twisted into a knowing smirk. "A bit rough around the edges? A bad boy? Is that why your father would not approve?"

"Yeah, that's *definitely* it," I said. "He's a bad, bad boy. So he's not appropriate to bring." I threw a glare at Sydney. "At *all*."

"Okay, but seriously," she said, her voice solemn. "Who else can we call?"

I opened my mouth.

Nothing came out.

A beat of silence passed, and then another, and then Anne-Marie's room was full of silence and tension and a distinct hopelessness that was making my stomach curl.

"Well," Anne-Marie said slowly. "I think it is time to consider something you do not want to consider, *chérie.*"

"I'm not asking JP," I said.

"Nellie—"

"He's not even available," I said. "He's got a dinner meeting in Sherbrooke."

She frowned. "How do you know that?"

Fuck. I stammered for a second before remembering I was an idiot.

"I saw him in the kitchen," I said, holding up the glass. "When I was getting chocolate milk. He mentioned it when I said hi."

I thought that would explain everything, but amusement crossed Anne-Marie's face. "Milk, you say?"

"Uh... yeah. What's weird about that?"

"Nothing." She half-shrugged. "Just, that glass is empty. And looks sparkling clean."

"Well, that's because I"—'forgot to put the milk in the glass because I was busy kissing your brother' was what screamed through my head, but I held it in—"changed my mind and had water instead."

"And finished already?" Anne-Marie said. "But brought the glass with you anyway?"

"Look, we have bigger things to discuss than Nellie's idiosyncrasies right now," Sydney said.

If she hadn't nearly pushed me under the bus by bringing up Ben, I might've kissed her for diverting the subject. "Thank you."

"Like if JP would consider cancelling his dinner meeting so he could be Nellie's date tonight," she continued.

Well, now I definitely wasn't going to kiss her. "Are you for real, Syd?"

"Yeah," she said. "Maybe he would. Like, if you explained what happened."

"How many times do I have to say this?" I set the empty glass down on the vanity and lifted my hand to count off on my fingers. "First of all, no. Because no. Second, no because fuck no. Third, not in this lifetime. Fourth, your brother hates these events as much as I do." I picked up my empty glass, then realized my fourth point might have sounded like I knew more about JP than I should have. "Uh, doesn't he? He used to, I'm pretty sure."

"Smooth," Sydney muttered, her voice low enough that only I could hear her.

"I bet he would go with you if you asked him," Anne-Marie said, folding one leg over the other. "He went to *La Nuit Rose* with Chantel because she asked him and I do not believe he likes her all that much."

"He went with her as a favour," I said.

Anne-Marie's eyes shot to mine like lasers. "How do you know that?"

Fuck. I knew JP had gone with Chantel because she'd given him—in his words—an insane blowjob. But I only knew that because he'd said it to me at the beginning of the summer when he was explaining why he wanted to fuck me again.

"Bruno told me," I said. "He knows someone who knows someone."

She pursed her lips. "Who does he know that I do not? Because I had not heard that."

Fuck.

"I don't know," I said. "Maybe it was because, uh, of why. Why he owed her the favour."

"Which was...?"

I swallowed hard. "I think he said JP owed her the favour because she gave him a blowjob. And whoever heard that probably thought since you're his sister..."

Anne-Marie scoffed. "That has never stopped anyone from telling me anything about Jean-Paul. If half of the stories I've heard from his conquests are to be believed, he is both the biggest they've ever seen and also the smallest."

Well, those people were lying or not getting laid enough. JP wasn't *huge*, not like the guys they had in porn. But I could confidently say he was on the higher side of average. Like, he wasn't the *biggest* I'd ever seen, but the biggest I'd actually enjoyed since getting punched in the cervix was not my idea of a good time.

Not to mention that JP knew how to use what he had.

"How many people do you know who've seen his dick?" Sydney asked.

Anne-Marie shrugged. "Probably more than will admit it. Regardless of size, my brother does not seem to know how to keep it in his pants. And why I am surprised anyone would bother hiding a rumour about Jean-Paul putting his dick in someone's mouth."

"Jesus, Annie," I muttered. "Can we stop talking about your brother's dick now?"

"You brought it up, *chérie*."

"Whatever," I said as Sydney cackled far harder than was necessary. "The point is that no, I'm not asking JP and even if I did, he wouldn't go."

"Then what else are you going to do?" Anne-Marie asked, her voice dripping with exasperation as she started scrolling through her phone again. "No one is available. You cannot go with Clinton. Unless you are planning on dressing Sydney up in a tuxedo and calling her Sid Cunnilinginton the Third or something ridiculous like that, I do not see what other option you *have*."

I stared at her for a moment, then looked at Sydney. Sydney blinked, then pressed her lips together and looked at Anne-Marie, who was still staring at her phone screen. But when she realized Sydney and I had gone silent, she looked up.

"What?" she asked.

"Annie," I said. "You're a fucking genius."

Chapter Ten
Sid Cunnilinginton The Third

"I STILL THINK THE top hat is a bit much," Anne-Marie muttered.

A man and woman walked past us to enter the hall. The man looked at us from the corner of his eye, his eyebrows raised, and the woman stifled a giggle as they passed.

"It makes it less obvious that her hair doesn't match her mustache," I replied, taking Sydney's elbow and guiding it into a bend so I could entwine my arm with hers. "Otherwise it would look weird."

"Because *that's* what would make this look weird."

"It's not my fault you didn't have an eyebrow pencil that matched her hair."

"Sydney *also* did not have an eyebrow pencil that matched her hair."

"Excuse me for being born with perfect eyebrows," Sydney said.

A group of older women dressed in outfits that would've never made it off the rack save for the designer label attached to them caught sight of us. A couple of them scoffed, but a woman with platinum blonde hair and a cane grinned, her eyes sparkling.

"I'm still not sure why you needed to draw the mustache on," Remy said as he guided Anne-Marie into the hall. "Or borrow my tuxedo."

Sydney adjusted her top hat. "Are you saying I don't look *fantastic* in this?"

"Of course not," Remy said. "It suits you more than it does me."

There was no derision in his statement; he said it as if it was fact, which it arguably was. Sydney was wearing the *hell* out of the tux, like it had just been sitting in her closet waiting for the opportunity to be paired with an eyebrow-pencil mustache. The jacket hit the perfect spot on her wrist, only letting the silver cufflinks on her dress shirt peek out when she moved a certain way. The pants were almost too long, which was surprising considering she was nearly the same height as Remy until one remembered that between the two of them, Remy was the one blessed with the bubble butt.

"But I don't understand why you couldn't go as yourself," Remy continued. "It would have made more sense to borrow one of Anne-Marie's dresses and attend as Nellie's plus-one."

"One would think," Anne-Marie said.

"Sure, if one hadn't known my dad for nearly her entire life," I said. "You know as well as I do that this was the best option. And besides"—I bumped Sydney with my hip—"she looks legit enough in this that if we keep my distance from my dad, he might not even realize it's her."

Anne-Marie and Remy exchanged a silent glance.

"Don't do that," I said.

"Do what?" she asked.

"That couple thing where you're talking to each other with your eyes so no one else can understand you," I said.

"Oh, my apologies," she said, her voice light. "I thought it would be obvious that we were agreeing you are insane."

"She almost fooled Bruno," I pointed out.

Anne-Marie gave me a silent but skeptical look, which was understandable since that was an exaggeration. Bruno had caught sight of the four of us as we entered the lobby and stopped walking so suddenly that Niko was ten feet in front of him before realizing he'd left Bruno behind.

"Nellie!" Bruno had called, waving at me as he dashed across the foyer, the brightness of his voice as uncharacteristic as the relief in his eyes. "Hey!"

"Hi, Bruno," I'd said, trying not to sound annoyed even though I was definitely still annoyed.

"Hey," he said again, then nodded at Remy and Anne-Marie. "Hi, Remy."

"Bruno," Remy said, his voice flatter than normal.

"Anne-Marie, you look lovely," Bruno said.

"I always look lovely," Anne-Marie said, her voice cold and her expression stony.

Bruno forced an awkward laugh as Niko caught up, putting a hand on Bruno's lower back as he joined us. "True. Well, um, you all know my date, Niko." He gestured to Niko, who was wearing a suit that was a little too tight around his thick neck. "And Nellie, you found a date?"

"Sure did," I said.

He'd smiled expectantly like I was going to introduce them, but faded when I didn't. His throat flexed as he swallowed before looking at Sydney.

"Well, hi, I'm Bruno. I wanted to say thank you," he started. "I'm the one who kinda—"

And then he cut himself off as he took an *actual* look at Sydney.

"Well hel-*lo*," Sydney said, adopting an accent that made it sound like she'd given up a weekend at her daddy's beach house in the Hamptons to be here. "Pleasure to meet you. I'm Sid Cunnilinginton the Third and my preferred method of travel is 'yacht.'"

There was a thick, heavy, almost unbearably awkward silence. Then all at once, Bruno blinked, Anne-Marie snorted, and I cackled so hard I had to pinch my thighs together because I almost peed.

"Oh God," Bruno had said, half-leaning on Niko as he pressed a hand to his chest. "I don't know whether to keep feeling bad about ditching you or to take half the credit for allowing this ridiculousness to happen."

"You should keep feeling bad," Remy said bluntly.

Bruno's mouth dropped open and he looked at Anne-Marie. So did I, actually, because I assumed she was going to nudge Remy and subtly hint that this wasn't the time or place, but she just looked back at Bruno with a withering stare and slipped her arm beneath Remy's supportively.

"Why should he feel bad about taking his *boyfriend* as a date?" Niko said testily.

"It's one thing to break a commitment," Remy said. "And another to do it hours before an event when the consequences involve putting someone in an arguably dangerous situation with the creep he was brought in to avoid in the first place."

Niko's eyes widened. "What?"

"I'll explain later," Bruno said, his face going red. "I just—"

"Why didn't you tell me that?" Niko pressed.

I would've loved to know the answer to that, too. I had my guesses, like that this was another example of feelings making people act stupid, but the desperate look on Bruno's face as his eyes darted to me sent a reluctant and not entirely welcome sensation of pity through me.

"Don't forget I said it was fine when you both asked," I said to Niko. "And it got sorted out. I'm here with someone and that someone is masculine-presenting, which means I'm technically doing what my dad wants."

"And technically correct is the best kind of correct," Sydney said.

"Do you think being technically correct will stop your dad from being upset?" Anne-Marie asked pointedly.

The answer to that was no, obviously. Not in the slightest. People always said that it was easier to ask for forgiveness than for permission, but that wasn't true for my dad. It wasn't easy to ask for anything from him.

I'd known from the moment I thought of it he'd be upset with me for bringing Sydney. I'd known he'd be even more upset that I drew a mustache on her.

And I'd done it anyway. I'd put all my options on the scales, weighing them to see what would be the best outcome.

Showing up solo was worse than showing up with a date he didn't approve of.

Bringing a woman as a legitimate date was worse than poking fun at the whole thing by bringing a woman with a mustache drawn on.

Facing my dad's anger was better than facing a night with Clinton Thibault.

So no, being technically correct wouldn't stop my dad from losing his shit at me, but I could probably argue that I did the best I could considering it was so last-minute and promise that I'd find a suitable date for the Diamond Gala, which was the only big event left for the summer.

Plus, there was the whole brunch thing earlier in the day. He had to know I was upset about it, so maybe there would be some leniency. He was an asshole who made me cross my boundaries for his newest girlfriend; I was an asshole who wasn't even technically wrong. It had to even out.

To the credit of the stuffy assholes who usually attended these kinds of events, most of them found it amusing, and more than I'd expected outright laughed and complimented Syd on her outfit and creativity. I gladly let her take credit for that, even though technically the concept of Sid Cunnilinginton was Anne-Marie's idea and the mustache was *definitely* my idea. But Sydney deserved it for the way she made people smile, especially as her introductions got more and more unhinged.

"Hi, I'm Sid Cunnilinginton the Third. My favourite food is gold leaf."

"Nice to meet you, I'm Sid Cunnilinginton and my family summers in the lost city of Atlantis."

"Sid's the name, living off the money my great-great-great-grandfather made after discovering an underground reserve of ancient barefoot sandals is the game."

"I'm Chasidy Andrew Cunnlinginton the Third because my mother didn't know the meaning or spelling of 'Chastity,' but you can call me Sid for short."

"What do I do for a living?" Sydney was repeating to a woman we were talking to after we'd filled up our plates at the chocolate fountain. "Mostly breathe, I guess. Also I have a heart rate."

"No," the woman laughed. "Like, what do you do for a job?"

"Oh, good Lord," Sydney said. "Luckily, it hasn't come to that so far. Though, if my uncle Gorbert steals Mummy's black card and sneaks down to Vegas again, who knows what might happen."

I tried not to laugh, mainly because I was talking to the man she was with.

"So when I graduate, I want to work with a lab, but I'm not sure which one yet," I said. We'd been making small talk until he asked what I did for a living—which I didn't respond to nearly as cleverly as Sydney had—and then seemed interested in hearing about my degree. "It'll depend on who has openings and—"

"There you are, Nellie," a different man's voice interrupted.

"—and what specialization I aim for," I finished without acknowledging him.

"That's fascinating," the man said.

"It is. And actually, what's even more—"

"Excuse me," he said again, and a second later a disgustingly unwelcome hand was touching the bare skin on the back of my arm as an even more disgustingly unwelcome person sidled up on the other side of me. "I hope you don't mind if I steal her attention for a moment."

"Actually, I—oh," the man said as he realized who was touching me. "Of course. Not at all, Mr. Thibault."

Fuck.

Before I could plead with him not to, he took his date's arm and they politely said goodbye to me and Sydney.

"It's good to see you," Clinton said after they left. "How's it going, Nellie?"

"Fine," I said, my tone clipped as I batted his hand away.

He waited as if I was going to say more, his eyes fixed to me. I refused to look at him, instead staring at a fixed point somewhere far beyond his right shoulder.

"I'm doing great. Thanks for asking," he said when I didn't respond.

"I'm sorry to hear that," I replied.

He frowned. "I said I'm doing great."

"I heard you."

He scoffed. "Wow. What did I do to deserve that?"

"Interrupted me because some kind of misguided sense of self-confidence makes you think your presence was more important than my conversation."

"Aw, I wasn't interrupting," he said. "I just thought you'd want to say hello."

"What indication have I ever given that I want you to talk to me?"

"Some people like persistence."

"I don't."

He chuckled. "Well, selfishly, I also wanted to size up my competition. I saw Bruno back there with someone else and since I thought you were going to call me up if you couldn't find a date, I figured I could see who took my place."

"Trust me, Clinton. You were never in the competition," I said.

"We'll see about that." He glanced at Sydney. "You've probably heard of me. I'm Clinton Thib—"

And that's when he actually *looked* at Sydney, who was glaring at him.

"Hi," she said, not even bothering with her fake rich person accent. "I'm Sid Cunnilinginton the Third and I'm better than you."

Clinton stared at her, then turned to me, his grey eyes darkening into a stony shade of grey that was so much like my dad's, I wanted to run.

"Are you serious?" he asked, his voice low with disbelief.

"What?" I asked.

He gestured at Sydney. "You didn't ask to go with me so your friend could play dress up instead?"

"No, I didn't ask to go with you because I don't like you," I said.

His eyes narrowed even more, the joints of his jaw bulging from how hard he'd clenched it. I stared back, refusing to look away as much as I wanted to.

"Oh my God, *chérie*!" Anne-Marie's voice broke through the tense air between me and Clinton. "I have been hoping to see you all evening, Nellie!" She walked up briskly, stepping between me and Clinton so she could hug me. "Clinton, you do not mind if I steal my dear friend? It has been much too long since I've seen her."

Clinton didn't look like he believed her, but just let out an annoyed huff before turning to Sydney.

"Your 'mustache' is smeared," he said snidely, then turned and walked away without another word.

"It's not," I whispered as Sydney lifted a hand to her upper lip.

"Ooo," Anne-Marie said, her voice quieter than usual as she let go of me. "I think he is insulted, *chérie*."

"Good," I said. "Maybe he'll leave me alone."

"I hope so," she said with a solemn earnesty, though there was a worried line between her eyebrows. She glanced at Remy, who put a hand on her lower back and nodded before looking in the direction Clinton had stalked off.

Them and their fucking silent conversations.

"It'll be fine," I said, taking Sydney's arm. "I've got my big strong date here. No one's gonna mess with someone named Sid Cunnilinginton, even if his mummy stopped paying for riding lessons because he was too tall to be a jockey."

And then the most horrible, gut-wrenching, spine-tingling, hair-raising sound pierced my eardrums.

It was so staggeringly alarming that it took me a moment to figure out it was coming from the mouth of a woman standing nearby, and a few more worrying moments to figure out that the sound, reminiscent of a snow plow dragging along bare asphalt, was actually laughter.

It was one of the worst laughs I've ever heard, but it didn't overshadow two much more interesting things about her: one, that she was hot as fuck, and two, I'd never seen her before.

While I couldn't quite guess her age, I would've said she was in her thirties or *maybe* her forties based on the fact that unlike many of the attendees at the benefit, she didn't look like she had any plastic surgery, but appeared to be older than twenty-five. Her tall, slim frame was flattered by the perfectly tailored tuxedo she was wearing, though unlike Sydney, she hadn't drawn a fake mustache on her peach-white skin to go with it. Long brown hair hung past her shoulders in gentle waves and her face had a mischievous quality to it, with sparkling eyes that were almost too big for her face and pointed features that had a distinctly elf-like quality to them.

The woman standing next to her was younger by a few years and was looking at the first woman with a half-amused, half-adoring expression. She had hair that was somewhere between dark blonde and light brown, a round face with pink tinting her pale beige cheeks, and a sweet smile. She also had the same sort of short, curvy-chubby body type that I did, which was only important because I immediately fell in love with her silky green dress and wanted to ask where she'd gotten it.

But before I could, the cackling woman started talking through her laughter.

"*What* did you say their name was?" she asked, still choking on the horrendous sound.

"Sid Cunnilinginton," Sydney answered. "The Third."

"Of the Southern Cunnilingintons," I added.

"The ones who made their fortune by claiming they invented a new style of dictionary?" the shorter woman asked.

Sydney burst out laughing, her face turning red beneath her freckles. More surprisingly, Remy chuckled too.

"I am afraid I do not understand the joke," Anne-Marie thankfully said, since I didn't get it either.

"They were cunning linguists," Remy said.

Sydney grinned. "Which is extra hilarious since I'm getting my degree in linguistics."

"Sid Cunnilinginton the Cunning Linguist," the first woman said, shaking her head as another rasping chuckle bubbled up. "Thank God they have my kind of people here. Well, minus a decade or two."

"What kind of people are those?" I asked.

"You know." She waved vaguely. "A little less, ah..."

"Stuck up?" the other woman suggested.

The first woman nodded. "Most of the time, there are at least a few people you can find who are down to poke some fun at these dumpster-fire events. But we've never been to any in Montreal before, so I wasn't sure what to expect."

Anne-Marie's eyes widened as the events she revolved so much of her life around were labelled as dumpster fires, a crack in the otherwise refined social mask she usually wore. But it was the only crack; she still had a polite and warm smile on her face as she extended her hand.

"I thought I had not seen you at any events before," she said. "I am Anne-Marie. This is my boyfriend, Remy. You've met Sydney—excuse me, Sid—who is here with Nellie."

"Claire," the woman in the tuxedo said, reaching forward and shaking each person's hand as Anne-Marie introduced us, then gestured at the other woman. "This is my sugar baby, Julie."

"Claire!" Julie gasped.

Claire grinned. "You know I'm joking, princess." She took Julie's hand and held it up to show off a glinting jewel on her finger. "It's a recent development, so this is the first time I get to say this is my *fiancée*, Julie."

Anne-Marie clapped her hands together as Julie's face went delightfully pink. "Ohmigod. Congratulations! Is that what brings you to Montreal?"

"Oh, no," Claire said. "We came for, ah, business reasons. Scouting out some potential opportunities for expansion in Quebec. But it worked out well since Julie and I hadn't been to Montreal together before, so—"

She said more, but I didn't hear it. My eyes had been pulled to the side almost by instinct, a little past Claire's left shoulder and in the general direction Clinton had stormed off. I wasn't sure why I was drawn to look; it wasn't like he'd seen me first, since I watched the moment my dad caught sight of me.

He was with Kimberlee, his hand on the small of her back as they walked away from the bar. There was a social mask similar to Anne-Marie's on my dad's face, something I easily recognized considering I'd spent my whole life seeing it. It was an expression strategically built to look both welcoming and daunting, the corners of his mouth forced into a curl that wasn't quite a smile. Focused eyes made it clear he was attentive, but hid the fact that every word, every interaction, every observation was being processed and calculated in his mind.

Those eyes met mine and at first, I didn't know if he knew what I'd done. I didn't know if his anger was hidden behind his mask. If he was so good at hiding things that even I couldn't catch the subtle differences anymore. My heart didn't quite jump into my throat, but it prepared itself, bending whatever a heart's equivalent to knees are and standing on the edge of wherever hearts jump from, waiting to see what my dad would do.

"—unfortunately that means duty calls," Claire said, putting a hand on my shoulder. I almost flinched at the unexpected contact before realizing she was stepping around me to go... well, wherever duty was calling her, I guess. "It was great to meet you all. I'm sure we'll see you around again."

I returned the sentiment with some kind of vague response before looking back at my dad.

And my heart didn't bother jumping.

It just joined the rest of my body in trying to implode on itself, like if all my organs and bones and muscles folded themselves up, I'd end up small enough that my dad wouldn't be able to see me anymore.

"Oh," Anne-Marie breathed from beside me, and I didn't need to look at her to know she was seeing the same frozen fury in my dad's eyes as he and Kimberlee walked towards us. "I, um, do not know if he is going to laugh this one off, *chérie*."

"He will," I said, knowing full well he wouldn't. "I'll explain."

They weren't far from us now. I forced a smile and four steps later, he was beside us.

"Hi, Dad," I said as sweetly as I could. "Hi, Kimberlee. Are you having a good—"

And then they were gone, walking by us without my dad so much as glancing in my direction, let alone making eye contact again.

"Shit," Sydney said, her eyes following them.

"It's fine," I said.

"Are you certain, *chérie*?" Anne-Marie asked.

"Of course," I said, then tried to laugh. "I mean, I just discovered a life hack for getting him to ignore me for a while." I took Sydney's arm and tugged her towards the bar. "Come on. Isn't my date supposed to buy me a drink or something?"

Anne-Marie and Remy exchanged another silent glance. I pretended not to notice.

Chapter Eleven
Expectations

"Get rid of this one," my dad said.

Without looking away from my closet, he held out a ruched black Amoren Viole mini-dress that still had the tags on it.

"Dad, no," I said, trying not to sound like I was begging as Kimberlee reluctantly took it from him. "I wouldn't wear that to an event. It's for going out to the bars and stuff."

"This is brand new, Max," Kimberlee said softly.

"An unfortunate waste of money, then," he said, examining another dress in my closet.

I'd expected my dad's anger. I'd expected consequences. I'd even insisted that Sydney not cancel her plans with Olivier to come back to my dad's house so she wasn't around when he got home.

Partly because I didn't want her to give up her night with Olivier. But mostly because I didn't want her around when my dad lost his shit on me. Because that's what I thought would happen.

I hadn't expected to hear my dad and Kimberlee return from the benefit an hour after I did and go straight to bed without saying anything to me.

And I definitely hadn't expected him to be collected and calm in the most terrifying of ways over breakfast that morning, not addressing the situation at all before casually stating he would be going through my closet when we finished eating.

"This is excessive," I said as my dad held up a floral maxi-dress for examination.

"It is not," my dad replied, putting the dress back in the closet. "I would like to make sure you have an acceptable outfit to wear."

"I have plenty of—"

"*Acceptable*, Eleanor." A short black-and-pink dress was held out to Kimberlee without comment.

"And that requires you to get rid of half my clothes, of course," I said. My voice didn't shake, but only because it was so dry it might have broken. "That makes perfect sense when the thing you're mad about didn't even have to do with my clothes."

"Not this time." He took another dress with a plunging neckline from the closet. "But it has become a priority to mitigate the risks associated with trusting that you will not embarrass yourself at these events."

"I told you, I thought it was the best choice given the situation," I said.

He didn't reply, just removed a black babydoll mini-dress from the closet.

"You said I had to have a date. I thought it would be better to bring anyone than it would be to show up alone."

The babydoll dress went on the pile next to Kimberlee, followed by my backless Givenchy dress I'd worn to *La Nuit Rose* a few months earlier.

"Almost everyone we talked to thought it was charming."

A pink dress with a tulle skirt that I'd bought *for* the Diamond Gala three years earlier joined the pile.

"Like, I *know* now. I won't do it again. And if you want me to apologize, I already said—"

I cut myself off as he picked up my red bikini from the shelf with all my swimsuits on it, passing it to Kimberlee.

"Dad, please," I said.

He handed her the spare pink bikini I always left here.

"I said I was sorry."

A fistful of colourful fabric. I didn't even know what was in it.

Silently, I watched as he went through the dresses hanging on the other rack. He handed two more things to Kimberlee, then wordlessly considered the remaining options before turning away from my decimated closet.

"Order something for Eleanor to wear to the gala," he said to Kimberlee. "Nothing black. She has plenty of that already."

"*Had* plenty of that," I whispered, looking at the neat stack of clothes Kimberlee had put on my bed. A moment later, the black volleyball team hoodie I'd had since high school joined it. My nose stung as I stared at my favourite sweater in silence.

"Black is a classic colour, Max," Kimberlee said. "And many of the dresses here would be more than appropriate—"

"It would be nice to have her not appear to be in mourning for once," he said, cutting her off. "Although perhaps we should save one for her to wear for the next time one of her debacles nearly costs me one of my biggest investors."

"How did this almost cost you an investor?" I asked, though I was still staring at the pile of clothes.

"I am certain my daughter is smart enough to understand she was humiliating someone by bringing a farce of a date instead of reaching out to him," he said, his calmness finally marred, but by condescension instead of the anger I'd thought would be there.

I sighed. "Okay, but—"

"But if that wasn't enough, you also rebuffed his attempt to show there were no hard feelings by being the bigger person and introducing himself to your date. In fact, Mr. Thibault said you made a point of insulting him in front of a group of other attendees."

I stared at him, partially in disbelief. "Clinton told you that?"

"He did. While I was speaking with his father, no less."

"So he tattled on me," I said. "Clinton Thibault tattled on me to my dad because I don't want to date him."

"Clinton expressed his disappointment in your actions," he corrected. "And again, I am certain that *my* daughter would understand that puts *my* reputation with the Thibaults on the line."

He was bluffing. He had to be. "I don't think they'd stop working with you over something like this."

"They won't," he said. "Not this time."

"So it'll all be fine."

"It will," he said.

"Okay, so—"

"After you attend the Diamond Gala with Clinton."

"No," I said.

"Yes," he responded patiently. "And even though I apologized on your behalf when I informed Clinton you would attend with him—"

"You *didn't*," I said, bitter and bile-like panic rising up my throat. "Dad, please. *Please* tell me you didn't."

"I did," he said. "And—"

"No. I can't. I *can't* go—"

"Stop interrupting, Eleanor." Each word was clipped, the only hint at the anger I'd been expecting the whole time. I fell silent, even though there was something screaming in the base of my chest. "You will attend the Diamond Gala with Clinton and you will call him to apologize yourself."

"No," I said. "No fucking way."

"Language," he said, his voice almost mild. Everything from his tone to his stance spoke composure, the placid expression on his face stoking the rage boiling in my stomach. "And yes. You will. You insulted Clinton and his family. I then had to spend my evening mitigating the offense *you* caused so I did not lose one of my current clients, meaning I was not able to connect with the person attending from the Martelle group. And considering taking a step towards gaining a massive account was the entire *point* of the event—"

"I thought the point was to support music and arts programs for at-risk youth," I said.

He looked at me, unimpressed. "You do not get to pull the garbage you did last night and not face any consequences."

"Consequences? You threw out half my clothes!" I said, trying not shriek. "And on top of that, you want me to go to *another* event with this absolute fucking pig—"

"Language," he said again.

"He is!" I made a noise that was almost a laugh. "He doesn't know how to keep his hands to himself. I wasn't even there with him last night and he was being creepy. I don't understand why you're so set on me and Clinton going to things together when I keep saying I don't want to!"

"You may not like Clinton, but I have been asking, as a favour, that you be civil with him," my dad said. "I have not stepped in or asked you to attend any other event with him so long as you have another date. But when you personally insult the son of one of my biggest investors and potentially cost me the business of another prospective investor, what would you expect me to do?"

I wanted to say a lot of things there.

Like "I'd expect you to stand up for me."

Or "I'd expect you to understand why I'm uncomfortable with him."

Maybe even "I'd expect you to be horrified at the prospect of me having to be alone with someone who could realistically hurt me" or "I'd expect you to at least pretend that his dad's money is less important than me," if I was feeling spicy.

But since all those words wanted to come out, none of them did.

And since I couldn't tell my dad what I expected him to do, he assumed that meant I didn't know.

"You see," he said, holding his hand out as if the lesson was sitting in his palm for me to look at. "We are aware that Clinton would like to know you better. Which means we know the solution to the issue you've created is for you to attend the event with him."

"You realize how fucked up it is that he's insisting on this, right?" I asked.

"Sometimes we have to do things we don't like in life, Nellie," my dad said. "And if this is one of those things, so be it."

"Like making me choose a restaurant because it's what your precious girlfriend wanted even though you know the last time I did that, you and Mom got divorced?"

My room must have been a vacuum because I didn't say the words so much as they were pulled out of me, and once they were, they filled the space around us. My dad wasn't looking at me, but I could see Kimberlee turned towards me, her mouth half-open.

"You know that was not what happened," my dad said, his voice even. "Regardless, the misconceptions of a child are not relevant. You are not throwing that into the conversation to avoid the consequences of your actions."

The air left behind after he spoke was heavy.

Really fucking heavy.

And somehow, Kimberlee was the first one strong enough to lift it.

"Max," she said. "There must be another—"

"There is not another way." My dad's tone was clipped. "Nellie will be going to the Diamond Gala with Clinton."

"And what if I already had another date?" I asked.

"You don't," my dad said.

"I do, though," I said, my heart beating so fast it was almost vibrating. "I... I knew you'd be mad. About this. So when... when one of the people I asked said he wasn't available last night, he offered to come with me to the Diamond Gala. So I said yes and—"

"Who," my dad said. It was probably a question, but he said it tonelessly.

"What?" I asked.

"Tell me, exactly, who you are attending the Diamond Gala with who was not available last night, who you are just bringing up now, and who I am going to grant my approval to? Because we are talking about the Thibaults and I am not about to risk offending them further, nor am I going to risk the opportunity to connect with the Martelle group again." He set an icy gaze on me. "Who would that be, Nellie?"

Afterwards, I told myself I'd been desperate and panicked at the prospect of having to see Clinton, so blurted out the first name I thought of. I told myself that even at that moment, I picked him because I knew it was the one and only name my dad would even consider.

And he did.

He blinked at me, almost like he was surprised, then glanced at Kimberlee with his eyebrows raised. She didn't return his amused look, her face scarily blank and unreadable. My stomach tightened, preparing itself for the gut punch of him laughing in my face for even suggesting there was a way to get out of going to this with Clinton.

"Alright," my dad said.

Holy fuck.

"I will tell the Thibaults you express your apologies but unfortunately already committed to the Diamond Gala with someone else."

My stomach relaxed. "Thank—"

"There are conditions."

Of course there were. "What conditions?"

"You will still apologize to Clinton personally," he said.

Shitty, but expected. "Okay."

"Kimberlee will select an appropriate dress for you."

Whatever. "Sounds good."

"You will come to Montreal two days earlier so I can ensure you are adequately prepared for the gala. And you will come *alone*. No friends joining you."

Definitely shitty, but still doable. "Alright."

"And Eleanor? I want no further surprises. I do not know if you do it because you are rebelling or simply bored, but you will control your instinct to do anything and everything to make things difficult. Do not show up in a different dress than the one Kimberlee selects. Do not *modify* the dress. Do not dye your hair, decide you need to pierce your nose, or get some horrid tattoo across your chest. Do not inadvertently insult the Martelles. And do not, under any circumstances, show up with any date other than the one I've approved unless that date is Clinton Thibault. Do you understand?"

I nodded.

"Good," he said. "Because if you are lying about who will be escorting you, Eleanor, I expect you will need to find a new, less expensive place to live for your last year of school."

Rage saturated every part of my body, head to toe, in a sudden crashing wave that washed away any control I had as he turned and walked towards my bedroom door. "You can't keep holding that over my head!"

"Watch me," he said.

"Max!"

I was almost shocked to hear Kimberlee's voice again, but I was too focused on the spot my dad had been standing to care. My fingernails dug into my palm, my fists clenched as tightly as my jaw was. For a blissful minute, there was no sound, so all I had to do was focus on not letting the rage-filled tears that had washed up into my eyes spill over.

And then she had to speak.

"Nellie—" Kimberlee said.

"Regret it yet?"

I almost didn't recognize my voice. Bitterness had warped it, made it low and raspy and cold in a way so reminiscent of my dad that I wanted to puke.

Kimberlee sighed. "He is being unreasonable."

I almost laughed. "You fucking think so, Kim?"

She didn't call me out for shortening her name. "I will speak with him for you."

"I don't need you to do anything for me."

"Trust me, Eleanor"—oh, she wasn't calling me out. Just being snarky—"it is not just for you."

I didn't know what that meant, nor did I have the capacity to care at that moment, so I didn't respond.

"What colour would you like your dress to be for the Diamond Gala?" she asked.

"Black," I said.

"And if not black, what colour would you like it to be?"

"I don't care."

"Nellie—"

"Puce," I said. "Mauve. Magenta. Baby shit green. I don't fucking care."

She sighed. I waited for her to finally leave, but instead, she walked over and put a comforting hand on my shoulder.

"I am sorry," she said, her voice quiet. "For yesterday morning. I did not know. And I am sorry for... for all of this today."

I didn't say anything. I couldn't say anything. She wasn't supposed to be nice to me. She wasn't supposed to be on my side. She was supposed to be shallow and conniving and call me a spoiled brat who deserved to be cut off.

Instead, I stood there, refusing to look at her as she walked over to my bed to collect the pile of clothes before leaving the room.

It wasn't until I went to sit down after she closed the door that I realized the black Amoren Viole dress, my red and pink bikinis, and my volleyball hoodie were all still sitting there, neatly folded.

Chapter Twelve
Is The Hot Dog Water Off The Table?

IF PROCRASTINATION WAS AN Olympic sport, I would've never won.

Mainly because I would've put off attempting to qualify until it was too late and missed the deadline.

I was not an "eat the frog" kind of person. The worst tasks were always saved for last like I thought maybe they would go away if I waited long enough. And I could *wait*. When I didn't want to do something, I could talk myself into doing literally anything else.

So I wasn't quite sure what it said about me that I not only started figuring out how to deal with the date I'd lied about to my dad about only a couple of minutes after Kimberlee left my room, I was frustrated that I had to wait until she and my dad went to church a little while later to do anything about it.

I was impatient enough that as soon as I heard voices in the downstairs foyer, I pushed my bedroom door open and tiptoed into the hallway so I could leave the second they were gone.

"—will not soften discipline just because it seems unpalatable to you," my dad said. He was speaking in rapid French, but I could still catch most of the conversation.

"It was *cruel*, Max," Kimberlee replied, her French just as clipped and rapid. "I am not talking about discipline, I am talking about—"

"It was not cruel. Her behaviour was unacceptable and somehow Nellie has never learned that her actions have consequences. And regardless, we have discussed this before. You do not get to tell me how to handle my daughter."

"I do when you use me in your so-called discipline," Kimberlee snapped. "When you make me stand there as if I'm going to agree with you that taking her things away is normal. When you disrespect her boundaries on my behalf and do not even have the decency to tell me!"

My dad didn't say anything.

"Do you believe that is reasonable? Do you know how you hurt her with all that? How you hurt me by using me like that? You are acting like the person people warned me about and I told you I would not tolerate that."

Oh, *shit*.

There was more silence, but this time, Kimberlee didn't break it. My best guess was that my dad was giving her the cold, finalizing stare he used on all the women he'd been with when they dared to contradict him, either by argument or by strengthening into the kind of woman who would stand up to him. It was a look that made people retreat, like standing in the glacial aura pouring off him would turn them into brittle ice sculptures he'd shatter half a breath later when he dismissed them from his life. And he'd given that look and that dismissal to women for far, *far* less than what Kimberlee was doing and saying.

But apparently, he really liked Kimberlee or something.

"I did not use you," he finally said. "I would not and will not do that."

No one could see me, but I knew the shock was showing on my face all the same.

"My attempt to provide you with what you wanted may have been misguided, but I was not using you."

"Max—"

"Please," he said. "Kimberlee."

There was more silence, then the closing of the front door. I frowned, slightly frustrated that I hadn't heard anything more and desperate to know what the hell had just happened, but I didn't have time for that. If I wanted to be gone by the time they were back from church, I had to go *now*.

Spinning around, I grabbed the bags I'd packed with the things my dad hadn't taken away and raced down the stairs. Slipping my shoes on, I rushed as slowly as I could outside, my heart slamming in my chest as I threw my bags in the car and tried to appear nonchalant.

Then I closed my trunk, locked the car, and turned to walk across the stretch of lawn between my dad's house and the Marchands'.

Before I could even knock, the front door opened. I worried for half a second that it wouldn't be him, but JP was standing there, his hair wet like he'd just gotten out of the shower—thank God for that—and wearing a perfectly fitted polo shirt tucked into a tan pair of chino shorts.

And, of course, a brown leather fucking belt.

His typical jovial, cocky, infuriating smile crossed his face as he saw me striding purposefully towards him. "Hey, Nel—"

I didn't let him finish before grabbing his shoulders and pulling him in to kiss me.

"—lie," he mumbled against my mouth. "Shit, what are—"

I interrupted him by slipping my tongue into his mouth. Another noise of disbelief escaped before he kissed me back. Strong arms wrapped around my waist, which were very helpful for when I pushed my body against his to make him stumble back through the doorway into the foyer of his house, praying that JP hadn't lied about having the house to himself when I'd texted him to see if he was home.

I mean, I wouldn't have put it past him. He would've thought it was funny, probably, if I'd knocked on the door and his mom or dad or, God forbid, Anne-Marie had answered, making me scramble to explain what I was doing there. And I'd hesitated when he said he was home alone, since I'd planned to ask if we could go to the parking lot we usually hooked up in. My dad's assistant, Pierre, was still downstairs, doing some cleaning or tidying or something, so there was always a chance he'd see me.

But I knew Anne-Marie and Remy had stayed at his place after last night's benefit. And I knew Della and Mr. Marchand were probably at church already, too. Which just left Marc-Andre unaccounted for. So I'd decided to risk it and luckily for both of us, JP hadn't been lying.

As soon as the front door swung shut, I let go of his shoulders and shoved my hands between our bodies. JP chuckled as I pulled the end of his belt through the buckle.

"Babe, it's been at most a day and a half since you got laid," he said. "How are you already this desperate?"

It wasn't a complaint. I didn't think so, anyway. His hands were almost as busy as mine, sliding down my sides so he could push his fingers beneath the hem of my t-shirt. An involuntary shiver ran through me, almost like electricity was dancing from the tips of his fingers to my skin, but I still didn't say anything.

He tried to push those fingertips further up my shirt after I got his belt undone, dipping down to capture my lips. I let him kiss me, but nudged his hands away so I could get to the waistband of his shorts. He tried to get his hand up my shirt again and I shoved his hands away harder before pushing on his chest. A startled laugh puffed against my mouth as I made him turn, switching places so I could push him against the front door.

"Nell," he said through his chuckles. "What are—"

And then whatever he was going to say turned into a throaty, almost breathless noise. Probably because it had only taken one smooth movement for me to pop the button on his shorts open, another to pull the zipper, and a third to tug his boxers down and free his cock before dropping to my knees in front of him.

"Holy fuck, what—ah." He grunted as I wrapped my lips around his semi-erect cock. "Jeez, Nellie. You—*ugh*..."

I could feel his eyes on me, his cock twitching in my mouth and thickening against my tongue as I sucked him. He groaned again, his hand pushing my hair back again before he threaded his fingers through it. A hiss of pleasure left his lips a moment later, his hips jerking forward as his tip hit the back of my throat. I swallowed around it, moving forward until my nose pressed against his pelvis.

"*Fuck*," he grunted. "Holy sh-*shit*."

I didn't look up until he was fully stiff, my lips stretched around his shaft as I started bobbing my head. He wasn't looking at me when I did; he'd tilted his head back, resting against the door heavily as he relaxed into the blowjob. His breath came in deep inhales that weren't quite gasps but still betrayed how good I was making him feel.

And fuck if that wasn't so goddamn hot.

That was all I focused on. How much I liked listening to his breath as I sucked his cock. How he was so hard I could feel his heartbeat with my tongue. How he pushed his hips forward, making heat rush through my body and my nipples harden in my bra because I knew he couldn't stop himself from doing it.

I didn't think about anything else. Not about how angry I was with my dad or how hurt I was or why I was on my knees attempting to give the best blowjob of both my life and JP's. I focused solely on him, on how he felt, how he tasted, how his hand felt *so* good on my head and how I almost wanted to reach down and slip my hand into my own shorts because *fuck*.

Fuck, this shouldn't have been turning me on so much.

It shouldn't have been turning me on at *all*.

Wet noises echoed the foyer as I bobbed my head. JP's fingers tightened whenever I did something he particularly liked, which was often, and by the time his stomach started tensing like he was trying to stop himself from writhing, he had a consistent fistful of hair clenched in his hand.

"Nellie," he mumbled. "Oh my God. Oh my fucking *God.*"

He finally opened his eyes and looked down, watching as I spoiled his dick with my mouth. His eyebrows knitted together, an expression that wasn't pained as much as it was pleasure.

"Look at you," he muttered. "Look at you fucking me with your mouth. You're—*ugh.*"

He shuddered as I shifted my head back and forth, like I was trying to work his cock even further down my throat.

"Nellie, you—" I cupped his balls and added the pressure of a gentle, careful squeeze. "—ah fu-ucking *crisse d'*fucking *ciboire* goddamn *tabarnak!*"

I almost laughed. I was pretty sure I'd never done anything that made JP swear in French before, let alone let out a string of mixed French and English curses that I wasn't sure I'd ever heard *anyone* say before.

His other hand found the back of my head, grabbing another fistful of hair, and I knew. I knew he was about to groan, and I knew it was going to be staggered and stilted and desperate, and I relaxed as much as I could because I knew we were almost at the inevitable moment when he would shove his cock the rest of the way down my throat.

"Nellie," he gasped. "Babe. I—"

He grunted again and a moment later, his cock pulsed. I tasted the first drops of his cum before he pushed my head down, holding me in place as he emptied himself in my throat, my eyes stinging with tears as the urge to choke fought with the physical limitations of doing so.

When he finally loosened his grip on my hair, I pulled back, gasping for breath as a mix of saliva and cum dripped onto my chin.

"F-Fuck," he panted. "Sorry."

I ran the back of my hand over my mouth before glancing up and grinning. "You'd think with how many times we've done this, you'd figure out you can stop apologizing."

He laughed, the sound still breathless, and reached down to help me to my feet before pulling his pants and boxers up. "Right. Because as if it wasn't enough that you stomped over and sucked me off like you were cheating on me with my own dick, you also think gagging on it is *hot*."

"Yeah, well..."

He chuckled again and finished buckling his belt, then dipped his head down and kissed me. I let that kiss linger, though not long enough for him to start returning the favour before looking up at him through my eyelashes.

"So," I said. "I have a favour to ask."

I had never seen JP laugh so hard before. Not even the time when I'd baa'ed at him after he told me I sounded like a goat when I came.

"I swear you should've been a lawyer," he said, still chuckling. "Like really, babe. You'd be so good at it."

"No thanks. I might be a sleazebag, but you're living proof I'm not enough of one to be a lawyer."

"I'd tell you to suck my dick, but you just did, so..." He kissed me again, his smile still on his lips. "Alright. What's the favour?"

"I need you to be my date for the Diamond Gala."

I said it the same way I would've pulled the first wax strip off my legs after a long, hairy winter: without thinking too much about what I was doing so I couldn't chicken out, and as fast as I could because if I *did* chicken out, it would be ten times more painful. And much like the expression I made when I looked at that first wax strip full of hair, JP was staring at me with a mix of fascinated horror and concern, the smile having been ripped off his face at the same time I'd spoken.

"Uh... what did—"

"I know," I said. "It's ridiculous for me to ask. It's... this... this thing"—I motioned between us—"is not a dating or dating-adjacent arrangement and you told me the other day that you didn't want to go to stuff like this and I *get* that. I swear I wouldn't be asking if I wasn't desperate."

"I'm so flattered," he said dryly.

"You know what I mean." I bit my lip. "Please. I really need help."

He looked over my shoulder. "Nellie, I... Look, the Diamond Gala isn't for a while yet. You have time to find someone else."

"It's not time that's the problem," I said.

He sighed, the sound almost aggravated. "There's really, honestly no one else you could ask?"

"No one else my dad will be okay with."

There was no mistaking the absolute horror on his face as his eyes snapped back to mine. "You told your *dad*?!"

"Not... no. I mean, yes, but not about—" It was so uncommon for me to get flustered, it took me a moment to realize that's what was happening. "I told him you'd agreed to it. And after what happened last night, there's literally no one else he'll be okay with."

"What happened last night?"

Right. Anne-Marie hadn't come home yet. So he didn't know.

"I, uh... couldn't find another date," I said. "So I might've... dressed Sydney up in a tuxedo and drew a mustache on her and introduced her to everyone as Sid Cunnilinginton the Third."

JP pressed his lips together. "And you thought your dad—"

"—would be less mad about that than if I showed up alone," I said.

His laugh slipped out. "Oh God. I almost wish I'd seen that." He flicked his eyes to mine pointedly. "Not enough to actually *go* to a benefit, mind you."

Fuck.

Fuck.

Fuck.

I'd really hoped the blowjob would be enough. And if not the blowjob, mentioning that my dad wouldn't be okay with any other date. I really, *really* hadn't wanted to tell him the last bit because it would go one of two ways: either I'd feel bad that I'd guilted him into agreeing, or he would reveal he was as bad as the rest of them.

But I didn't have much choice.

"If you don't, my dad says I have to go with Clinton," I said. "No one else."

JP stared at me.

Then he closed his eyes, tilted his head back, and groaned defeatedly. "Damnit, Nellie. It *had* to be that piece of shit, didn't it?"

"His dad told my dad he was going to pull his investments or something," I said. "Because Clinton was insulted that I took Syd instead of agreeing to go with him. And because of that, my dad also didn't get to meet with some other rich person who might want to invest with him, so that's entirely my fault, too."

"And your dad thinks you going with Clinton will fix that," he said, not as a question but as a statement.

"Yes."

"He knows about Clinton and what's been said about him, right?"

"He says there's no proof so there's nothing to worry about."

JP studied me for a moment, then sighed again. "Drinking the old hot dog water from La Belle Provence isn't on the table to get me out of this?"

"I'd be right there chugging it with you if I thought it would work."

"And you don't think my sister will lose her fucking mind if she sees us together?"

"She'll be planning the wedding before dessert," I said.

He half-laughed, though it was more of a huff. Looking back at me, his eyes darkened into an accusatory glare.

"I know what you're doing," he said. "Don't think I don't know."

He wasn't going to agree.

Fuck.

Fuck.

I almost threw all dignity aside. I almost begged. I almost gritted my teeth and got on my knees again and apologized for bringing him into this, even though I hated apologizing more than I hated begging. I almost promised him anything he wanted.

I almost cried. And no, not to guilt him even more than I already had, but just because...

Because *fuck*.

Thankfully, I hesitated for the brief moment it took to force my chin to stop trembling. Because that's when JP's glare flickered into a roguish smirk, a glimmer appearing in his eyes as his teeth raked over his lower lip.

"What do I get out of this?" he asked.

I flicked my eyes down, then back up. "I just sucked your cock."

"I can get that from you anytime."

"Was it better or worse than the one you got when you agreed to go to *La Nuit Rose* with Chantel?"

A laugh escaped his lips. "You're asking me to compare?"

"Well, you said it was insane, but did she make you swear in French and refer to it as... what was it? Cheating on you with your own dick?"

"Had I known it would be used against me, I would've never said that."

"Not my problem. You should've had better representation."

Another laugh made him shake his head. "Alright. Your admittedly exceptional blowjob can be a retainer for the favour. The actual doing of the favour, though..."

It was my turn to let a laugh escape. "You're such a fucking lawyer."

"And you're fucking a lawyer you want a favour from." He half-shrugged, a nonchalant expression on his face. "Those are the terms, babe."

"What is it you want, then?"

I didn't think I'd ever be quite sure what went through JP's head at that moment. If he was being flippant. If he was trying to pick something that would make me decline so he didn't have to go through with being my date. Or if he was testing the waters to see how far I'd go. Because even then, even as his eyes trailed down my body with so much heat I could almost feel it and as his tongue poked out to wet his lips, even as his eyes flicked back up, his eyebrow twitching to reveal the gleam hidden away behind the blue of his pupils, I doubted he actually meant it as anything more than a joke.

"I don't think it'll matter," he said. "You won't say yes."

"How would you know that if you don't tell me?"

His mouth twitched. "Because I know you."

"You don't know me as well as you think you do. Tell me."

"Mmm... you sure?"

I folded my arms. "Stop being a bastard about it."

A smirk tugged the corner of his lip up, giving a lopsided wickedness to his face. "But you're sure? *Really* sure, babe?"

"I'm really, really, *really* sure, bastard."

His eyes flicked down and back up again one more time before he spoke.

"What I want," he said, his voice low and smooth and purposeful, "is to fuck your ass."

It took *everything* in me not to laugh in his face.

Like, everything. Fighting not to gag on his cock when it felt like the tip of it was past my vocal cords and my nose was buried in the curls of hair on his pelvis was easier than fighting that laugh. I fought back that laugh like it had a reverse bob haircut and was trying to grab the last eighty-percent-off TV at six am on Black Friday. I did whatever the mental equivalent of body slamming is to that laugh.

Because if I'd laughed in his face, JP would've thought he was right instead of realizing that I'd wanted to do that very thing for ages.

So I didn't laugh. I didn't shoot him down. I bit my lip, looking at a spot somewhere over his left shoulder as I pretended to mull it over, then inhaled deeply.

"Okay," I said.

JP blinked, the arrogant smirk disappearing. "Okay?"

I shrugged. "Yeah. What else am I gonna do? I need a date for this, so yeah. You can."

His eyebrows pinched together. "That—"

"After the gala," I said. "I'm guessing my dad and Kimberlee will stay at the hotel since my dad usually does for that event. So you... you can come over."

He stared at me, not quite gaping, not quite disbelieving, not quite certain of what had just happened. And fuck if I didn't *love* being responsible for unsettling him like that.

"You're sure, babe?" he finally asked.

"Yeah. Aren't you?"

A scoff-like laugh was his response. "Of course. I'm the one who asked for it."

"So we have a deal?"

His throat flexed as he swallowed and there was no mistaking the little smile that played on his lips. "What colour tie should I wear?"

Chapter Thirteen
Boink?!?!

"THAT RACE MUST HAVE been quite the experience," Ben said as he walked up to me.

I leaned forward, my heel resting on the seat of the wooden bench and the muscles along the back of my leg burning through the stretch. "Why do you say that?"

Amused lines appeared in the corners of his eyes. "I thought you said once it was over, you were done with any cardio that didn't involve orgasms."

I finished stretching, shaking out my leg and standing up straight. "I did. But I figured it would be nice to hang out before you go see your ex-wife for a week and then leave me forever."

"Not forever," he said with a chuckle. "And I'm planning to see you in the two days I'm back before I leave for California."

"Well, yes, but then how am I supposed to be dramatic about it?"

He shook his head, still grinning.

Ben had taken me running on a few different trails, but when I'd texted him earlier that day, I'd suggested we jog along the Rideau Canal. There were trails on the Rideau River that I preferred, but they were farther from my apartment than the one I liked at the canal and I'd just wanted to get out as soon as I could.

"So the run went well then?" Ben asked as we started to jog along the path.

"Pretty well," I replied. "I might do it again, actually."

"Really?"

"Maybe. It was fun. We did a Jello shot at the start line. The foam pit was fun. JP and I fucked in the bushes. Bruno fell into a garbage can. It was my kinda race, you know?"

He almost tripped. "You did... what?"

"A Jello shot," I said. "At the start. It wasn't technically part of the race, I guess. It's more of a toast for this guy who died. I think JP probably knew him. But it's always nice to start with a shot, you know?"

"Right, of course." He half-coughed. "And the, uh, other thing you said you did?"

"The foam pit?" From the corner of my eye, I caught his unimpressed look and I laughed. "JP?"

"You hadn't mentioned he would be there," he said.

"I didn't know he would be."

The conversation faded and we ran in silence for a while. It was the good kind of silence, or at least, as good as silence can be. It wasn't awkward or tense or heavy; it was just there, accompanying us the same way as the footsteps on pavement and the gentle rush of water in the canal and the constant murmur of thoughts in my mind.

Normally while we ran, I had to remind Ben a couple of times that he was a weirdo who trained for marathons and this all started because I lied about jogging so I could get laid so he would slow down a bit. That time, though, I didn't say anything, just did my best to keep up with him, panting for breath as my heart rate rose in time with my footsteps.

When we reached a couple of benches, Ben looked at me.

"Quick break to catch our breaths?" he asked.

I nodded and he slowed down, pulling his water bottle out and handing it to me.

"Thanks," I said, trying not to gasp as I opened it to take a sip before passing it back.

"You're quiet today," he said before taking a sip himself.

I snorted. "I don't think I've ever been described as quiet before in my life."

He offered me the water bottle again. "Quieter than usual, then."

I shrugged as I took it. "I like to give people a break from my voice once in a while."

"Well, I enjoy listening to your voice," he said. "What's on your mind?"

"Nothing really," I said. "Just the usual eight million things."

"Eight million?" he repeated as I took another sip of water.

"Give or take."

He chuckled. "Want to tell me about some of them?"

"It's not anything interesting," I said.

"I bet that's not true."

"I am capable of being boring, you know."

He scoffed, almost offended. "Well, I *know* that's not true."

I laughed again, but I couldn't quite bring myself to say anything. Instead, I handed Ben back his water bottle. He took another sip and with a natural sort of ease, silently agreed to start walking down the paved path. The quietness fell again and I scratched at the side of my thumb.

"So this weekend my dad made me pick a restaurant for brunch even though I hate picking restaurants," I said after a cyclist zipped by in the other direction.

"I see," Ben said, though it was pretty obvious he had no idea where I was going with that. Neither did I, to be fair. It sounded as stupid out loud as it did in my head.

"Then he threw out half my clothes," I said.

"He threw out your clothes?" Ben repeated.

"Or donated them, maybe."

I wasn't looking at him, but I could hear the frown in his voice. "Did he give you a reason for that?"

"Because my date cancelled on me for the event I was attending this weekend."

"Uh…"

"And I couldn't find another date," I continued. "So I dressed Sydney up in a tuxedo and fake mustache and told everyone her name was Sid Cunnilinginton."

"Sid Cunnilinginton," he repeated.

"The Third. Which I thought was better than showing up alone because earlier in the day he told me I absolutely couldn't show up alone to any events because he wants me to get together with the creepy son of one of his clients, so he decided I can't be trusted and took anything he thought might be inappropriate for the Diamond Gala out of my closet. Including some bikinis and my volleyball hoodie, except Kimberlee secretly gave those back. Because oh yeah, he did this in front of his girlfriend, who even called him out on it."

"The girlfriend you don't like?"

"Yeah."

"It sounds like things might be going better with her, though?"

I rolled my eyes. "No way. She's gotta be hiding something. There's no reason anyone decent would be with my dad."

There was a hint of anger in his voice. "Given what you're telling me right now, I can't exactly disagree with that."

"Yeah." I sighed. "So anyways, now I owe JP anal."

Ben tripped.

Like fully tripped and nearly went down on the pavement, but I reached out and grabbed him before he fell. He steadied himself, then looked at me with wide, semi-frantic eyes, and I couldn't help but laugh.

"He's going to be my date for the gala," I explained. "Because there's no one else my dad would approve other than Clinton."

Ben's eyebrows knitted together. "Understandable, but if he's saying you *owe* him—"

"I'm half-messing with you," I said. "I want to do it."

"Okay, but did you offer? Or did he ask for that in... ah... exchange?"

"I mean, he asked, but—"

"Nellie." His voice was firm, but the touch on my arm was gentle. "That's not okay."

"He wouldn't actually make me," I said. "I thought his eyes were going to fall out when I said yes."

He didn't look convinced. "You're sure?"

I nodded. "He was totally thrown off by me saying yes. And you know that any time I can have the upper hand on JP is a good day. He might be a sleazy lawyer and arrogant dirtbag and an annoying bastard, but he's not the kind of guy who would ever make someone do something like that."

"He better not be," Ben said, and I was almost surprised by the heat in his voice. Just like I was almost surprised by the warmth that heat put in my chest.

"Why? Would you go beat him up for me?" I asked.

"I'm flattered you think I can beat up a guy who's, what, fifteen years younger than me?"

I frowned and tilted my head. "No, only like... twelve. Or eleven, maybe. But you run and stuff."

"It barely makes up for the hours of sitting around I do." He pulled out his water bottle and took a sip, then offered it to me. "And given that you saw him at the race, I'm guessing he does as well."

"Yeah. And he goes to the gym." I rolled my eyes as I took his water. "The weirdo."

"But he's a weirdo who would be good to you?"

I started to say yes, then re-processed what he'd said. "Don't do that."

"Do what?"

"That."

He half-laughed. "I don't know what you mean."

"Say he'd be *good to me*." I slugged back a sip of water. "Like it's some kind of *thing*. It's not."

"I wasn't saying it was."

"Good." I handed the water bottle back to him more aggressively than intended. "Because it's not."

"Mmm," he said, lifting the bottle to his lips and taking a sip.

The warm feeling from Ben's protectiveness sparked into annoyance. "You better believe me."

"I certainly do."

"Right. And the reason you sound so skeptical when you say that is...?"

"I'm not skeptical, Nellie." He put his water bottle back in his running belt. "I know you and JP are only friends."

"I don't even think we're friends," I said, and that was a bit more aggressive than I wanted it to be, too. "JP and I just fuck. But it's different than you and me. Like, you and I fuck too, but we're also friends. Or at least, I think we are."

He stifled a cough. "Yes. Of course we are."

I wrinkled my nose in realization. "Oops. Right. You don't like calling it fucking. You and I... is 'boink' a better word?"

"*Boink*?!" he repeated.

We'd just started walking under a bridge, so the sound of my relatively formal former professor's voice saying the most ridiculous word in existence echoed. I cracked up, grabbing Ben's arm so I didn't accidentally trip as the "*boink...oink...oink*" bounced around us. His laughter joined mine as he steadied me.

"Or do you prefer 'bone'?" I said through giggles as we walked out from under the bridge.

"I prefer whichever gets me inside you, honestly," he said.

My laughter stopped as I looked at him in impressed astonishment. "*Ben*."

He glanced back at me, eyebrows raised. "Yes?"

"We're in public."

"That's never stopped you from making jokes like that."

"Well, yeah, but it's always stopped you."

He half-shrugged, though there was almost a look of pride on his face. "Yes, well, friends make jokes like this together. Don't they?"

I tried not to smile and failed. "Yeah, they do."

And maybe that was weird. That we were friends, I mean. On the surface, we didn't have a lot in common. He was a tenured professor with an ex-wife and a career taking him to work with some of the most renowned psychologists in the world. I was a student who didn't want a relationship beyond friendship and fucking.

And from the outside, it probably looked like something different. Neither of us were ignorant to what an older guy hooking up with a younger girl *looked* like. What people would assume he wanted from me and what I wanted from him.

But it was deeper than that while not being deep at all. We knew where we stood and it was refreshing to have that confidence with someone.

"You would tell me, right?" I'd asked one night a few weeks after the whole thing had started. We'd been lying in his bed, naked of course, and he was trailing his fingers up and down my arm in a lazy, hypnotizing pattern.

I hadn't said anything else, but he'd known what I meant. "If I... what did the song say? 'Catch feels' for you?"

I'd let out a short huff of laughter. "Yeah."

"I'm still impressed you knew every word."

"I've been listening to it on repeat for, like, a month now."

"Just that song?" he'd asked, amused.

"Yeah. I'll get sick of it soon and never listen to it again." I'd yawned. "Then it'll be something else with completely opposite vibes."

He'd made a knowing noise. "A stim song."

I'd frowned. "A what now?"

"It's a term Isabelle—my ex-wife—uses. Or used to use, at least. I don't think it's an official term but it's something she talks about with her patients."

"What patients?"

"Children, mostly. She's a pediatric psychiatrist."

"Do I want to know where you're going with this?"

He'd chuckled. "It's just a characteristic of some types of neurodivergent disorders. Stimming is a type of repetitive behaviour that some use to cope with emotions or stress. To lean on stereotypes, something like hand-flapping or rocking would be a 'stim.' And since some songs seem to 'itch' part of the brain, as it were, listening to them on repeat can be a type of stimming."

"Oh. Does that mean there's something wrong with me?"

"No. Partly because neurodivergence wouldn't mean there's anything *wrong* with you, but mostly because it's not a behaviour exclusive to neurodivergent disorders. The term just carries over well." I'd nodded slowly and he'd walked his fingers up my bicep. "Back to your original question, yes. I'd tell you if I developed feelings for you."

"But for real?" I'd pressed. "None of this 'Oh my God I have the feels and now I have to hide them because that historically goes well in every book, movie, and sitcom that's ever existed' shit?"

He'd chuckled again, his hand moving up to my hair and twirling the end of it around his finger. "Yes, for real, I'd tell you. But I don't think you have to worry." A beat passed before he'd tensed. "I mean, as lovely as you are, and as fun as this is—"

"No offense was taken," I said. "You know that."

He'd sighed. "I know. But it still seems weird to tell someone you don't think of them as relationship material. Especially given our current, ah... position."

"Trust me, I'd be far more offended if you told me I was girlfriend material. I've worked hard to make a relationship with me as undesirable as possible." I'd twisted my mouth to the side. "Well, I guess aside from the fact that I definitely put out."

He'd laughed again and reassured me again that he wasn't expecting more from me. And maybe not everyone would have taken that at face value, but I did. Ben and I agreed that we wanted a good time, not a long time, like that Trooper song my mom used to blast on repeat said. Of course, I wasn't exactly looking forward to losing a regular source of face to sit on, but it wasn't tearing me up inside or anything.

"We're near your apartment," Ben said, breaking me out of my thoughts again.

I blinked, surprised by how far we'd walked in relative silence and seemingly without me being aware of it. "I guess we are. Are you tired already?"

He chuckled. "No. But you're tense."

"Uh... thanks?"

His mouth twitched. "You've had a lot going on lately. And as good as a run is for, ah... stress relief, it's also important to make sure you're not overexerting yourself."

A knowing smile spread across my face. "I see."

"Mm-hmm." After a quick glance behind us, a daring hand ended up on the small of my back and he guided me off the path and towards the sidewalk. "I think a post-run treatment is in order, Ms. Belanger."

Chapter Fourteen
A Post-Run Treatment

BEN HAD GIVEN ME a lot of post-run treatments in the few weeks we'd been jogging together. Those had varied from hot, steamy showers with his face between my legs to hot, steamy showers with his cock in my mouth to hot, steamy showers followed by hot, steamy fucking in his bed followed by more hot, steamy showers.

However, all of those hot, steamy showers had taken place at his apartment since he had a massive shower that was perfect for fucking in, with dual shower heads and even a bench in it.

My apartment was pretty nice, as far as student apartments went, but my bathroom had the standard tub-and-shower combo. And while that was also a perfectly acceptable place to fuck, I'd definitely been spoiled by Ben's shower.

So I wasn't quite sure what kind of "post-run treatment" I was in for this time. I figured it would still start the same way, but was surprised when Ben kissed me before taking my hand and leading me to my bedroom.

He started by lifting the tank top I was wearing over my head before stripping off my lavender-and-blue patterned sports bra with a touch deft enough that it was clear he'd done that before. He set it to the side and I waited for him to peel off the matching skintight running shorts because even though I was fully capable of undressing myself, I knew Ben liked to unwrap me like I was gift wrapped in hundred dollar bills. But once I was topless, he dipped his head down to press a kiss to each of my breasts before nudging me backwards.

"On the bed," he said.

"But my shorts—"

"Face down."

"Oh," I said. "You meant an actual post-run treatment."

"Maybe I did," he said as I climbed on the bed, then followed so he could straddle my hips and lean forward. "Maybe I just wanted an excuse to touch you for as long as I can."

"You don't need an excuse for tha—*ohhh*." My eyes fluttered shut as he started rubbing my lower back. "Fuck, Ben."

"Good?"

I made a soft humming noise, then sighed as Ben gave me one of the most magical massages I'd ever had. Like, I would have paid for that good of a massage. Even if he hadn't used the opportunity to do one of the hottest things I'd ever experienced in my life.

It started as nothing. As a consequence of circumstance. As a bulge bumping my ass cheek whenever he leaned in to deepen the pressure or move his hands further up my back or just because it probably felt nice to have something brush against his cock. As a promise for later, once he'd finished spoiling my body, to let all those muscles he loosened tense right back up as he made me come.

Then it became a hint of something. His bulge pressed a little harder against one ass cheek and his next breath was shaky, and two breaths after that, a quiet exhale hinted at relief after he shifted so his erection nudged against my ass crack.

Not too long after that, he leaned in under the guise of adding pressure to my shoulder blades, but the almost inaudible groan and slight pump of his hips made it clear it wasn't just about me anymore.

Especially not after I lifted my pelvis slightly to press my ass harder against his cock and his groan turned from nearly inaudible to needy.

"Nellie," he murmured, then ground his hips forward again.

"You can take my shorts off whenever you want, you know," I whispered.

"Not yet." He hit the Ts of each word hard, giving them a sharp sort of admonishment to his voice, like hinting that he could get me naked and fuck me anytime he wanted was offensive somehow. "I'm not done *treating* you."

"If you say so."

"I do say so, Ms. Belanger." He dug his thumbs into a knot beneath my shoulder and it took everything in me not to whimper. "Don't rush me."

"Yes, Professor Cameron," I whispered, and smiled into the pillow, especially after he rubbed his hips forward again.

And again.

And again.

He kept touching my back, trying to continue the massage, but the pressure seemed to lessen each time he thrust himself forward, until his hands were resting on me and his hips were moving at a steady pace.

"Goddamn," he breathed, and I bit my lip to hold in another smile. My nipples were hard, pressing into the bedspread, and warmth was pooling between my legs. He moved his hands off my back, bringing them down to my hips, and I thought he was going to finally pull my running shorts down. But instead, he ran his palms along the stretchy, skintight fabric.

"You know exactly how good your ass looks in these, don't you?" he asked.

"I wouldn't have bought them otherwise."

His fingertips moved to the bottom of my shorts, slipping along the hem before he nudged them underneath. I stifled a gasp as he worked the fabric up higher and higher, pulling my shorts up until the curve of my cheeks were hanging out the bottom. He ran a finger along my ass crack, molding the fabric to my body and making me shiver.

Once he was happy with what I was trying very hard not to think of as the sexiest wedgie ever because I didn't want to ruin the moment even though that was funny as *fuck*, he sat back. His hands moved away from my ass and there was a soft rustling sound. When he rested against me again, the fabric-covered bulge was gone, replaced by the thickness of his bare cock, so swollen that I could feel the heat of it through my shorts. There was a heaviness to the air, something heady and full of anticipation and excitement.

And then Ben eased his hips forward so he could rub his cock against my ass.

My core throbbed. He pulled back, dragging the head of his cock along my ass before pausing and rocking forward again.

"God," he breathed, though it came out as more of a hiss. "Why... fucking *why*..."

He didn't finish the sentence, but he didn't have to for me to know both the questions and the answers. He wanted to know why he liked seeing my ass eat my shorts like that. Why it was so fucking hot to pull his cock out and rub against fabric instead of skin. Why there was a perfectly good pussy *right there*, and he was choosing to hump me instead of fuck me.

And the answers to each of those questions, in turn, were: because it felt good, and because it felt good, and because it felt fucking *good*.

Even for me. Like yeah, I wouldn't come from it. I was lucky enough to not always need something on my clit to come, but everyone knew you couldn't come from someone grinding against your ass.

Hopefully they knew, anyway. I mean, the guy I'd "lost my virginity" to after losing it to JP asked me if I came after he'd tried to fuck my belly button, so who really knew what people thought.

But I fairly sure Ben knew I wasn't going to come from this. And that made everything even hotter. He rarely did anything that was just for him—more than once, I'd had to plead with him to relax and let me suck his cock, promising him that sucking him off really *did* do something for me—so listening to him moan softly as he used my ass was turning me on more than I could have ever thought. Imagining what his cock looked like, sandwiched between my ass cheeks and pressed down by the hand he was holding over it, was making my nipples harden, pressing almost painfully into the bedspread beneath me.

And then he shifted. His fingers lifted the edge of my shorts and a moment later, the head of his cock slid beneath the fabric and between my legs. I bit my lip as he leaned forward, resting more and more of his body against me, angles changing and the heat from his shaft gliding against the wetness coating my pussy lips, until—

"Ben?" I whispered. "Not that I'm not open to talking about it, but—"

"No, no." His lips pressed against the back of my neck. "I wouldn't without asking. I promise. I just want... I mean, feeling you—" He stopped, making an aggravated sound as he couldn't find the words. "I want to touch you like—"

He eased his hips forward the same way he had when he was on top of my shorts. My breath hitched and both of us shuddered as the head of his cock pushed between my pussy lips before brushing against my clit.

"—like that." His voice was choked. "Is this okay?"

"Mmm..." I said, my voice high-pitched. "Maybe. Can you do it one more time so I can see?"

His lips curled into a smile. Without a word, he pushed his hips forward, and I had to slam my eyes shut as a soft *ungh* sound escaped my lips.

"How's that?" he growled in my ear.

"T-Try it once more," I gasped. "Just to be sure."

Both of us moaned as he thrust again, and then again, and then a hand slid underneath me and cupped my breast as Ben started fully *fucking* my thighs, coating his cock with my wetness and grinding against my clit with every movement. I cried out, the pillow muffling my moans as he pinched my nipple and kissed my neck, his breath hot on my skin as he both fucked me and didn't fuck me at the same time, my pussy getting wetter and wetter until my body couldn't take it anymore.

His thighs held my legs in place as bliss rushed through me. I tried not to buck my hips, but I wasn't in charge of my own motions anymore; my body writhed in Ben's arms as an intense surge of electrical pleasure took over. And that probably wasn't a good thing, considering neither of us meant for the angle to change enough that his tip nudged against the entrance of my pussy, but Ben hurriedly pulled back instead of sinking into me the way I would've probably begged him to had I been capable of speaking at the time.

But that single second of almost being inside me seemed to be it for Ben. A low, heady rumble started and he thrust forward harder, then immediately pulled back, the heat of his cock disappearing from between my legs and his hand moving out from under me. Barely a breath later, warmth flooded the backs of my thighs, soaking through my running shorts and pooling in the place where my legs pressed together.

He sat heavily on my legs for a moment, just long enough to take a deep breath, then forced himself to move off so he wouldn't crush me.

"Sorry," he whispered as he reached over to the nightstand to grab some tissues. "I came all over you."

"Do I look like I'm complaining?"

He carefully began to wipe up the mess. "I would hate to think I ruined these lovely shorts."

"If by 'ruined' you mean I won't be able to wear them when I go jogging anymore because I'll get too turned on thinking about the time you came all over them, then yeah, I guess you ruined them. Otherwise, I have questions about your inability to wash cum out of fabric."

"Well, I've never had to wash it out of this kind of fabric." There was a smile in his voice as he started peeling my shorts off so I could roll over without spreading the mess onto my blankets.

"I guess they don't make socks out of this type of material, hey?"

"Socks?" he repeated, then realized what I was saying and scoffed derisively. "I don't use *socks* as cum catchers."

"Oh, I'm sorry. Wash cloths? Towels? Or are you one of those kinky guys who has a collection of panties he uses to—"

I cut myself off with a giggling shriek as Ben spanked my bare ass cheek. "Kleenex, Ms. Belanger. Or a shower."

He didn't stay over too much longer after that since he was heading out of town to visit his ex and her wife for a few days and needed to finish packing, both for that and for his move to California. After he left, I ran a load of laundry to wash the shorts he came on, and then a second one a few hours later when I realized I'd forgotten to put the shorts in the first load. As I was setting a reminder on my phone to switch loads, it vibrated with a new message.

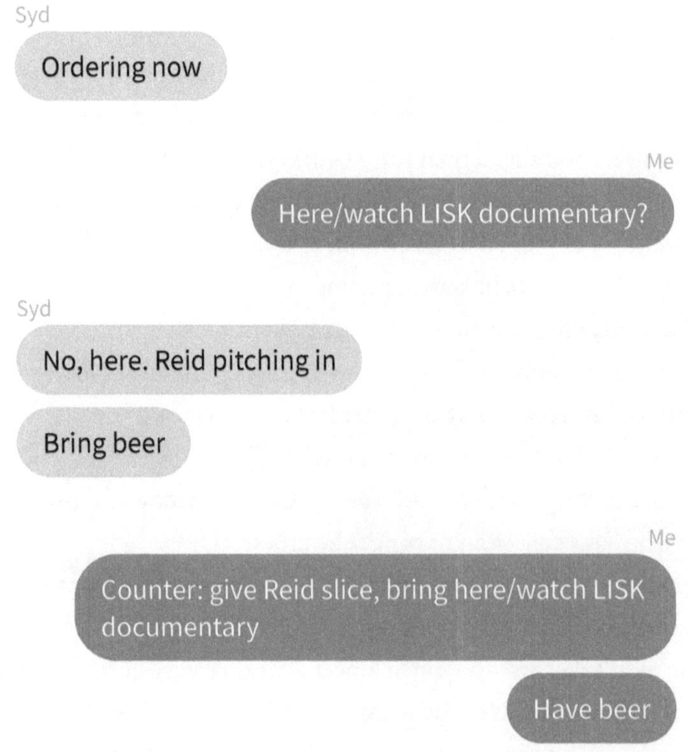

She sent an eyeroll emoji and told me we'd watch the rest of the documentary later and to just come down to her apartment to eat. Slipping on a pair of shoes, I grabbed six random beers from my fridge, shoved them in one of the cardboard six-pack holders I kept stacked in my front closet instead of recycling them like a normal person, and went down to their apartment.

It made sense once I got there why Sydney wanted to stay at her place. Not that there was anything wrong with her, but Reid had a bleary look to him and clearly wanted to stay in. He clearly hadn't expected me to show up, either, since he looked kind of greasy and was wearing old grey sweatpants and a ripped T-shirt when I first walked in.

"Thanks," Sydney whispered after he excused himself to change. "Alison's been calling him non-stop and being totally toxic. And he thinks she stole his Adderall because he asked—well." She huffed. "I think he just forgot to refill it but the pharmacy said he's not allowed to get a refill for another week. I figured inviting you over would at least get him to shower."

"You could've just told me that," I whispered back.

"Yeah, but I wasn't sure if you were still down from the weekend."

I frowned. "So you thought tricking me to use me was better?"

She shrugged shamelessly. "How's the saying go? Feed two moping drama queens with one pizza?"

"I'm not moping. I've been fine since we got back," I said despite the fact that I'd been mopey enough to ask Ben to go for a run with me. But Sydney didn't need to know that since things seemed a lot better once I'd had an orgasm. "And you better have ordered more than one pizza."

"Well, I haven't seen you since we drove back," she said. "But I'm glad you're doing better. Have you talked to JP?"

I cracked one of the beers I brought open and gave it to her before grabbing another for myself. "Why would I have heard from him? I'm not in Montreal."

She shrugged and sipped her beer. "I dunno. I thought maybe he'd follow up on the gala."

"I mean, he asked me what colour tie he should wear, but I don't know what colour dress Kimberlee is going to pick." I tried not to sound bitter. "It's not like I talk to him other than to figure out when and where we're hooking up. We didn't even know we were both going to be at Illumi-Nite last weekend."

"Makes sense," she said. "And your dad?"

I snorted. "The silver lining about pissing off my dad is that if I make him mad enough, he tends to not want to see me for a while. He won't call until next week."

Of course, since I said that, my dad had to go and make me a fucking liar not twenty minutes later, immediately after a freshly showered Reid had set two steaming boxes of pizza on the coffee table.

"You've gotta be kidding me," I said as my phone vibrated, the screen lighting up with my dad's name.

Sydney frowned. "I thought you said he wouldn't call until—"

"Yeah. So this means he needs something from me." I hesitated, wondering if I could get away with just ignoring it, but couldn't bring myself to let the call go unanswered. Sighing, I picked it up and tapped the screen.

"Hello?"

"Good evening, *ma fille ange*," my dad said.

"Hi," I said.

He didn't bother with small talk, which was fine with me since it meant we'd get off the phone faster. "You will need to come to Montreal. There is an unexpected event I require your attendance at."

And maybe it was because Sydney and Reid were sitting right there, listening to my side of the conversation. Maybe their presence made me feel more confident than I usually did when I talked to my dad. Or maybe I was just tired of the fucking audacity he had to ask me for more after throwing out half my clothes and ignoring my boundaries.

Whatever it was, I held myself up a bit straighter, my shoulders square as if standing up to him required physical effort.

"I can't. I'm busy that day."

"I did not tell you a day, Eleanor," he said, his voice flat.

"I'm not coming to Montreal again," I said. "I told you I'd be there for the Diamond Gala. I'm already coming there early for it. I have a life outside of the stuff you need me for."

"This is important."

"It's important to you," I said. "Not me."

Sydney pumped her fist in the air, opening her mouth in a silent cheer before giving me a thumbs up. That bolstered me even more, so when my dad let out another impatient sigh, I was ready.

"I understand you are frustrated after last weekend," he said in a cold tone that made it clear he didn't understand at all. "However, I need you in town this week. Friday during the day at a minimum."

"Dad, unless someone has literally died, I'm not coming to Montreal this week," I said.

"Well," he replied. "I will see you Friday, then."

Chapter Fifteen
An Event To Die For

I'D NEVER GIVEN INTO the temptation of asking Anne-Marie to use her powers of gossip for my own benefit.

Mostly because I'd never had that temptation since it was pretty hard to be tempted by something you never had to ask for.

Because no matter what, no matter if I knew a person or not, no matter if she was told it in confidence or witnessed it first-hand, no matter if it was actually of interest to literally anyone in the world but her, Anne-Marie would tell whoever would listen everything she knew.

Unfortunately, that didn't seem to be the case at Arthur Kroft's funeral. Because the information I *wanted* wasn't important information at all, but Anne-Marie seemed infuriatingly incapable of talking about anything aside from the situation at hand.

No matter how hard I tried to direct her towards the topic.

"They are saying it was a heart attack," she whispered as we slowly entered the sanctuary of the Notre Dame Basilica before the service. "But I have it on very good authority that it was a—" She cut herself off and glanced around. Whether it was to make sure no one was listening or to make sure someone would definitely overheard, I didn't know, but once she was satisfied, she leaned towards me again, accidentally making Remy veer in the same direction. "—a cocaine overdose."

"Really?" I murmured. "I thought he was in his sixties."

"That does not mean he doesn't use cocaine. Or, well, did not use cocaine. I imagine that is part of why his daughter is so destroyed since she was in rehab just last year. But some people are saying she's destroyed because he had a huge stake in the Martelle group and it's all been left to her sister, which is simply ridiculous." She scoffed. "I swear, people will say anything these days."

"That's the ridiculous part?" I asked.

"Of course, *chérie*."

"You told me he left a Manhattan penthouse to an albino fennec fox that you then said died five years ago after his groomer mixed up pet shampoo with neon yellow hair dye."

"Yes, but he did not have two daughters," she said. "There is no way Paige Martelle has a sister I have never heard of."

"Right," I said, glancing around as I spotted my dad and Kimberlee talking to Anne-Marie's parents, along with Marc-Andre, in a pew about halfway through the sanctuary. "Although, speaking of siblings..."

"Oh, yes!" she said, her volume pitching up a bit more than intended and cutting through the indistinct chatter underscoring the mournful music in the church. "That is right. I'd also heard his *brother* is attempting to claim Arthur's stake in the Martelle group. But Pia—the actual founder of the brand—is adamant that it stay in the family, and since she and Arthur were not married, that does *not* include him, and he's refusing to attend the funeral because of it."

"Wow," I said. "I can't believe someone's brother wouldn't attend a funeral."

"I know." She shook her head. "It's so sad."

"Like, imagine if one of your brothers didn't attend your other brother's funeral. What would cause something like that?"

"Oh, I cannot begin to imagine," she said, shaking her head again. "I am sure they would have a good reason for it, though. My brothers are much more reasonable than Arthur Kroft or his brother seems to be. Although—oh!" She pressed her hands together in a soft, single clap. "You will never guess what *Remy's* brother did last week!"

I glanced at Remy, trying not to grit my teeth in frustration. "What'd your brother do?"

A proud half-smile spread on Remy's lips. "He proposed to his girlfriend. Fiancée, now, I guess."

Which I begrudgingly had to admit *was* exciting for him, even if it did make Anne-Marie launch into a spiel about who she thought Remy's brother's fiancée would ask to be in her wedding party and why she thought she might be on the list. That tangent went on until we'd joined our respective parents in the pew, so I didn't have time to fish for information again despite sitting beside Anne-Marie. Partly because the funeral mass started before she'd finished, but mostly because my dad was sitting on the other side of me and would've probably decided it was time for me to make peace with the Lord for embarrassing him if we talked through the service when I was supposed to make him look good.

Because that was why I was there.

Prior to his funeral, I had no idea who Arthur Kroft was. I'd never heard of him, let alone met him. But unfortunately, I hadn't watched my language when my dad called earlier in the week. So now, since the client my dad missed out on talking to because of how I'd offended the Thibaults at Harmonies for Hope might be here, I had to go to the funeral for a guy I'd never been in the same room with.

And that was really saying something, considering how many rooms I'd been with the people who had filled the sanctuary of the Notre Dame Basilica to pay their respects to a man who didn't seem to deserve much respect.

It was the perfect backdrop for the funeral, though the funeral itself seemed to be a veil thinner than the one on the mourning hats some of the women were wearing for what was just another ostentatious social event. The soaring arched ceiling and rich colours complemented by gilded decorations and patterns housed air that had a melancholy stuffiness to it, that somehow smelled of rumination and stillness despite the hushed bustle of activity in the aisle and pews.

In hindsight, I should have expected it. I'd only attended a few other funerals in my life, and the ones I could actually remember were all like this. And I had a feeling the one I couldn't remember was probably similar, since it was for my dad's father, but I'd only been two when he died. My dad was in thirties when I was born, but his dad had been in his forties when he was born, so I had no memory of my grandpa.

I didn't have many memories of any of my grandparents, actually. My dad's mom had died when he was a kid and while his dad had remarried, my dad despised his stepmom and refused to talk about her or visit her. And my mom's relationship with her parents had been tense ever since she got knocked up at twenty and married a guy significantly older than her. We'd visited their house in Newfoundland a couple of times when I was a kid, but those visits had stopped after my parents' divorce. I didn't understand it, but my mom didn't like to talk about it.

Regardless, the point was that the only funerals I'd ever attended were for people my dad said I had to pay my respects to. They were always big affairs, most of them at the Notre Dame Basilica just like this one was, and I was never there because I needed the closure, whether that was of the casket or something else.

No, I was supposed to make my dad look like he had a heart. I was a prop to show off the caring, supportive, family-oriented man he claimed to be and earn him some brownie points with whoever he was supposed to be impressing.

So I couldn't spend the service trying to pry more information from Anne-Marie. Which was fine. There was an exclusive, invite-only wake after the service that I'd been invited to for some reason and I'd be able to get answers from her then.

And then Arthur Kroft went and screwed me over.

"What does he mean, *both* their daughters?!" Anne-Marie hissed during the homily, when the priest mentioned Arthur finding peace with the Lord would surely be of comfort to his life partner, Pia, and both their daughters. "*Both*?!"

She wasn't the only one stunned by the revelation that Arthur did, in fact, have two daughters. A wave of hushed astonishment rolled through the church, the kind that made it clear that this was *big* news.

Which meant that Anne-Marie couldn't be swayed into talking about literally anything else.

"Wow, there are a lot of people here," I said as she, Remy, and I sauntered into the parish hall for the wake. "Pretty much everyone who's anyone."

"And you think at least one of them would *know* something," Anne-Marie replied, her forehead wrinkled with a mix of grumpiness and calculations as she tried to figure out the puzzle of Arthur Kroft's other daughter.

"Yeah, that's crazy that no one knows," I said. "But you'd have to have a pretty good reason not to be here, eh?"

"Yes, exactly." She sighed, twisting her mouth to the side as she observed the room. "Perhaps she is also dead."

"His other daughter?" Remy asked.

Anne-Marie nodded. "It would explain why only Pia and Paige were part of the funeral procession."

"They would have mentioned that in the homily," Remy said. "Or in the program. It said he was predeceased by his parents and sister, so if he had a daughter who died, they would have included her."

Anne-Marie's mouth scrunched into a tight pucker. "Yes, I guess so."

"What a mystery." I sighed and glanced around performatively. "I wonder if there's anyone missing from here we should tell about this."

"Oh, I am certain everyone will know by the end of the day," she said, then caught sight of someone she knew. "Oh! *Bonjour,* Michele!"

"Anne-Marie!" A curvy girl with fiery red hair and skin so smooth it looked like she had a live filter on it side-stepped a few people to make her way over to us. "You must tell me, what did you make of hearing about—"

"The other daughter?" Anne-Marie finished. "I know. Is it not *astounding* that—"

I groaned internally, tuning out Anne-Marie's voice and glancing around the room.

The parish hall was a large space with marble floors and an old stone wall along one side of the room. Along with a catering spread, there were wine spritzers and a cocktail people kept calling a Cheeky Sham-Sham, which was a signature drink Arthur Kroft said he invented. I wasn't entirely sure Arthur Kroft was the first person to put Chambord in champagne, but I'd call it whatever they wanted to call it as long as they kept serving them. The room itself was filled with a sea of black-clad mourners, some faking an appropriately solemn tone so they looked like they were better people than they were and others not even bothering to pretend it was anything but an excuse to be seen at a who's who event.

My dad was one of the former, currently wearing a serious, intent look as he spoke to a group of men. Next to him, Kimberlee had her hand on an older woman's forearm, a sympathetic look on her face as the woman spoke. After the service, I'd hung behind while Anne-Marie stopped to talk to someone or another, promising my dad I'd catch up with them at the wake so I would be around to prove that Max Belanger was more than an ice-cold businessman.

But he was busy and probably wouldn't want me to interrupt him. And since Anne-Marie was preoccupied and also useless in answering the thing I *wanted* to know, it was up to me to figure it out myself.

Because yeah, *someone* might have insisted he'd rather drink hot dog water than go to an event, but I would've thought funerals were an exception to that. If he'd found a way to get out of going to funerals, I wanted to know what it was so that if it ever came up again, I'd be able to get out of it, too.

That was obviously the only reason I pulled my phone out of the small clutch purse I was carrying.

No other reason at all.

Me

So how'd you get out of this

JP was usually pretty quick to respond, so I watched my screen after it sent. Still, I was a bit surprised when the checkmarks showing he'd read my message appeared almost instantly.

Bastard

Hello to you too. Get out of what?

Me

The fashion show/funeral. How'd you convince your parents you didn't have to come to the most morbid fashion event of the season?

The checkmarks appeared right away again, but unlike the first message, his response didn't come through right away. It was long enough that I saw the bubble appear to show he was typing, but it disappeared a moment later. Biting my lip, I tapped my fingers on the side of my phone.

Me

Come on. Help a girl out so she doesn't get dragged to the next one

Again, the checkmarks appeared, followed by the typing bubbles. I didn't know what could possibly make JP hesitate like this before responding, but the whole thing was leaving a squeeze of anxiety in my chest that I wasn't a fan of.

Though, that disappeared completely when the most boring reply in existence came through.

Bastard

Unfortunately, I just couldn't make it. Give my condolences to everyone in the room who has to suffer through the absence of my presence.

Me

Asshole

Bastard

I thought that had to wait until after the Diamond Gala, but if you're offering…

I scrunched my nose, trying not to laugh, even though there was no way for JP to know if I'd laughed or not.

"What's so funny?" a voice asked.

I barely looked up before an arm slid around my shoulder and barely processed the arm belonged to Clinton Thibault before turning my screen off as quickly as I could.

Unfortunately, Clinton was tall—not quite as tall as JP, but taller than both Anne-Marie and Remy—and not only had been looking at my phone, but given the disgusting leer on his face, had *definitely* seen what the messages said. I panicked for all of a second before my brain caught up and reminded me that JP had been in my phone as "Bastard" from the moment he'd texted me at the start of the summer.

Even still, I tried not to show the way my heartbeat tripped over itself and squirmed away from Clinton. "Nothing. Why are you touching me?"

He chuckled but thankfully lowered his arm instead of reaching for me again. "I just wanted to say hi. And *something* seemed to be pretty funny. What was that about the Di—"

"It's literally none of your business," I snapped.

He stuck his lower lip out, faking a pout. "Oh, but unfortunately, it *is* actually my business."

"How is it your business, Clinton, dear?" Anne-Marie asked, her voice cold as she abandoned the conversation she'd been having so she could turn to me. "Since Nellie is not your date for that event, I do not see why it would be relevant to you in any way."

Clinton's tongue poked out, wetting his lips so a small smile grew on his face like mold. "Well, that's exactly *why* it's relevant, Anne-Marie. I don't think it's any secret that I'd love to get to know Nellie better, so I'm playing along with her little game of 'hard to get.'"

"I'm not playing hard to get," I said. "You're just hard to *want*."

I blurted the words without thinking first and nearly winced as I remembered the consequences of insulting Clinton. But instead of another fake-pout or a sneer that said he was about to go tell his daddy on us for being mean to him, his mouth twitched into a wider smile that was the visual equivalent of cockroaches scuttling across a floor.

"Tell me who you're going with and I'll tell you why I'm the better option," he said.

"I don't know who I'm going with yet," I lied, since Anne-Marie was *right there* and the last thing I needed was for this to be how she found out JP and I were going to the gala together. "But it won't be you. I don't know how to make it any clearer that I don't like you, Clinton."

"Give me a chance and I'll change your mind."

"I guarantee you won't," I said, then almost shivered because my voice was so cold it reminded me of my dad. "It's pretty bold of you to think you even could."

"Bold of you to think I couldn't," he replied. "Seeing as even your dad keeps suggesting we get together."

"Her dad makes her go with you as a punishment," Remy said, his deep voice soft but firm. "You know that, right, man?"

"Maybe he makes her go with me because he knows what's best for her," Clinton replied, his eyes still boring into mine before he flicked them down, then back up, the slime of his gaze making my stomach roll with nausea. "Kind of like I do. Because I know I'd be good for you, Nellie. Better than whoever that *bastard* you're texting is."

Luckily for Clinton, he punctuated his statement by walking away, as if leaving me hanging would make me want him or something. Between that, Remy stepping forward, and Anne-Marie grabbing my arm, I couldn't reach Clinton in time to make him the second dead body in the church that day.

Chapter Sixteen
Without Me, It's Just Eral

It was Clinton's fault I pissed my dad off.

I was all for taking accountability. At least, until I was the one who had to actually take accountability. But I wasn't just shifting blame onto him so I didn't have to admit I was the one who fucked up.

"What part of *you do not need to say anything* confused you?" my dad hissed after Pia Martelle set a withering look on me before snorting and telling my dad he had to try harder next time.

"How was I supposed to know that would offend her?" I asked.

"It does not matter." He glanced to the side to make sure no one was listening, his lips pressed in a flat line that held in what was probably a mountain of rage. "Had you listened to me, Eleanor, it would have been a non-issue."

"I forgot."

"You *forgot*." He almost scoffed, but settled for shaking his head so it wouldn't draw attention. "I told it to you not thirty seconds before we—"

"And it's a funeral! That's what you're *supposed* to say at funerals!"

"Max," Kimberlee said. "She was trying to be sympathetic."

My dad's jaw clenched and he drew a breath in through his nose, then exhaled.

"It's fine," I said. "I'll go home and then you don't have to worry about—"

"No," he said. "You will stay until the end of the wake so that if there is another opportunity to make a good impression on Pia Martelle, you can take it."

I bit back my response, which was a multi-part retort including such gems as "Do you seriously think there's a way to make a good impression when you're literally trying to gain her as an investor at her life partner's *funeral*?" and "How am I supposed to make a good impression on someone who thinks 'I'm sorry for your loss' is the finance industry's code for 'Hey hun *butterfly-emoji* I know this is so random but are you tired of fighting with your current *puking-emoji* financial management? I'd love to have you try *strong-arm-emoji* hiring my dad as your *moneybags-emoji* hedge fund manager!'"

Instead, I mirrored the way he'd clenched his jaw and nodded, then went to track down Anne-Marie so at least I could stand near someone I knew while I waited for a break in the lineup of vultures trying to impress a multi-billionaire cosmetics mogul at a fucking *funeral*.

Despite her name being synonymous with "extrovert," Anne-Marie was the perfect friend to be around when I didn't want to talk to anyone. She flitted around the parish hall, collecting gossip like the book of condolences near the entrance was collecting signatures from all the esteemed guests. Other than nodding occasionally and shaking a hand or two when I "*had* to meet So-and-So, whose father is a Some Kind Of Job With A Big Paycheque," I could stand there, letting Anne-Marie chitter and chatter to her heart's content.

She was standing with a group of people I didn't recognize, so when I rejoined her and Remy, she took a moment to introduce me before going back to her conversation. I nodded mindlessly for a moment, then subtly slipped my phone out of my purse again.

Where I had another message waiting from JP.

Bastard

The silent treatment? It was a joke, babe. Unless you're legitimately offering your asshole tonight, in which case, I've never been more serious in my life

Me

Maybe I would've considered it if you hadn't wormed your way out of this funeral

Bastard

You miss me that much?

Me

Of course not. But now I can't cross "at a funeral" or "in a church" off my depraved sexual bucket list

He sent back a laughing emoji, but the bubbles showed he was still typing. I looked up, pretending I was listening to some guy with brown hair talk about... polo, maybe? Or horse racing. I wasn't sure. Whatever it was, I nodded like I cared until my phone vibrated again.

I sawed my fingernail back and forth across the side of my thumb, staring at the messages and trying to figure out if there were more to them than the words on the screen.

Because yeah, I hadn't talked to JP since The Blowjob Incident. That wasn't unusual. It wasn't like we talked very often, outside of texting each other to figure out when and where we'd be hooking up next. Or to check when the next time I'd be in Montreal was and if he'd be around. Or if we needed to share some kind of relevant gossip from Anne-Marie. Or if she told one of us an interesting piece of gossip that the other person might find hilarious. Or if there was, like, a particularly relatable meme we thought the other person needed to see.

So it wasn't *that* often. But this time, I hadn't messaged him to let him know I'd be in town that weekend. And that was only because I might've been able to drive back to Ottawa as soon as the funeral was over and not have to spend another night here.

It wasn't because I was avoiding him after the Blowjob Incident or something.

Probably.

Maybe I was. Maybe things were weird now. Not that they should be. I mean, yeah, I felt a little guilty for asking JP to be my date for the Diamond Gala, but he'd agreed to it. And I'd promised him something in exchange for it, too.

That was all it was. I'd asked a favour. He'd agreed to it. So things shouldn't be weird.

But if they were…

I mean, maybe it would be better if I didn't see JP this time around. Then at least I wouldn't be risking my date for the following weekend. Now that my dad was insisting I stay to the end of the wake, it was unlikely I'd have time to drive back to Ottawa because he'd want to go for dinner or something too. But that was okay. Maybe I didn't really *need* to get laid and—

The thought startled me so much that I nearly laughed out loud. Me? Choose not to get laid?

Who the fuck even *was* I?!

And that was it, wasn't it? Who the hell was this person standing here, overthinking to the point of potentially choosing to not get laid when getting laid was my whole *thing* because some guy I was fucking *might* be weird about things?

It had to be Clinton's fault for throwing me off the way he had. Because this wasn't me. And if I wasn't weird about things, JP wouldn't be weird about it, either. JP was just being JP, a snarky asshole who liked getting under my skin as much as he liked getting under my clothes.

Me

Is that on the table?

Bastard

That seems a little TMI, but if you must know, no. I usually use a tissue or clean up after myself if you're not around to swallow it

Me

Not your cum, perv. I'm going for a "jog" tonight to that place nearby with the empty parking lot. What time will you be there?

Bastard

What if I already have plans?

Me

What plans?

Bastard

I might have a date.

I rolled my eyes. He was so full of shit. Dating wasn't a requirement for getting laid. I couldn't speak for JP, but for myself, I didn't date at all, even casually.

I wasn't looking for people to spend time with.

I was looking for people to fuck.

And I knew damn well that was what JP wanted, too.

Me

Who'd want to date you?

Bastard

If you're jealous, you can just say that, babe

Me

Why would I be jealous of Alexhandra?

Or are you switching it up tonight and going with Palmela?

I assumed he saw the message right away, but before I could even see if he'd read it, a hand clamped down on my arm and I nearly dropped my phone.

"—remember Nellie Belanger!" Anne-Marie said excitedly.

I blinked, looking up at the woman standing in front of me. Like many of the other people in the room, she was wearing black, but her outfit was more like a standard funeral outfit. She was wearing a modest dress with three-quarter length sleeves and black boots with a low heel. Even though she had distinctive auburn hair and blue eyes, it took me a moment to figure out why she looked familiar.

"Oh!" I said when I recognized her. "Ms. Travers!"

"Nellie! What a surprise!"

There was an awkward moment where I wasn't sure how to greet her. When it came to former elementary school teachers, I didn't know if I was supposed to shake her hand or go in for a hug or put my hands up to protect my face because technically she could slap me without repercussion now that I wasn't eleven years old anymore.

But Ms. Travers extended her hand for a handshake, despite the look of discomfort in her eyes.

"You still know who I am?" I asked, hoping I might be a repressed memory.

"Somehow I have a hard time forgetting students who burn my eyebrows off."

I tried not to wince, but it was hopeless. "I honestly didn't see the foil on my lunch that day. But I am still sorry about it, even if it was a mistake."

"The time you coloured all the desktops with permanent marker, on the other hand?"

My face went warm. "Yeah, that was pretty bad."

"Not as bad as the acrylic paint-splosion," she said pointedly.

I grimaced. "It was, um, a rough year for me. But I *am* sorry, Ms. Travers."

"Right," Ms. Travers said.

There was a beat of discomfort before Anne-Marie graciously disrupted it. "Well, Nellie is still mischievous as ever, but she has gotten a touch more mature. I imagine you did not see each other, but Nellie did the Illumi-Nite run this year."

"Did you?" Ms. Travers asked, looking both surprised and impressed.

"She did." Anne-Marie turned to me. "Ms. Travers is heavily involved in the HueManity Foundation as well. We would not have half the success we do without her."

"It's a great organization," I said.

Ms. Travers waved a hand nonchalantly. "It's an important cause and frankly, a bit selfish on my part. The more resources there are for neurodiverse students, the better it is for us teachers. But you know—" She tilted her head thoughtfully. "If you are looking to be more involved, Nellie, I know HueManity could use the support. We are always looking for ADHD mentors and I think it would be a, ah, *valuable* experience for you to work with some of the younger students."

"Oh, um... thanks," I said uncertainly. "But I'm not living in Montreal anymore."

Anne-Marie looked confused. "And I thought the mentors generally shared a diagnosis with the students they work with, do they not?"

Ms. Travers glanced at me. "Oh. Yes. And you... don't."

I shook my head. "Nope."

She forced a laugh. "Of course. Well, you can't blame me for being confused. You were a... a real handful. But I guess you were just like that."

I gritted my teeth together. "I guess so."

Ms. Travers excused herself a few moments later. I smiled politely at her, then made to follow Anne-Marie as she flitted to another person so I could excuse myself without her knowing.

But for once, luck was on my side.

"Anne-Marie! I need to speak with you." The curvy redhead Anne-Marie had been talking to before—Michele, I think—stormed up with a fiery look on her face.

"Have you discovered something new?" Anne-Marie asked, but Michele's face darkened even more.

"Privately," she muttered, then took Anne-Marie's hand and tugged her away. "Come to the washroom with me."

Which was fucking perfect. I looked at Remy.

"While she's busy, I'm gonna go pee," I said.

He nodded uncomfortably and I turned, going in the opposite direction Michele and Anne-Marie had gone, despite knowing they were going to the bathroom.

Because the key to surviving any social event, at least for me, was to know where the *least* convenient bathrooms for the venue were. Those bathrooms were the best hiding places. They were out of the way enough that I could escape people for a bit, but if anyone did stumble across me, I had a legitimate excuse to be there.

Even if the actual reason was that I needed a fucking minute.

Because yeah, I'd been a little shit in Ms. Travers' class.

But looking back, she hadn't even had to put up with it for very long, since that was the same year my parents got divorced and my mom pulled me out of school to move to Toronto partway through the year.

That didn't make it any less embarrassing to remember, though. Especially since it almost sounded like she thought... well, I wasn't sure. Maybe she thought there was some other reason I'd been such a bad kid in her class.

Sighing, I used the bathroom, since I was there anyway, then went to wash my hands, intending to waste time on my phone after. But while I was at the sink, the door banged open and a loud voice echoed through the room.

"I can't *take* it anymore!"

"I know it's hard, but it's just an afternoon and—"

"It's *bullshit*, Princess! You know this is why I didn't want to come to this sham of a funeral for a guy who was too—"

And then they saw me standing at the sink and stopped in their tracks.

Funnily enough, I knew who it was. Claire, the woman with the awful laugh who'd been wearing a tuxedo at the Harmonies for Hope benefit and who'd laughed about Sydney's fake name, was staring at me with a semi-alarmed expression on her face.

She wasn't wearing a tux this time. Instead, she was rocking a black jumpsuit that was entirely out of place given its chic minimalism, with tapered legs, flouncy sleeves, and a deep V-neck that showed off one of my absolute *weaknesses* when it came to women.

Not cleavage. I mean, cleavage was great, obviously. But Claire had small-ish breasts with a wide, shallow valley between them. I don't know what it was about women with chests like that—maybe because of the subtlety of the gentle curves or the inviting expanse of skin or because it meant they probably weren't wearing a bra—but god*damn* did it do it for me.

Behind her, her fiancée—whose name I couldn't remember for the life of me—was biting her lip. She was wearing a short-sleeved black wrap dress and opaque tights along with a concerned frown that knitted her eyebrows together.

For a moment, they both stared at me, Claire with a wary look on her face.

"Don't mind me," I said, turning off the tap and grabbing a paper towel. "You can pretend like I'm not even here. Also, I fully agree with this being a sham of a funeral."

Claire blinked, then let out a soft chuckle that didn't have the same gratingness as the full-body laugh she'd had at Harmonies for Hope.

"So this is the hiding-out bathroom, then?" she asked.

"Depends," I replied. "Are you hiding from someone?"

"Depends," she echoed, heaving a sigh. Her heels clicked as she crossed the tile floor and she hauled herself up onto the counter, letting her legs dangle lazily. "Is everyone someone?"

"Depends," I said. "Are we talking 'everyone' or everyone *here*?"

"What's the difference?" Claire's fiancée asked.

"Well, if it's everyone here, I'd say it's a fifty-fifty split between people who think they're someone and people who are the results of the animal testing the dead guy was involved in. So I wouldn't count those ones as people."

Claire's fiancée's mouth dropped open, her eyes going wide on her round face. She looked from me to Claire, then back at me. I panicked for a moment, wondering if I'd found the only two people at the service who actually liked Arthur Kroft, but before I could say anything, Claire started laughing.

And *actually* laughing, that horrible, creaking crack of a laugh that probably made the glass of the mirror behind us vibrate.

"I like you," she said, wagging a finger at me. "You're fun."

"I had to bring the fun," I said. "Otherwise we'd just have 'eral.'"

Both of them frowned.

"Earl?" her fiancée repeated just as Claire got the joke and let out another honk of laughter.

"Because she puts the 'fun' in 'funeral,'" she said, snorting on one of her crackling giggles. "You're fucking morbid, darling."

"Are you sure—" her fiancée started.

"It's okay, Julie," Claire said, waving a hand. "That was just what I needed."

Julie, that was it. A reluctant smile spread on her lips. "Leave it to you to let a joke like that cheer you up."

"What can I say?" Claire said, heaving another sigh before tilting her head so she could bat her eyelashes at me. "Funny, pretty, curvy girls are my weakness."

Aside from certain situations involving certain bastards, it was pretty hard to fluster me. But that... well. I wasn't sure if the blatant flirting she was doing *directly* in front of her fiancée or her boobs being my weakness were more at fault, but Claire's words made a rush of heat crawl up my neck and into my cheeks.

"Uh... thanks," I said.

Julie tsk'ed, though the apples of her cheeks rounded as amusement flitted across her face. "Don't make her uncomfortable, Claire."

"Oops," Claire said, though it wasn't very convincing considering she batted her eyelashes at me again. "Sorry."

"It's fine," I said. "I'm not uncomfortable."

Claire grinned. "Good. Because you have nothing to worry about. You're a gorgeous little thing but I'm getting old." She heaved another loud sigh. "And my roster's getting a little full these days."

"I mean, that tends to happen once you get engaged," I said.

Julie and Claire exchanged an amused glance.

"And you're not old," I added belatedly. "You don't look it, anyway."

"No?" Claire said, her mouth twisting into a smile. "How old do you think I am?"

I studied her for a moment, then shrugged. "Like, thirty-ish at most."

Julie snickered as Claire pressed a hand to her heart and fake-swooned.

I laughed. "What? How old are you?"

"Nearly thirty-seven," she said.

I rolled my eyes. "That's not *old*. One of the—I mean, this... guy I know. Who I'm friends with. He's the same age. And he's *definitely* not old."

"I take it back," she said. "I might have some room on that roster after all."

"Like hell you do," Julie said, but her eyes were sparkling good-naturedly.

We talked for a few more minutes before I excused myself, since my dad would probably lose his shit if I didn't come back soon. It wasn't until I got back to the parish hall that I remembered I hadn't checked my last message from JP, and that was only because my phone vibrated with another response.

Bastard

Looks like I can switch some things around and squeeze you between Palmela and Alexhandra

Let me know when you're available

Chapter Seventeen
Closer

"The things I do to get laid," I grumbled as JP slid the patio door open.

"Text someone and then show up at their house?" he replied skeptically.

I gave him an unimpressed look. "You know what I mean."

"Not really."

He closed the door behind me. When he turned around, he found me frowning at him.

"What?" he asked.

"What's wrong?"

His eyebrows flicked up. "What do you mean, what's wrong?"

"I dunno. You seem weird."

"Pretty sure you've told me multiple times that I'm not normal."

"That's true, but you're extra weird right now."

"I'm fine, babe."

"Don't call me babe."

And maybe if he responded like he usually did, I would have assumed JP's initial weirdness was me reading things wrong. Like, maybe I was still stuck on the worry that things were weird because I'd asked him to be my date at the Diamond Gala. Or maybe he was a little tired or extra horny and couldn't think straight. But for the second time in the thirty seconds since I'd snuck into the Marchands' house, JP didn't run his mouth in response to something I'd said like he always did.

"Whatever you say," he said, not even throwing an infuriating "babe" at the end, but before I could accuse him of lying to me, he gestured towards the staircase. "Come on. Let's go upstairs."

"I swear, you only want one thing from me," I huffed as I walked past him to the staircase. "No 'hello,' no 'how are you,' no—"

"I thought that was your preferred way of doing things," he said, following me. "But you can tell me how the funeral was while we go."

"Why? So you can put my mouth to better use once we're in your room?"

Finally, he chuckled. "Obviously."

Unfortunately, I probably shouldn't have taken JP up on the offer to tell him about things as we walked up to his room. The Marchands had a big house, but it wasn't nearly a long enough walk to tell him everything that had happened that day. When we reached his room, I'd only managed to cover my general feelings about Arthur Kroft and the kind of person he was and had just started to tell him about Arthur having two daughters even though only one of them was in the funeral procession.

"That's crazy," JP said as he opened the bedroom door. "Sounds like I didn't miss much."

"Oh, you missed tons," I said. "That doesn't even get *into* the fact that Clinton was there being his usual prick self. You wanna know what that asshole said to me?"

"Uh... sure," he said.

"Okay, well, first of all, he almost caught me texting you," I said. "Luckily I don't have your actual name in my phone."

"What do you have me in your phone as?" he asked.

"Bastard."

His lips curled downwards in concession. "Fair."

"I know." I pulled the bedroom door closed behind me. JP was standing near the edge of his bed expectantly, but I didn't go to him right away. "He legitimately thinks I'm playing hard to get. Like, he thinks me outright saying he disgusts me and I want nothing to do with him is a game. Like I'm flirting."

"He is pretty disgusting," JP agreed.

"Right? And my dad still thinks I should give him a chance."

"Sounds like you need something to help you forget that."

"Like anyone could *forget* that." I huffed, turning away from JP as an echo of the rage from earlier perked up, and paced past the foot of his bed. "But what can you expect from a guy who thinks a funeral is the best place to talk an investor into working with him? Oh, and not just *any* funeral. The funeral of that person's *partner*."

"Not much, I guess," JP said, his tone resigned.

"Exactly. He doesn't see the problem with that." I let out a dry laugh, looking out JP's window. "To the point he asked me to drop everything I was doing and drive out here for a thirty-second introduction to this person. Which, of course, I screwed up by having the audacity to give my condolences to a seventy-something year old woman who, again, *just lost her partner*."

It wasn't quite a conscious decision to let my feelings about the day spill from my mouth like that. It just happened, words blurting themselves out as I paced JP's room, reliving every annoying moment of the day from my interaction with Clinton to my dad's reaction to my screw up and even seeing Claire's cleavage in the bathroom. The occasional hum of agreement or mumble of understanding underscored my rant, but apparently I'd gotten so swept away that I stopped looking at him at some point.

"Oh, and that was all after Anne-Marie dragged me over to say hi to Ms. Travers, who decided to—" I stopped speaking and moving, staring at JP. "You're not even listening to me."

JP, who was sitting on his bed, flipped a page of the book he was holding. "Yes, I am."

"You're reading a book."

"I can do two things."

"You're literally reading a book and ignoring me," I said, trying not to sound as hurt as I felt.

"I promise you, I was listening," he said, finally glancing up. "You have to remember I have ten years of experience listening to the AMNN. This is *hauntingly* similar."

"You read while Anne-Marie talks to you?"

"Talks *at* me, but yes. I read the whole *Hitchhiker's Guide to the Galaxy* trilogy over multiple updates about Ives Clement's affair and can still tell you every last detail." He tilted his head to the side. "Though, I did put the book down for a bit when the whole hitman thing came into play."

"The what now?"

"Hitman." He put his book down beside him. "Ives and Stacia, the woman he was having the affair with, allegedly tried to hire a hitman to kill his wife so he could inherit her money, which he wouldn't have gotten if he divorced her because of the prenup. Fortunately, not only is Ives an idiot, it wasn't the first time Stacia tried to pull the same thing, so they ended up trying to hire an undercover cop. And the whole thing went down over the course of, like, two weeks."

"Oh my God."

"I know, right? I can't believe I read five books in two weeks, either."

"Not that," I said. "The fact that Anne-Marie knows someone who—and *wait*." I pointed a finger at him. "You're full of shit."

"I'm not. It's only 'allegedly' because Ives claimed it was a misunderstanding and that he didn't know what a hitman does."

"Not that. You said it was a trilogy. Now it's five books?"

"*The Hitchhiker's Guide to the Galaxy* is a trilogy of five."

"For all the Latin you lawyers use, you'd think you'd know that *tri* means three."

He nodded towards the bookshelf beside his desk. "Second from the top, about a third of the way in from the left. Count 'em."

"I'm not going to look just so you can laugh at me." I glared at him. "And anyway, it doesn't matter. You seriously don't see how you sitting there reading a fucking book while I'm talking is rude?"

"I'm not saying it's not," he said.

"Oh. So you're being rude on purpose."

"It doesn't mean I'm not listening." He sighed. "I just... you said you didn't want to talk about it. And I thought you were here because..."

He didn't finish the sentence. Probably because he realized how much of an asshole it would make him. But it didn't matter because I finished the sentence for him.

"Because we both wanted to get laid," I said. "Which is reasonable, I guess, because that's what this whole thing is."

"Nell—"

"Whatever. You're right. We're not friends or anything, so it's not fair for me to make you sit there and listen to me. Especially when regardless of what you said, you *are* acting weird."

"I'm sorry," he said.

"Don't be." It came out snappier than I intended. "It's fine."

He sighed. "It's not. You're right and I'm sorry. I was being rude."

"And petty."

"And petty," he agreed.

"And shallow."

"Like a kiddie pool in a drought," he said. "But I promise, I *was* listening."

"Don't lie to me."

He raised his eyebrows, studying me in silence, then took his book and moved it to the nightstand.

"You were about to tell me about Ms. Travers—who I'm guessing is Sylvie Travers, who was one of Anne-Marie's teachers and works with the HueManity Foundation, which is probably why Anne-Marie was introducing you—and what she said to you," he said. "Right after whatever that was, you ran into a woman named Claire and her fiancée, Julie, when you were all hiding in the bathroom, but you aren't sure what they were hiding from. There was a tangent about how good Claire's boobs looked and that she said you were funny and pretty after you joked about the dead guy being involved in animal testing. And that segues nicely into your rant about Arthur Kroft, who you thought was a gem of a person so long as we're talking about the way kid's jewellery sets from the dollar store have 'real gemstones' on them."

I bit my lip. "Well—"

"You also thought it was arrogant that he claimed to have invented the 'Cheeky Sham-Sham,' which is just Chambord in champagne. And this goes a little off book, but I'm assuming this is all at odds with your frustration about how fake and performative everything was because you *wanted* to be offended on his behalf, but he's a massive asshole, so you don't feel all that bad about it."

"I... object," I said, frowning. "Speculation."

A puff of laughter escaped his lips. "On top of all that, Clinton was being Clinton and your dad was being your dad by trying to turn a funeral into a business opportunity, which I fully agree was slimy of him because said business opportunity involved the widow of the deceased. Oh, and despite gossiping about everyone and everything, you couldn't get Anne-Marie to spill why I got out of the funeral, so had to take on the onerous task of asking me yourself."

He looked at me expectantly, though not sarcastically. It was more hopeful, like he genuinely wanted me to acknowledge that he'd heard everything I said.

"See? I knew you weren't listening," I said.

He made an incredulous noise. "What? What did I miss?"

"They weren't married. So she's not a widow. He was her 'life partner.'"

He let out an exasperated breath, but a small smile tugged at the corner of his lips. "Fair enough, babe. Why don't you come sit here and tell me what Sylvie—sorry, what Ms. Travers said that got you upset enough to hide in the bathroom."

I rolled my eyes, even as I let his words draw me a step closer to the bed. "I wasn't *upset*. I just needed a break."

"Right. But what she said contributed to that."

"Well, yeah." I pinched my fingers together, not looking at JP. "I was kind of a brat when I was in her class."

"You? A brat?" he said.

"More than usual." I tapped my fingertip to my thumb. "I was enough of a little shit that she still hates me, like, ten years later."

"That seems unfair."

"Yeah, especially since I kind of had a reason for it."

"You did?"

I nodded. "That was when my parents were getting divorced."

He made a knowing sound. "That makes sense."

"Not to her, apparently." I scoffed. "She said I'd make a good mentor with HueManity because apparently she thinks I have something wrong with me. But when I said I don't have ADHD she was like, 'Oh, I guess you're just *like that*.' Because obviously it couldn't be that my parents were splitting up and fighting all the time. There has to be something wrong with me."

"Having ADHD doesn't mean there's something wrong with you," he said.

"The word 'disorder' is literally in the name. Disorder, aka something that's out of order."

"It's a condition, not a—" He stopped and sighed. "Look, I'm not saying what she said was appropriate, but I've been running for Illumi-Nite for seven years. Anne-Marie puts more hours in for HueManity than I do. One of the most brilliant people I've ever met was—" Another pause, followed by a shake of his head. "He had ADHD and yeah, that made some things in his life harder, but it didn't mean there was something *wrong* with him, okay?"

The words came out more heated than I think he intended. I flicked my fingertip across my thumbnail nervously, not sure how I was supposed to respond. JP looked down at his hands, like I wouldn't be able to see the way his face had reddened a bit.

"You're smart as fuck too," he said. "There wouldn't be anything wrong with you, either. If you did have it."

"Okay, seriously," I said. "What's going on with you?"

He looked up. "Why do you think something's going on?"

"You just called me smart."

"So?"

"And didn't even add 'for a blonde' or something to it." I crossed my arms again. "Like, you're kinda cranky for someone who somehow got out of going to a funeral today, but you're also all... distant or something."

JP stared at me. I thought he was going to cave and tell me what was going on, but he shook his head a moment later. A moment after that, a familiar roguishness was sparkling in his eye.

"If you think I'm distant, maybe you should come closer."

It wasn't an order, just like it wasn't a suggestion. It was an invitation and a challenge all at once, something woven through the gravelly tone of his voice. I almost shivered, but tightened my folded arms and stood firm. "Tell me what's going on first."

"It was a long day." He shrugged. "I'm sorry. Let me make it up to you."

I raised my eyebrows so it was clear I wasn't buying it. "JP, come on."

"I'd love to, but my aim isn't good enough to hit you from all the way over here."

For as many times as I'd tried not to laugh at JP because I didn't want him to know how funny I thought he was, sometimes I couldn't help it. A laugh slipped out and the smile on JP's lips grew.

"Come closer, babe," he said.

And maybe I shouldn't have.

Maybe I should've kept listening to that little voice, like the tingling of a bell, warning me not to let it go.

But that little voice seemed to support decisions that didn't get me laid, so I took half a step forward, bringing my legs against the foot of JP's bed.

"Closer," he said.

I unfolded my arms and knelt on the edge of the mattress. JP's eyes took on a heavy look.

"Closer," he said again, his voice going soft, and softer still when he repeated it after I inched forward, and again when I crawled forward, and again until I was on his lap.

"Just a little more," he whispered.

"Any closer and you're gonna end up inside me," I said.

"And they say blondes aren't smart."

"You're blonde, dumbass."

"No one said I was smart."

"Since when do you consider yourself no one?"

He chuckled, his face close enough to mine that his breath puffed against the tip of my nose. His hand moved to my hip, tracing over my running shorts and up my sides until his fingertips were caressing my cheek.

"You've had a shitty day," he said, so quiet I felt his words more than I heard them. "Let me take your mind off it."

"How're you gonna do that?"

His mouth twitched, the corners tugging up into a smirk that was becoming far too familiar.

"I'm gonna make you come"—all at once he twisted, so sudden and so confidently that I was on my back before I even realized we'd moved—"here, babe."

Chapter Eighteen
The Warning Bells Are Ringing

FOR AS MANY TIMES as we'd fucked, I'd only been naked with JP twice.

The first was three years earlier, obviously. I'd dropped his robe to the ground and stood in front of him fully naked, my heart pounding out of my chest as I lied about not being a virgin. The second was the beginning of this summer, since that was the last time we'd been somewhere I didn't have to keep my shirt tucked under my armpits while JP licked and sucked my nipples in case someone pulled into the parking lot and I had to tug it back down before their headlights caught my headlights.

Or somewhere that I hadn't purposely worn a skirt so all he had to do was bunch it around my waist and push my panties to the side to enter me.

Or where we weren't trying to stay quieter than the trees and leaves rustling around us, my pants keeping my legs trapped together as they circled my thighs and his tugged down just enough that he could take his cock out.

I told myself that was why he luxuriated in the act of stripping me, why he peeled off my tank top and unhooked my bra like he was one of those nerds who saved the wrapping paper off a gift instead of tearing it to shreds to see what was beneath. He was indulging in the space around us, not confined by the backseat of a car or stuck kneeling on an air mattress.

After getting me topless, he pressed quick kisses to each of my breasts before reaching for the waistband of my shorts. Before he could pull them down, I pressed my thighs together, reaching down and touching his wrist. He looked up, eyes patient but curious.

"Shirt off," I said.

I half-expected him to tease me for wanting to see him shirtless, but he didn't say anything before pulling his T-shirt off. And yeah, maybe I didn't get to slowly luxuriate in the way he got naked the same way he had with me. But I couldn't deny the way he reached behind his head and tugged his shirt off by the neck before dropping it unceremoniously to the floor was hot as *fuck*.

I was going to stop him again once he had my shorts and panties off to insist he take his jeans off, but before I could speak, he put a hand on each of my thighs and parted them. Moving between my legs, he dipped down and took one of my nipples in his mouth.

"Fuck," I breathed as JP's teeth dragged along my nipple, sending shocks of arousal skimming across my skin. He smiled against the swell of my breast, reaching up to flick his thumb across one nipple while tugging gently at the other with his teeth, and the breathy moan dancing in the base of my throat twisted into a whimper. I squirmed uncontrollably beneath him, like it would soothe the sudden fire in my core, and JP hummed a low rumble of appreciation.

"Do you know how addictive it is to hear you make noises like that?" he asked, releasing my nipple so he could soothe it with his tongue.

"Like what?" I gasped.

He nipped at my nipple a third time, pressing a tender kiss to it before I'd even finished crying out.

"Like that." He buried his face in my cleavage, kissing between my breasts as he squeezed one in his palm. "There's only one thing more addictive than biting your nipples and making you squeal."

"Let me guess," I said. "Staring in the mirror at your own reflection while jacking off."

He laughed. "That's a close third."

"Third?"

"Mm-hmm. Second is this." He moved his lips to my nipple and tormented it with his teeth again. "And first..."

He didn't finish the sentence, but I figured it out anyway. All it took was a few of the quick kisses he peppered down my ribs and stomach, pressing one after another to the spot above my belly button piercing and below it, then to the curve of my belly, top of my mound, and—

"F-Fuck," I stammered as he worked his fingers between my folds and spread me open so he could place a kiss directly on my clit.

"In a bit," he murmured. "Gotta eat first."

And he fucking *ate*.

I couldn't keep still as he licked me. His tongue was everywhere, not like he couldn't find his way around a pussy but like he was tasting every inch so he could pick his favourite spot, comparing and contrasting and narrowing things down until he could decide.

And luckily for me, he decided on my clit.

"JP," I gasped as he slipped two fingers inside of me and curled them so heated pleasure radiated from my core. "I'm getting close."

He lifted his head for all of a moment, just high enough that I could see my wetness coating the lower half of his face. It was so slick I thought it might drip off his chin like juice and his eyes were wild, like he was so drunk on the taste of me that he wanted to drown in it.

"Grab your tits," he said in a mumbled rush.

"Huh?"

"Tits." He grabbed my wrist and shoved my arm up until I let it fall onto my breast. "Touch."

I almost laughed at the pseudo-caveman speak he'd resorted to, but he lowered his mouth to my pussy again and started sucking on my clit. Lightning jolted through my body, along my skin and down to my bones. Moaning, I grabbed my breast as he'd directed, pinching my nipple between my fingers. He pushed his other hand between my legs and traced down my slit until he reached my asshole. So much of my wetness had collected on his finger that he dipped it in without warning, slipping it into the tight ring of muscle and sending me past the point of cognition and into a realm of sensation.

Slamming my eyes shut, I squeezed my breast harder. My other hand ended up woven in JP's hair and my back arched off the bed. An orgasm erupted through me and I tensed, not able to stop myself from writhing, from hooking my leg over his shoulder so I could use it to both grind against JP's tongue and push him closer, from nearly choking on the overwhelming pleasure that escaped as moans from my throat.

The whole time I was coming, his tongue didn't stop. He kept licking, kept fingering, kept drawing out my pleasure until every moment of bliss had passed and all I could do was relax back against the bed. Only then did he slowly withdraw his fingers from my ass and pussy, dragging his tongue along my slit for one last lingering taste before sitting back on his knees, eyes on me as he ran the back of his hand across his grinning mouth.

He'd barely finished wiping his face before I was sitting up and curling my legs under me so I could dart forward and get his pants off.

"I didn't make you come hard enough to need a recovery period?" he asked as I worked his button open.

"Are you saying you don't want me to fuck you?" I asked, tugging his zipper down.

I expected him to laugh, but he didn't.

"Don't put those fucking words in my mouth," he growled instead, and it was a surprising enough sound that I glanced up. Darkened blue eyes met mine, hungry and deep and eager, and a second later my hands were swatted away so he could take over and get his pants off.

The gravel in his voice might have been unusual, but the eagerness and urgency of his actions weren't. The way he pushed his jeans down, the way he twisted on the bed, the way I crawled back onto his lap: there was so much familiarity in all of it that it went unspoken. I knew he wanted me on top, wanted me to sink onto his cock in that one smooth, sudden motion, wanted us to go from stripping to kissing and kissing to grinding and grinding to riding, skin to skin and thick cock buried in wet pussy.

I knew he wanted me to fuck him, really *fuck* him, bouncing on his dick like all that existed was our bodies and our pleasure. He wanted to feel me stretch around him as much as I wanted him to stretch me, the sound of our skin slapping together a beat to the melody of gasping breaths and primal moans.

I knew all of that because we'd done this so many times. Which meant I also knew how long it should have taken to make him come.

And when that time passed and passed and *passed*, and I made myself come on his cock again and was working my way towards a third and he *still* hadn't finished, I knew I'd been right about something being weird.

"JP," I murmured, slowing my pace.

"Mmm?" His fingers were digging into my hips and he had his eyes closed, his head tilted back.

"I know I'm not doing anything wrong because I'm really good at this—"

He made another humming sound, paired with a soft chuckle. "You are, babe. You're so fucking good at this."

"...but?"

His breath hesitated in his chest. I bit my lip.

"You can tell me if you need something different," I said. "If this isn't working for you."

A heartbeat passed before he opened his eyes and looked up at me. "Yeah?"

"Yeah."

"How different?"

I gave him a scolding look. "*That* doesn't happen until after the Diamond Gala."

He laughed again, his hands tightening on my hips. "But something a little... more different?"

I had no idea what that was supposed to mean. My guess was something kinky. And while I was usually up to try something kinky, I wouldn't try it with just anyone. But with JP...

Well.

With JP, I would.

"Yeah. More different is okay."

His tongue poked out and he hesitated for another moment, then sat up, his cock still inside of me.

And yeah, I'd said we could do something different.

But I didn't know it would be different like *that*.

That it would make something ring through me, something like a warning.

That the little voice I'd ignored to fuck him and fucked him to ignore would rise, barely more than a whisper but as clear as calm water.

I didn't know any of that would happen. But it did, and the hands that had been squeezing my hips one moment were around my waist the next.

One moment, he'd been watching my tits bounce. The next, his eyes were boring deep into mine.

One moment, I was riding him hard, giving our bodies what they'd been craving.

The next, his chest was pressed against mine and he was kissing me, giving into a different kind of craving. Our pace slowed to a stop and I fell in his arms, letting him guide me onto my back again.

Suddenly we weren't fucking. Not the way we usually did. He was moving inside me, his body connected to mine, quiet words brushing my lips as he whispered how good I felt.

How he'd been dreaming of being inside me.

How hard he got when he remembered how hot and how wet and how smooth my pussy was.

How much he'd needed this.

How he'd needed *me*.

My legs wrapped around his waist and my arms around his back. His cock was buried inside me as I held him close, kissing him back as our breaths synced and pleasure built and built and built, and it wasn't fucking.

That wasn't *fucking*.

And I...

"Fuck," he said, the words a breathless gasp.

Fuck.

"Nellie."

I opened the eyes I didn't remember closing, looking up into blue ones hazy with need and clouded with confusion.

"God, what are—" He cut himself off with a groan, bowing his head as he pushed deep.

I liked it.

"Why is this—"

"I don't know," I whispered. I wouldn't have known even if he had finished what he was saying. "Just don't..."

Fuck.

We couldn't. Shouldn't. But...

Fuck.

"...don't stop."

He groaned, moving his face so it was buried against my neck.

"Keep holding me," he whispered. "Please."

That sensation of ringing rushed through me again, something silent that resonated around my spine, but I kept my arms wrapped around him. I held him like that until I came again, shaking in his arms and clutching him against me.

And that should have gotten him over the edge. It wasn't like I had a magical pussy or anything, but I mean, if it felt good when I made a girl come with my fingers or my face, I imagined it had to feel *amazing* on someone's dick. But when I finished, he still wasn't done. I turned my head, pressing a kiss to the side of his. There was another soft groan, desperate, his breath hot on my skin.

"God, I can't... fucking..." he mumbled, then trailed off.

"Can't what?" I asked.

He shuddered, his shoulders trembling beneath my palms. I tried to finish the sentence for him in my mind, telling myself that he couldn't hold back, that he was close, that he was going to come inside me and then we'd figure out what the actual fuck was going on here.

But a moment later, he lifted his head, blue eyes full of contradiction like he was holding back and pleading with me at the same time.

"This is gonna sound stupid," he whispered as he slowed his thrusts.

"Most of what you say sounds stupid," I whispered back.

He laughed. "Can you lie to me?"

"Lie?"

"Yeah."

"About something specific or...?"

"Can you just say something like, uh..." He trailed off, his throat flexing as he swallowed. "Say you're mine."

I blinked. My lips parted but nothing came out and JP winced, looking down.

"Nope, you're right," he said. "That sounds, uh... I shouldn't have—"

And he was right. He shouldn't have.

But I should have.

I should have said no.

Should've pushed him off of me.

Should've stopped things.

I *shouldn't* have lifted my hand, cupped his chin, and forced him to look up at me.

I shouldn't have stared into his eyes.

I shouldn't have let him feel my lips move. Another warning bell vibrated through me along with a million echoes that this was a bad idea. That I'd been right when I thought something seemed off about him.

But, another part of me reasoned, I wasn't doing what he asked.

"JP," I whispered. "*You* are *mine*."

A second that skipped and staggered and hung on a breath too long ticked by, JP's eyes wide and round and staring into mine.

And the second after that, his eyes slammed shut.

"Ah-*fuck*," he grunted, and shoved his cock in as deep as he could.

He came as hard as he came unexpectedly. JP's body tensed, his back hunching as staggered gasps and shuddering groans escaped his mouth. He pushed forward, pressing his body to mine like he was desperate to be even deeper despite his hips already locking against me.

Then he kissed me, both of our eyes closing as he rested his forehead on mine until we caught our breaths.

And the moment he pulled out, everything hit me at once.

I swallowed hard as JP sat back before settling beside me. For a moment, there was only silence, tense and terrifying and awkward.

"So," I finally said, curling my hand into a fist and trying not to pick at my nail. "That whole, um... 'mine' thing..."

"Oh my God," he groaned, but started laughing at the same time. "I know. It came out of nowhere."

"So did you."

He laughed harder and I couldn't stop a reluctant smile from spreading on my face.

"I think I just learned something about myself that I didn't want to know," he said.

"Right," I said. "But you know that was, like…"

He looked over at me, raising his eyebrows, and I'd never been so grateful to be on the receiving end of that mocking, skeptical look of his.

Because it made him look like the JP I knew: the snarky, arrogant asshole version of himself, crooked tooth flashing on the left side of his smile and the corners of his eyes crinkled.

"Babe," he said. "You've always been a good liar. Why do you think I asked you to lie?"

"Right," I said. "I'm amazing. And you… you're a liar, too."

"Of course," he said. "You didn't think—?"

"Of course not."

"Well, I mean, if I was good enough that I convinced you…"

"You're a soulless sleazebag lawyer," I said. "You couldn't convince me the sky itself is blue."

He laughed again. "Right. Of course. I just, uh… you know." He shrugged. "Like, you were kind of right, I guess. I was going through some shit today. And I guess I needed something… like that. But that's all it was."

"Alright," I said, nodding. "Cool."

And part of me wanted to leave it there. There didn't need to be more to it. Whatever JP was going through was his business and I didn't care, obviously. We weren't even buddies unless the word "fuck" was in front of it and we weren't currently fucking. So it wasn't my problem.

"So what was that all about, then?" I blurted.

Shit.

It was fine, I told myself. I just didn't want to be a shitty person who ignored something that was obviously bothering him. JP would say he didn't want to talk about it because it was personal and I'd say okay and that would be that.

And that was almost the case. JP's jaw twitched awkwardly and I prepared my response of "It's all good, I'm not offended you don't want to tell me."

But after taking a breath, he paused and looked down at his hands.

"Do you still want to know why I didn't go today?" he asked. "To the funeral?"

No, I told myself.

"Yeah," I said.

"It's kinda personal."

He said it like a warning.

"I'm okay with that."

I said it like it was true.

His throat flexed as he swallowed. "I'm, uh... not good. At funerals."

"I don't think anyone's really *good* at them," I said. "Other than maybe the person who it's for since all they have to do is... you know. Lie there."

He half-laughed. "Fair. But I, uh... I mean, my dad was pissed. I dunno if Anne-Marie mentioned that."

"Anne-Marie didn't mention anything," I said. "It was annoying, actually, because I—"

And that was when it hit me.

Anne-Marie would tell anyone who would listen anything she knew.

Or so I'd thought. Because even having known her for a few years shy of two decades, I underestimated her sometimes.

The woman knew everything.

And what she didn't know, she was *determined* to find out.

But her constant chatter was a cover. She was strategic about how she *shared* the information she knew. Sure, it might seem like you'd have better luck hauling sand with a bucket made of wet single-ply toilet paper than getting Anne-Marie to keep a secret. That was by design.

Because what better way to pretend like you didn't know a key piece of information than by making it seem like you couldn't keep a secret to save your life?

She'd been hiding the reason on purpose.

"I don't go to funerals," JP said.

"Why?"

He wasn't looking at me when he responded. He wasn't looking at anything, I don't think.

"Because the last time I went to one, it was for someone who died because of me."

Chapter Nineteen
Sam

I BARELY KNEW ANYTHING about JP.

That wasn't supposed to bother me. At all. It was part of why I'd decided *he* was the one I wanted to lose my virginity to three years earlier. I knew enough about him that he wasn't anonymous, but not so much that he meant something to me.

That's what I told myself, at least. Because as cold as it sounded, it was what I'd needed.

And it wasn't all that cold. It wasn't supposed to make me feel like an asshole. JP didn't seem to think I was an asshole for it because that was what we'd agreed to.

Somehow, though, that made it bother me more.

Whatever it was, it didn't change the fact that I stared at JP and wondered *how* I didn't know that about him. Because yeah, I knew how his cum tasted and he knew what the inside of my butthole felt like—with his finger, anyway—but I didn't know he'd apparently *killed* someone. And even if we didn't know all that much about each other on a personal level, Anne-Marie was my best friend. I would've thought she'd mention that at some point.

And then he started telling me what happened and I realized two things: JP should probably go to therapy and I *had* known this about him.

Sort of.

"His name was Sam," JP said as he pulled his boxers on, though it seemed like he was doing it more for something to do than because he felt the need to dress.

"Sam," I repeated. I hadn't exactly expected the name, but I wasn't surprised by it, either. "The same one you had on your T-shirt at the run?"

He nodded. "We met in CEGEP. The very first day. We hit it off, ended up going to law school together, decided to try taking the same classes as much as we could, that sort of thing."

"You were close," I said.

He nodded, not looking at me. "Yeah."

I bent my knees, pulling his bedspread up to my chest and settling against the headboard. "What happened?"

"There was a car accident."

I tried not to show it, but I was confused. I would've *definitely* remembered Anne-Marie telling me if her brother got into a car accident bad enough to kill someone.

"We were at this party," JP said. "While we were there, he sort of, like…" He gestured vaguely. "We had a fight. I'd told him some personal stuff and he told someone else and I was pissed. Hurt that he'd do that, you know? So I was petty and left the party even though I was supposed to be DDing for him. I told him he could find his own way home and went back to my dorm."

I stayed quiet, watching him. JP still wasn't looking at me, instead staring at the wall across from his bed like there were a thousand miles between it and him.

"When I got home, he'd already texted to apologize. I just texted back that it was fine, we'd talk about it in the morning, and went to bed. I didn't ask if he still needed a ride or… When I went down to grab breakfast the next day, someone told me—" He stopped, swallowing hard. "He'd gotten a ride with this other guy. And that guy was high. I don't think Sam knew when he got in the car."

He went silent, not saying the rest because he didn't need to. I stared at him, trying to figure out the right thing to do.

"That's not your fault, JP," I finally said. "You couldn't know—"

He held up a hand. "I know. Trust me. I've been down all the roads here and I know, logically, I wasn't driving that car. But that doesn't make the fact that he wouldn't have gotten into that car if it wasn't for me go away. It doesn't make any of this… you know." He sighed. "It doesn't make it *stop*."

I nodded, looking down at my hands. "What happened to the guy who was driving?"

JP scoffed, a snarl of anger flashing across his face. "When he finally went to court to get sentenced for the whole thing, he said he understands if 'Sam's loved ones can't forgive him' and that he 'wishes they could trade his life for Sam's if it would help.'" He snorted. "His life isn't worth a half-melted Iced Capp. But I'd trade it even just to find out if Sam saw the message I sent."

"There were no read receipts or anything?"

He shook his head and laughed. "Sam had the cheapest, oldest, busted-ass phone you can imagine because he constantly lost or broke his phone. He… he's the one I said earlier was brilliant. He had ADHD and that made him insanely good at some things, but he'd misplace his own dick if it wasn't attached. And he could remember the stupidest little details about obscure cases from decades ago, but after he spent months planning Illumi-Nite, he forgot his shoes for the run. Did the whole thing barefoot." JP grinned. "Luckily we had a bunch of Jello shots so he didn't seem to realize how bad his feet hurt."

"So he was the originator of the Start Line Jello Shot?" I asked.

"And the Holi powder cannons," JP said, still smiling. "And also the first one to get pelted with powder at the finish line. He was super passionate about the run and organized it the first year. We've kept it going because it was important and he would've loved how big it's gotten. And, you know, knowing how many kids it's helped. Like, he was just a good guy. Here, let me show you what he…"

He trailed off, twisting to grab his phone off the nightstand, and tapped the screen a few times before turning it towards me to show me the picture he'd pulled up on his social media account of him and a man with reddish-brown skin, thick black hair, and dark, sparkling eyes.

"Oh!" I said. "Him."

JP looked at me, startled. "You know him?"

I didn't *know* him, but I'd seen him before. And I'd thought he was cute. Not that I was going to tell JP that, or the fact that I'd seen this same photo because Anne-Marie had showed it to me when she was trying to convince me to let her brother pop my cherry.

"No," I said. "But I saw a picture of him at… must have been at the run, maybe?"

JP shrugged. "Maybe. I'm sure someone had one somewhere. This was taken after a fundraiser he helped with for immigration legal services. He put in a sixteen-hour day during finals to do that because he said it was more important to make sure people who needed help got it. And that's more the way I want to remember him. Because his funeral was just… shit."

"Why?"

His jaw twitched and he hesitated before responding, like he was trying to decide if he actually wanted to tell me how all of this led to him not going to Arthur Kroft's funeral.

"He would've hated it," JP finally said. "There were all these people there who didn't know him. All our friends and profs and his family, of course, but like... it turned into something that wasn't about him. My parents came, despite never having met him. Your dad might've been there too, actually. Because Sam's dad was in politics, so people knew who he was.

"And funerals are just a day that drills in that the person is fucking *dead*. It hits you again and again and again and it's supposed to help you, what, get closure? I don't even know. I showed up with my friends and we were... you know. Upset. And after I hugged Sam's sister and things were a little, um... emotional, my dad came up to pull me to the side and gave me shit for acting like that because there were all these people watching."

My mouth fell open. "He what?"

"There were a lot of 'stakeholders' and 'important names' there, according to my dad, and he didn't want me to 'hurt my reputation' because I couldn't hold it together in public." JP sighed. "And I listened to my dad for everything. So I went back and sat there, holding it all together while everyone told stories about Sam and broke down around me, pretending I was totally unaffected burying my friend." His voice caught and he cleared his throat. "So I just... I don't do funerals. If I can help it." He rubbed the back of his neck uncomfortably. "Sorry."

"For what?"

"I, uh, haven't really... talked about this much before."

I studied him, not sure if I was stunned or horrified or devastated on his behalf. The Marchands were involved in a lot of the same social circles as my dad, but I'd always thought they were at least marginally better than he was about being semi-decent human beings.

And JP was just... *fuck*. At Illumi-Nite, their shirts had said they'd been running for Sam for six years. Which meant he'd been my age when this all happened. When he'd lost his best friend and had to sit there pretending because his *dad*—

I didn't fully decide to reach out and touch JP's hand. It just sort of happened. He didn't look at me and I didn't look at him, even after he flipped his palm over so I could weave my fingers through his.

"JP," I said. "I'm sor—"

"Don't."

"What?"

"Don't say you're sorry." His voice was sad, but there was a hint of teasing behind it. "You never say you're sorry."

"I do too!"

He laughed, his eyes on where our hands met. "You do not, babe. Not unless it's big. It's one of the things I—" He stopped, laughing again. "—I, and *everybody* else, knows about you."

I huffed, almost but not quite offended. "Fine. I'm not sorry, then. I—" I thought for a moment. "I'm sad."

He tilted his head to the side. "Why are you sad?"

"I'm sad you had to go through that." I bit my lip as JP's thumb rubbed along mine. "Thinking about losing someone like that... like... like if that was Sydney or Anne-Marie and it was me... it just hurts. And I'm sor—sa...ddy. I'm saddy you went through that."

He chuckled, the corners of his eyes crinkling. "Thanks."

"Will you tell me more about him?"

He looked up, a confused line appearing between his eyebrows. Which was fair, because I was a little confused, too. The question had just slipped out and it wasn't until I heard myself say it that I understood why.

"I just thought you might want to talk about him," I continued. "You were close and you said you haven't talked about it much and he sounds... you know. Important to you."

He held my gaze, something swirling behind his eyes. I thought it was more confusion, but there was something else storming there, something so heavy I wasn't sure how he could hold it all up. It was so big and so encompassing that I felt it walk up my spine, ringing and prickling and sparking as the moment locked around us. My heartbeat was in my ears, silent and thundering all at once.

And I was scared, but in that way where I couldn't look away. Where I didn't want to look away.

JP's lips parted. The air was so thick, it seemed to move around us as he took a breath. The heartbeat in my ears got louder, the thundering turning into a thumping, a pounding, something that was more like footsteps running up a set of stairs, like a—

Wait.

Those...

Those were footsteps running up a set of stairs.

"Jean-*Pa*-aul!" screeched Anne-Marie from *far* closer than I would have liked.

I yanked my hand away like his skin had been getting hotter and hotter and was suddenly boiling. "I thought you said she wasn't supposed to be home tonight!"

JP's eyes were wide with panic. "She wasn't!"

"It sure fucking sounds like she is!"

"Nell, I swear to God, I—"

"What do I do?" I asked desperately. "I have to... I have to—"

"*Chérie*, you have a lot of explaining to do," Anne-Marie said, and three loud knocks landed on the door before the handle twisted.

And I didn't wait for an answer.

I didn't think.

I just dove.

Chapter Twenty
And Another Thing

Surprisingly, there were only two things I regretted about JP.

It wasn't that I hadn't made a ton of mistakes with him. I had. Getting distracted by an inappropriately emotional conversation with JP was a mistake.

Fucking in his room instead of meeting in our usual hookup spot was a mistake.

Hell, it could be argued that everything I'd done with, for, and about Jean-Paul bloody Marchand from the moment I'd entered his bedroom three years earlier was one big goddamn mess of a mistake.

But mistakes didn't have to be *regrets*. I didn't regret losing my virginity to JP. I didn't regret the orgasms he'd given me. Even being there that night, Anne-Marie pounding on the door as I leapt bare-ass-naked off JP's bed, wasn't something I regretted.

What I did regret was, firstly, the whole part where I dove off his bed bare-ass-naked. The second I hit the floor, I realized I could've just thrown his bedspread over me and pretended I was some random other girl who was going to stay hidden until his sister left.

That realization came at the same moment I realized there was no way in hell I was going to fit beneath JP's bed, which had apparently been my instinctive hiding spot instead of some place smart, like his closet. There was no more than six inches of space between the base of his bed and the floor. All I could do was press my body as tightly as I could to the frame and hope against hope that Anne-Marie would stay on the other side of the room so she couldn't see this side of his bed.

The second regret I had was telling JP he was mine.

Mainly because after about ten seconds of lying there, my heart racing fast enough to leave me light-headed, I got cum on the floor. And sure, it wasn't *my* floor—or my cum, obviously—but in order for it to get on the floor, it had to drip out of me and onto my leg and I couldn't even reach down to wipe it up, which meant all I could focus on was the annoying sensation of it sliding from my leg to the floor.

And that sensation cemented the moment in my memory, making it a stark snapshot. A freeze-frame where I stared at the wall and wondered what was wrong with me.

How, exactly, I'd gotten here and what, in the fuck, I was doing with my life.

But by the end of it all, I would've given almost anything to go back and erase the memory of his chin in my hand. To forget the resistance of his neck as I turned his head to me and the echo of the rasp in my voice as I stared him dead in the eye and told him the opposite of what he thought he wanted to hear.

JP barely got the bedspread over his lap and yanked his book off the nightstand before his bedroom door banged open. I sucked in a breath, holding it so my heart would stop vibrating in my chest before letting it out as soundlessly as I could. On the wall across from me, abstract shadows cast by the mix of light between JP's window, the hallway, and the lamp beside his bed shifted into the indistinct form of my best friend, who took two harrowing steps into the room before pausing.

"You're home early," JP said, his voice unnervingly casual and unbothered.

"It is not that early, dear brother," Anne-Marie said. Her shadow-form shifted like she'd folded her arms and leaned against the wall next to the door. I jammed my fingernail against my thumb, praying to any deity who might take pity on a joyfully promiscuous girl that Anne-Marie would stay there the entire time. Dionysus, maybe. Or Aphrodite, or literally any of the Erotes, or Bacchus and Venus if the Romans had been right instead of the Greeks. Or there was Freyja, who was Norse. The Hindu goddess Rati. Tlazolteotl from the Aztecs. And a bunch more that I'd learned about because besides the typical Greek mythology phase I'd had as a teenager, I'd spent a couple of weeks nerding out over every god or goddess that represented sex or lust or vice after embracing my slutty side in the first year of university.

"I thought you'd be staying at Remy's," JP said. "Or is he waiting in your bedroom because Mom and Dad got a hotel tonight?"

"No, Remy is volunteering in the morning," Anne-Marie said, her voice almost wistful. "Plus I already tired him out tonight, so—"

"Jesus Christ, Anne-Marie," JP muttered.

Anne-Marie snorted on a laugh. "Since when are you such a prude, Jean-Paul?"

"I'm not." I could almost hear him rolling his eyes. "I'm just not in the mood for an AMNN broadcast tonight."

"What is an AMNN broadcast?"

"Oh. The Anne-Marie News Network. Because your, uh, updates are like a news broadcast."

There was a moment of silence. On the wall across from me, a shadow shifted, and in my mind I imagined Anne-Marie had tilted her head thoughtfully. "You know, I *would* make a wonderful news anchor."

"As your only current viewer, I'll be a reference for you," JP said. "Now, if that's it?" Apparently I could also see the aura of JP's movements because the shadows shifted again as if he'd held up his book. "I was in the middle of a good part."

"That is not it and you know it," Anne-Marie said.

"Do I?" JP asked, his voice tired.

"What are you doing home?"

"What do you mean, what am I doi—"

"Jean-Paul. Do you take me for stupid?" she interrupted.

"Only most of the time," he replied.

She ignored the jab. "You were supposed to go out with Michele tonight."

"It sounds like you have your nights mixed up."

"Oh, do I?" Anne-Marie asked. "Did Michele also have her nights mixed up? Because she mentioned when I saw her at the funeral this afternoon how much she was looking forward to your date, and then halfway through the wake, she pulled me aside to complain that you cancelled on her, and for what? To... read?"

My lips parted, but not even a breath came out.

"It's a good book," JP said.

"It must be to be better than Michele. As much as I do not want to know a single thing about your sex life"—I almost snorted at the disgust in her voice. Anne-Marie was *way* too comfortable knowing about JP's sex life—"she has *repeatedly* told me she would do anything with you."

"I mean, Michele's hot, but... like, not to be a dick, but it's a *really* good book," JP said.

"Funny. I do not believe you, for some reason."

Neither did I. Because I'd seen Michele and she *was* hot, and no book was better than hooking up with a hot redhead, and also I was lying—still bare-ass naked—on JP's bedroom floor because he'd...

He'd picked me.

The same sensation of ringing curled up my spine, warning signals making my palms sweat as my heart rate picked up again, pattering out a beat that sounded something like *oh-god-no-please-no-not-this-not-him-he-promised.*

JP let out an exasperated sigh. "What does it even matter to you if I cancel a date?"

"Because it is not like you to cancel a sure thing."

"Maybe I wasn't feeling it."

"And maybe I am being a concerned sister." Something in her voice softened. "Is it because of the funeral?"

"Don't," he said.

"I know things like this are—"

"Seriously," he said, his voice stony. "Stop."

"JP, please." I almost sat up in surprise. I didn't think I'd ever heard Anne-Marie call her brother JP instead of Jean-Paul. "I want to make sure you are alright."

"So you came home to check on me?" he asked.

"Yes," she said plainly. The shadows moved on the wall and I figured Anne-Marie had lifted her hands in surrender. "But I will stop, if you tell me you are really okay."

"I am fine," JP said. "Seriously. I am."

It looked like Anne-Marie nodded. "Okay. Well, Michele told Sonique LaPlante that she is not going to give you another chance, so you know."

"I'm positively devastated," JP said.

"Don't be," she replied, ignoring his obvious sarcasm. "We all know she is lying. Michele will drop her panties the second you look in her direction. But then again, she would probably—"

Her voice dropped mid-sentence. Silence filled the room and my heart seemed to climb my ribcage so it could settle itself in the base of my throat.

"Speaking of panties," Anne-Marie said, her voice pitching up. The shadows slid forward as she took a step forward and floated up as she lifted something. "What... are these?"

Oh no.

Oh.

Fucking.

No.

"I've started an online business," JP said smoothly. "Figured I'd earn a little extra on the side."

Anne-Marie shrieked and the shadows on the wall jerked wildly. A second later, I nearly let out a shriek of my own as something pink and silky and literally my fucking *panties* pitched over the side of the bed and landed on my forehead. Slamming my teeth together, I held it in, but couldn't bring myself to move and take my thong off my face.

"You are *disgusting*," she spat.

JP was laughing, somehow. "You asked."

"You are not selling *used panties* online, Jean-Paul. Or worse—oh, *crisse d'ostie*, you are not selling, ah, photos of yourself or something, are you?!"

"For fuck's sake, Anne-Marie," JP said. "Of course not."

"So you are a liar."

"And you're the one asking questions you clearly know the answer to."

Fuck. Did she? Had she spotted me or—

"I do not know shit, Jean-Paul. That is why I want you to explain to me what these panties are doing here," Anne-Marie said.

"What do you *think* they're doing here?"

"I think you have been collecting souvenirs from your conquests," she sniffed.

"Bingo," JP said.

Anne-Marie let out an offended scoff. "That is disgustingly misogynistic, Jean-Paul! And rude, besides. Do you even know how expensive panties are?!"

"It's not like I'm stealing them," JP said defensively. "They're giving them to me."

"And what are you even going to do with them?!" she demanded.

JP's shadow shrugged. "Make a quilt, probably."

"And you had these out because you were taking measurements?" Anne-Marie asked sarcastically.

JP was silent. A long beat went by, neither of them speaking, their shadows still on the wall across from me. Then:

"Oh, *ewwww*!" Anne-Marie squealed, and JP started laughing. "You are *disgusting*, Jean-Paul!"

"I didn't say anything!" he said through his laughter.

"Ugh," she grumbled. "Whatever. I came to make sure my brother was okay since he was acting unusual and I was trying to be a thoughtful sister given the circumstances, but clearly you are fine if you've had time to blow your own horn while sniffing panties."

"No one said I was *sniffing* them," JP said.

"I should tell Michele you would rather sit at home and play with your own ding-a-ling than have sex with her. It would serve you right to miss out on that."

JP laughed. "*Ding-a-ling*?! Are you seven?"

"Whatever!" Anne-Marie said again. There were three loud stomps accompanied by a shadow moving across the wall and then JP's bedroom door slammed closed.

Beautiful silence filled the room, pouring around us like refreshing water, muffling even the way my heart was still drumming in my ears. I counted one moment, then two, then twenty before the shadows on the wall shifted and JP's face appeared over the edge of the bed, his eyebrows raised.

"Nice hat," he said.

"Thanks."

He reached down and gently took my panties off my forehead. "She's gone, you know."

"I was making sure she wasn't going to do that whole 'And another thing' thing where she bursts back in the second I sit up," I said.

JP chuckled. "I think we're in the clear."

I forced a laugh as I shifted from my half-twisted position and sat up. "I thought she'd never leave."

"I'm surprised she did, honestly," he said, sighing. "Normally, she—"

The door flew open again.

I hit the ground hard so hard I nearly gave myself whiplash.

"One more thing," Anne-Marie said, her tone so bright you would've never known she'd just stormed out. "Do you know who was at the funeral today?"

"Who?" JP asked, and I was stunned again by how casual he was able to sound.

"Nellie," Anne-Marie said.

My throat went dry.

"Okay," JP said.

"And do you know, she still has not found herself a date for the Diamond Gala," Anne-Marie said.

I stiffened slightly. Of course I was putting off telling her, and of course she'd heard me tell Clinton I didn't know who I was going with yet earlier that day. I knew I'd have to tell her at some point, but I kept telling myself it was a bridge I'd cross when I came to it.

"Okay," JP said.

"Well, I just thought it was interesting, since if she does not find a date before this weekend, her father will make her go with Clinton Thibault. And you know what he was saying about her before."

"Why don't you help her find a date, then?" JP asked.

"You know how Nellie is."

"No, I don't," JP said.

"You do." Anne-Marie's shadow moved as she leaned against JP's wall again. "She ignores things until she can't ignore it anymore and is left scrambling. Then she panics and wonders why she gets into these impossible situations like they are not entirely avoidable. I love *ma chérie* to pieces, but she is so lazy sometimes."

I blinked as the watery sensation of time slowing settled around me.

"That doesn't seem very nice," JP said.

Anne-Marie sighed. "I know, but it is like she doesn't even try. I have stepped in to help her so many times and I cannot keep fixing all her problems simply because she does not want to."

I blinked again, another watery sensation beginning to prickle in my eyes. Staring at the wall, I watched the stillness of the shadows, an oddly blank feeling in my mind.

"So if you don't want to help her, why are you here telling me about this?" JP asked.

"Oh, because she nearly punched Clinton today and it was *amazing*," she gushed, then told him an embellished version of Clinton approaching me at the funeral. JP's shadow moved as he nodded along, interjecting occasionally like he hadn't already heard the story.

"Wow," he said when she finished. "Well, good for her."

"I know." She sighed again. "I sure hope she finds someone else to go to the Diamond Gala with. We would never allow Clinton to harm her, of course, but it would be much easier if she did not have to spend the evening with him next weekend."

"I bet," JP said.

There was a moment of loaded silence and despite everything, I had to fight not to laugh. Anne-Marie was clearly hinting that he should offer to take me. And maybe that would've worked out. JP could offer to take me, then we could tell her we were going to the gala together and I wouldn't have to figure out how to actually tell her.

Then again, I guess that was just another example of me being lazy and letting other people solve my problems.

Finally, Anne-Marie let out another noise of annoyance. "God, I wish you two stubborn shits would get some sense knocked into you."

JP laughed, startled by her sudden change of tone. "What?!"

"*What*?!" Anne-Marie mocked sarcastically as her shadow on the wall moved.

"Good night, Anne-Marie," JP called out as his bedroom door closed for the second time.

"Good night, dickhead," Anne-Marie replied, her voice muffled through the door.

And again, silence filled the room.

It was less beautiful that time. Less refreshing. I didn't count moments or heartbeats or breaths. I just stayed there until JP leaned over the edge of the bed again.

"As much as I wouldn't complain about having you permanently naked on my bedroom floor, I think the housekeeper may have some questions," he said.

"I'm not moving until I know she's not coming back," I said.

"I heard her bedroom door close," he said.

"And which side of it was she on?"

"Presumably the one in her bedroom."

"You don't know that, though."

The mattress shifted as he stood up and I listened to his footsteps as he padded to his door. It opened and he walked into the hall, returning a moment later and closing the door.

"Her shower is running," he said. "So you've got at least an hour, depending on how hot she's got the water."

I swallowed hard, then slowly sat up. My face was burning and heated even more when I glanced at JP, who was standing near the door in his boxers. "Where, um, are my clothes?"

"Right." He stepped forward and pulled the bedspread back, revealing where he'd hidden my shorts and tank top and bra. "Sorry I, uh, missed your panties."

I forced a laugh as I grabbed my things. Neither of us said anything as JP pulled on a T-shirt and a pair of shorts and I dressed quickly, running a hand through my hair to smooth it down.

And fuck, it was awkward.

"Alright," I said when I finished. "So, I'm gonna head out. I'll see you next weekend?"

"Yeah, for sure," he said, then cleared his throat. "Uh, about tonight—"

"It's fine."

"Sorry." He half-laughed. "Things got, uh, unexpectedly deep."

"You mean your dick?" I asked, trying to laugh.

"Are you implying my dick's gotten bigger since the last time we fucked?" he asked.

I shrugged. "Maybe."

A smile flickered on his face, then faded. "And um, what she said—"

"It's fine," I said again.

"Nellie—"

"She didn't know I was here." I shrugged. "She's not wrong. I am lazy."

He sighed. "You know how Anne-Marie is."

I shrugged. "She says things behind everyone's back. It was just my turn. Whatever. It's fine."

"If you say so. And, uh, about the whole... date thing. I didn't feel like going out tonight. Michele can be a lot to handle and I..."

"Of course," I said. "Like you said, it was a hard day."

"Right. And it doesn't mean anything."

"Yes it does." I ran my hand through my hair again as JP looked up with wide, startled eyes. "It means I've got a great pussy."

He laughed, the sound relieved. "Yeah. Exactly."

"Cool. Okay. I'm gonna, um, head out."

"Yeah, for sure," he said. "Bye, Nell."

I nodded, then went to JP's door. After opening it carefully and listening, I left, closing it behind me without looking at him before creeping down the hall and disappearing down the stairs so I could sneak out using the route my best friend and I had discovered years earlier.

Chapter Twenty-One
Take Care, Ms. Belanger

"IF I'D KNOWN YOU still had a table, I wouldn't have got Chinese food."

Bewildered laughter escaped Ben's lips as he followed me into his kitchen, which had far more furniture in it than I'd expected.

"Can I ask what the connection is there?" he asked as I set the bulging plastic bags on the table.

"Isn't it a whole thing to eat Chinese food out of the boxes while sitting on the hardwood floor? Or, like, a mattress without a bed frame? Or do I just watch too many movies?"

"I think that's more for moving in, but same concept."

"Oh." I untied the bag handles. "Well, there goes my joke."

He chuckled, then put a hand over mine before I could pull the boxes out of the bag. "There's nothing stopping us from eating Chinese food out of the boxes in bed, you know."

I'd been somewhat surprised when Ben messaged me earlier that day asking if I'd come over for dinner that night. Not that I wasn't happy about it; I'd just thought that we'd have a quick get together to say goodbye and fuck before he left for California. But it was one of those moments that highlighted the years between us.

Me

You know I'd love to, but don't you want to go out with your friends or something?

Professor Sexy

I saw most of them last weekend

Me

Yeah, but it's your last night here. No one wants to take you out?

Professor Sexy

It's also a Tuesday night.

Me

…and they don't want to miss Taco Tuesday?

Professor Sexy

Well, most of my friends and colleagues don't take summers off. It's a work night.

I'd been embarrassed about not realizing that, but before I could type a response, Ben messaged me again.

Professor Sexy

But I would hate to miss my last Taco Tuesday with you…

So that was how we ended up sitting on Ben's bed, passing boxes of chow mien and sweet and sour pork and beef and broccoli back and forth. Unfortunately, I'd made the mistake of taking my phone with me and setting it on the bed, so when it started vibrating incessantly, Ben noticed.

"Not that it's any of my business—" he started when the third message in as many minutes came through.

"Ah-Ma-ee," I said through a mouthful of chow mien, then chewed aggressively and swallowed. "Anne-Marie, I mean."

"You're not talking to her?"

"No, I am," I said, reaching over and spearing a piece of sweet and sour pork on my fork without looking at him. "I just... need a break."

"From what?"

Semi-reluctantly, I told him what had happened with JP over the weekend, though I skipped a few of the more important parts, like why he hadn't been at the funeral and that he'd cancelled a date because of me and that whole "You are mine" thing. So mainly, just that Anne-Marie had nearly caught us and what she'd said while I was lying naked on JP's bedroom floor.

"It's fine, though," I said. "Everyone says stuff behind other people's backs. Confronting her about it would probably lead to questions like 'Why were you in my brother's bedroom?' and 'So I'm your maid of honour, right?' It's not like I'm holding it against her. I'm just taking some space."

"You are still allowed to feel upset when someone says something hurtful about you," Ben said. "You don't think she'll notice you're not talking to her?"

"I'm not ignoring her completely. Just... not responding. Which probably doesn't seem weird because apparently I ignore problems until they go away and she's freaking out because she thinks I don't have a date for this weekend."

He nodded again. "It might be easier to tell her you're going with JP, you know."

"And give her the extra time to plan a surprise wedding during the Diamond Gala? No, thank you."

He chuckled and scooped some vegetables onto his fork. "She seems very passionate about getting you and JP together."

"I don't even understand why. We're both sluts."

The word made Ben wince. "That's not—"

"It's not a bad word," I said, popping another piece of pork into my mouth.

"I would argue that it, at the very least, has negative connotations," he said.

"Why?" I asked pointedly. "Because it's such a bad thing for people to sleep around and not commit to one person?"

He tilted his head. "Good point."

I moved a piece of green pepper out of the way so I could get to more of the pork. "It's not my problem if people think that's something to be ashamed of."

"I just don't want you to think you have to reclaim a label in order to be proud of who you are," he said. "Especially one I know hurt you before."

"Isn't that the same as being ashamed of it?"

"It doesn't have to be."

I helped myself to more chow mien, chewing in a quiet thoughtfulness as I processed what he said. Ben ate another bite before studying me in the silence.

"What's going through your head?" he asked.

"The usual eight million things," I replied.

"Do you always have eight million things going through your head?"

"Give or take."

He nodded slowly like I'd said something telling, but he replied before I could ask why. "Tell me one of them."

"Just one?"

"To start."

When I started humming the Jurassic Park theme song, Ben nearly choked on a piece of sweet and sour pork as he started laughing.

"What?" I asked, grinning. "You didn't say it had to be a *thought*."

"I didn't," he said, coughing. "That's true."

"Although I guess I'm also wondering why it's stuck in my head," I said. "Got any ideas on that, Professor Cameron?"

"Oh, God," he said, blowing out a breath like it was a heavy question. "I mean, they're designed to do that, in some ways. Music triggers the auditory cortex. And like much of your brain, the auditory cortex loves patterns, so it 'sings along' and anticipates where the song is going, even after the music is gone. It's why pop music is exactly that—popular. It scratches an itch. Much like a stim song does when you listen to it over and over again."

"Okay," I said. "But that's a choice. The rest of me is a little tired of my auditory cortex scratching the 'da-na-NA-na-na, da-na-Na-na-na' part over and over again."

"Well, yes, because earworms—songs that get stuck in your head—are more like bug bites. With them, the more you scratch, the worse the itch gets. And the way you scratch a song in your head is—"

"—repeating it over and over again."

He grinned. "Exactly. So you hear a song you like, your brain latches on to part of it and 'loops' it, and now you're thinking about dinosaurs."

"Okay, except I *didn't* hear it," I said.

He raised an eyebrow. "What do you mean?"

"Like, I haven't watched Jurassic Park in years. I'm sure I haven't heard that song anywhere."

"Well, brains can be odd in what triggers them, so it doesn't always have to be something you've heard. Maybe the last time you watched Jurassic Park was in Montreal. Or after a funeral." He lifted his fork. "Or when you were eating Chinese food. Something may have triggered the memory to play and, along with it, the song. Although it's more likely it played over the speakers at the grocery store and you subconsciously picked it up."

I stared at Ben's bedspread as the Jurassic Park theme song played in my head, underscoring flashes of a memory from years earlier. Not one that featured Chinese food or a funeral, but a rainy day and handfuls of popcorn being thrown at an obnoxious teenager who was ruining the movie for everyone.

Swallowing my mouthful of chow mien, I suppressed that memory with everything I had in me and nodded. "Yeah. That must have been it."

Ben didn't seem to buy it. "Are you sure?"

"Mm-hmm."

"Remember that whole thing where it's part of my job to tell when people are lying to me?"

"No, not at all. What's your job again?"

He fought back a smirk. "What else is going through your head, Nellie?"

"If I want to be on top of you for the last time we fuck or if I want it on my hands and knees."

"I... what?"

I blinked to break the hold his bedspread pattern had on me and reached for the chow mien, helping myself to another forkful. "I considered missionary since I do like looking up at you while you're fucking me. But I also *really* like the noises you make when you let loose and pound me from behind. The problem is I *also* like watching your eyes follow my tits when I bounce on your cock."

"Right." He cleared his throat and set his fork in one of the other containers. "All excellent reasons."

"What's going through your mind?" I asked, then ate my chow mien.

"That there's no reason we can't do all those things." He reached out and took my fork from my hand, setting it in the same container as his before moving it to the nightstand beside his bed. "But I want to start with dessert first."

And I wasn't about to complain about that. Especially not when he finished his dessert, dug a condom out of the carry-on suitcase sitting next to his closet, then flipped me over to fuck me from behind for a while before deciding he wanted second dessert and pulling out to take a few more bites—well, licks, technically—from the back to make me come on his tongue a second time.

"That's it, Ms. Belanger," he murmured, his breath warm on my pussy lips and his fingers buried deep inside me as I quivered on them. "Fuck, am I gonna miss how good you come for me."

"I'm gonna mi—*ahh*." I gasped as he flicked his tongue on my oversensitive clit, making my whole body shudder. "I'm gonna miss coming for you."

He groaned, lifting himself away from my pussy and slipping his hands beneath me so he could pull me against his body. His lips pressed to the back of my neck, soft and warm and enticing, before he helped me turn in place so I was facing him. But before I could crawl onto his lap, he stopped me, moving forward so I had no choice but to lie on my back.

"Relax, Nellie," he whispered.

"I wanna ride your cock," I whined as my head hit the pillow.

He moved between my legs and dipped down to kiss me. "Let me fuck you like this."

The word slipped through the haze and I blinked. Ben had kind of aversion to the word and I was pretty sure he'd never said he'd wanted to *fuck* me before. I looked up at him and a wicked smirk spread on his lips as he pushed my legs wider, then positioned his cock at my entrance.

"Is that okay?" he asked.

"Fuck me, please, Professor," I whispered, and both of us groaned as he slipped his cock back inside me.

He fucked me hard. *Hard.* The only noises we made were grunts and cries and moans, but somehow, it was like I could hear his thoughts in all those things. In the way his hips moved and the way his body slapped against mine. In the way he kissed, heated and primal, like he was driven by instinct and need and pleasure as he pounded me into that mattress on the floor.

And it seemed like he could hear my thoughts too, somehow. Like he knew from the way my hands tightened on his back that an orgasm was building up, fast and urgent and unexpected. His response was to fuck me harder, to reach down and put an arm under each of my thighs so he could push them back and make sure I had as much of his cock as I needed to clench around.

"Come," he demanded, and a second later every nerve in my body exploded at once, nearly making me pass out at the overwhelming amount of pleasure being demanded from my body. I writhed as much as his body would allow me with how I was pinned to the mattress and how his arms were holding my legs up, my back arching and his sheets clenched in my palms while light burst in my eyes.

He lasted exactly as long as it took me to finish that orgasm before he pulled out, reaching down and practically tearing the condom off before wrapping his hand around his cock and stroking hard. His eyes scrunched shut and he let out a low, rumbling groan as hot cum spilled onto my mound and lower belly.

"Fuck," he gasped. "*Fuck*, Nellie." He kept pumping his cock until every drop was out, dripping into the pool of cum on my body, then leaned down for a kiss before collapsing on the bed beside me.

He stayed there for all of five seconds, barely enough time to catch his breath, before sitting up and going to the bathroom to get tissues so he could wipe up the mess on my stomach. After that, he crawled back into the bed next to me and I shifted so he could collect me in his arms.

It was a moment that both highlighted and blurred the differences between us. I didn't usually cuddle after sex, not when I was getting fucked in parking lots and pool houses and parks. Not with anyone but him. But for Ben, it was natural beyond the point of expectation. Natural enough that it didn't require thought. That it made it easy to forget this summer was a coincidence of circumstance, that our paths had crossed in the oddest of ways before diverging in other directions.

Maybe that should've made me sad. We didn't have to be in a relationship for me to know a good thing was ending. But maybe it was one of the many things that seemed to be wrong with me because I didn't have any sadness about this being my last time with Ben while I was lying there in his arms. It was all good.

Good memories.

Good feelings.

Good conversations.

And a weird feeling, a strange sort of excitement that he was getting to go off and do something he was so passionate about.

The sensation that I was *losing* something wasn't there. We'd always known about the time limit and that neither of us wanted more than what we were. And it wasn't like I didn't have other things in my life to keep me feeling full. Like sure, Ben's dick wasn't filling me anymore and no one could fill me quite the same way, but I had other people to—

Or did I?

I blamed the fact that I'd come so hard for the extra moments it took me to notice the hazy way JP had floated his way into my mind, bobbing into the path of my thoughts like a cloud instead of the out-of-control U-Haul that he was.

This wasn't how it was supposed to be. JP was supposed to be a good time. He wasn't supposed to be my date for a gala. We weren't supposed to cancel dates for each other. I wasn't supposed to be his confidant, someone holding his hand and waiting for whatever stormy thing was unsaid behind his eyes to come to light.

Neither of us were supposed to want *this*, like what I was doing with Ben. JP and I were supposed to be fuck buddies who met each other at the same level of horniness and need and, honestly, skill level, because I was pretty confident in saying that I was at *least* as good in bed as JP was and—

"Want to tell me one of the seven million, nine-hundred-and-ninety-nine thousand, nine-hundred and ninety-seven things on your mind?" Ben murmured.

I half-laughed, but it came out a bit more despairing than I'd intended. "How am I supposed to pick one?"

His arms tightened around me. "Pick the one most relevant to where you are right now."

"It's nice being held," I said.

"It is," he agreed.

"Why?"

He chuckled. "What do you mean, why?"

"Like, why... do people want to cuddle after sex? When he knows—I know—when I know it's just a casual thing?"

If Ben caught my slip up, he didn't call me out on it. "Psychologically speaking, it makes sex more satisfying."

"Seriously?"

"Mm-hmm. Obviously in traditional monogamous relationships, you'd consider it increasing the bond between partners. But even in situations like ours, it comes down to the endorphins experienced post-intimacy. Instead of being a measure of increasing connections in a relationship, it's more of a relaxing indulgence." He chuckled again. "Honestly, if we could cuddle with ourselves after masturbating, we probably would."

"So it means nothing," I said. "My body just likes being touched."

"Something like that." He shifted, his head twisting so he could look down at me. "Is that, ah, a... problem?"

I buried my face against his chest. "Not right now."

Ben's body stiffened. "Nellie, you know this can't—"

"No," I said quickly. "No, not *this*. Like, not that you're not great, but I know what this is. That hasn't changed."

"Okay," he said, not sounding entirely convinced.

"I mean it's not a problem right *now*. Like not... not with... *you*."

The statement seemed to hover above us as he realized what I meant. The tension faded from his body and he didn't say anything else as he pulled me in closer.

And honestly, it was a testament to how well Ben had gotten to know me. Because while anyone else in the world might have pressed me to say more or guessed at what I meant or told me it was okay to change my mind even though it *wasn't*, he said nothing.

He just held me and let me process what I'd just said out loud, along with the seven million, nine-hundred-and-ninety-nine thousand, nine-hundred and ninety-five other things on my mind until the room was dark and I was roused from half-sleep by a kiss pressed to the side of my head.

"I would love for you to stay," he whispered. "But I know you like to sleep in and my flight is first thing in the morning. I have to be at the airport at five."

"Rude," I murmured. "You could've taken a later flight, you know."

He chuckled. "Had I known you would make this the summer of a lifetime, I would've. But I booked this flight in April."

Ben only pulled a pair of jeans on while I got dressed, so he was still shirtless when he walked me to his apartment door. After I put on my shoes, there was a moment where we just looked at each other.

Then his face broke into a smile and we reached for each other. I squeezed my eyes shut, listening to his heart thump steadily in his chest.

"Thank you," he whispered, his voice muffled by my hair. "For this. All the conversations. The absolute pleasure it was getting to know you."

"No problem," I whispered back, because if I spoke any louder my voice might come out watery and I couldn't have that. "Thanks for all the orgasms."

He laughed as he let go of me.

"Take care, Ms. Belanger," he said.

"Goodbye, Professor Cameron."

Chapter Twenty-Two
I'll Cross That Bridge When I Get There

My phone vibrated to wake me up the next morning. Groggily, I pulled it off the nightstand, hoping maybe it was a selfie and a goodbye text from Ben.

Then I realized I was stupid because Ben's flight had taken off three hours earlier and we'd agreed that things were over and also, it was Anne-Marie.

Annie

> Remy's coworker Jorge mentioned he was looking for a ticket to the Diamond Gala

I groaned, closing my eyes again, then told myself I needed to text her back and reopened them.

I wish I could've said it was because I finally decided to be the bigger person, but it wasn't like Anne-Marie knew I was trying to be the bigger person. But the Diamond Gala was only a couple of days away and if Anne-Marie thought I'd been avoiding her to keep the secret of who was taking me, she'd think there was even more going on than there actually was.

Not that I was ready to *tell* her that secret. I'd cross that bridge when I got there, even though Anne-Marie was doing her best to cast a line off the riverbank near that bridge in her hunt for details.

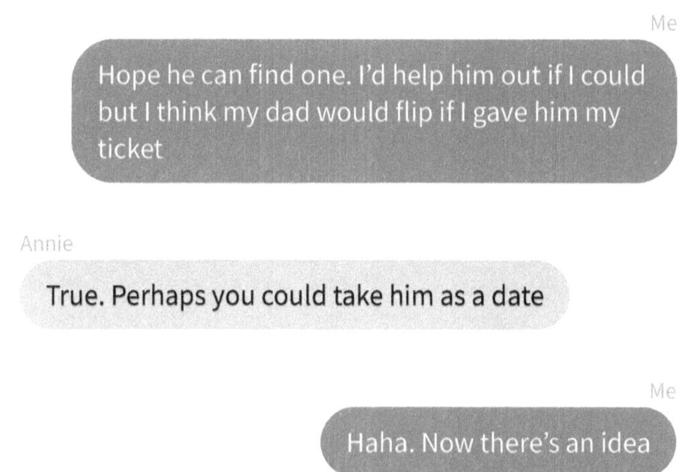

It wasn't the best response on my part since it opened the door nicely for her to ask why I couldn't take Jorge or who I was going with instead, but maybe Remy was too chivalrous when it came to opening doors for her or something because Anne-Marie didn't even try to turn the knob.

Though she knocked on the metaphorical door again a few hours later, and the next day, and again after I'd arrived in Montreal on Thursday afternoon since my dad had insisted I come to town two days early so he didn't have to risk me not showing up.

The answer to that was technically no, since I'd already had a date the last time I saw him. But it was also yes, since... well.

I hadn't heard from JP since that night. That wasn't exactly weird, but part of me was worried he'd changed his mind. I kept trying to tell myself that was unfounded, that JP wouldn't do that to me, that the whole... *whatever* that had happened last time wouldn't be enough for him to decide I wasn't worth helping anymore. Just because everything had gotten weird and deep and serious didn't mean he was going to back out on me.

And if he was, well, that was another bridge I'd cross when I got to it.

Except when I'd arrived in Montreal earlier that day, I'd glanced at the Marchands' driveway for no reason other than that it was there and noticed a certain BMW parked in its usual spot for no reason other than it *wasn't* there.

Which, like, wasn't a big deal. It was Thursday afternoon and he was a fancy lawyer with a day job and clients and shit, so he was at work.

Probably.

Except, I told myself after bringing my suitcase to my bedroom, that bridge was *really* going to fuck me over if it turned out it had collapsed before I got there. And then I'd be scrambling to build a raft or a swinging rope or *something*, scrambling at the last minute just like Anne-Marie said I always did.

So to spite her, even though she had no idea I was doing it in the first place, I flopped onto my bed and pulled out my phone, then thought for a minute or eight before messaging him.

I sent it, cringed, and quickly typed a second message.

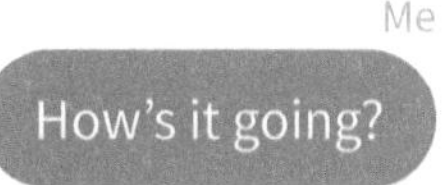

He saw both messages almost immediately, which was good, and when the bubbles appeared to show he was typing, I let out a tense breath.

Bastard

I'm trying to figure out the professional way to tell a client to stop fighting with the other party via redlines on the contract instead of scheduling a fucking phone call to discuss why a termination for convenience clause is even necessary, since I am not, in fact, a fucking babysitter and doing another round of redlines just so they can be sassy is, in fact, a waste of their fucking money.

Yikes.

JP wasn't shy about swearing, but three "fuckings" in one text message made it sound like he was a *little* on edge. Maybe that meant it wasn't the best time for me to badger him about Saturday.

Or, I thought, twisting my mouth to the side, maybe it was the best time.

Me

"While I understand the desire for my involvement in the base-level discussion for what necessitates a termination for convenience clause, it would be unconscionable for me to not advise that this is both outside my scope as legal counsel and an inefficient use of your retainer. This matter would best be discussed via phone call prior to redlining the contract a fucktonillianth time."

He read the message right away, but the typing bubbles didn't appear before his response of five laughing emojis came through.

Bastard

Not doing much to convince me you weren't born to be a lawyer, babe

My heart skipped a beat and my body felt about eighty pounds lighter when he called me babe. Not because he called me *babe*, which I'd told him not to do a fucktonillian times, but *because* he called me babe.

That had to be a good sign.

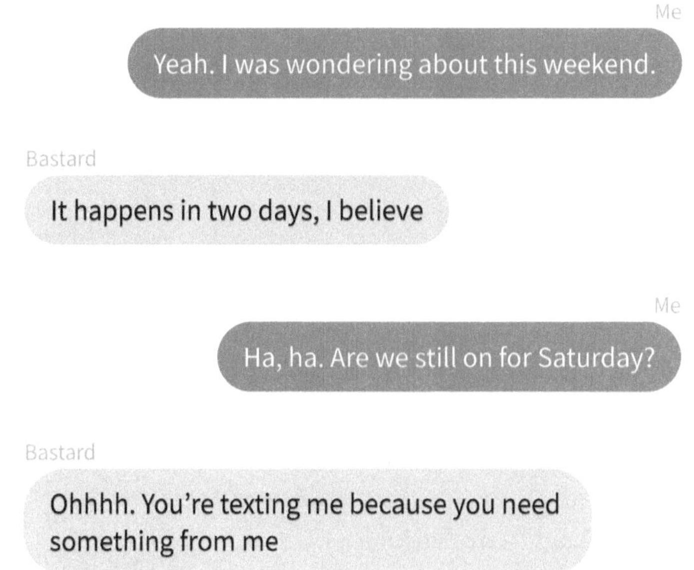

I chewed on my bottom lip, then propped myself up a bit so I could bend my left leg under my right knee and sit on it while I thought of my response.

The lightness faded and I bit my lip harder. Yeah, it could be hard to read tone over text, but that didn't exactly sound like playful teasing.

My stomach dropped like a rock.

No, not like a rock.

It fell like a bullet shot at the ground. Explosive and destructive and painfully loud, shrapnel bursting out around it in a blasting circle and making me freeze in place, staring at the phone with my heart in my throat and a stinging blurriness in my eyes.

Fuck.

Just... *fuck*.

He wasn't wrong. He wasn't right, either; I hadn't been giving him the silent treatment, but I definitely hadn't texted him the colour of my dress. In fairness, I didn't know what colour it was. I wasn't trying it on until later that night. But I could've messaged to check on him after everything that went down last weekend. It would've probably been the nice thing to do considering what he told me after the funeral.

But also, JP and I weren't friends.

We weren't friends.

Not like that.

Not at all, really, if he was going to do something like that to me. But there wasn't much I could do about it now.

Me

Alright. I understand.

I put my phone face down and flopped backwards on my bed, staring up at the ceiling.

This was it. There was no other option.

I wasn't sure if I should tell my dad right away. If I put it off, maybe Clinton would break both his arms and fall into the river before Saturday. There was a whole Friday to happen still, after all. Or maybe I could get Anne-Marie to tell me where I could find Ives Clement and see if he'd ever found an actual hitman.

Not that I'd hire a hitman to kill Clinton, per se, but maybe just... you know.

Break his arms a little.

And then take him swimming.

Beside me, my phone vibrated once, probably with JP telling me good luck or something. I ignored it as I reminded myself that two days wasn't a lot of time to find a quality hitman and that I wouldn't do well in prison.

Then it buzzed again, and again, like it was ringing.

Which it was.

I nearly dropped the phone onto my face when I saw the name Bastard flashing on the screen. Sitting up so aggressively I nearly punched myself, I jammed the phone to my ear. "What the fuck are you doing calling me?!"

"Great to hear your voice too, babe," JP said, chuckling.

"Ha fucking ha," I said. "Why the hell are you *phoning* me? What do you want?"

"Can't a guy call to get sworn at without having a reason?"

"I'm hanging up on you."

He laughed. "Okay, alright. I wanted to make sure you got my last text telling you I was joking before you went and did something stupid like tell your dad you need Clinton to be your date."

Joking.

He was fucking joking.

"You thought that was a good thing to joke about?" I asked.

"I mean... yeah." He didn't sound entirely confident, but still managed a laugh. "I was definitely joking, Nell. Of course I'm still coming on Saturday."

I gritted my teeth. It was a stupid fucking thing to joke about, but... well, I wasn't sure what would come from me pointing that out.

"You'll be at the event too, though, right?" I asked, trying to sound light-hearted.

"As long as you didn't ask Clinton the Fuckwit to take you."

"I didn't."

"Okay," he said. "Good."

"Is it?"

"Is it what?"

"Good?"

"Of course. I've gotta go through with it to get my end of the deal. And by my end, I mean your back end."

I made a noise of disgust, which made him laugh. "I thought you were at work."

"I am," he said through his chuckles.

"And that's how you talk to people while you're at work?"

"While my office door is closed, sure," he said.

I raised my eyebrows, surprised. "You have an office to yourself?"

"Once in a while, I lean into the nepotism," he said, but there was a hint of bitterness behind it.

"I mean, I might too, if it got me a private office."

"Yeah, well... it comes with a cost."

I picked at my thumbnail. "Right. Okay, well. If that's everything...?"

"One more thing, actually," he said. "I need you to be serious with me for a sec."

Shit. "Why?"

"Because we need to talk about something important."

Shit. "We do?"

"Mm-hmm."

I tensed. "Alright. What is it?"

"I need you to tell me the honest truth, okay?"

Shitshitshit. "About what, JP?"

"What colour is it?"

I blinked. "Huh?"

"The dress, babe. What colour is your dress."

The fucker. "Oh. I don't know."

He laughed incredulously. "How do you not know?"

"I haven't seen it. But I have a fitting tonight. I'll... I'll send you a picture."

"You better. And then send another one after you put the dress on, okay?"

"Bastard," I muttered, and hung up on him while he was still laughing.

Chapter Twenty-Three
Well, Well, Well, If It Isn't The Bridge I Said I'd Cross When I Got There

"Eleanor Belanger, how very *dare* you!?!"

My bedroom door burst open. I nearly toppled off the dressmakers' stool I had been given strict instructions to remain on by a seamstress with a thick Ukrainian accent and surprisingly nimble fingers. "Jesus *Christ*, Anne-Marie!"

Anne-Marie bumped the door with her hip, letting it swing shut. There was a look on her face like a mountain lion who had just discovered the door to the butcher shop was left open.

Which was, apparently, the look she took on when she was in full AMNN journalist mode.

"Details, *now*," she demanded.

"Details on what?"

"Do not play me for stupid, *chérie*!" She wagged a finger at me as she stomped across my bedroom. "You ask—*ow!*" She plunked herself in the accent chair that usually sat by my window, but leapt up when she realized the seamstress had been using it to hold her pins. "*Crisse d'ostie de tabarnak*, that hurt."

"Oh, damn. Are you okay? Maybe you should go—"

"Not a *chance.*" She wagged that finger again. "You asked my brother to be your Diamond Gala date and did not even *tell* me?!"

Ah.

Well.

If it wasn't the bridge I said I'd cross when I got to it bringing itself to me with a maniacal grin and a squeal of glee.

"I cannot believe you," Anne-Marie said, dancing in place, though I wasn't sure if it was because she'd poked herself in the ass with a bunch of dressmakers pins or because she was excited. "After everything, after *years* of telling you that you would be perfect for each other, you finally do this and did not even let me *celebrate* with you!"

"That's not—"

"Is this why you ignored me last weekend? Wait, no, start by telling me how you asked him. No! How? *How* did you make him *agree* to this?!" She gasped as though she'd had a sudden realization even though the entire thing had definitely played out in her head multiple times before she walked over. "Are you *together*?!"

"It's not like that," I said, even though it was sort of like that in the sense that Anne-Marie was basically asking if I was fucking her brother and I *was* fucking her brother. But I also wasn't about to tell her that, *or* tell her that I'd gotten him to be my date by agreeing to let him fuck me in the ass.

"Of course it is not, *chérie,*" she said, the smirk on her face making it clear she didn't believe a word I'd said. "Look at you. Look at that *dress.*"

Ugh.

The dress.

To be honest, it wasn't actually that bad of a dress: a bright turquoise Elie Saab design with one shoulder and a flowing skirt. It was a colour I would've never picked and a style I would've never chosen and made of silk, which I would have never worn, but it was a designer I liked, at least.

The thing was, it felt like the kind of dress people wore to hide their insecurities, and I didn't have those. Well, at least not physical ones. I had *plenty* of other insecurities, but the "worst" I felt about my body was indifferent, and that was to the few stretch marks on my hips and stomach that had appeared when I gained weight a few years earlier. I'd never been as slim as Anne-Marie or as athletic as Sydney, but after I stopped playing volleyball in high school and started university, I'd put some pounds on.

The thing was, I loved it. I'd known for a while that I was attracted to people regardless of their gender, and when it came to women, I'd *always* loved bigger girls, the soft curves and cute bellies and the way things *moved*.

So when I gained weight, all it did was make me more of my type, and I didn't see how that was a problem. I had no problem thinking I was hot because I was, and anyone who didn't think I should admit that could go be sad in a corner by themselves. The way my hips curved was hot and my breasts were bouncy and jiggly and hot and my thighs rubbed together because they were thick and strong and *hot*.

So I liked to dress to show that off. I liked clothes that fit tight, that highlighted my curves, that turned my ass to "a work of art," as JP had once described it. I liked stretchy running shorts and miniskirts and low-cut tops.

The dress Kimberlee picked, on the other hand, covered my cleavage and swished around my legs and hid all the parts of me I liked beneath flowing fabric.

But, I realized after I tried it on, it wasn't totally hopeless.

At least not yet, though I figured that would change almost as soon as the seamstress showed Kimberlee the things she was planning to do. Take in the waist a bit, shorten the shoulder strap, hem the whole thing so it skimmed the ground when I wore the strappy silver heels I'd picked to go with it.

When she got to the mid-thigh-high slit, I held my breath.

I figured it had been a mistake. That Kimberlee hadn't noticed that part and that showing off that amount of leg would go against the standards my dad had, which were higher than the slit in my dress. And like, *I* wasn't going to point it out to her, but the seamstress had to.

"And the height here?" the seamstress asked, taking the skirt and swishing it so Kimberlee could see how much leg was showing.

"What about it?" Kimberlee asked.

"She cannot wear shorts under," the seamstress said. "So her thighs will rub."

"Does that bother you, Nellie?" Kimberlee asked.

"Uh... no," I said.

"Then it's perfect," Kimberlee said without looking me in the eye.

Which was good, because it meant she didn't see my startled expression.

The seamstress nodded and had me turn in place so she could show Kimberlee the back. Kimberlee asked her to shorten the shoulder strap a touch more since apparently it was sitting funny under my other arm, but that was the only other change she made.

"Are you happy with it?" Kimberlee asked when I turned back around.

"Uh... yeah," I said, still surprised.

She smiled. "That's all that matters."

"Well, no," I said. "What matters is if my dad okays it."

Kimberlee practically brushed it off. "He will. If you are happy with the fit, I will go get him now to see how it looks."

I'd agreed to that, so she'd left me in the room with the seamstress and gone to get my dad from his office. Which, of course, was when Anne-Marie had burst in.

"*T'es ben chix, chérie,*" Anne-Marie said as stood, circling the stool I was standing on. "You are *glowing*."

"I'm not pregnant."

She ignored me. "This is the best dress you have picked for anything all summer and you expect me to believe it is not a *tiny* bit because of your date?"

"Yeah, I do," I said, trying not to sound icy. "Considering Kimberlee's the one who picked it."

She waved a hand again. "Sure, sure."

"She did."

"Mmm." She threw herself on the edge of my bed, bouncing a bit as she tucked her legs under her. "So. Details. *Now.*"

I stared at her, lips parted. "Why would you even want that?"

Her lips puckered in excitement. "So there are details?"

"Of course not," I snapped. "I meant if there *were*. But there aren't, because I'm not doing anything with your brother. It's not like that."

"You keep saying that," she said, her voice full of thoughtful consideration. "What is it not *like*, Nellie? Because it must be like something, then."

"It's not *like* anything. He's helping me out so I don't have to go with—" I stopped, glancing at the seamstress, who had been sitting on a stool nearby the whole time while we waited for Kimberlee to come upstairs and look at the alterations she'd pinned and who was currently staring up at the ceiling pretending not to listen. "—you know who."

Anne-Marie looked at the seamstress, then back at me with a frown. "Well, yes. But that does not actually explain why Jean-Paul agreed. I mean, when did you even ask him? I am assuming last weekend since it was only this week you were ignoring me—"

"I haven't been ignoring you."

"You responded to my messages with only an emoji three times and have not given me an ounce of information when I've asked about your date for this weekend."

"Because you never actually asked."

"Hmm," she said, her voice pitching high. "Because perhaps you did not want to admit I was right that you two are perfect for each other?"

"Because I was naked on his bedroom floor and heard you say I'm lazy and it hurt my feelings," was what my heart wanted to say, for some reason, and it felt like the statement was balled up in my mouth ready to be spat out at her. But somehow, I managed to keep it in.

"Maybe it's because I knew you'd respond like this," I said instead.

"Appropriately, you mean?"

"Insanely."

She cackled an insane laugh. "So? When did you ask him?"

I sighed. "Last week. After the funeral."

"You ran into him while he was out that night?"

I never thought I'd be thankful for Anne-Marie's interruption the previous weekend, but just then, I almost prayed to the same deities of lust and sex and vice I had before to thank them she'd burst into the room so I didn't give myself away. "Out? He was at your house all night."

Anne-Marie looked surprised that her clever little plan hadn't worked. "So you... went to see him? At my house?"

"Yes," I said. "Well, no. I went to your house to... to ask you for help." I said it as begrudgingly as I could. "I was panicking after seeing—" I glanced at the seamstress again. "After the funeral. And thought maybe you would have some ideas."

"You knew I was out with Remy."

I shrugged, trying to look miserable. "My dad had made a comment. I was upset and forgot. But JP was home. I told him what was going on."

Anne-Marie looked even more incredulous. "And he... offered to take you?"

"No," I said. "I asked. I was desperate and I knew he wasn't going and that my dad would be okay with him as a date."

She folded her arms. "That does not sound like him at all. What is Jean-Paul getting out of this? There must be something."

"Anal," was the answer that floated through my head.

"Nothing," was what I actually said.

Anne-Marie snorted. "The idea that my brother is getting nothing from this is laughable. If you are telling me a lie, you must work harder than that." She wiggled her eyebrows at me, grinning. "Are you lying to me, *chérie*?"

"I'm *not*," I said. "I just owe him a favour. That's it."

"Oh, like the favour Chantel did for him before *La Nuit Rose*?"

The base of my neck to the tips of my ears burned. "I have no idea what you're talking about."

"Are you certain?" She lifted an eyebrow at me. "Because if I remember correctly—and I do—*you* were the one who told me he went with Chantel because she su—ah! Hello, Mr. Belanger. Hi, Kimberlee."

"Anne-Marie," Kimberlee said, smiling as she led my dad into the room. "What are you doing here?"

"Oh, I popped by quickly when Nellie told me how excited she is about the dress you selected." Anne-Marie stood up. "It is stunning on her. But I will head home. I just wanted a preview of my *dearest* friend in her stunning dress. You know she is practically a sister to me."

Kimberlee looked at me. "You do like it, Nellie? I was so hoping you would."

Fucking Anne-Marie. I tried not to glare at her as she waved before gliding out of my room. "Yeah. Of course. I like how it has, uh, half the expected number of shoulders."

Kimberlee's smile widened and she looked at my dad. "What do you think, Max? It looks perfect on her, no?"

The way my dad proceeded to examine me gave me an exceptional amount of empathy towards horses. He circled the dressmaker's stool much like Anne-Marie had, only he did it like he was trying to determine an eighteen-character-or-less name to submit to the Jockey Club.

Beside him, Kimberlee watched, and beside her, the seamstress who had intimidated me into standing in place and not moving had her hands clasped together.

"Turn," my dad said, making a circle with his index finger.

"Which direction?" I asked flatly.

My dad's mouth tightened and the forked wrinkle appeared again. "Around, Eleanor."

Taking small, careful steps on top of the dressmaker's stool, I turned in place, rotating clockwise until I was facing away from him so he could see how low the back was. My shoulders tensed as I caught sight of him in the dresser mirror, only relaxing when he nodded brusquely.

"Good," he said. "Turn again."

Part of me wanted to make that another slow turn, since if I did, the skirt might not move as much and he might not see the thigh-high slit. Luckily, a much smarter part of my brain reminded me that Kimberlee was on the hook for this dress and if I hid it, he wouldn't notice until we were at the gala, where he would probably think I'd added it myself last-minute or something.

Which might have been her plan.

Maybe.

I still didn't know what Kimberlee's deal was, so I couldn't discount that she might be trying to make me look bad. It wouldn't be the first time one of my dad's girlfriends tried to pin something on me to make him hate me even more.

So planting my foot firmly, I didn't just turn.

I twirled.

The skirt flared out as I did a full three-sixty, then swished back around my legs as I halted myself and spun the other direction for a final half-turn to face him. Cool air and silky fabric brushed against my thigh as it peeked out. My hair bounced against my face, blocking my vision for a moment before everything settled around me.

The seamstress was staring at me with cautious excitement, like she was thrilled at how well her alterations had turned out, but was too terrified to say anything. That was likely because my dad's face was turning steadily redder as he stared at me.

Which meant he was pissed, just as expected. My eyes darted to Kimberlee, who I thought would be glaring at me for ruining her plan.

But her eyes were full of delight.

"*Parfait*," she said. "I thought of you immediately when I saw it, Nellie, and it is exactly as I'd hoped. Elegant, classy, and still brimming with so much personality." She blinked innocently at my dad. "What do you think, Max? I know it is a *bit* different than you requested"—I nearly snorted as she admitted to his *face* that she'd gone against his wishes—"but turquoise is much more on trend this season than pink or red."

My dad said nothing.

He set his gaze on her, not doing a single thing to hide his annoyance, but kept his lips pressed together tight. Kimberlee blinked prettily again, but there was a hint of a challenge in her soft smile. After a moment, my dad turned his eyes back to me, a muscle in his jaw tightening before he opened his mouth.

"Do another twirl, Nellie," he said.

It took me a minute to process that, since I'd been expecting him to say there was no way in hell he'd let me out of the house with a skirt slit that was higher than some of the miniskirts I owned. But once I had, I spun in a circle again, though not quite so extravagantly that time. Not that it mattered; the skirt swished the same way, my thigh peeking out as saucily as it did the first time, and when I returned to my starting position, my dad's mouth was tight again.

Then he took a breath through his nose, not so deep as to be an obvious deep breath, but enough that *I* noticed it, and let it out as he nodded.

"Excellent," he said. "You look lovely, *ma fille ange*."

What?

I... *what*?!

"Uh... thanks," I said.

He nodded again, a brisk, single jerk of the head. Kimberlee pressed her hands together.

"Wonderful," she said. "Nellie, you can get changed and give your dress to Oksana. Max, I was thinking for her hair—"

My dad didn't meet my eye again as Kimberlee explained the rest of her vision to him. He just nodded, not speaking, until she'd finished showing him the jewellery she'd selected and the small clutch purse she'd decided I would carry.

"You have thought of every detail," he said.

"Of course," Kimberlee said.

"Has Nellie thanked you for all your efforts?"

"Of course," Kimberlee said, the lie so smooth it almost sounded true. It wasn't enough to convince my dad, though, and he looked at me, unimpressed.

"Thank you, Kimberlee," I said.

"It was no problem at all, Nellie," she said graciously.

"And it will remain not a problem," my dad said.

The beaming look disappeared from Kimberlee's face. "Max—"

He ignored her and stepped towards me. "As a reminder, this is the exact dress you will be wearing on Saturday. No changes. None of your own 'alterations.' Do you understand?"

"Yes, Dad."

"You will do your hair as Kimberlee says. You will wear the makeup she recommends. You will not alter your appearance in any way before Saturday."

"My hair might grow about a millimeter by then," I said. "Will that be okay or should I ask for them to trim it before they style it?"

"Eleanor—"

"I was joking," I said.

He finally seemed to take my word for it and nodded again. "Good. You may get changed. I have to send a few emails and complete some paperwork, but once I am done, we will go for dinner together as I'd originally planned."

As soon as he left, the seamstress undid the zipper and I pulled the dress off. She took it and breezed out of the room without another word. The second I was alone, I grabbed my phone.

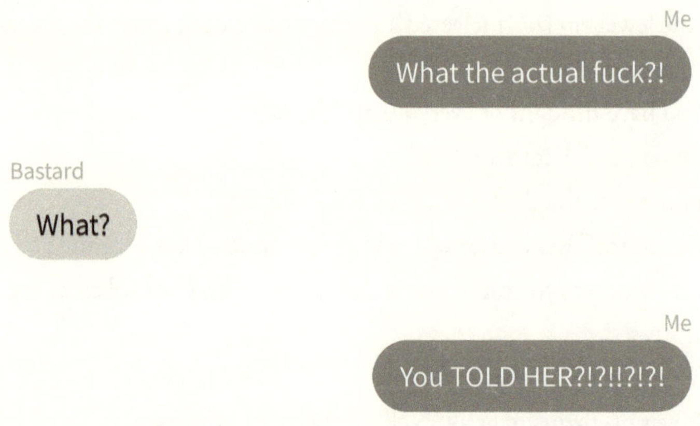

I didn't know what I was expecting, but it wasn't laughing emojis.

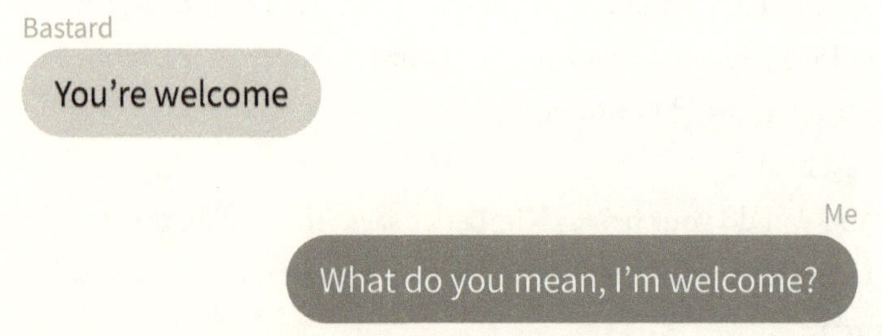

Bastard

You wanted her to find out when she saw us arrive at the gala together? You don't think she'd start picking names for our hypothetical babies and cause a scene that would make your dad lock you in a tower for the rest of your life?

I bit my lip, glaring at the phone for a minute.

Me

You could have at least given me a head's up

Bastard

But then I wouldn't have gotten another random text swearing at me and you know how much I look forward to those.

Anyways. You're welcome. For both things.

Me

Both things?

Bastard

Telling her, and then the quick thinking I just did when she burst into my room to cross-examine me about why I'd agreed to be your date and why I didn't tell her because someone didn't give me a head's up, either

Me

I was busy. She showed up while I was getting my dress fitted

Bastard

And yet somehow I still don't have a picture

Shit. I'd forgotten.

Me

It's turquoise

Bastard

I know. AM has put herself in charge of making sure my outfit matches yours because she doesn't want me to bring down how hot you look. She's debating between two ties right now. I think she's going to pick the striped one, which means I'll wear the monochrome one

Me

She's there now?

Bastard

Yep. So don't worry about sending me the dress pic.

I'll still take the other one, though

I rolled my eyes. I mean, I also stood up and went to my mirror, lifting my shirt so I could take a decent tit pic, but I was flipping off the camera while I was doing it.

Chapter Twenty-Four
A Perfect Gentleman

I REGRETTED ASKING JP to be my date the moment he arrived to pick me up for the Diamond Gala.

For one, I'd told him he didn't need to. He lived next door. I was capable of walking across the yard to his car, since he'd said he'd drive us.

For two, it was degrading to know my dad didn't trust me enough to pick a dress that wouldn't embarrass him at the gala, but trusted JP enough to believe he'd make sure I showed up to the gala instead of making the two of us share a town car with himself and Kimberlee.

Although, he made it clear that if I pulled something like not bothering to attend because he wasn't there to make sure I left, I could kiss my apartment goodbye.

Begrudging though it was, I had to admit getting out of going to the venue early was a relief, regardless of the reason. Kimberlee was on the board for the charity the Diamond Gala supported and my dad was giving a speech during the event because he donated a bunch of money or something, so they had to be at the venue early. At least this way I didn't have to sit around the hotel for any longer than I had to.

The doorbell rang at the exact time I said I'd meet JP on his driveway. Annoyed because I fucking *knew* it was him, I took my time touching up my lipstick. My hair and makeup had been done by the people Kimberlee hired to come over earlier in the day, but my dad's assistant, Pierre, had brought all-dressed bagels from Fairmont Bagel that morning along with a large pack of smoked salmon and a bunch of cream cheese. And yeah, there would be plenty of food at the gala.

But also, bagels.

So I'd helped myself to one before brushing my teeth so my breath didn't smell like salmon, and then fixed my lipstick because obviously I'd smeared it while both eating and brushing my teeth. Tucking the tube into the Kimberlee-approved clutch purse, I made my way down the stairs and didn't bother looking through the peephole before flinging the door open.

And fuck

Fuck.

I'd fucked up.

Because the third reason I regretted asking JP to be my date was now standing in front of me.

JP had always been good-looking. The childhood version of me would never in this lifetime admit to it, but had thought that the boy next door was the cutest thing I'd ever seen, even though I didn't know what to do with a thought like that until I was in my teens. He was the easy kind of handsome that just didn't seem fair. The golden hair, the blue eyes, even the single crooked tooth in his otherwise perfect smile because it meant you couldn't even write him off as plastic, as a Ken doll with an empty head or the result of thousands of dollars of plastic surgery.

He was real, and it was unfair.

Especially when you considered everything else about him. He wasn't a Ken doll anywhere else, either; I could definitely attest to that. He had money—too much money—and he was smart—too fucking smart—and I hated it.

I fucking hated it.

Because he wasn't just those things. He was also funny and logical and principled and thoughtful.

Because he represented the thing I was desperately trying to squirm away from.

Granted, he seemed to despise it, at least a bit. So at least there was that. Sure, it may be because he found galas and benefits boring or a waste of time. But there was that hint of resistance in him, too, that spark of displeasure with the way things were even though on the surface, he had it all. And along with that, the uncertainty of how to express how much it bothered him.

Because I had that, too.

I had the shame of complaining, of being unhappy, of crying because my dad threw out all my designer clothes and might not pay for my apartment and made me go to fancy parties. I had the shame of knowing there were people out there with bigger problems who would love to have *these* problems, who would love to play the golden child to get their tuition covered, who would have laughed at me for daring to wish for more.

Even though the "more" that I wanted was something you couldn't get with money.

The point was, JP was part of this. He was part of the lifestyle my dad loved. He was part of the back room business deals and corner offices that went to someone's son. He was part of the designer names and fancy cars and who-knew-who.

JP looked like those things. He came from those things. He was part of that horrible, shallow, deceivingly ugly world.

And he proved it wasn't all bad. It wasn't all ugly. It wasn't all plastic.

The man standing at my door was outlined by the glow of the sun behind him. He was wearing a suit that wasn't quite navy and wasn't quite royal blue with a cream-coloured shirt. His hair was pushed back from his face, though it wasn't overstyled, so it looked thick and natural as it caught rays of that golden sunlight.

Oh, and the tie he'd been so fucking worried about.

It wasn't the exact same colour as my dress, so it didn't look too high-school-prom. Instead, he'd gone with a slightly darker and more muted shade that complemented my dress perfectly and set off the blue of his eyes, making them pop even more. Small crosses were embroidered in the same colour thread to give it some texture, and the knot sat tied beneath his collar, so flawlessly knotted that made me want to yank it open and mess it up.

In short, *fuck*.

"I know I look good, but you're going to have to tear your eyes away eventually so we can get going," JP said. "You're already running late."

"Don't flatter yourself," I shot back. "I was trying to figure out how to ask if *that* was what you were really wearing or if you were planning on changing before we have to be seen in public."

He laughed, showing off the crooked tooth on the side of his mouth. "Is your dad still home?"

"No," I said. "The town car left a while ago."

"Good."

Before I could ask why that was good, he stepped through the doorway, lifting his hand in a smooth motion and cupping my cheek. A surprisingly heated kiss was pressed to my lips and I did my best not to melt. But if there was one thing JP was good at—besides the many things I had to begrudgingly admit JP was good at—it was making me feel like an ice cube clutched in a bare hand, layer upon layer turning to liquid and dripping to the floor until I was nothing but a puddle.

"We don't have time for this right now," I forced myself to say against his lips, though I couldn't quite pull away.

"For what?" He slipped a hand behind my back, pulling my body closer to his. "For kisses?"

"Mmm… yeah." It came out more breathlessly than I intended and my face burned. I pushed him away and glared up at him through my eyelashes. "I don't have time to fix my makeup again or wait around while you try to get rid of an inconvenient boner."

"You wouldn't help me with said inconvenient boner?" he asked, feigning hurt.

"What's in it for me?" I asked dryly.

He laughed again, then leaned in for one more kiss, giving me plenty of time to push him away before his lips met mine.

And I didn't, of course.

"You look good, Nell," he murmured, his voice low. "Really good. I can't wait to tear this dress off and fuck you in the ass tonight."

I shoved him away again and he cackled, catching himself before he stumbled into the door frame.

"Come on," I grumbled, turning to put my shoes on. "You said we were late already, so let's get this over with."

"The gala, right?" JP asked, holding his hand out so I could use it to balance as I shoved my feet into the heels I'd been told to wear. "Because I plan on taking my time with the anal thing."

Despite every effort, I couldn't hold back my laugh. "Yes, the gala, you fuckwit."

"Fuckwit!" He faked a gasp, then let go of my hand once I had both heels on and held his arm out in a way that was completely unnecessary given that no one was around to see us. "Careful now. Let me remind you which of us is getting fucked in the—"

"You're obnoxious," I said, taking his completely unnecessary arm so he could lead me to his car. "Anne-Marie is already suspicious. If you keep acting like this while we're there—"

"I won't," he said. "I'll be such a gentleman, babe."

"Off to a good start," I said with a fake sniff as we walked outside and I spotted his car parked in its usual spot on the Marchands' driveway.

"A gentleman wouldn't have made me walk across the lawn to his car in these heels."

"Hmm," JP said thoughtfully. "You're right. Should I carry you?"

I rolled my eyes. "You'd hurt yourself trying to lift me."

He scoffed. "I would not."

"Well, you might hurt me when you drop me."

"I wouldn't *drop* you, babe. You're not—"

"Don't say it." I lifted a hand, glaring at him. "I know I'm hot as fuck, but I'm not small, JP."

The smirk that played on his lips wasn't unexpected, but only because JP was smirking about eighty percent of the time. "I was going to say 'heavy enough for me to drop,' for the record."

"Whatever. You can't ca—*ahh*!"

JP let go of my arm and dipped, making me shriek as he lifted me into a princess carry in a single swift motion. An instinct I didn't know I had, having never been fucking *carried* before, scrambled to clutch at him, but I missed his shoulder. Instead, my fingers wrapped around his perfectly tied tie and succeeded in messing it up like I'd wanted. Flailing, I kicked my legs, and my left heel went soaring about ten feet down my dad's driveway and thunked against the side of my Honda Civic.

JP then proved my point about not being able to carry me, though it wasn't because he dropped me. He just started laughing so hard that he had to put me down, nearly doubling over once I was back on solid ground and trying to steady myself despite being three inches taller on one side than the other.

"What the *hell*, JP?!" I hissed. "You can't just *lift* someone!"

"I just did," he chuckled, reaching up to fix his tie before going to get the shoe I'd kicked off. "Though next time, I'll probably do a fireman's carry so you don't strangle me while launching shoes all over the neighbourhood."

"Bastard," I muttered, but I doubted he heard me.

He bent over to pick up my heel and brought it back, but instead of putting it into my outstretched hand, he dropped to his knee in front of me. I barely had time to be unsettled before he was lifting the hem of my dress, only then noticing the high slit that revealed my left leg.

"Hmm," he said, tracing a finger up my bare leg from my ankle to my knee. "This might be convenient."

"You need to stop," I whispered, though the trail of goosebumps beneath his finger said otherwise. "What if someone's watching?"

"Everyone's gone already." He moved his hand back to my ankle, guiding my foot up with one hand so he could slip my heel on it with the other. "Your dad and Kimberlee left ages ago. My parents are staying at the hotel, too, so they checked in this morning and are getting ready there. Anne-Marie went to Remy's to get ready. And Marc-Andre went on a bender at one of his friend's cottages this weekend." He leaned in, eyes flicking up as he pressed a kiss to my thigh. "It's just you and me, babe."

And anyone in the neighbourhood who was looking right around then, I wanted to add, but the words were caught in my throat and didn't make it out of my mouth before he rose to his feet.

"So, should we try this again?" he asked, reaching for me, then snickered as I batted his arms away.

Thankfully, he seemed to think it was because I was annoyed with him, and not because the sheer delight of having someone pick me up like that had made my legs wobbly. Because if he did it again, there was a very good chance we'd have to fuck in the backseat of his car before getting to the gala and I did *not* have time for that.

"I can manage myself," I snapped, starting towards the Marchands' yard.

"I thought you wanted me to be a gentleman!" he said, following me.

"Yeah, at the *gala*."

"Oh, thank God," he sighed from behind me. "I was wondering how I'm supposed to be a gentleman when I shove my dick in your—"

"For fucks' sake," I grumbled, and JP dissolved into laughter again as I stomped away from him.

He caught up once we were on the driveway, jogging slightly so he reached the passenger door before me. He didn't make another smart-ass comment, so I didn't give him shit for opening it for me, and flipped the visor down so I could touch up my lipstick again as he walked around the car and got in.

Neither of us said much as we started driving. It wasn't until I'd put my lipstick away and we were turning out of the neighbourhood that JP cleared his throat.

"So," he said. "We haven't really talked about last time."

Fuck.

"What about last time?" I asked as nonchalantly as I could.

"Shit got a little intense," he said.

"I mean, if you consider that intense, I guess."

He sounded amused. "You don't?"

I kept my eyes facing straight ahead, staring at the road in front of us. "I've had intense...r."

That earned me a chuckle. "Okay. Well, even if it wasn't the intense-iest thing you've ever experienced, I wanted to make sure we're cool."

"I'm cool," I said. "You, on the other hand, are a fucking nerd."

From the corner of my eye, I saw him grin. "That means you're fucking a nerd, then."

"So? I fuck pretty much anyone. You're not special."

He laughed harder. "Seriously, though. I'll take that as a yes, then?"

I pressed my lips together, picking at the side of my thumb. "I mean, yeah. I'm okay. If you're okay."

"I am, yeah."

"Okay. Then... great."

"We're cool?"

"We're cool."

There was a weird sort of beat there, something that was relieved but still heavy with awkward tension.

"I do, uh, want to say thanks, though," JP said.

I wasn't sure I liked the seriousness in his voice. "For what?"

He cleared his throat, turning his head to glance out the driver's window before looking forward again. "For, ah, letting me tell you. About... him. Sam. And just being around that day."

"Oh," I said. "Um. No problem."

"Seriously," he said. "It meant a lot."

"It's really okay," I said. "I mean, you're welcome, but it's not a big deal."

"It is, though," he insisted. "At least to me. I don't think I've ever had someone do that for me before or ask to hear more about him and I wanted you to know I appreciate it, okay? Because it's... it was... nice."

I tapped my foot nervously in the wheel well. "Stop it, JP."

"Stop what?"

"You're talking like things aren't cool."

Something about my voice made JP glance at me, which I only knew because I saw his reflection in the windshield as I kept my eyes glued to the front of the car.

"Oh," he said, and his voice lightened. "My bad. I mean, I wanted to say thank you for working so hard on not sounding like a bleating goat when you come. I noticed a marked improvement over the last time, so—"

"Oh my *God*," I groaned as he started laughing. "You're a fucking nerd."

"Not currently," he said. "Right now I'm just a nerd, but later, when I've got my dick buried in your—"

"JP!" I nearly shouted. "Oh my God. You can't act like that when we get there. You promised to be a gentleman."

"I know, babe." He reached over, putting a hand on my thigh and squeezing. "Don't worry. I'll be a *perfect* gentleman."

Chapter Twenty-Five
Oops

JP WAS A PERFECT gentleman in the same way that a rectangle was a perfect square.

As in, it might be able to fool a few people since all squares are rectangles.

But not all rectangles are squares, and JP... well.

JP was JP.

The Diamond Gala was the event of the summer. It was held in the ballroom of a large historic hotel downtown and was the epitome of glamour. All of the stuffy, pompous elitists who had been at all the other galas and benefits and luncheons and fundraisers practically battled for tickets to this one. They flocked here, making it the most ostentatious of the displays. It was the last opportunity of the summer for them to puff out their chests and display their plumage and open their wallets not to help whatever the actual cause of this event was—which I couldn't have told anyone even though Kimberlee was on the charity's board—but to show off how thick the wads of cash inside were.

Women wore dresses in every colour, though there was a serious divide between the ones embellished in beads and sequins and details embroidered in gold thread and the ones in simple, straightforward gowns that screamed money only because the label on the inside had an impressive name on it. Many of the older men wore tuxedos while the younger ones opted for suits in various shades of pitch black and grey and blue, some with the occasional hint of texture or a pop of colour in the tie. The scents of expensive perfumes and colognes clashed together in the lobby, mixing into a smell that reminded me of the cheap perfume stores at the mall that left a dizzying cloud for people to walk through.

I hated it.

But not as much as I hated that JP was the only saving grace.

Because he might not have been a perfect gentleman, but he knew damn well how to play the game. He knew how to poke fun at the situation, how far he could push things without dropping off the edge of too far, which was something I'd never gotten the hang of since I was there, with him, after doing just that.

And given that he disliked these games just as much as I did, that made him dangerous in the best way.

"Do you need to stop at the coat check?" he asked when we first walked in.

"Do I look like I'm wearing a coat?" I asked.

"You can check other things in a coat check," he said innocently. "Umbrellas. Bags. Panties. Hats."

"You can't check panties into a coat check," I muttered.

"Are you saying you've tried before?"

"You're an assho—" I cut myself off as his eyes flicked up in eager anticipation of the setup. "Bastard. You're a bastard."

"I might've been premature, but my parents were married when I was born six months after their wedding," he murmured.

I frowned. "Wait, really?"

"Mm-hmm. I was a healthy, hefty ten-pound 'preemie.'"

"Jesus. So you've been wrecking vaginas since day one, then."

JP's bark of laughter turned way more heads than I'd intended, but none of those heads belonged to my dad, so I didn't quite mind.

A few minutes later, he took my arm to escort me through the doors and into the ballroom. It was already full of people milling about as servers dressed in all black wove between them, some with trays of hors d'oeuvres or champagne. I figured that between getting one up on him with the comment on his mom's vagina and the fact that we were now at the actual gala, JP's sass would disappear.

Of course, I was wrong.

"I am glad to note you have corrected your posture, *Mademoiselle* Belanger," said Madame Vivienne Villeneuve, who had come over to admonish me for taking a glass of champagne off a tray before my date took one for himself. My parents had sent me to her for etiquette lessons when I was eight or nine because that was the trendy thing for parents to do that year. She was a petite woman whose stick-straight spine was rivalled only by her stick-straight hair, the ends so even and severe it seemed like they'd cut through the scissors instead of the other way around.

"Thank you, Madame Villenueve," I said.

"Mostly," she continued. "You do not seem to have quite grasped the correct angle of your chin, of course, but it seems you've learned to keep your shoulders back, finally. Especially given the additional weight in the front."

"Sure have," I said, pretending not to notice the jab at my weight or let on that my posture correction was a result of trying not to jump when JP went to put his hand on my lower back, only to place it *much* lower than my back.

As in, low enough that his fingers were playing in the spot where my legs met my ass cheeks, his palm warm against the curve of my ass as I tried to keep a straight face.

Thank God we were standing in front of a tall, black-linen-clad cocktail table so no one could see behind us. Or Satan, since that table was the only reason JP had done it.

Madame Villenuve pressed her lips together, her nostrils pinching themselves closed in disapproval. "The correct verbiage would be 'I certainly have,' if you would like to speak so casually."

JP shifted as if he was about to take his hand away, but froze when I pushed my hips back and leaned into him.

"Of course," I said. "My apologies, Madame Villeneuve. I'm rusty on some of the specifics."

"You should consider a refresher," she said curtly. "Especially as etiquette for young ladies is much less forgiving than it is for children."

JP's finger traced up my ass crack and I smiled brightly. "I will certainly keep that in mind. I would hate to cause any offense."

"Hmph," she said, snuffling as disappointment flashed through her steely, beetle-like eyes. "Well, hopefully your posture has improved enough to make up for the lack of speech etiquette. I seem to remember you had some resistance to sitting still with your legs properly positioned. I had better luck with most of the boys in my little gentlemen's class keeping their ankles crossed than I did with you."

"That is definitely not the case anymore, Madame Villenueve," JP said before I could respond. "Nellie is exceptionally adept at keeping her legs closed. When she wants to, that is."

He pinched my ass hard and I let out the most proper laugh I could, despite wanting to double over at the look on Madame Villenueve's face.

"Bastard," I muttered, finally taking a sip of my champagne after she walked away a few minutes later.

"Me?" he said, feigning offense as he set down the flute of champagne he'd finished while I was stuck talking to Madame Villeneuve. "What did I do?"

"Your hand is *still* on my ass."

"I mean, you practically sat on it mid-air to keep it there."

"Oh, and it's my fault that you started groping me in front of my former etiquette teacher?"

"Well, I had to see if any of the lessons stuck," he said.

I twisted my head to look at him, eyebrows raised. "And you think they teach you how to keep a straight face when someone's grabbing your ass in social etiquette lessons?"

He hesitated, then grimaced as the realization dawned on him. "Ah. Yeah. That came out—"

"Horribly? Offensively? Crudely?"

"It may not have been my top jokes, that's for sure."

"And considering how bad some of your jokes are, that's saying something."

The corners of JP's eyes crinkled. "Don't worry, babe. I'll make it up to you later tonight when I top your—"

"Don't even, JP," I said, though I was trying not to laugh.

"Alright, alright. I'll stop, but"—he squeezed my ass one last time—"and it's a big butt—"

I couldn't help it. I laughed, half-snorting as I tried to suppress it, and JP grinned broadly.

"Oh, you seem to be having such fun, *chérie!*"

Anne-Marie floated up to us looking like the kind of person Madame Villeneuve would have been proud to say was a former student. She was dressed in a blue gown that had a slight train, delicate ruffles making up the flowing skirt. Drop sleeves circled her biceps and her hair was twisted in a complicated-looking updo, drawing attention to the long line of her shoulders and neck. Her arm was looped through Remy's, who was wearing a black suit paired with a shirt in the same shade of blue as Anne-Marie's dress. He'd gotten braids done since I'd last seen him, cornrows with larger braids in straight rows paired with smaller curved ones that wove between them.

"Hi Anne-Marie," I said as JP moved his hand off my ass. "Hey, Remy."

He nodded at me solemnly, then at JP. "Good to see you both."

Anne-Marie shot me one of her maniacal smiles, white teeth nearly gleaming in the soft light of the hall. "You are having a good time then, Nellie?"

"Depends on your definition of 'good,' I guess," I said dryly.

It didn't seem to deter her. "And you, Jean-Paul? You are treating my dearest friend as wonderfully as she deserves?"

"I'm ensuring she makes the best use of her *assets* to impress everyone," he said.

If I could have, I would've kicked him. Instead, I tried to change the subject to the one thing I figured Anne-Marie wouldn't be able to resist. "Have you heard anything interesting tonight?"

"Oh, have I!" she said, letting go of Remy's arm and clasping her hands together gleefully. "Did you know, I saw that woman again. The one we saw at the Harmonies for Hope Benefit and who joked about the cunning linguists?"

"The what now?" JP asked interestedly.

"Nothing," I said, knowing she meant Claire. "She's still in Montreal? I thought she said she wasn't from here."

"She's not, but I have it on good authority that she will be part of these events a bit more commonly now, because you will never guess who she is," Anne-Marie said.

"Who is she?" I asked.

Anne-Marie grinned. "Guess, *chérie*."

"You just said I'd never guess. How am I supposed to—"

"Nellie," said a voice from behind us.

It was pure instinct that drove my shoulders back, pulling my spine straighter as if I'd been caught doing something I wasn't supposed to, even though I hadn't. Beside me, JP put a hand on the small of my back, not so much to guide me but as a comforting sort of support as we turned.

"Hi, Dad," I said as he and Kimberlee joined us.

He nodded curtly before looking at JP. "Good to see you, Mr. Marchand."

"And you, Mr. Belanger." JP extended his hand, shaking my dad's firmly before extending it to Kimberlee. "Ms. Dunn, you look lovely. Nellie told me you were involved in the planning for tonight?"

"I was, yes," Kimberlee said, smiling. "It has always been one of my favourite events, but I am feeling extra fond of it this year."

"Why is that, Kimberlee?" Anne-Marie asked.

A look that I wasn't sure I'd ever seen crossed my dad's face as Kimberlee glanced up at him.

"Well, of course, this is where Max and I met last year," she said. "So it is even more special than it usually is. To me, at least."

My dad nodded in agreement.

"That is so sweet," Anne-Marie said. "Don't you think so, Nellie?"

"Of… course," I said.

"And perhaps you will end up with a similar fondness for this event," she said, a hint of lunacy returning to her smile as she glanced from me to JP.

"We're here as friends," I said, trying not to sound exasperated.

"Which is surprising, if I'm being honest," my dad said. "Pleasantly, of course. I wasn't aware the two of you were such close friends. Although, Nellie, you could certainly do far worse than Mr. Marchand here."

I almost snapped.

Almost.

His approval alone would have been enough to make me tell JP the deal was off, that I was done, that I'd find a new apartment to live in because I'd rather sleep in my car than have my dad think JP and I should get together. On top of that, saying it in front of Anne-Marie, whose eyes brightened like she'd just been handed a magical book that contained every scandal that existed in the world and told she could keep it?

Un-fucking-forgivable.

But JP's hand was still on my back. It was still there, connecting me to the ground and stopping me from blurting out something I couldn't take back. So I bit back the urge to set my life on fire and smiled.

"You mean like Clinton Thibault?" I asked, then took a sip of my champagne.

Kimberlee winced. Anne-Marie tried not to look like the magical book of scandals also came with a bonus audiobook that she would be the first person to ever hear. My dad stared at me, nothing changing on his face except how dark his eyes seemed.

"Well, it has been lovely seeing you," Anne-Marie said graciously. "But you will have to excuse us for a moment; I have spotted someone I have been meaning to catch up with all summer."

As she and Remy escaped the awkwardness of the situation, JP shifted casually beside me.

"Well, I appreciate you saying that, Mr. Belanger," he said, his voice smooth. "It certainly is surprising how deeply I've gotten to know Nellie, but I can assure you we're just friends. There's no need to worry about me sneaking in the back entrance."

The bastard.

The funny fucking *bastard*.

"Well, there's no question that you're a trustworthy young man," my dad said as if JP wasn't going to be sneaking into his house later to fuck his daughter in the ass. "Certainly with a sense of prudence that I am sure Jean-Luc is grateful for at his firm."

"Thank you, sir," JP said.

My dad waved a hand. "It is not something to thank me for. Any parent would be appreciative of a child with such a developed sense of judgement and practicality."

"Max," Kimberlee said softly.

Because of course my dad had glanced at me when I said it. Of course he was standing there implying I was a disappointment compared to perfect golden boy JP. Of course I wasn't supposed to respond, just allow myself to be subtly chastised before reflecting on my life choices and what I could do to make my dad proud of me.

So I decided to kill two birds with one stone, as it were, and try to get out of the conversation while getting back at JP.

I just used a little stone, though. My dad might never forgive me if I did the first thing I thought of, which was to "accidentally" spill the rest of my champagne on JP's suit and then escape to the bathroom.

But the small cocktail napkin they'd handed me when I took my champagne was still in my hand, so I let go of it and watched it float to the floor.

"Oops," I said. "How clumsy."

"Oh, let me—" JP started, moving to pick it up.

"I've got it," I said, quickly stepping a half step in front of him and bending over in one quick motion.

And yeah, the dress Kimberlee had picked didn't cling to my ass the way I would've liked it to, but that didn't matter. Partly because JP seemed to like my ass no matter what was covering it, and mostly because after grabbing the napkin and standing up, I stumbled backwards, nudging my ass against his pelvis. JP steadied me, which was great because it gave me another moment to rub against the front of him.

"Oops," I said again as I used his bicep to steady myself. "Gosh, I'm clumsy today."

"And you're not even a full glass of champagne in yet," JP said, his voice hoarse.

Perfect. That was one bird.

"Hmm," my dad said, unimpressed before looking at JP again. "Well, certainly you are well-suited for your career. Your father mentioned you've been doing well in your role. He says you're working in contracts and negotiation?"

JP nodded distractedly. "Yes, for now."

My dad raised his eyebrows. "For now?"

JP blinked, bringing his focus back to my dad with a smooth smile. "Well, yes," he said. "We never know what the future holds."

"Certainly, but I imagine there are few alternatives open at a firm like Jean-Luc's," my dad said. "So unless you are intending to work with another firm, I do not see how it could be a 'for now' type of position."

Shit. Apparently the stone had hit both birds, but also summoned a much larger, much more agitated bird attracted by something JP clearly hadn't meant to let slip.

"Of course," JP said, his voice still casual even though I could sense the tension rolling off him. "But there are always plenty of opportunities to expand my knowledge and skills in ways that would be more, ah... beneficial. To the firm."

My dad looked skeptical, but nodded. "Well, as I am certain Jean-Luc said the plan was still for you to step in as managing partner one day, I suppose that would be advantageous."

JP nodded, Kimberlee said something that redirected the conversation far more effectively than my bend-and-shove-my-ass-at-JP moment did, and a few moments and a couple of pleasantries later, my dad and Kimberlee excused themselves. JP and I watched them disappear between designer gowns and crisp suits. JP still had a confident look on his face, but a muscle in his neck was taut and for once, he was quiet.

Shit.

"What did you mean, for now?" I asked.

"What?" he asked, keeping his voice even.

"That's what's bothering you."

He didn't answer right away, but his jaw tightened as he stared in the direction my dad had walked off to. After a moment, he sighed.

"I don't know many people who went to law school intending to sit around and review contracts all day," he said. "I wanted to make a difference."

"So then go make a difference," I said.

He laughed, but didn't have its usual warmth. "Thanks, babe. Couldn't have figured that one out myself."

"You don't have to be a dick about it," I said.

He finally looked at me and if I didn't know any better, I would've said something apologetic flashed across his face. I did know better, though, and decided I was seeing things.

"Right," he said, his voice curt. "I don't. And I didn't have to come here to be your date and put up with all these questions while you're trying to distract me, but for some damn reason, I did anyway."

Well, clearly I'd been seeing things, because he was *definitely* a dick about that. I tried not to let his words hurt, but there was a sting behind them I couldn't ignore. JP seemed to realize it as I turned and took another long sip of my almost-finished champagne.

"I just mean instead of bending over and shoving your ass in my crotch so I was busy trying not to get hard in front of your dad, you could've poured your champagne on my shirt so we could've escaped the conversation all together."

"We?" I asked dryly. "You don't think I would've still been stuck here talking to them?"

His tongue poked out and his eyes flicked down. "Why should I do all the clean up when you're the one who spilled it?"

My face was guarded as I looked at him. He stared back, one eyebrow raised. Without a word, I held out my almost-empty champagne flute. I paused and when he didn't so much as move, I tipped it forward, letting the final mouthful spill down the front of his shirt.

"Oops," I said again.

Chapter Twenty-Six
Messy Little Princess

"You know, you're fucking unfair," JP whispered.

"I thought we agreed you're a nerd," I said.

His laugh vibrated against my lips as he worked the slit in my skirt up to my panties, shoving the fabric to the side before using his lower body to press me against the wall.

"That would require you to be fucking me," he said, nipping at my bottom lip. "Instead, you're pressing your ass against me in front of everyone so all I can think about is how I'm going to stretch it open with my cock in a few hours, making all these lewd comments and teasing me—"

"Oh, of course, *I'm* the one making lewd comments," I joked as he used his knee to nudge my thighs apart. "I'm the one constantly reminding you about how hard it's going to be for you not to nut in ten seconds like a fucking chump because my tight little virgin butthole is gonna choke the tip of your cock and—"

"See? Exactly like I said." He pushed his hips forward, his voice a low growl. "You're fucking *unfair*. This whole night, I've had to look at you all prettied up in your fancy dress with your gorgeous hair and flawless makeup like you're one of these perfect little princesses."

He buried his head against my neck and bit down, making me gasp as the sensation of his teeth sent shockwaves bursting through me. "I'm n-*not* a princess."

"Of course you're not. But I'm supposed to act like you are. Like I don't know what you look like on your knees with my dick halfway down your throat. Like I'm not going to mess up your hair and smear your goddamn lipstick all over your mouth as soon as we're alone."

He bit my neck again, then brought his hand to my chin and held my head in place as his eyes bored into mine, dark and eager and despite everything he was saying, safe.

I never felt like I wasn't safe with him.

"But we both know this makeup's gonna run down your face when you're crying out because my cock is stretching your cute little asshole *so* wide and you're coming so hard you can't even remember your name. Don't we, babe?"

"Yes," I breathed, captured by his eyes and responding without even really thinking.

"Fuck." He let out another dry, choked groan. "How am I supposed to behave like a gentleman when you've got me hard as a fucking rock, Nellie?"

The hardness he was referring to was pressed against the thin fabric of my panties, though it was still restrained by JP's suit pants. I made a soft noise, then slipped my tongue into his mouth. He groaned, his cock throbbing so intensely I could feel it through the layers of fabric as he ground it against me, using my body to relieve some of his need.

The Diamond Gala had been held at this hotel every year for as long as I could remember, and while I didn't go every year, I'd been to plenty of them in the past. That meant that while I knew the bathrooms we were supposed to use were right outside the foyer to the ballroom, there was a single-stall accessible bathroom at the top of a staircase with no elevator nearby—which was obviously the best place for an accessible bathroom—down a hall that led the opposite direction of the ballroom.

Unfortunately, that bathroom had been out of order and locked up, so JP and I were in a small alcove around a dark corner, praying that no one would venture this far down. It sucked since I'd been planning to sit on the bathroom counter while he fucked me—flexible as I was and strong as he was, standing and fucking me against a wall came with a serious risk of messing up my dress, whether by crumpling it or tearing it or dripping cum on it because there was so much fucking fabric to deal with—but I figured I'd go down on him and if we had time, he could finger me until I came.

"Maybe you should let me take care of that," I said, moving to unbutton his pants to free the hardness he was blaming me for.

"I thought you were here to help clean up the drink you spilled on me," he said, his hands joining mine.

"Are you trying to talk me out of playing with your dick?"

"Nah, but if you're gonna make a mess of me... maybe I should make a mess of you."

I raised my eyebrows, intrigued. JP smirked, kissing me one more time before unzipping his pants, then nudging my hands out of the way so he could grab the waistband of my panties and tug them down. I bit my lip to stifle a moan as he stuck one of his fingers between my folds, a pleased noise escaping along with a smile as he realized I was already soaking wet for him. He rubbed, spreading that wetness along my lips, then took his hand back.

"What are you doing?" I mused as he pulled his cock out of his boxers.

He didn't respond, instead guiding his cock forward and holding my panties down so he could push his cock past them. I stifled another noise as his tip brushed against my clit, then let out a shaky exhale when he pushed between my folds. Using my waistband to keep himself pressed against my pussy, he thrust forward, both of us struggling to keep our noises restrained as his shaft slid between my lips. He pulled back and I grabbed his shoulder, steadying myself when the ridge of his crown dragged along my clit and sent an electric quiver shooting through me.

Then I dug my fingers in, clenching my jaw to keep from crying out when he shifted. He thrust forward again and my legs shook as his entire length dragged along my clit.

"Fuck," he breathed, shuddering as he paused with his pelvis pressed to mine. "This is more unfair than anything."

"What is?"

"That this—" He pulled back and his voice caught, forcing him to squeeze his eyes closed. "How?"

"How *what*?"

"How does fucking you like this feel better than most of the other women I've fucked?" He shook his head and his voice dropped to an almost introspective whisper. "I'm not even *inside* you, Nell."

I bit my lip, heat rising up my spine and spreading across my collarbone at the same time that it pooled in my stomach. Tilting my head back against the wall, I focused on the sensation building in my core, starting from that place deep behind my pelvis and growing each time his cock caught the sensitive nub aching for release.

He wasn't wrong. I couldn't pinpoint what made it feel so good. Maybe it was the circumstances or the boiling tension or the angle that we were rubbing together. Maybe it was the way I rolled my hips to grind against his shaft or the heat of it, the way he throbbed between my legs, the head of his cock sliding past my entrance as he fucked between my thighs.

Whatever it was, it didn't matter. It was fast and hard and carnal and even though I was pretty sure he'd thought he was doing this for himself, I pulled JP forward, squirming against him and whispering in his ear that I was about to come.

"Fuck yeah, you are," he hissed. "Come for me, babe. Come for me so I can come for you. And you know where I'm going to do it?"

"My mouth?" I guessed.

"Mm-mm." His teeth grazed against my neck. "I'm gonna come in your panties. Then I'm gonna watch you walk around the rest of the night talking to all the other princesses like you down there with your cute little panties full of my cum."

"No," I breathed.

He lifted his head, an eyebrow raised as he slowed his thrusts. "No?"

I shook my head, struggling to keep myself from moaning as I moved my hips, urging him to start again. "I'm not a princess."

His eyebrow lowered and a smirk played on his lips. "You don't think so?"

"No." My voice shook and oh, God, I was so fucking close it almost hurt, balancing on the edge and not quite being able to fall over it yet. "I'm—"

I choked on a moan and JP lifted one of his hands, letting it hover over my mouth but leaving just enough space for me to whisper to him.

"You're what?" he urged, pushing his cock against me. "If you're not a princess, what are you? Tell me, babe."

"I'm a slut."

The word fell out of my mouth almost thoughtlessly, almost breathlessly, almost like it had been waiting there to be said for so long, I'd forgotten to notice it. It came out quiet and needy and powerful, a vocalized whimper as much as an unspoken demand and a bashful request.

Because for some reason, something about that heated, all-encompassing moment had sent me back to that conversation with Sydney a few weeks earlier. I wasn't sure what, exactly, was making me think of something she'd mention as part of a humiliation kink. I mean, JP constantly made fun of me and I didn't think it was *hot*.

Or did I?

No.

No, I didn't. I didn't want him to humiliate me. I wanted him to say it more than I wanted anything in that moment, but not because I got off on him making fun of me.

I wanted him to say it because it was *him*.

Because it meant the same thing to him that it did to me.

"I'm a s-slut," I repeated, my eyes squeezing shut. "I'm a messy slut who's letting you use my pussy to jack off and fill up my panties with cum and fuck me in the ass later."

JP's mouth twitched, his eyes dark with what I thought at first was need, but his hand moved out of the way and he covered my mouth with his.

"You're both," he said, his voice almost a growl. "My perfect, messy, slutty little princess."

Of those final six words, two were correct.

I was messy.

I was slutty.

But I wasn't a princess.

I wasn't perfect or little.

And I wasn't *his*.

I should have been more concerned about that, but my body didn't seem to give a single flying fuck about it because before I could even process the whole "my princess" part, JP's hand was clamped over my mouth to cut off the high-pitched whine forcing its way out of my throat. Leaning forward, he kissed my neck as my orgasm hit.

I writhed, hips bucking as I used his cock to extend my bliss, his hand muffling the moans I was desperate to let out as my legs shook uncontrollably. As soon as the overwhelming pleasure faded, I sagged against the wall he'd pressed me against, letting a heavy breath out against his palm. He took his hand back and reached down immediately.

"Watch," he demanded, and I looked down as he wrapped his hand around his cock and dragged it up. I nearly jolted as he pressed the tip between my folds right at my clit, the oversensitive nub throbbing almost painfully from the unexpected stimulation. He started jerking himself hard and fast and I'd barely caught my breath when he shuddered and came, hot ropes spilling against my pussy, dripping down my folds and leaving an absolute *mess* in my panties.

And I wasn't mad about it.

Not one bit.

I was still watching when he wiped the head of his cock against my mound. Neither of us said anything or even looked at each other as he tucked his cock back into his boxers. Before zipping up his pants, he reached forward and hooked his fingers in the waistband of my panties, and it was only then that I glanced up. JP didn't; he kept his eyes down as he pulled my panties back up. It wasn't until he let my skirt drop down, the fabric swishing around my legs as the hot stickiness of his cum coated my pussy, that he looked up at me.

"Thanks," he said. "That was much needed."

Oh, good. We weren't talking about what he said.

"Very," I said.

He reached forward, wiping his thumb along the edge of my lower lip. "You're gonna need to fix that."

"I figured." I reached forward and wiped a smear of lipstick off the side of his mouth. "You're gonna need to clean that up."

He smirked. "So are you. Because I hope you know I'm still fucking you in the ass later."

"You better be."

He blinked, surprise flashing through his eyes. "What?"

I pressed my lips together, trying not to laugh, but it was futile. "Come on. Clean up so we can get back. Someone's going to notice we're gone and you *know* chances are that'll be Anne-Marie."

Chapter Twenty-Seven
Don't Fake It

"And where were you, *chérie*?"

Anne-Marie gave me a pointed look as JP and I walked up to the table she was sitting at with Remy.

"What do you mean, where was I?" I asked as JP pulled a chair out for me. I went to sit down, then hesitated when I remembered my panties were soaked and wondered if they'd leave a mark on the skirt of my dress, but figured the lining was thick enough to hide anything that might leak through and sat.

"Oh, I simply mean no one seems to have seen you for a significant amount of time," she said, her voice light enough that it almost masked the predatory demand for information. "I thought you and Jean-Paul were up to no good, perhaps."

"Jesus Christ, Anne-Marie," I muttered, my face going red.

"*Au contraire*," JP said, his voice smooth as he sat beside me. "Nellie was up to plenty of good."

Anne-Marie's mouth twisted in excitement. "Was she?"

My heart hammered in my chest as I looked at JP, trying not to let the betrayal show on my face. "Was I?"

"Of course." He slung his arm casually on the back of my chair. "Nellie spilled some of her drink on my jacket and insisted on helping me clean it up. I'd say that was pretty good of her, wouldn't you?"

Anne-Marie didn't seem to buy it. Her eyebrow flicked up in skeptical disbelief and she folded her arms. "That seems like the kind of thing Nellie might tell you to do your damn self, regardless of who spilled it."

Damnit. She was right about that.

"She did," JP said. "That's the story, anyway."

"I knew it." Anne-Marie's grin widened to Cheshire Cat levels. "And the truth?"

JP glanced to the left and right before taking his arm back and leaning across the table as I prayed he knew what he was doing.

"The truth, dear sister, is that I saw Clinton floating around," he murmured loud enough for the four of us to hear. "So I didn't want to leave Nellie unattended since the whole reason I'm here is so she doesn't have to deal with him, isn't it?"

Anne-Marie glanced at me, then sighed. "Yes, that is true, Jean-Paul."

Thank God.

"I just thought perhaps that *finally* you two might get together so I could stop hassling you both," she continued.

"Anne-Marie!" I said, my face turning red. "What the hell?"

A casual, easy smirk crossed JP's face and he sat back, putting his arm around my chair again. "Don't worry, sister. I wouldn't do something like that to you. Your friends are firmly off-limits."

"You're so full of shit," I murmured when one of Anne-Marie's other friends came up and distracted her a few minutes later. "How many of her friends have you fucked?"

"Like six," he muttered back. "But you're my favourite."

I tried not to snort. "Sure I am."

"You think I've fucked any of her other friends more than once?"

Before I had to answer, we were thankfully interrupted by a tall, slim woman wearing a tailored tuxedo folding herself into the chair next to me.

"Well, well, well," Claire said loudly. "If it isn't my weakness."

I burst out laughing. "Hey again. You're becoming a regular at these things."

"I know." She sighed heavily. "What a fucking chore."

"They aren't that bad," Julie said, pulling out the chair next to Claire and settling into it. "At least you've made friends."

"That might be my reminder that I'm allowed to think you're funny, pretty, and curvy, but in a friends sort of way," Claire stage-whispered, her eyes darting to JP. "So your boyfriend doesn't have to worry."

"He's not my boyfriend," I said.

"Not her boyfriend," JP said at the same time.

"They aren't together," Remy also said in unison.

"Not yet," Anne-Marie added in a sing-song voice.

Claire let out one of her horrific laughs. "Oof. I stumbled on a nerve, apparently."

"Not a nerve," JP said warmly. "We're friends and I'm here as a favour to Nellie, despite Anne-Marie implying otherwise." He stuck out his hand. "JP. Nice to meet you."

"Claire," she replied, shaking his hand firmly. "And my fiancée, Julie."

"It is *so* good to see you again, Claire," Anne-Marie gushed, and I finally noticed that she was practically vibrating with excitement. "And I hope we will be seeing more of you, too. My friend Bella said you are coming to Montreal permanently?"

Claire's expression shifted, not quite enough to be obvious but enough that I saw the hint of tension that wasn't there before.

"Possibly," she said. "We're not divulging any specifics yet."

"Oh, of course." Anne-Marie waved a hand. "Forgive me. I just know how honoured so many people would be to have you in attendance."

"Right," Claire said, though the smile on her face was forced.

"We'll see what the future brings," Julie said with a gracious diplomacy that confused me even more. "Of course, we had to check out tonight's event since everyone talked about how extravagant it is. A few of our friends even came to town to enjoy it with us."

"I certainly hope we get a chance to meet them, as well," Anne-Marie said. "I imagine they must—"

"Anne-Marie, there you are."

If Anne-Marie wasn't as good at covering her emotions with socially acceptable manners, she probably would have screamed in frustration at the interruption. Instead, a practiced and patient look graced her face as we turned to see Michele, the curvy redhead I'd seen at the funeral and who JP had cancelled his date with so I could sneak into his bedroom, sidle up to the table.

"I need to speak with you," she said pointedly.

"Right now?" Anne-Marie asked.

Michele's eyes flicked towards me and JP. "Mm-hmm."

"Hi Michele," JP said pleasantly. "Good to see you. I appreciate you being so understanding I had to cancel last week when I was sick."

"Not enough to call, apparently," she said.

"Alright," Anne-Marie said brightly, clapping her hands together as she stood to interrupt the obvious tension. "Excuse me, everyone. Remy and I will be back shortly."

Remy got up and followed Anne-Marie and her friend dutifully. Once they were gone, Claire sighed again.

"She's one you have to watch out for, isn't she?" she asked.

JP snorted. "Oh, absolutely."

Julie looked amused. "You seem to know that well. Is she a former girlfriend or something?"

The laugh that burst out of me was so sudden and unexpected that I clapped a hand over my mouth. JP chuckled and shook his head.

"No, but she is my sister," he said.

Julie looked mortified. "Oh, God. I'm sorry."

"I'm not," Claire said, then winced like someone had just kicked her under the table. "Kidding. I definitely am."

"Don't be." JP waved a hand. "But you also don't need to worry. She's not interested in corporate espionage or anything. More like who's dating who and what their ex thinks of it."

Claire nodded, though she still looked suspicious. An awkward beat of silence passed.

"Well, your makeup looks great tonight," I said, mainly because I couldn't think of anything else to say and since unlike the other times I'd seen her, Claire was wearing a rainbow eyeshadow look with a bold eyeliner and subtle glitter.

"Oh," Claire said, her voice dipping into disappointment. "Thanks."

Confused, I glanced at JP, who had a practiced, casual look on his face that did nothing to help me figure out what the hell was going on.

"Did you, um, do it yourself?" I tried.

Claire exchanged a look with Julie. "You think I do my own makeup?"

I wasn't sure if it was her tone or the implication that I might have said something stupid or just the impatience of not knowing what the fuck was going on, but annoyance flared through me. "I was just asking. I like the colours and thought maybe you knew what brand it was or something."

"What... brand?" Claire repeated incredulously.

The annoyance switched to aggravation. "Oh my God. Yes. Like what makeup brand you or your artist used because I like the colours. Yeesh."

"Nell," JP said, laughter in his voice.

"No, no, it's okay," Claire said, shaking her head. "You just, uh, confused me. It's fine."

"Okay," I said, also confused.

"I didn't do it myself," Claire said. "My girlfriend did it for me."

"Fiancée, you mean?" I said, looking at Julie.

"No," Claire said, twisting in her chair so she could gesture at a nearby table, where a chubby woman with wavy brown hair was sitting between two men. "My girlfriend."

"Oh, sorry," I said. "I thought you meant, like, a romantic girlfriend."

Julie looked amused, the corners of her eyes crinkling. "Wait until she finds out how you and Tess catch up."

I must have looked completely lost when Claire snickered because Julie finally took pity on me.

"She means girlfriend as in *girlfriend*," she said. "For a while they were girl-friends-not-girlfriends but when I got promoted to fiancée, Tess decided she wanted the title after all." She gestured at the woman again. "The guys she's sitting with are her partners."

I blinked.

Then I blinked again.

Then I practically whirled towards the table they'd been mentioning and studied the people there. This time, I noticed the man on the left, who had brown skin and dark brown hair, had his hand on the woman's thigh. And the man on the right, who looked almost too tall to fit into a standard gala chair and had shaggy blonde hair tied into a low ponytail at the base of his neck, had his arm around her chair... and his hand on the other man's shoulder.

"Wait," I said. "You're all fucking?"

Claire's crackling bark of laughter turned heads around us, but I didn't notice them.

"The three of them are partners," Julie said. "Claire and I are together. But Claire and Tess also hook up regularly."

"Don't forget that you and Tess also used to hook up," Claire added. "*And* your ex-boyfriend is one of her partners."

"Yes," Julie sighed. "It's all very complicated."

"And you just go out to events and stuff together?" JP asked, sounding amused.

"Not always," Claire said. "They all live in Vancouver. But my, ah… mother's been looking at business opportunities in Quebec and having an office here would make that much easier. Julie and I were only supposed to be here for a couple of weeks coordinating things but my mother keeps asking for more and more, so I figured I'd fly them out to see us. Plus it's a good way to see what the reactions would be like."

"Your mom doesn't know?" I asked.

"She does," Claire said. "And doesn't care at all. She's surprisingly accepting of things, especially as she's gotten older. But my sister is obsessed with appearances and business-wise, appearances matter, apparently." She rolled her eyes. "The things we do for family."

I half-laughed. "Tell me about it."

"I just did." Claire shifted in her seat and crossed one leg over the other. "But now you're going to tell me about it, because *that* sounds interesting."

"Not really," I said. "I'm mainly just at these things to make my dad look good."

"I see," Claire said. "What's your dad do?"

"He's a hedgefund manager," I said. "And also an asshole."

She let out a bark of laughter. "Relatable. My father was also a massive asshole."

"Yeah, well, did yours make you go to a funeral because he was trying to impress the life partner of the dead guy so she'd hire his company and then get mad at you for offering your condolences because she thought it was a total front?" I asked sarcastically.

JP's hand found my leg under the table, urgent and demanding. "Wait, Nell—"

"Shh." Claire held a finger up at JP, her eyes sparkling, and he hesitated, then nodded in concession. "This was the funeral last week?"

I nodded. "He's been trying to get in contact with this company all summer and I keep fucking it up for him, apparently. He was trying to meet someone at that other event we saw you at, but Sid Cunnilinginton the Third offended the creep who thinks he's entitled to be my date and my dad was dealing with that all night."

Claire nodded, then exchanged a look with Julie that I couldn't quite interpret before looking back at me. "Do you want to impress your dad?"

"Does 'yes and no' make sense as an answer?"

"As a fellow fierce babe with daddy issues, absolutely." Standing, Claire gestured for me and JP to follow her. "Come. Both of you."

"Well, I can try, but I can't usually do it on demand," I said.

"And I'm not sure how your fiancée or girlfriend will feel about that," JP said as he rose.

Julie rolled her eyes, but Claire snorted. "Are you two sure you're just friends?"

"Yes," we said, instantly and in unison.

She let out another offensive shriek of laughter, which thankfully seemed to distract her from the way I had to adjust myself because my panties were sticking uncomfortably to my skin because of JP's stupid cum.

"Nell, listen," JP breathed as we followed Claire, who was walking with a confident and quick stride, through the ballroom. "Be yourself."

I frowned, looking at him with confusion. "What?"

"When you meet her."

"*Who*?" I asked.

JP almost laughed, but he held it in. "Pia Martelle."

Pia—

"*What*?!" I shrieked in the quietest hiss I could manage. "No! Why... *how*?"

He shook his head. "You are so smart sometimes, babe, but other times..."

"Shut up." I glanced wildly ahead of me, my heart jumping into my throat. "My dad's going to be furious, JP. I can't—"

"You've already impressed her daughter," he said reassuringly.

"Whose daughter?" I asked.

JP pressed his lips together, drawing in a breath. "Pia Martelle's daughter. Claire."

Oh.

Oh, fuck.

Oh fucking *no*.

Now that JP had basically spelled it out for me, it made sense. Heat rose up my cheeks, embarrassment at it taking me this long to put two and two and two together and realize that Claire was the mysterious other Martelle sister.

That explained Anne-Marie's reaction and Claire's response to my question about her makeup.

And it also meant I'd insulted Claire's father to her face at his funeral.

Although apparently Claire had issues with her dad, too, and had also taken a liking to me, so now we were going to meet her mom because I'd also told her my dad was trying to get in with her mother *and* that he was a predatory asshole.

And now I was on my way to be introduced to the billionaire founder of one of the biggest cosmetic companies in the world in front of a gala full of people with my panties full of cum and no idea what to do.

But before I could tell Claire to stop, that I didn't want to meet her mom, that seriously, this was just going to make things worse because I was *not* good at making good impressions and my dad was going to lose his shit if I fucked things up even more for him, JP put a hand on my lower back, not so much to guide me as to steady me.

"Stop panicking," he murmured. "Be yourself."

"Except I suck," I breathed back.

"Yeah, and you're damn good at it." His hand moved in a small circle. "Trust me. I would know."

"Perv."

The corners of his eyes crinkled. "Listen. Just be genuine around her. Don't fake it."

I didn't have a chance to tell him that was a horrible idea before we reached a table near the front of the room surrounded by a group of people. Claire slowed, though she still walked confidently.

"Mother dear," she said cheerfully, and the group parted to let us all pass through, revealing the small frame of Pia Martelle sitting at the head of the table holding a flute of champagne that looked gigantic in her tiny hand. "I have someone you need to meet."

"Do you, darling?" Pia said, her tone almost bored.

"Mm-hmm." She stepped to the side, drawing me and JP forward. "This is Nellie and her date, JP."

Pia had eyes like a hawk, beady and predatory and aware of every detail around her. She set her gaze on me, so piercing I almost shivered.

"Nellie," she repeated. "You look familiar."

Crap. "Um, yes. I met—"

"Do you remember I told you about the girl who dressed up her date as a man and drew a mustache on him?" Claire interrupted.

"I do," Pia said.

"Same girl," Claire said.

Pia looked from me to JP. "Has she upped her game? This one seems more convincing than what you described. And he doesn't have a mustache."

"I didn't have the pleasure of being Nellie's date to that event, unfortunately," JP said.

"Hmmph," Pia said. "Too bad. I would've liked to see that."

"I can show you a picture," I offered.

She set her hawk-like eyes on me again. "Let's see it, then."

So that was how I ended up showing selfies of me and Sydney to Pia Martelle, who snickered almost immaturely as she examined them.

"Well, your technical skills leave something to be desired," she said, passing my phone back to me. "But you know damn well how to make a statement."

Somehow, I didn't feel insulted by her critique of my makeup skills, probably because she wasn't wrong. "Thanks, Ms. Martelle."

"And what was your name again, darling?"

"Nellie," I said. "Nellie Belanger."

Her eyebrows pinched together. "Belanger, eh? Any relation to that hedgefund manager? Max?"

Fuck.

"Yes," I said. "He's my dad."

"Mmm." She looked unimpressed and glanced at Claire. "Is that so?"

"Don't worry, ma'am," I said. "I'm not happy about it, either."

And then I heard the worst sound I'd ever heard in my life.

Pia Martelle's laughter was a mix of nails on a chalkboard meeting squealing Styrofoam meeting a fully booked transatlantic flight on its way to a colicky baby convention. The sound was *horrendous*, and even worse, it was loud. I wish I could have said I'd never heard anything like it, but the truth was, it was a more grating version of Claire's laughter, which joined the cacophony as Pia threw her head back in amusement.

"Well, I'll be damned," she chuckled. "Either Max Belanger copulated with the most beautiful clown in existence or the stick in his ass is actually holding in a sense of humour."

"Well, he did meet my mom at a circus," I said, which was a lie, but another peal of laughter scratched eardrums throughout the ballroom.

I wasn't sure if it was the first bout of laughter or the second or if someone just told him I was spotted walking around with Claire Martelle, but at least one of those things caught my dad's attention because Pia hadn't even stopped laughing when he pushed his way through the crowd around us.

"Eleanor," he said, his voice steady and even but his eyes cold. "Are you bothering Ms. Martelle?"

"Oh, lighten up, Belanger," Pia said dismissively. "Your daughter is a delight."

Holy *shit*.

I wasn't the only one who thought it; my dad looked stunned as Pia snapped her fingers and a handkerchief appeared there from an assistant who moved as undetectably as a ghost. She patted the handkerchief beneath her eyes.

"Thanks, Ms. Martelle," I said.

She waved a hand. "Call me Pia." She snapped again and the assistant reappeared. "Therese, schedule a call with Max Belanger to discuss those accounts he's been harassing me about."

"That would be wonderful," my dad said, and to anyone else, he probably sounded as smooth and confident and in control as he always did, but the way his eyes darted to me betrayed his shock.

"Well, if it'll get you off my back," Pia said, sniffing before she turned to JP. "And you."

"Yes, ma'am?" JP said.

"Take care of that girl," she said.

"We're just friends," I said, alarmed.

JP smiled good-naturedly. "I've always known she's out of my league, ma'am."

Pia snorted. "Well then, *when* you two get your heads out of your asses, hold onto her. You won't find another like her."

My face burned and JP looked amused, but another spine-tingling laugh from Claire kept us from saying anything more and when she stopped cackling, Pia turned her gaze to the next people vying for her attention. In the whirlwind of her dismissal, I thanked Claire and tried to apologize for what I'd said about her dad, but she waved it off. Moments later, I ended up a few tables away, JP standing on one side of me and my dad standing stiffly in front of us.

"Well," my dad said. "That was a pleasant turn of events."

"It was," I said.

He nodded stiffly. "I suppose I must say thank you—"

"You're wel—" I started to say.

"—Jean-Paul."

My voice fell to nothing.

"Pardon?" JP said.

My dad, oblivious to the fact that I was pretty sure my heart had fallen out of my chest and was squelching along the floor beneath my skirt, motioned towards Pia's table. "For facilitating that interaction. I'll be certain to mention to your father how helpful it was."

"I didn't do shit, Mr. Belanger," JP said bluntly.

My dad's eyebrows went up to nearly his hairline. Mine didn't, but only because I felt like I was made of stone, every atom of my being frozen in place.

"You do not give yourself enough credit," my dad said. "I have been attempting to meet with her all summer and—"

"And Nellie was the one who made friends with Claire," JP interrupted. "*Nellie* impressed Claire when she dressed Sydney up at the one event. *Nellie* cheered Claire up at her father's funeral. *Nellie* made Pia Martelle laugh like a possessed robotic magpie with the batteries running out. She's the one you need to thank. I had nothing to do with it."

A beat of tension thumped between us. My dad's lips were pressed in a line and his eyes were trained to JP.

Then he nodded stiffly. "You have my gratitude, Eleanor."

And without another word, he turned and walked away.

"God, your dad's a dick," JP said, no trace of a smile on his face as we watched him go.

"Are you kidding?" I forced a laugh. "I don't know if he's ever thanked me for anything. That was a huge milestone."

JP didn't say anything, just put his hand on my lower back again. I let it sit there for a moment so I could indulge in the warmth of his touch.

"Nellie—" he said after a moment, his voice so soft it made my skin prickle with pain.

"Come on." I shook his hand off. "I need more champagne to get through the rest of this shit show."

Chapter Twenty-Eight
Countdown

IN THE MIDDLE OF my dad's speech, my phone went off.

It wasn't loud or anything. I'd told JP to remind me to set it to vibrate before we got to the gala. Which meant he knew it was on vibrate when he texted me as my dad took the stage.

Bastard

We're leaving as soon as this is done, right?

Me

Yes

Bastard

Good. 60

I frowned at my screen, then glanced at JP, whose full attention was on my dad as he talked about... uh...

"—the importance of this event to maintain the cultural value of Montreal's heritage. Your donations mean the *Societe de protection de l'histoire de Montreal* can continue their hard work—"

...protecting Montreal's culture or something.

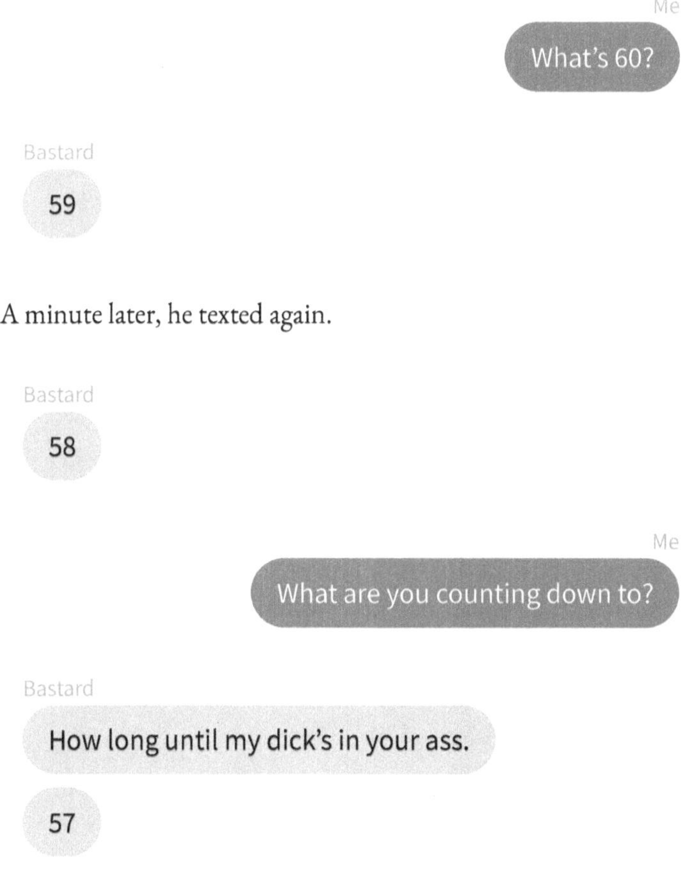

A minute later, he texted again.

I rolled my eyes and put my phone back in my purse. Beside me, the corners of JP's eyes crinkled.

I thought ignoring his messages would make him stop, but JP was dedicated to his countdown.

"Fifty-one," he whispered when we stood to applaud my dad's speech.

"Shut up," I muttered.

"Forty-six," he said after we said goodbye to Kimberlee, who promised to let my dad know we'd actually said goodbye to her before heading out.

"Forty-four," he said when we exited the lobby two minutes later. "Lucky you."

"How is that lucky?" I asked dryly.

"I miscalculated how long it would take us to get out of there. So I guess you get a bit more foreplay before I shove my—"

"We are in *public*," I hissed.

"Forty-three," he said.

He'd opted not to bother with valet parking, which ended up being good because we didn't have to wait in the lineup of people leaving, so it took less time than he'd expected to get his car.

"Let me get that for you," he said when we got there, moving past me so he could get the door.

My heart fluttered momentarily, a light feeling that almost made me feel sick because it was too romantic, too couple-like, too not-a-casual-thing for him to do.

But then he paused, used his body to push mine against his car door, and captured my lips with his. When he pulled back, I was breathless, and there was a grin on his face.

"Thirty-nine," he whispered.

"Are you counting to sixty each time or something?" I asked.

He just grinned wider. "Excuse me. I can't get the door for you when you lean against it like that."

Heat rose in my cheeks and I shoved him away. "Fuck you."

He chuckled, his lips brushing against my cheek as he opened the door for me. "Soon. In the ass. Remember?"

"No, I'd most definitely forgotten." I climbed in, continuing only after JP walked around the vehicle and slid into the driver's seat. "And are you sure that's what you want out of this? I mean, you haven't brought it up at all. I can't think of a time you mentioned anything even remotely related to fucking me in the ass."

"Babe, I want nothing more."

"Don't call me babe," I grumbled.

JP turned the key in the ignition. "Thirty-seven."

We didn't talk much on the drive back, but it wasn't a bad thing. Partially because it meant JP wasn't counting down every minute on the minute, but also because it wasn't uncomfortable. There was tension in the air between us, but it wasn't the same crawling, awkward tension that had come up at the gala when he said something he hadn't wanted to say in front of my dad. No, it was more of an excited, alluring, anticipatory sort of tension. More than once, I caught JP tapping his fingers against the steering wheel when we were waiting at a light, and there was definitely a bulge in his suit pants that betrayed just how excited he was about this.

At least as excited as I was. Because while I might not have the parts to make my pants bulge when I was turned on, I had to assume the light, aching, craving sensation in the pit of my stomach that wanted to urge JP to drive a little faster had to be pretty similar.

"Fourteen," JP said when he parked in his usual spot on the Marchands' driveway and turned off the car.

"You're pretty confident my butthole isn't gonna need a lot of prep, hey?" I asked as I opened the car door.

He chuckled as he followed me, but didn't say anything as the twin sounds of us closing our car doors echoed through the night. It wasn't until we'd stolen away to my dad's house, my heart racing as I opened the door and resisted the urge to creep up the stairs even though I knew he wasn't home, and reached my bedroom that JP spoke again.

The moment I closed the door, he pulled me in for a kiss. I tried not to melt against him, tried not to make a noise as he ran his hands down my sides and pulled my lower body against his so I could feel how hard he was.

"Eleven," he said.

"Mmm, about that..." I said.

Air puffed against my face as JP chuckled. "Oh?"

"You might need to reset your counter."

I felt the smirk on his lips. "Let me guess. You're backing out on me."

Both of us were probably surprised when that offended me. Him because he probably didn't expect it to; me because I didn't think it would bother me that much.

"Of course not," I snapped. "I just need a shower first."

"Oh, sure," he teased. "So you're procrastinating your way out of it?"

He tried to kiss me again, but I dodged his lips and wriggled my way out of his arms. "No, stupid. I want to make sure everything's clean before you stick your dick in my ass and I'm guessing it's going to take more than two minutes of foreplay for you to get me ready enough that you don't literally tear my asshole open."

For once, JP didn't have a witty response ready on the tip of his tongue. After letting go of me, I caught a moment of something on his face, which I thought was just surprise that I'd thought of something he hadn't. Whatever it was, I ignored it, ducking into the bathroom before he could recover and do something stupid like suggest joining me.

Which was only stupid because I didn't want to listen to him make fun of me as I put a shower cap on.

It didn't take me long to shower. I'd shaved that morning, so all I had to do was scrub myself down, spending a little extra time making sure I got all the cum JP had left in my panties off, and dry myself. I didn't even bother getting dressed, just wrapped my fluffy white bath sheet around myself, since it seemed pretty pointless to get dressed when JP was about to tear my clothes off again. Leaving the silk gown heaped on the floor,

I took my shower cap off and stepped back into the bedroom barely ten minutes after I'd left it.

JP was sitting on the edge of my bed. He'd taken his suit jacket off and set it beside him and loosened his tie, but surprisingly enough, was otherwise dressed.

"I thought you'd be naked by now," I said.

He looked up at me. The warmth of the shower faded all at once, my skin coated in ice and my feet frozen to the carpeted floor, as I saw the serious expression on JP's face.

"We need to talk," he said.

My stomach twisted, spinning around itself like the handles of a plastic grocery bag tightening painfully around a pair of fingers. "Talk?"

JP nodded, his throat flexing as he swallowed.

"Look, Nell," he started. He thought for a moment, then sighed before continuing. "I wasn't *joking*, exactly, about wanting to fuck you like that, but I wasn't serious, either."

"You weren't?"

"I already knew I was going to say yes. I was giving you a hard time, but when you agreed… I mean, I kind of ran with it because you surprised me. But while I might be an asshole, I don't want to be *that* guy. I don't want to be like him."

We both knew he was talking about Clinton. "Okay."

"I thought you were going to back out and I was going to tell you then that it was okay." He looked up at me with an expression that mixed a plea to believe him with disappointment in himself. "This doesn't have to happen. I would never make you do this, okay?"

Relief washed over me, strong enough that it must have shown on my face, but JP mistook its reasoning and grimaced.

"Fuck. See, I knew—Jeez, Nellie. I'm so sorry." He started to stand up. "I'll go. We're not—"

"Oh, we are."

I unwrapped the towel and let it fall to the ground. JP froze in an odd position, not quite sitting but not standing either. His mouth was still open, but it was round with shock for a moment before he shook it off.

"You just looked like you'd been given a last-minute pardon while on death row," he said bluntly. "There's no way—"

"Yeah, because I thought you wanted to *talk*," I said. "Like, talk-talk. Like 'We need to talk' kind of talk. And there's nothing for us to *talk* about like that."

It was a statement, not a question, and it was the truth. There was nothing for us to talk about because there was nothing between us that *needed* that sort of thing. But JP looked like he wanted to say something, so I continued before he could.

"You and I are... whatever. 'Friends,' sort of. That's it," I said. He nodded. "So I don't want to 'talk.' I *do* want you to fuck me in the ass. I mean"—I scoffed, shaking my head—"I was trying not to let on that I wanted it so you'd think you were getting something out of this."

"Seriously?" he said, amused.

"You know I haven't before. Did you think I *wouldn't* want to try it sometime?"

The amusement turned to a reluctant chuckle and he shook his head in defeat as he sat back on the edge of the bed. "I should've known."

"Yeah. You should've." I took a step towards him. "But if you don't want to—"

"I *never* said I don't want to," he said.

"Good." I took another slow step, then another. "Have you... ever? Done this before, I mean?"

His throat flex as he swallowed and he shook his head. "Not... really."

"What do you mean, not really?"

"I tried, once." He cleared his throat. "Like, with permission, obviously."

I hesitated. "What happened?"

"Nothing bad," he said quickly. "It just, uh, didn't work out. With that person."

"She changed her mind?" I took another step towards him.

"Something like that." He reached for me, even though I wasn't quite close enough to touch yet. "Have you ever done this?"

"Nothing except, you know. Fingers. Mainly with you." I moved a bit closer. "Do you know what you're doing?"

His arrogance shone through, a smirk playing on his mouth. "Don't worry, babe. I'll take care of you."

I let the pet name slide, mostly because another step brought me close enough that he could grab me. "Get on with it, then."

He slipped his hand around my hip and urged me forward, bringing me between his legs. His other hand reached up and cupped my cheek, guiding my face to his so he could press his eager mouth to mine. I made a soft noise as his hands moved, tracing up and down my body, caressing my waist and cupping my ass and feathering along my hips. After nipping at my lower lip, he pulled back, bringing his head down and taking my left nipple into his mouth.

"Fuck," I whispered, then steadied myself on his shoulders as my whole body trembled because he nibbled on the sensitive little nub. Then I cried out, almost shaking, as he sank his teeth in harder.

He kept up the attention on my breasts, licking and sucking and kissing, as his fingers explored my ass more thoroughly. They dug in as he squeezed it, then inched closer and closer to my crack. When one of his fingertips finally slid into the valley, he paused, looking up with wide eyes and my nipple still pressed to his lips.

"You're sure?" he asked.

"Ten," I said.

He frowned. "You're ten percent sure?"

"I want your cock in my ass in ten minutes."

Chapter Twenty-Nine
Shattered

TEN MINUTES WAS AN ambitious estimate.

"I thought you were sure, babe," JP teased as he pulled his finger out of my ass a few minutes later.

I whimpered miserably. "I *am*. I just..."

"You need to relax." He kissed my nipple, still holding me close.

"I'm trying."

And I had been. I'd been trying from the second he traced his fingers down to my pussy and realized just how *sure* I was. Which hadn't been hard when he'd dipped his finger inside my pussy to collect some of the wetness there and used it to work the tip of his finger into my ass, slipping it past the tight ring of muscle and inside me.

But once it was more than just the tip of his finger, I'd tensed up.

"I have a bunch of lube, you know," I said. "Maybe that would help."

"It will," he agreed. "But it'll work a lot better if you can relax a little more first."

Again, I tried focusing on loosening my muscles, but my body didn't want to cooperate. A frustrated noise escaped my lips and JP's other hand made a soft circle on my lower back.

"You're sure you want this?" he asked.

"I *do*," I muttered. "I just... I don't have many 'firsts' left and this is one of them. So I'm... nervous. I guess."

He placed a kiss on the side of my breast. "This coming from the girl who impaled herself on my cock before mentioning she was a virgin?"

"This coming from a girl who's gotten a lot smarter since then."

I felt him smile as he kissed between my breasts before looking up at me. "Look, it's probably obvious I'm an ass guy."

"You have always been an ass."

He smirked. "I've wanted to try this basically since discovering it was a thing. But I also don't do serious and I'd say most people want to do it with someone they're going to be with seriously for a while. I've learned a little more since the first time I tried it with someone and if you're willing to trust me, I think I can help you relax."

If I was willing to trust him. As if I didn't trust him completely already. "Okay."

He pulled me onto the bed with him, kissing me before directing me onto my stomach. I stopped only to reach over to the nightstand and grab the lube I'd bought to prepare for that night. Before standing to remove his clothes, JP grabbed a pillow and tucked it beneath my stomach, propping my ass up in the air, then slid off the bed.

I craned my neck to watch him undress. When he caught me looking, he grinned, slowing down the unbuttoning of his shirt.

"You can tip after the show," he teased, shrugging the shirt off his shoulders.

"Don't flatter yourself. I need something to watch while you get yourself organized and it's either you or the headboard."

He unbuckled his belt. "I'm better than the headboard? Careful, Nellie. I might start to think you actually like me."

"Yeah, well... you might have your moments."

His eyes lingered on mine for a second too long after I said that, but a moment later he was fully naked and neither of us addressed it.

He crawled onto the bed, bringing himself alongside me. Warm lips pressed to mine, his kiss weaving itself through my bones and curling around my entire body. After stealing my breath, his mouth left mine, moving first to my neck and then to my shoulder.

"You trust me?" he asked again.

"Only God knows why, but yes," I replied.

His chuckle vibrated against my skin and he shifted, moving behind me. I turned my head, but I couldn't really see him. I could feel him, though; his hands were on my back, tickling their way down my spine until he was touching my ass again. Then his lips followed, tracing the same path, his breath warm on the back of my neck and his tongue flicking out to trace the occasional lazy pattern along my skin.

I expected him to stop kissing me once he reached my ass, but he didn't. The first few kisses were just against the swell of my ass, but when his tongue finally dipped between my cheeks, my eyes widened and I gasped. His hands slid beneath my hips and pulled me up from the pillow.

"JP?" I whispered.

"You're gonna like it, babe," came the muffled reply.

And if the heat in my core was any indication, he was absolutely right.

"Okay," I said.

He groaned, and a moment later, he licked my ass.

He *licked* my *ass*.

I didn't relax immediately. Tension clutched at me, though it wasn't from fear or nerves or anything; it was like my body knew what was about to happen and tried to preemptively prepare itself. But JP's tongue circled my hole and he slipped a finger into my pussy, making me moan and relax into him.

"*Mmm*," I heard from behind me, and his face pressed against me harder.

I moaned, my pussy clenching around his finger, and he made another noise of approval before licking even more enthusiastically.

And just... *fuck.*

Between the pillow and his hand, I barely had to support myself, yet I still felt like I was going to collapse, maybe through the mattress and floor and crust of the earth itself. I'd never expected something like that to feel so intense, but every sensation in my body was stemming from where his tongue swirled against me.

He was eager at the same time he seemed to relish me with every lick. Maybe it was that, more than anything, that made my body shake and my stomach tighten and my legs tremble. Just the knowledge that JP Marchand was *licking* my *ass* and loving every second of it—

"JP," I gasped after way less time than seemed reasonable, and some deep-seated instinct made me struggle to prop myself up on my elbows like I knew I was going to need the extra support. "JP, I'm c-c-clo—*ahhh.*"

He wouldn't let me finish the word. Or at least, I was blaming him for it. Because as soon as I started trying to tell him I was close, he slipped another finger in my pussy and buried his face even harder against me. A moment after that, his tongue stopped lapping around the outside of my hole and dipped inside me.

In-fucking-*side* me.

"God," I choked, and he thrust it in harder or deeper or I don't know, I couldn't tell what the hell was happening because my eyes rolled back in my head. Or maybe I squeezed them shut. I had no fucking idea. My body was shaking and I clutched at my sheets, balling them in my fists as he tongue-fucked me, his fingers curling and stretching my pussy. My body was on fire as he kept licking, kept fingering, kept moaning against me until I wasn't sure if I'd gone blind or if my eyes were closed or if that was just what the back of my skull actually looked like because I was coming so fucking *hard.*

The orgasm consumed me so much that I barely noticed when JP took his fingers out of my pussy. I collapsed against the pillow and wouldn't have even registered the final kiss he planted on my ass except that it was lower than expected, right at the spot where my leg met my ass cheek. I was still trying to catch my breath when I heard him flip the cap of the lube open. I almost didn't notice the finger coated with cool gel pushing into my ass and only tensed slightly when a second one joined it.

By the time I regained some sense of what was going on, JP was fingering my ass slowly, but deeply. I sighed, relaxed as I pushed back against his hand.

"You okay?" His voice was hardly recognizable, aside from the dripping, craving tone that underlined each word.

"I'm okay," I whispered.

"Think you're ready?"

I didn't hesitate, didn't even think. "Yes."

He pulled his fingers out and I whimpered, not because it hurt but because the loss of sensation was disappointing, even though I knew something better was on its way. Shifting, I craned my neck to look over my shoulder.

JP wasn't looking back at me, preoccupied at that moment with pouring some of the lube into his hand. He was as hard as I'd ever seen anyone, his cock dripping with pre-cum. I licked my lips as he stroked himself, watching him spread the lube evenly along his length, and it was only when he paused that I glanced up and met his eye.

"You're so hot," he said.

"I know," I said.

A smile flitted on his lips, but there was an uncharacteristic seriousness on his face as he moved his hand to my ass and caressed it.

"I'm serious," he said. "Nellie, you... I don't think I've ever been this hard before in my life. I want you so fucking bad right now."

"Guess you better do something about it," I replied, and shook my ass for emphasis.

His eyes were trained to the sight in front of him like what was there wasn't real. "You're sure? Really, really fucking sure?"

"Yes."

"I'm gonna try to, you know… but it's probably still gonna hurt a bit."

"I know."

He almost shuddered, patches of pink on his cheeks as he looked longingly at me. His throat flexed and he grabbed the lube again, adding a bit more to both my ass and his cock.

"You'll tell me if it's too much to handle?" he asked.

"I will."

He apparently decided that I was as certain as I would ever be, and moments later my hips were lifted off the bed. I held myself up as he spread my ass cheeks, took a breath as soon as I felt his thick head pushing against my entrance, and willed my body to relax as he guided himself forward.

There was resistance. I couldn't control that, no matter how hard I tried to relax, so JP pushed his cock steadily forward. I took a deep breath, relaxing into the intense sensation of pressure as I stretched around him. All I could think about was the feeling, the way that ring of muscle was inclined to protest its penetration and the way I was willing myself not to let it. Further he pushed, and further I stretched, and just when it was almost too much, the tip of his cock was completely in.

He stopped, letting me adjust even though I could hear him breathing heavily behind me and practically feel his desperation to just let go and start fucking me. I knew he could feel how tight I was; *I* could feel how tight I was, how the head of his cock was completely enveloped inside of me. He was forcing himself to be patient, probably struggling to hold back, telling himself he *had* to take it slow, he *had* to let me adjust.

At least, he was probably telling himself that until I started pushing back.

"Nellie?" My name was strangled, a groan that had twisted into a plea. "Babe, what—"

He choked, still frozen in place, though his fingers were digging into my hips as I shifted further back. I was hyper-aware of his length, and after pushing another inch inside me, I had to stop and take a gasping breath.

"Babe," he gasped again. "Are you—"

"Yeah. I just need—" I sighed, content, then started moving again.

"Oh, *fuck*," he breathed.

"In a bit," I said, almost surprised by how dreamy my voice sounded. "Need to get it in first."

He couldn't hold himself still any longer, though he managed to take it slow. It was almost a lean forward, a gentle pressure increasing as he pushed inside me, despite his hands simultaneously pulling me back onto him. It took some time but inch by inch, he filled me, and I felt all of it.

It was intense. It was the only way to describe it. I was so full, so intensely full, and when JP's hips finally pressed against my ass cheeks and he was completely buried inside me, I whimpered.

"Holy fuck," he gasped. "Nellie, I'm... holy fuck."

"Yes," I squeaked.

When he pulled out, I nearly came. It was hardly even an exaggeration; the feeling of his cock sliding back out of me was relieving in a way that was consuming, yet when only his tip remained inside me, I wanted more.

"Again," I pleaded, and he made a noise that was barely recognizable as human.

"Can I go faster?" he asked after the next repetition.

"Thought you'd never ask," I said. "More lube first."

Another one of those strange, beautiful, deep sounds erupted from his throat. I couldn't see him, but I could almost hear his hands shaking as he squeezed another dollop of lube onto his cock. The thick tip nudged my hole again and he thrust inside me, just a bit faster than before, and pulled back out. I couldn't stop the high-pitched squeal that left my throat when he plunged inside me again, my eyes squeezing shut.

"Nellie?" he asked, half-groaning and half-concerned.

"Harder," I whispered.

"What? But—"

"*Harder*," I demanded.

"Babe—"

"God*damn*it JP, fuck my ass harder or I'll do it my damn self!"

"Fine," he said, and shoved his cock in.

And that was the last clear thing I remembered.

He fucked me hard. I knew that much, knew he was pounding my ass as hard as he'd ever pounded my pussy. He enjoyed every second of it, I knew that too. I knew each time he pushed his cock in me, I felt it, like my nerves were exploding from the sensation. I knew I felt full, achingly full, almost uncomfortably full, until he pulled back out and I craved it again, and again, and again.

My hand shook as I slipped it between my legs, fingering my clit as he took my ass. I cried out as I rubbed the swollen nub, my pussy soaking wet. After that, things melded together, a mixture of sensations and sounds and pleasure and gasping, breathless, amazing pressure.

There was a hazy moment where I realized I was going to come, and a clearer moment where I knew it was going to be like nothing I'd ever felt before. I pushed my fingers against my clit harder. Everything seemed to be happening with ten times more intensity than usual, and my legs started to shake hard enough that I thought they might break.

"Gonna come," I squeaked.

"Yes," he grunted, and I was almost surprised he'd heard me at all. "Come on. Come for me."

I cried out, rubbing my clit harder, and my stomach tightened. He hunched forward, his hand slipping beneath me and batting mine out of the way so he could take over.

"You're so convinced you're not a princess?" he breathed. "Then fucking prove it. Show me what my messy little slut looks like when she comes with a cock up her perfect ass."

Oh, God. "Don't s-stop."

His fingers moved faster and pleasure sparked beneath them, guiding me closer and closer to the edge. "You take it so good for me, baby. You're letting me wreck this ass so fucking good."

Fuck. "JP–"

"Do it, Nell." His arms jerked me closer. "Fucking *shatter* for me, princess."

"Don't s-stop," I gasped, practically sobbing. "Don't s-stop, please don't stop, I'm gonna, I'm, I, I—"

My orgasm hit and I screamed his name.

Maybe.

I could have sworn his name was on my lips, could have sworn I tasted it, the sweetness of those letters filling my mouth as I did what he said and shattered on his cock. But it must have sounded like nonsense, like something that wasn't even words, because I couldn't imagine that JP would hear me literally scream his name and let me live a single moment without teasing me about it.

But I couldn't help it. I lost control. I had never—fucking *never*—come like that and it was so heated, so overwhelming, so painfully all-encompassing that I couldn't help myself.

I needed his name.

JP was almost right about ruining my makeup; if I hadn't taken it off in the shower, mascara and eyeliner would have been dripping down my cheeks, not from pain but because I couldn't even breathe. When I looked back on that moment, I never pictured what I actually saw—darkness and white light flashing in my eyes as I came, followed by a view of the blankets since my face was buried against the mattress—but what we must have looked like, what JP would have looked like with his cock buried inside me as I exploded in his arms.

He came at some point. I barely registered it happening, aside from thinking that the sound of him coming was one of my favourite sounds in the world, and the sudden feeling of him spilling inside me. I felt each spurt of cum inside me, felt it in a way that was almost better than feeling him come inside my pussy, and then JP was resting heavily against my back.

He stayed there for a moment before pulling out and collapsing beside me. His face was shining with sweat and his hair was matted against his forehead, but his eyes were closed and a smile of pure elation played on his lips.

"JP?" I murmured.

"Babe," he breathed, and his eyes opened as he reached for me.

Luckily, our eyes met first.

Because oh, fuck.

There was something there.

"Nellie," he whispered. "I—"

"Can you pass me the towel?"

He blinked. "Huh?"

"The…" I gestured towards the foot of the bed. "It's, um… I need to clean up."

He blinked again, then nodded. "Right. Yeah. Let me—"

He sat up, grabbing the towel I'd left on the floor so I could awkwardly shuffle to my bathroom and clean up. I took my time, hoping that when I returned, he'd have gotten dressed, but when I came back out wearing panties and a T-shirt, JP was lying on my bed with the sheet pulled over himself. His eyes were closed and one arm was tucked behind his neck.

"You've made yourself comfortable," I said.

He chuckled, his eyes dragging themselves open and fixing on me.

"Come here," he murmured.

Fuck.

He noticed me tense and sighed, a pained look on his face.

"Come on, Nellie," he asked. "Just... come sit with me for a bit."

"Is that a good idea?"

"Maybe not. But... please?"

It was the tone of his voice more than anything that made me even more certain I shouldn't go to him, and at the same time, made me disregard that certainty and crawl beside him on the bed. The arm tucked behind his head curled around my shoulders and we both exhaled, almost relieved as our bodies touched.

When JP and I hooked up, it was supposed to be fun. We didn't take things seriously, we laughed and teased each other, we fucked hard and fast and passionately.

But that night...

That couldn't really be described as just fun.

It was fun in the way that was unexpected.

It was fun in the way that I came hard enough that I might have had a legitimate out-of-body experience.

It was fun in the way that I could see it happening again, in the way that I almost yearned to curl up against his body and rest with his arms around me.

But JP and I weren't like that. It was one thing with Ben, but this...

This was comfortable.

This was content.

This was completely terrifying.

"This isn't serious," he whispered.

"Not at all," I replied.

"You just feel nice."

"It's a biological reaction. Makes sex more satisfying."

"Did Professor Sexy teach you that?"

"Yes, actually. After sex, while he was holding me."

We both laughed, JP's chest jostling my head, and it was only when he pulled me in to kiss me that we stopped. It lingered just a little too long, and both of us refused to acknowledge it. We refused to acknowledge the fact that I fell asleep against his chest, that he woke me up a few hours later when he got dressed to go back home, and that he kissed me again in the darkness of my room, softly and sweetly and so unlike JP that I thought I might have dreamt it.

Chapter Thirty
You Could've Just Asked

"It would be very helpful for you to be there," my dad said.

I gritted my teeth, staring into my bowl of yogurt. "I can't commit to any more events. Classes are starting and I don't know what my schedule will be like."

"I am not asking for much, Eleanor," he said.

"It's Nellie, Max."

I blinked and looked up at Kimberlee, who was sipping sparkling water in her spot across the table from my dad. My dad looked back at her, his face unreadable, before clenching his jaw.

"Nellie," he said. "I am asking for one, maybe two additional visits."

"And I am telling you, I need to figure out what my semester is going to be like," I repeated, trying to keep my voice calm.

He looked unimpressed. "Fine. What about Thanksgiving?"

"What about it?"

"You could attend something that weekend, no?"

"I go to Mom's for Thanksgiving."

He sighed impatiently. "It is *one* holiday—"

"And I spent it with you for seven years in a row," I interrupted. "I saw Mom for one weekend this summer. I'm not giving up Thanksgiving just to impress a client you don't even have yet."

"Fine." He picked up his coffee cup. "I will keep this in mind."

"Please do."

He set a stony look on me. "I hope you will keep in mind how much support you receive and reconsider your opinion on this."

"Well, if I don't, you can always ask JP if he'll go and impress the Martelles for you."

The air between me and my dad didn't get any less tense over the rest of breakfast. But I wasn't sure I actually cared. Because of course, my dad wanted more from me. Of *course* he saw that I'd made a connection with someone Very Important, and now he wanted to use that for his own benefit.

But I'd done what I'd agreed to. I'd held up my end of the deal.

I didn't owe him anything else.

Once breakfast was over, I went upstairs and finished packing, making sure to take anything I was certain I didn't want to leave behind. Because theoretically, this was the last time I had to be in Montreal.

I didn't know if I could actually cut myself off from my dad. Not because I might need something from him, but because beneath it all, beneath the negative assumptions and all the ways I knew I disappointed him, he was still my dad.

But just in case, I wanted to make sure I took my favourite dresses and swimsuits and hoodies, my shoes and mementos and the one pillow on my bed that was way better than the pillows I had at my apartment.

When I went back downstairs, my dad pretended we hadn't been fighting over breakfast and I played along like I always did, hugging him goodbye and pretending to insist I didn't need Pierre to carry my bag out to the car for me.

Although, this time, I didn't insist quite so hard and actually did let him carry it out.

After all, it's not easy to pretend you're not walking stiffly when you are indeed walking *very* stiffly, and it's especially hard to do that while carrying a heavier-than-usual suitcase.

It wasn't that I was in pain. My ass itself didn't hurt, which was a relief because... well, obviously that was something that could happen. No, I was walking stiffly because of just how hard we had fucked.

Which was fair, because it had been *so* hard.

But I didn't exactly want that to be obvious.

Unfortunately, even if I didn't make it obvious, it was an obvious enough risk that someone had put a Post-It note on my windshield during the night.

> *Text me before you leave*
> *Xoxo*

I rolled my eyes, then took out my phone while Pierre loaded my bag into the car.

Me

What do you want?

Bastard

One sec.

Sighing, I waited impatiently for his response, but I didn't get one until Pierre had closed the trunk and told me to drive safe before walking away.

And then, it wasn't the response I'd expected.

"Morning, Nellie!" JP said cheerfully as he strode across the Marchands' lawn.

"What the hell?" I asked, glancing behind him. "What are you doing here?"

"Saying goodbye," he said as if it was the most obvious thing in the world.

"Why?"

"Isn't that what friends do?"

"Are we friends?"

He shrugged, smirking. "And also making sure you're doing okay."

I rolled my eyes. "You could've just asked."

"Yeah, and you would've just lied."

"Well..."

We both chuckled.

"So you're okay?" he asked.

"I'm fine."

"Good."

There was an awkward pause and I swallowed hard.

"Okay," I said. "So, if that's everything—"

"Not really."

He cleared his throat and my stomach dropped.

He lifted a hand to his head, running his fingers through his hair, and my chest clenched.

His eyes looked to the side, like he was drawing strength by looking away, and every warning bell in my body clanged at once.

"I was thinking about stuff after I got home last night," he started. "And I just wanted to know if maybe... like, I know we... but would it really be so bad if—"

"Yes."

He fell silent. I felt guilty.

"Don't do this to me," I whispered.

"I'm not doing anything."

I swallowed hard, then reached out and nudged his arm.

"Come on," I said, trying to sound light-hearted and keep my voice down at the same time. "I'm your sister's annoying friend. Remember that time I glued all your deodorant and body wash bottles closed?"

"I do," he said, his mouth twitching.

"I make fun of you all the time. I call you a sleazebag. You should be trying to get rid of me."

He laughed, an easy, casual sound that had a sense of relief in it. "Right. And you think I'm hideously ugly."

"Just the worst. I can't even look at you."

"And Anne-Marie would never let us live it down."

"Never. And I'm also done with Montreal."

"You are?" He sounded surprised.

"I mean, that was the last event I needed to go to, so..."

"Right. Of course." He looked like he wanted to hug me or something, but that would've been too much. "Congrats. You made it through the summer."

"Thanks." I bit my lip. "Although, I mean, I might be back."

"Yeah?"

I shrugged. "My dad mentioned he might need me to come to some other things, I guess. And I might have to, like, visit or something."

"Well, you know where to find me if you do," he said, then smiled. "Have a safe drive, babe."

"Bye, bastard."

And that was it.

Well, that should have been it.

"*Chérie!*" came a shrill shout just after JP walked away and I was about to get into the driver's seat.

"Fuck," I muttered, closing my eyes briefly before turning to watch as Anne-Marie barreled over from next door.

"You cannot be leaving without saying goodbye!" she said as she stomped up to me.

"I thought you weren't home," I said.

"Well, had you said goodbye last night, that would not be a concern." She folded her arms, though she was trying not to smirk. "I did not see you and Jean-Paul leave the gala."

"I mean, I tried to find you," I said, which was true. I'd kept an eye out for her so we could avoid running into her as we left. "But you know I was only there because I had to be."

"Yes, and you must have known I would want *all* the details about your little *tête-à-tête* with Pia Martelle." She leaned against my car, grinning. "I heard you impressed her *and* your father."

My face flushed red. "Apparently, she thought I was funny or something."

"Mmm. And then you immediately left, right after that?"

"No," I said. "I left after my dad's speech, like I told you I would."

"Hmm," she said again. "Do you know something funny, though?"

I had a feeling whatever it was, I wouldn't find it funny. "What?"

"My brother was not home when Remy and I returned last night." She tilted her head to the side. "You wouldn't happen to know anything about that, would you?"

"I think JP mentioned Marc-Andre's at a friend's cottage for a bender this weekend," I said. "So it would make sense he wasn't home."

She gave me an unimpressed look. "*Jean-Paul* was not home when we got home."

"Oh," I said. "I dunno. Maybe he went out after we got back. We did leave pretty early."

"His car was on the driveway, though."

Fuck. "Okay. Maybe he Ubered somewhere? You could ask him. He literally just walked back into your house."

"I did ask him," she said. "And it's so funny, because he says he did not Uber anywhere, but he went to a girl's place after the gala." She looked at me pointedly. "And he will not tell me who."

I stared back at her blankly. "I guess you'll have to ask him again. He didn't say anything to me about going to a girl's place after dropping me off."

Her eyes gleamed with laughter. "Jean-Paul said if I *really* wanted to know what he was up to, I could ask you, because he told you on the way home."

"JP is fucking with you, Annie. You know that as well as I do."

"Do I?" she asked.

"What's more likely?" I folded my arms. "That JP is playing a game with you? Or that I know all these details about a mystery girl he met up with last night?"

She twisted her mouth to the side and finally conceded that JP was probably just teasing her. After hugging me and wishing me a safe drive home and making me promise that we'd go out to the clubs the next time I was in Montreal, I got into the car and started it.

Just as I did, I noticed movement next door, and caught JP grinning at me as he walked out to his car. I could almost see his eyes sparkling as he raised a hand and waved cheerfully.

Rolling my eyes, I started backing out of the driveway. Once I was on the road, I glanced in the rear view mirror. JP was still standing there and he waved again, then blew me a kiss. Trying not to laugh, I flipped him off before driving away.

He was such a bastard.

Epilogue

JP

I WATCHED HER DRIVE away, my heart thumping the same refrain it had been pounding since I'd collapsed next to her the previous night, too high on bliss and too spent from the most intense sex of my life to silence the thing that had been brewing for way longer than I could admit:

I love her.

Fuck.

I love her.

Fuck.

I love her.

Fuck.

Fuck.

Fuck.

It was all I could do to smile, to blow her a kiss like nothing was wrong, to hold back the nausea of hoping this wasn't the last time I'd see her that battled with the nausea of hoping to *God* she wouldn't come back.

Because I swore I wouldn't do this. To her, yeah, but much longer ago, to myself.

I couldn't do this. I couldn't go through this.

Not again.

The story continues with Keep Me If You Can, coming October 10, 2024.
*Get your copy here: **bit.ly/iycbook3***

Acknowledgments

Book two is always the hardest book in a series, but I am so happy and excited that this is out in the world! Thank you to everyone who's followed Nellie's journey so far!

A massive amount of thanks to my editors, beta readers, proof readers, and cheerleaders: Nora, Jason, Charlie, Sam, Jenine, Kristi, Lisa, Lauren, and Becca.

Nazarea Andrews from Inkslinger PR is amazing and keeps me sane.

Paul M, Kevin Matheny, PM, KJ, MidNyt, RP, Alex, and GW, and all my incredible supporters on Patreon are amazing. Thank you all so much for joining me on this journey!

Thank you to all my friends and family who are so supportive and amazing. I am truly humbled every time one of you recommends my books or tries to convince a new reader to try me out. It means the world to me to have so many positive people behind me and keeps me going when things are tough. You make such a difference in my life. A special thanks to Kaylie because I forgot to thank her last book even though the story of the bachelor party at the bar asking the girls to participate in a scavenger hunt panty-stealing setup (the chapter titled Stealing A Cowboy's Panties) was shared and lived by her. Thanks, Kaylie!

To my husband, who makes everything in my life sparkly and wonderful: thank you. I love you.

Xoxo, Cheryl

A Note About Neurodiversity

Neurodiversity representation in media is an important but complex topic.

In addition to my own diagnosis, this book has been reviewed by multiple other neurodiverse readers and a large amount of due diligence has been done in ensuring neurodiverse characters are depicted in a respectful and accurate way.

That being said, "diversity" is a key component of neurodiversity. My experience is different from my beta readers and their experiences are different from the countless others with neurodiverse brains. I have done my best to represent multiple experiences in an accessible way, which means that not every aspect of the characters may match the experiences other members of the neurodiverse community have.

My intent is not to ever invalidate anyone's experience and I want to assure you that your experience is valid, even if it differs from or opposes the small slice of neurodiversity represented here. In addition, language, knowledge, and research is constantly changing. I have done my best to keep facts accurate and use accepted/supportive language, but if something is standing out as glaringly wrong, *please* do not hesitate to reach out to me directly at info@cherylterra.com.

En Francais, S'il Vous Plait

Or, a List of Quebecois Words and Phrases In This Book

As the If You Can series is set partially in Montreal, there are several Francophone and bilingual characters. For practicality's sake, the book is mainly written in one language and it may be noted in the text whether a character was speaking French or English. However, there are points where specific words or phrases are kept in French. For those who would like a translation, they are listed on the following page.

> *Je sais pas* - I don't know. A shortened version of *Je ne sais pas,* may be pronounced like "shepa."
>
> *Bien tenté* - nice try
>
> *ma nouère* - Quebec term of endearment for a friend, like "honey" or "sweetie," specific to *Joual* (kind of like a dialect - form of Quebecois spoken specifically in Montreal). Derived from "*ma noire*", translated as "my black" but specifically refers to hair colour, NOT skin colour (similar to *ma blonde* as a way of saying "my girlfriend")
>
> *il est un trou d'cul* - he's an asshole
>
> *Maintenant, sans plus attendre* - Now, without further delay
>
> *Prêts, partez, feu* - On your marks, get set, go (literally translates as Ready, Go, Fire.")

C'est gentil. Merci. - That's very kind. Thanks.

mon minou - my kitten - term of endearment

CEGEP - *Collège d'enseignement general et professionnel* - General and professional teaching college - specific to the Quebec school system - students graduate high school earlier than in other provinces. This is one option for post-secondary education, often for students intending to go to university. Like the first semesters of a traditional university.

Député - a member of parliament

chien sale - dirty dog - vulgar, more like "asshole" but not the way you'd jokingly call your friend an asshole

Il est un esti de mange de marde - he's a shit eater

ma fille ange - angel girl/daughter

T'es ben chix, cherie, - you're hot, dear

Parfait - perfect

Societe de protection de l'histoire de Montreal - society for the protection of Montreal's history

Character List

This page is meant to be a reminder of basic character information and appearances in the context of what you've read so far. This means that while no spoilers for this book will appear here, additional revelations or information may be different in later books of the series.

Nellie Belanger: Justified main character syndrome on account of being the main character. Rosy white skin, slightly chubby, blonde hair, brown eyes, 21 years old. Forensic science student attending Ottawa Tech, currently living in Ottawa but spending much of her summer in Montreal. Known for being joyfully promiscuous and unapologetically against commitment.

Maximillian Belanger: Nellie's father. Mid-50s hedge fund manager who places a high level of importance on appearances. Greyish blue eyes, straight nose, light olive-toned skin, thick black hair, shorter than average. Lives in Montreal.

Kimberlee Dunn: Max's current girlfriend. Appears to be in her mid-thirties, light brown skin, dark brown hair, large eyes, and about the same height as Max. Involved with a number of charities and associations. Lives in Montreal.

Anne-Marie Marchand: Nellie's childhood best friend and next door neighbour. Tanned medium white skin, dyed blonde hair, brown eyes, tall and thin. Flighty and slightly out of touch at times but loyal AF. Lives in Montreal and speaks with a distinct Quebecois accent, peppering her dialogue with both French and English phrases. Desperately wishes Nellie and JP would hook up despite not knowing that Nellie and JP have hooked up.

Remy Tremblay: Anne-Marie's boyfriend. Tall, dark brown skin, coiled hair usually kept in twists or braids, brown eyes. Stoic and serious. Autistic.

Jean-Paul "JP" Marchand: Disgustingly good-looking and aggravatingly smart lawyer who is the older brother of Anne-Marie Marchand. 26, tall, tanned light beige skin, thick wavy blonde hair, blue eyes, wide smile with one crooked tooth. Works as a junior associate at his dad's law firm, lives with his parents temporarily while waiting for his condo to finish being built.

Marc-Andre Marchand: The youngest Marchand child. He exists and has brown hair.

Jean-Luc Marchand: JP and Anne-Marie's father. Looks similar to JP, overly serious. Highly successful lawyer who has his own practice. His family comes from money.

Della Kinsley: JP and Anne-Marie's mother. Very involved in the charities, associations, and events. More down to earth than her husband.

Sydney Amhurst: Nellie's best friend. Tall-ish, pale skin, reddish-blonde hair, hazel eyes, athletic build. Currently lives in Ottawa and also attends Ottawa Tech. Regularly goes to Montreal to visit Olivier, who's not really her boyfriend but sort of. Definitely not in love with her roommate.

Ben Cameron: Forensic psychologist and professor at Ottawa Tech. Medium gold-beige skin, thick brown hair with a grey streak above the left temple, hazel eyes, average height. Sydney calls him Professor Sexy. Currently on sabbatical and moving to California for a year at the end of the summer.

Clinton Thibault: Son of one of Max's major investors. Lives in Montreal. Wavy blonde hair, pale blue eyes, and a distinct lack of understanding of the word "No." Despite Nellie's disdain for him, is interested in her, which her dad approves of.

Olivier: a police officer Sydney went home with after they met during a bachelor party Olivier was attending. Light brown hair, an inch or two shorter than Sydney. Lives in Montreal.

Reid: Sydney's roommate and childhood friend. Lives in Ottawa. Has ADHD.

Alison: Reid's girlfriend, who has a very high-pitched "squeaky toy" esque moan.

Bruno: Friend of Remy's who agrees to be Nellie's date for social obligations over the summer. Lives in Montreal. White skin, dark brown hair and eyes. In Nellie's words, looks like he's one hair straightener accident away from a 2006 Myspace photo.

Niko: Brown hair, mustache, swollen biceps, tanned beige skin, very distracting to Bruno.

Claire: a mysterious lesbian in her 30s. Long brown hair, white skin, impish face, often wears a tux to fancy events. Has a horrendously grating laugh.

Julie: Claire's sugar-baby-I-mean-fiancee. Also a mystery. Curvy with blondish-brown hair, white skin, and a pretty smile.

Pia Martelle: Multi-billionaire founder of a large cosmetics company called The Martelle Makeup Group.

Sam: A college student who passed away 6 years earlier. Reddish-brown skin, brown hair, had ADHD and was in law school in Montreal.

Vicki McCauley: Nellie's mother. Mid-40s, manages an LCBO liquor store. Left Max 10 years ago. Brown eyes, long, frizzy blonde hair, rosy white skin, taller than Max. Flighty and impulsive, doesn't drive. Lives in Toronto.

Join The Chaos

Every hot mess deserves a happy ending.

Get exclusive bonus scenes, short stories, novellas, and more by joining my newsletter: **cherylterra.com/newsletter▢**

Find even more bonus content, early access to new work, and weekly updates that I sometimes actually do post every week on my Patreon (free tier available!): **patreon.com/cherylterra**

Also By Cheryl Terra

Also By Cheryl Terra

Find all of Cheryl's books at cherylterra.com/stories

Aurora Flats Series

Fate and Fried Chicken

If You Can Series

The Boy Next Door
Kiss Me If You Can
Hold Me If You Can
Keep Me If You Can
Sleigh Me If You Can

Unicorn Confessions Series

The Unicorn Confessions
Unicorn For Sale
Death of a Unicorn

Love Across Canada Series

Get Over It
The Devil Made Me
Runaway
Finding Home

Standalones

When It Rains
Hearts at Play: Special Edition
One Little Question
What Happens In Vegas
Selfish Love
Another Last Call